BRIMSTONE

TAMARA THORNE

D1715578

BRIMSTONE

The Brimstone Grand Hotel, owned by reclusive former movie star, Delilah Devine, looms high on Hospital Hill, harboring long-buried family secrets that whisper of unimaginable horrors. Horrors that will echo down through generations.

When Delilah's granddaughter, Holly Tremayne, who has seen ghosts for most of her eleven years, first comes to live in the Brimstone Grand in the summer of 1968, she's delighted by its majestic western beauty - and its chilling history. But as she settles in, making friends and enemies alike, the nightmares begin.

Within the walls of the Brimstone Grand, the past has come back to life, and Holly and Delilah are faced with an ancient familial evil that rages just below the old hotel's serene facade. An evil that won't rest until it possesses Holly - body, mind, and soul.

PRAISE FOR BRIMSTONE

Tamara Thorne's **BRIMSTONE** is deliciously scary. Thorne's finely-etched 11-year-old heroine, Holly Tremayne, sees ghosts, but it never really bothered her until she moves to Brimstone, Arizona. She meets a fascinating, colorful cast of characters, each one harboring a dark secret from their past. Earthquakes, nightmares, aberrations and ghosts keep the reader constantly on-edge. **BRIMSTONE** is like a hair-raising, fun trip through a house of horrors. But it's not just one house, it's a whole city. - **Kevin O'Brien, the *New York Times* best-selling author of THEY WON'T BE HURT and THE BETRAYED WIFE**

"**BRIMSTONE** includes great characters, especially Holly. This little eleven-year-old girl is so endearing with her past and her heartbreaking relationship with her mother. The history and the Native American folklore with supernatural elements made this book one of my favorites of the year. I highly recommend this book; you will definitely not be disappointed." -**Book Review Crew**

"Tamara Thorne is the Mistress of Malignant Mansions, the Go-to Gal of the Grand Guignol; and her latest, **BRIMSTONE**, solidifies her place in the pantheon of modern Gothic storytellers. With a kaleidoscopic cast of characters, a rich sense of place, and ever mounting suspense, **BRIMSTONE** brims with chills and thrills. Highly entertaining and highly recommended!" - **Jay Bonansinga, the *New York Times* bestselling author of THE WALKING DEAD: RETURN TO WOODBURY, SELF STORAGE, and FROZEN**

"Yet another unforgettable landmark on Tamara Thorne's alternate map of haunted California—effectively expanded here to Arizona —**BRIMSTONE** demonstrates how much terror atmosphere and well-placed shocks can generate if handled with a deft hand. Not since the California Gothics of James Blaylock and Tim Powers has such a compelling vision of ghosts and monsters and the occult so ably tickled the spine and ruffled the short neck hairs ... The thundering climax is as satisfying and fulfilling as any Thorne has ever crafted. **BRIM- STONE** is a shivery delight from first page to last, guaranteed to keep you reading long past your safe bedtime. **-W.D. Gagliani, author of THE JUDAS HIT**

"Tamara Thorne has become one of those must-read horror writers. From her strong characters to her unique use of the supernatural, anything she writes entertains as much as it chills." *-Horror World*

"Tamara Thorne has an uncanny knack for combining the outrageous with the shuddery, making for wonderful, scary romps and fun read- ing." - **Chelsea Quinn Yarbro, author of Hotel Transylvania**

"Tamara Thorne is the new wave of horror--her novels are fascinating rides into the heart of terror and mayhem." **-Douglas Clegg, author of The Children's Hour**

"Think Mario Puzo meets Anne Rice ... Balance is what Thorne does best ... **CANDLE BAY** is a love story. A mob story. A family drama. A wise combination of creepy, thrilling, titillating, and good old vampire fun ..." **-Michael Schutz, Darkness Dwells Radio**

PRAISE FOR THORNE & CROSS

MOTHER

"**MOTHER** is about as disturbing as one can get. Thorne and Cross are seriously twisted individuals who know how to horrify and entertain at the same time." - **Fang-Freakin-Tastic Book Reviews**

"A great combination of strong characters that remind me of my V.C. Andrews characters, wonderful creepy twists, and a plot that will recall Mommie Dearest in an original take that shocks and delights at the same time. This is a full blown psychological thriller worth the investment of time and money." - **Andrew Neiderman, Author of The Devil's Advocate and the V.C. Andrews novels**

"**MOTHER** is a thriller in the truest sense of the word. What begins with a walk through a nice neighborhood in a nice town quickly becomes a chilling and unnerving descent into madness that is harder and harder to escape. Because I wear a fitness tracker I have scientific proof that the finale is a wild ride. Although I was curled up on the couch reading, **MOTHER** caused my heart rate to go up ten points! I'll never look at a neighborhood block party the same way." - **QL Pearce, bestselling author of** *Scary Stories for Sleep-Overs*

"Thorne and Cross bring the goods with **THE CLIFFHOUSE HAUNTING**, a clockwork mechanism of gothic chills designed to grab the reader by the scruff and never let go until the terrifying conclusion. Atmospheric, sexy, brooding, and brutal, the book manages to be simultaneously romantic and hardboiled. Highly recommended!" - **Jay Bonansinga, the New York Times bestselling author of** *The Walking Dead: Invasion*

"In **THE GHOSTS OF RAVENCREST**, Tamara Thorne and Alistair Cross have created a world that is dark, opulent, and smoldering with the promise of scares and seduction. You'll be able to feel the slide of the satin sheets, taste the fizz of champagne, and hear the footsteps on the stairs." -**Sylvia Shults, paranormal expert and author of** *Fractured Spirits* **and** *Hunting Demons*

Brimstone is dedicated to my friend and collaborator, Alistair Cross, with love and respect. You keep me on track, you make me laugh, and you make me think. I treasure you, our friendship, and our work. Long may we brainstorm! And giggle like ten-year-olds during our breaks.

ACKNOWLEDGMENTS

THANKS TO: Robert Thorne, for always being there, and Q.L. Pearce for your friendship and sage advice - and thanks to both of you for spending so many nights with me in haunted hotels during my research trips. Thanks, as well, to Berlin Malcom at BAM Literature for all her hard work, Mike Rivera for his great art, and Libba Campbell, for her eagle eye. And finally, thanks to the town of Jerome, Arizona, and The Jerome Grand Hotel for sparks of inspiration.

PROLOGUE

BRIMSTONE, ARIZONA

"Run! *Run! Run!*" The cry echoed in her head as the little girl clutched the book tightly against her chest with one hand and used her other to steady herself as she began her scramble down the rocky hill.

One foot caught in a rodent hole and she fell flat out, face in the dirt. "*Run!*" She rose, ignoring the pain in her ankle, the dust and dirt on her white pinafore apron. Clawing twigs of dry tumbleweed from her hair, never loosening her grip on the book, she limped toward the little cave, *her* cave, her secret hiding place.

"*Run!*" She glanced back, not sure whether the voice was real or not, but saw no one above the ridgeline, only rocks and desert scrub. She scanned. Below lay the town and the copper mines where men trailed like ants. No one was near - no one was watching her. Ignoring her ankle, unaware of the tears forging dusty rivers down her cheeks, she hurried on.

Halfway down the hill, breathing hard, she turned west, picking a path through the rocks and manzanita as she had dozens of times before; there was no visible trail, but she knew the way by heart. Just when she thought she couldn't go another painful step, she saw the tall tan and red stone that stood sentinel outside the little cave.

She thought she heard a scream, but it might have been the wind.

You can do it. You have to! She limped around the swirled sandstone rock then pushed past a stand of sagebrush. There, about two feet off the ground was the entrance; it was impossible to see until you were right on it.

She peered into the narrow opening, felt cool air that smelled of dust and desert, then set the black leatherbound book inside. Putting her hands on the ledge, she pushed herself up into the darkness.

Wishing for a lantern, she crawled in deeper, past the angled sunlight, past the Indian drawings halfway in, pushing the book along as she moved. It was a narrow passage and a dozen feet in, it suddenly became so tight that even a six-year-old could go no further. She turned around and settled, one leg crossed, the sore one straight out in front of her. She put the thick black book beside her and reached down to gently rub her ankle. It was hot and swollen.

The cave was too dark without a lantern, way too dark, but she concentrated on the shadowy light coming in from the entrance, watched the moving shadows of the sagebrush. It kept her calm, helped her not think about what she'd seen when she'd opened the basement door only a few minutes before.

She waited, unsure of what was happening above, knowing only that something was wrong, really wrong, and that Carrie and Addie were in trouble. She'd heard noises - voices and weird sounds - carrying up from the basement of the Clementine Hospital. She had opened the door and then Carrie, hair wild, face streaked with dirt, clothing torn and bloodied, had appeared in the lamplight and bolted up the stairs. She'd thrust a black book into her baby sister's hands. "Run! Hide it. Hide it where no one can ever find it! Promise!"

Below, she heard scuffling, then Addie screamed and Grandfather cursed.

"But-"

"Promise! Do you promise?" Carrie's blue eyes bored into hers, the gold fleck in one seeming to glow and pulse.

"I promise." She clasped the book to her chest.

"Good girl. Now, go!" With that, Carrie was yanked back into the shadows.

But the little girl just stood there, staring at the black book with gold letters embossed on it: INFURNAM AERIS. The words meant nothing to her. Nor did the symbol beneath it:

Uncomprehending, she simply listened as Carrie and Addie and Grandfather fought and yelled. Things fell over, there was a rushing sound, then something appeared in the lamplight at the bottom of the stairs, leering at her, tongue lolling, slobber glistening.

"GO!" Carrie screamed.

She ran.

Now, secure in her secret cave, she wept. For how long, she didn't know, but finally, she wiped her face on the hem of her dusty dress and looked up again. The sun was at a different angle now; it was getting late. Carefully, she undid her pinafore apron and pulled it over her head, then wrapped the leather book tightly in it. Pushing the book ahead of her, she crawled back toward the entrance, relieved as the cave widened. Beneath the Indian drawings was a neat pile of smooth rocks. She moved the stones, put the wrapped book in their place, then carefully piled the rocks on top of it.

Unable to see the drawings in the darkness, she touched the rocky wall, trying to feel them. *Petroglyphs.* Carrie had taken her to see the petroglyphs on Brimstone Peak a few months back and told her how they were hundreds, maybe thousands of years old. At least. There were lots more of them there than here, but these were her favorites because they were hers and hers alone. She felt like she knew the Indian who had drawn them. "Keep the book hidden," she whispered. "Promise?"

Outside, the wind sighed softly. She took it as a reply. "Thank you."

She crawled forward. Just before she climbed out, something

moaned deep in the earth behind her. There was a *crack!* and then everything was shaking. Dust and gravel showered her head. Coughing, she covered her face with her hands as the world rocked and fine earth sifted over her. She was afraid, couldn't breathe, and was terrified she was going to be buried alive like the miners last year.

Then it stopped. Instantly, she pushed herself out of the cave, crying out as she landed on her twisted ankle. She wiped dirt off her face as best she could then looked back into her little cavern. She couldn't see anything in the dusty darkness.

Taking a deep breath, she felt suddenly calm, knowing her plea had been heard; the book would not be found.

☙ I ❧

ARRIVAL

JULY, 1968

The town clung to the side of the hill, almost vertical, looking like it would tumble down the slopes if you so much as sneezed on it.

"We're going to live *here*?" Holly Tremayne glanced at her mother.

"Yeah, we sure are. For now." Cherry took a final drag on her cigarette then dropped it in the red dirt of the turnout and crushed it under her pink sneaker. She pointed. "See that very top building on the tallest hill?"

Holly followed her mother's red-enameled fingernail. "The tan one near that big white 'B' on the mountain?"

"Yep. That's where we're going to live. Over the river and through the woods, then out to the dried-up middle-of-nowhere to Grandmother's house we go."

"It's gigantic!" Holly edged away as her mother lit another Virginia Slim. "Do you think I can have my own room?" She hated the way the stink of her mom's cigarettes clung to her hair and clothes. It was gross. At their studio apartment in Van Nuys she could never escape the smell.

"She'd *better* give us our own rooms!" Cherry coughed. "That place is five stories and the first four are the hotel. I want hotel rooms so we don't have to live in her damned penthouse with her."

Holly heard the venom in Cherry's voice. "Why don't you like Grandmother?"

"She's a vain old woman; all she does is criticize. You'll see. You'll want to keep your trap shut around her or she'll pick on you. She still thinks she's a goddamned movie star." Cherry paused. "Trust me, kid, if she makes us live on the fifth floor with her, we'll be scrubbing crap out of her toilet and wiping her ass."

Though just eleven, Holly barely remembered her grandmother, but she hated the way Cherry talked about her. Delilah Devine was a glamorous movie star in the old days and she thought Cherry - she insisted Holly call by her first name - was just jealous. Cherry Devine was in movies, too - but last month she'd announced she was taking a break.

That's why they were moving to Brimstone, Arizona.

Holly knew it had to be more than that - Cherry didn't like her mother and probably needed money really bad to go live with her. 'Delilah Devine' was her grandmother's name. Cherry was Cherry Devine Tremayne, but she was only married about five minutes and never ever used her married name. Holly was secretly glad she had her father's last name instead of 'Devine,' which was just too much, especially since that fat guy who dressed in ladies' clothes hit the Hollywood scene. She heard about Divine a lot because Cherry kept laughing and saying she bet Delilah really hated him.

"Come on, kid." Cherry took a pull on her smoke. "Time to get a move on."

Holly nodded and got in the car, a red 1966 Ford Falcon - her mother called it "Cherry Red" - that she bought new a couple years ago when she played a stewardess in a movie called *Friendly Skies*. She called it "high class" but wouldn't let Holly see it. Cherry never let Holly see any of her movies.

Cherry pulled the Falcon back onto the narrow road that had twisted and turned for half an hour before they'd come to the turn-out where they finally got their first sight of the town. Now, they continued following its hairpin turns, and Holly caught glimpses of

Brimstone between trees and hills. It looked ramshackle and old. Really old.

Finally, they began passing ancient buildings - shacks, really - roof-less cabins, cement pads with nothing left on them, little clapboard houses with broken windows and no doors. Holly opened her mouth to ask if all of Brimstone was like this, but saw Cherry's hands gripping the steering wheel white-knuckle hard. Her face was set and deter-mined, her eyes unreadable behind big white-rimmed sunglasses. Her lips had another long cigarette in a death-grip.

Holly touched the passenger window - it was warm outside but not as hot as she'd feared. Still, she hoped there would be air conditioning where they were going. Or even electricity!

They passed a brown and white sign that read:

Welcome to Brimstone
Population 3021

"We're here," Cherry grumbled around her cigarette.

"I wonder what the school's like." Holly would be starting sixth grade in September and had been looking forward to it before the move. Now, she was worried; she hated the idea of being the new kid, but at least it wasn't like she had to walk into a strange classroom in the middle of the school year. That would be the worst.

"Schools and students are all the same." Cherry stubbed her smoke out in the overflowing ashtray. "There are girls who think they're better than everybody else if they're boobs are coming in." She glanced at Holly's flat chest. "Plenty of them aren't yet, don't worry. There are always boys who pull your hair because they like you, and boys who fight all the time. Girls who dot their i's with little round circles, or worse, hearts. Stay away from those girls, kid, they're weird. Usually stuck-up little brats. Then there are the kids who go to detention three times a week like I did." She laughed and ended up coughing. "Takes all kinds. You'll fit right in." She glanced over. "You always fit in, Holly. That's your special talent."

"It is?"

"Um-hmm. I've seen you. So many times, back when you were

little, I'd take you to the park and watch you. In five minutes, you had a new best friend, every single time. And that, Holly, is a real talent. Use it right and you'll be rich someday."

It didn't feel much like a talent. She just hated being alone all the time. Mostly Holly visited the park by herself, and her favorite trips were when her mother gave her change to buy an ice cream at Thrifty's on the way to hang out on the swings and monkey bars. That happened whenever Cherry brought home a boyfriend.

Holly stared out at the houses - mostly old and dinky - with rocks and manzanita, yuccas, and big junipers surrounding them instead of lawns and flower beds. There were quite a few trees, some tall sycamores, but mostly they were stunted oaks and smallish willows. As they wove higher into town, pines began dotting the landscape. It sure didn't look anything like Van Nuys. Neither did the brilliant blue sky and the white puffy clouds drifting on the wind; in Los Angeles the sky was so smoggy and yellow that some days it even hurt to breathe when she ran or played tetherball. "Why did Grandmother move here?"

"You got me, kid." Cherry glanced at her. "Get in my purse and get me out a stick of Juicy Fruit. You can have one, too. Watch it around your granny though - she's death on gum."

Holly pulled Cherry's white plastic purse into her lap and rummaged past extra packs of Slims, a handful of lipsticks, little Avon perfume sprayers, all kinds of eye makeup and powder and blush, and finally found the gum. She unwrapped two sticks.

"Put it right in here." Cherry opened her mouth.

Holly put one stick in Cherry's mouth, then one in her own. "Brimstone seems like a weird place to live."

"You think?" Cherry barked a laugh. Then coughed. "Hippies, bikers, artists, a lotta gun-toting desert rats. Religious nuts and Commie-haters judging by the number of American flags flying. And your grandmother." She shook her head. "And us. I hope we don't have to stay long."

"So, we're just here for a break?" Holly had wanted to ask before, but hadn't dared; sometimes questions like that made Cherry furious.

"Yeah. A break between jobs. The minute Larry calls me with the right gig, we'll go back to Hollywood where we belong."

But Larry Zimmer, Cherry's agent, hadn't been calling much lately.

"Look at that." As they drove into downtown, Cherry pointed at a big wooden buffalo standing on the sidewalk outside a saloon.

"Maybe there are real bison here," Holly said, half hoping. "Do you think?"

"Nah, it's just a cowboy-and-Indian thing. This town thinks it's part of the Wild West - and, you know, kid, they're pretty much right." Cherry snapped her gum. "Watch for a gas station."

They rounded a bend and hit Main Street proper. Holly stared up at the skinny false front buildings lining the narrow street. They loomed, seeming to lean forward as they cast tall shadows. She hadn't had time to research much before they left Van Nuys, but she had been at the library long enough to find out Brimstone was a copper mining town in the 1800s that pretty much died out around 1930. It was almost a ghost town until a few years ago when artists and other unusual-type people started moving in.

Some of the buildings looked empty but most had businesses in them. Holly spotted a stained glass shop, a couple of music stores (one blaring *White Rabbit*, one of her favorites because it was based on *Alice in Wonderland*, a book she loved), more bars and restaurants and markets, rock shops, and a bunch of souvenir shops. The musky scent of patchouli incense floated from one shop. Above all the businesses were crooked brick and clapboard second stories that looked like homes. She saw bicycles locked to haphazard wooden stairs, ferns hanging on porches, and curtains in windows; she smiled, thinking it would be a very adventurous place to live.

A black and white dog barked at them from the open window of a parked car as they wound up the curving street. Holly could have reached out and touched it, it was so close. "There. There's gas." She pointed at a tiny Humble station that seemed to be hanging off a cliff dead ahead, right where Main Street made a sharp turn and continued up the hill.

"Good, we're on fumes." Cherry headed into the lot and pulled up at one of the old-fashioned round-headed pumps. An elderly man in denim overalls and a red kerchief in his pocket came out and headed their way.

"Here, kid," Cherry said. "Go buy us some soda pop. I want a Dr. Pepper." She pressed change into Holly's hand.

As the old man went to Cherry's window to see what kind of gas she wanted, Holly hopped out and walked to the office, enjoying the feel of the warm, dry high desert air against her skin. There was a faded lost child poster in the window, a Pepsi ad, and a sign for the annual Fourth of July Picnic, just passed. She pushed the door open, setting off a cacophony of bells, then turned, looking for the soda chest.

"It's right behind you, honey."

Surprised, Holly glanced up to see an old lady sitting behind the counter. She could just see her face above the Baby Ruths, Jolly Ranchers, displays of Certs, and Juicy Fruit on the counter.

"Thanks!" She turned and looked with longing at an ice cream freezer, but opened the soda box and retrieved two Dr. Peppers, took them to the counter, and set them down with the dimes.

The old lady rose and came to the cash register. "Is that all, honey?"

Holly nodded. The lady, tall and slender, wore a print dress that left her freckled arms bare. There were lots of veins on the backs of her hands and a million wrinkles on her face. She stared at her like she'd seen a ghost as she rang up the purchase and pushed change back to her. "Want me to open those for you? Or you can do it over there on the machine."

Holly loved how the lady's wrinkles spread, accentuating her smile and wondered if her own grandmother would have as many lines on her face. "Would you?"

"Of course." The lady used an opener hidden behind the counter and put the sodas back up. Fizzy mist rose from the frosty bottles. Her eyes on Holly's, she asked, "Are you visiting or just passing through, honey?"

"My mom and I are going to live here," Holly said somberly.

"Well, welcome to Brimstone. My name's Adeline Chance and that old codger waiting on your mother is my husband, Isaac. What's your name, honey?"

Holly looked into the lady's eyes - despite the wrinkles, they were as clear and blue as the sky. "Holly Tremayne," she replied, staring hard. Adeline Chance had a big gold fleck in one eye.

"Holly. I like that name. Were you born around Christmas?"

Holly smiled. "No, I was born in May. I just turned eleven."

"A wonderful age. And where are you going to be living, Holly?"

"With my grandmother, up at the hotel."

Adeline Chance's smile faltered and she turned pale. "You don't mean the Brimstone Grand, do you?"

Holly nodded.

"Your grandmother is ..."

"Delilah Devine. She used to be an actress. Have you met her?"

"Yes, a long time ago." Adeline spoke slowly. "She was very young when her father sent her to live with her aunt in Boston."

"Wait! You mean my great-grandfather lived in Brimstone?"

Adeline hesitated. "Well, sure. You didn't know that?"

"I don't know much of anything about my family. Cherry - my mom - isn't into it. She says it's old news."

Adeline chuckled. "Well, then, you ought to know that your great-great-grandfather, Henry Hank Barrow, was one of the owners of the Clementine Mining Company. He was in charge of the hospital - in fact he owned it and the land it sat on."

"Hospital?" Holly asked.

"Your grandmother's hotel - the Brimstone Grand - used to be the Clementine Hospital. Your great-grandfather worked for him."

"Really?" Holly felt like she was going to pop with excitement.

"Really!"

"Was my great-great-grandfather a doctor?"

"No, he was an administrator. A businessman. You could say he ran things."

Holly nodded. "Mrs. Chance-"

"Call me Adeline, honey."

"Can I ask you something?"

"Of course."

"You have a gold fleck in your eye. Were you born with it?"

"Why, yes, I was." Adeline was quiet a long time. "My mother told me it meant I was special." She gazed into Holly's eyes. "I see you're pretty special, too. You have gold in *both* your eyes."

"Cherry told me they're flaws. See?" Holly widened her own blue eyes and stared up at Adeline.

"Light's not in my favor in this place," the old lady said. She bent down and squinted. "Well, I'll be ..." There was something in her expression that gave Holly goosebumps. The woman reached out and touched her chin, pushing just a little to turn her head so the light hit her eyes more. "Well ... in the light, I can see flecks of gold in both your eyes. They're very pretty."

"Thanks," Holly said, but Adeline was still studying her.

"Look at those tiny little motes, just like gold dust floating in a creek. I've never seen eyes so beautiful as yours, Holly." She smiled gently and let go of her chin. "I guess that means we're both special."

"What kind of special?" Holly asked.

Adeline looked thoughtful but said nothing for a long time. "I'm going to tell you something, but don't repeat it."

"What?" Holly leaned on the counter, feeling like Adeline was an old friend.

"It has to be our secret."

"Cross my heart and hope to die, stick a needle in my eye."

The old lady chuckled. "We're distant cousins, you and I."

"Really?"

"Really, though whatever you do keep your promise. Your grandmother wouldn't approve of my telling you."

"I promise, but why wouldn't she approve?"

"I come from the poor side of the family."

"Is that bad?"

Adeline searched Holly's eyes, the gold fleck shimmering. "It might be."

"That's so cool! I have a new cousin!"

Adeline smiled. "Me, too. And I'll tell you something else, young lady. Your great-great- grandmother Myrtle Delacorte had two daughters. One was your grandmother, Delilah, and the other was her big sister, Carrie. She was only a couple years younger than me and we were best friends. She had gold in her eye, too." Her smile faded. "So did your great-great-grandfather."

"He did?"

Adeline nodded. "Yes. And you know what they say about every one of us with gold in our eyes?"

Holly shook her head.

"They said we have the Sight." She leaned closer. "They say that about me - and they'll say that about you, too. Because of our eyes."

"Do we? Have the Sight?" Holly wasn't even sure what that meant. "Is that what makes us special?"

"We'll talk about it sometime."

Holly nodded. The only thing she knew about the Sight was that they sometimes referred to it on *Dark Shadows*.

"Holly," Adeline said. "Do you know what the Sight is?"

"Not really."

Adeline leaned closer. "Have you ever seen things other people can't?"

"You mean like a ghost or something?"

"Exactly like that."

She didn't hesitate. "Yes. At the park in Van Nuys where I go sometimes, there's a little girl on a swing. She's like maybe four years old and she's wearing this dress that looks like a party dress, all ruffly. It looks a little old-fashioned, but not much." Seeing Adeline was taking her seriously, she continued. "I've seen her three times and I didn't think much about it - she's just a little kid - but once, another kid ran up and jumped into the swing, right on top of her. He started swinging and the girl was gone. I think she was a ghost."

"I think you're right," Adeline said. "Did she ever make eye contact with you?"

Holly shook her head. "She just looked down, like she was sad."

"I see." Adeline spoke softly. "Holly, when you realized she was a ghost, did that scare you?"

"No. I love ghosts."

"Good."

"Why?"

"Because you are likely to see some up at your grandmother's hotel."

"Really?" Holly smiled. "Like what?"

"There's a nurse who pushes a rattling cart down one of the halls. A lot of people without the Sight can hear the cart or her footsteps, but I saw her a few times when I was young. She's not frightening. I haven't been in there in decades, mind you, but she's probably still there. There are other nice things, too, like the ghost of an old care-taker who rides the elevator. But there might also be some scary ones."

"Scary? I'm not scared of-"

"There's one who rattles door knobs. When you look, no one's there."

"Why is that scary?"

"I guess because whoever did that in life was a nasty person. If you're scary when you're alive, I'd say it's a safe bet, you make a scary ghost."

Holly nodded. "Are there any bloody ghosts? Gory ones?"

Adeline chuckled. "Not that I recall, but it's possible; after all, it was a hospital for many years. The point is, Holly, you have the Sight, so if there's something to see you may well see it. But there's nothing that can hurt you. They're more like movies than anything else. I guess they're always around, but hardly anyone notices. You have the sight, so you may see them - and if there are scary things, you'll likely see them too."

"I'm not afraid."

"Good." Adeline paused. "Sweetheart, I wouldn't bring any of this up - not about the ghosts and especially not about the family tree. I've talked my fool head off and I don't know why." She paused. "Or maybe I do."

Holly nodded. People told her lots of things. She figured she was a really good listener. "I won't tell anyone anything, I promise."

Adeline smiled and stood up. "Thank you. Well, young lady, now that you know your ancestors helped establish Brimstone and you're going to live here a while, do you think you might be interested in the history of this town?"

"Yes! I was interested anyway! But now I'm *really* interested! How'd you know?"

"You look like a girl who likes to know about things. A girl who loves books."

"That's me! I went to the library in Van Nuys, but hardly found out anything about Brimstone." The bells on the door jingled as the old man entered and handed some money to his wife. "I need $1.28 change." He turned a twinkling smile on Holly.

"Holly, this is my husband, Isaac," said Adeline.

"Call me Ike." The man grinned.

"And this is Holly," said Adeline. "And guess who her grandmother is."

"Well, I don't know. Is she the man in the moon?"

Holly laughed.

"Delilah Devine." Adeline spoke quietly.

"Oh, my." Isaac's laugh sounded strained. "Well, I'd better get this change out to your mother."

"See if you can't shoot the breeze with her for a minute or two so Holly and I can talk."

Isaac grinned. "Pretty lady like that? Sweet Adeline, your wish is my command." He was out the door.

"Holly, I want to give you something." Adeline rustled around behind the counter, grunting as she dug something out from below. "There it is."

Setting a white box on the counter, she wiped dust off the lid then opened it. Inside were flyers, brochures and booklets. "These are all about Brimstone." Adeline began rifling through the box. "You can take anything you want, but I suggest you start with this." She handed Holly a booklet with a faded blue cover that read, *The History of Brimstone*. "It talks about the hotel, about when it used to be the Clementine Hospital. You'll read about your great-great- grandfather-"

"Just a minute. I have to ask my mother for money ..."

"No, no. I'm giving these to you, honey."

"Really?" Holly didn't try to hide her glee. "Why?"

"Consider it a welcome present. Here are some flyers about places to visit in Brimstone. And here's a booklet about Brimstone today -

well, as of two years ago. Here's a pamphlet about the local Indian tribes that used to live here." She rummaged some more. "There's something else I think you'll really enjoy-"

The earth rumbled under her feet and Holly grabbed the counter.

"It's okay, Holly, it's just the ground settling. It happens once in a while."

"But that was an earthquake, right?" Holly had never felt one before, but they talked about them a lot back in California. It didn't seem so bad.

"Indeed, it was." Adeline looked kind of pale.

Holly wanted to ask why Adeline was upset but knew she shouldn't, so she picked up another booklet. *"Folklore and Legends of Brimstone, Arizona,"* Holly read. "This looks like fun!"

"By all means, take it, Holly. I love folklore, too."

"Are there any ghost stories in the folklore book?"

"I think so, but it's been a while since I've read it. Maybe you can tell me next time you visit." Adeline picked up the papers and booklets, put them in a small paper sack, and gave them to Holly. "Now, we'd better get you out of here before Ike bores your mother to death. Why don't you come back and see me after you've read a little?"

"I will. Thank you!" Holly, happy about the move for the first time, turned toward the door. Just as she put her hand on the latch, her mother tapped the horn.

And the shaking began.

The earth grumbled and the world rocked. Holly steadied herself against the cooler as soda bottles jingled against each other.

"It's a big one," said Adeline. Coins in the cash register rattled like rain on a tin roof. "Stay in the doorway, Holly."

Holly positioned herself, the earth moving beneath her feet. She felt as if she were riding a surfboard on a giant wave.

Outside, Isaac hunkered down and made his way toward the office. Cherry stared open-mouthed, frozen behind the wheel.

The Coca-Cola clock slipped off its place on the wall and struck the ground, its face shattering as the bells on the door rang in counterpoint to the soda bottles. Holly gripped her two open bottles, trying to keep them from sloshing as the ground rolled again. She watched a rack of postcards tilt, then right itself. A pair of sunglasses clattered from a display.

Isaac joined Holly in the doorway as Adeline disappeared behind the counter.

The gentle rolling stopped as the earth gave another angry grumble. And then roared.

A hard jolt sent the racks of postcards and sunglasses crashing to the floor. Fan belts skittered from a display and candy bars by the cash register flew through the air. Isaac grabbed Holly and held her tight.

It was over in an instant.

"You okay?" Isaac asked.

"Uh, huh."

"Adeline?"

"Right as rain," his wife called, coming out from behind the counter.

Cherry arrived. "You okay, Holly?"

"Fine."

"Jesus H. Christ, the last time I felt a quake like that, I was shooting a movie in Frisco. Let's get going."

Holly nodded, staring at Adeline Chance, "Do you have lots of earthquakes here?"

"No. Back when they were mining, there were quite a few, but honestly, Brimstone hasn't had a real quake in decades." She smiled but it didn't hide the nervousness in her voice. "I guess it's just your lucky day."

"It's an omen, is what it is." Cherry snapped her gum. "We should probably turn around and head straight back to Hollywood."

"No!" Holly said.

"What?" Cherry gave her daughter a surprised look.

"I mean, I want to at least meet my grandmother."

Cherry laughed, dry and brittle. "Don't worry, kid, you will."

"Goodbye, Adeline." Holly aimed her mother at the door. "Thank you."

"You're welcome, dear. Don't be a stranger."

"I won't! Here, Cherry, here's your Dr. Pepper. Let's go."

2

WELCOME TO THE
NEIGHBORHOOD

"Goddamned earthquakes, that's all these hicks are going to talk about now," Cherry complained as they continued climbing the hair-pinned road up to the hotel. They were in Brimstone's version of suburbs now. The houses - some beaten down and ramshackle, others neat and perfect - lined the narrowing road. Some were clapboard, some river stone, some brick. Most had dirt driveways, a few asphalt or concrete, and only a couple had lawns like Holly had seen in California. Most had dirt and desert plants and trees; many with low drooping willows tenting the ground with graceful branches. Dotting the neighborhood were taller oaks, manzanita, mesquite, and bright wildflowers. Smooth stones demarcated the driveways, many of which held motorcycles or VW vans. Others had bicycles or station wagons. There were plenty of pickup trucks, too, aging yellow Chevies, sun-faded turquoise Fords. Some yards had vegetable patches and even big gardens. Clothes hung on lines blew in the breeze - and lots of those were tie-dyed.

"Fucking hippies," Cherry muttered as they passed a white clapboard house with a big red, white, and blue peace sign painted on its tall peaked roof.

Cherry hated hippies; she said they were dirty and had lice. Holly didn't know about that, and was hoping to see some, but nobody was outside, which seemed a little weird after the earthquake. Maybe they were all at work or inside picking up broken dishes and sweeping and stuff.

"How many earthquakes have you been in, Cherry?"

"Oh, a few. The worst was in 1948, I think. Christmastime, though you wouldn't know it in Hollywood except for the decorations." She snapped her gum and gripped the wheel hard as the Falcon grumbled then roared up a sharp curve. "It was big - bigger than we just felt. It was a Saturday afternoon. My mother was in the tub getting ready for a night on the town, like usual. Everything started moving and she started screaming her lungs out that she was drowning or something. I remember that more than anything else, her freaking out."

"How old were you?"

"Oh, Jesus, kid, I don't know. Ten, maybe. Eleven. About your age." Cherry downshifted as the asphalt gave way to dirt and they started up an extra steep curve. "I hate this place; my poor car is getting filthy!"

"What were you doing? When the earthquake happened, I mean?"

Cherry shot Holly a glance. "You're full of questions. I guess this was your first quake, huh, kid?"

"Yes."

"You scared?"

"Maybe a little."

"Don't be. That was nothing compared to the one in '48. Nothing but peanuts." She coughed on the dust and closed the vent. "Christ! Anyway, your grandmother just freaked out. Refused to take a bath in her beloved tub for months - she'd only shower. I bet she's going to be a big old bundle of nerves when we get there."

"Why is she afraid of earthquakes?"

"You got me, kid."

They rounded a bend and as the main road turned east, saw a sign that read, "Hospital Hill. Elevation 5,300 Feet." To the west, a potted dirt track led toward a few old shacks, and beyond them, Holly saw a big wooden cross in the distance. "That looks like a ghost town. And maybe a cemetery!"

"You and your cemeteries, Holly. Yeah, that could be one, I don't know. All I know is that Brimstone is one big ghost town - by the looks of things, they don't tear nothing down in this town."

Holly couldn't wait to check out the cemetery - she loved them, mostly because she liked reading the names and making up stories about how the people died. But for now, she looked in the other direction. The road was much better and they soon passed a brown and white sign with an arrow pointing straight up: "The Brimstone Grand Hotel," Holly read. "Ahead 1000 feet. Historical Landmark."

"Jesus, I thought we'd never get here." Cherry shook her head. "I hate this place."

"You've been here before?" Holly asked.

"No. I just hate it."

The Brimstone Grand still wasn't in sight. Everything below and above the road was hidden by heavy desert scrub and trees. "Why is it a historical landmark?"

"It's old, so it's historical, I guess."

"But there are lots of old places that aren't historical. Why is this one?"

"You sure do ask a lot of questions." Cherry snorted. "I think if you let them put that sign up and make a turnout for people to park and gawk at something old, you get some money for upkeep from the state or something. I don't know."

"Brimstone Grand Hotel - Five Hundred Feet," Holly read another sign as the dirt road turned to gravel. Her stomach twisted with excitement and anxiety. She'd met her grandmother once, a long time ago, but barely remembered her, except that she had seemed tall and scary in her swooping black coat and veiled hat.

Then Holly gasped as she caught her first real view of the hotel. She could only see the top floors above the trees - a flat roof edged in adobe tile, then below, peachy-beige walls lined with windows, their frames painted burnt orange.

"It's huge," Holly said.

"It's a hotel," Cherry answered. "What'd you expect?"

"Not this!"

One more curve and the entire building, though still distant, came into view at the end of the long gravel drive. There were people milling everywhere.

"They're afraid of being inside," Cherry said, snapping her gum. "In case there's a bigger quake."

On the left, Holly saw a sign that said Clementine Park - it was just a lot of dirt crammed with a big slide, monkey bars of all kinds, an iron merry-go-round, a teeter-totter, a big jungle gym, and a couple of swing sets, tall and short. Holly smiled. Cherry kept telling her she was too old to play on those things, but she wasn't going to give them up yet, at least not until junior high. Even then, maybe not.

"Those kids look like they're around your age," Cherry said as they drove slowly by.

"Maybe." The kids in the playground were mostly just standing around, probably freaked out by the earthquake. She turned her eyes back to the Brimstone Grand.

The backside of the big rectangular hotel pressed up close to the mountain and she could see now that only the top two floors had balconies. The narrow end of the building faced them. It had a dozen broad curved steps leading up to big arched double doors with tall windows bookending them. Above them was an ornate gold sign that said, *Devine's*.

There were people on the steps and everywhere else, some staring up at the building, some out at the vista below. Holly glanced that way - the view was incredible; she saw the town, then the long ribbon of road slicing through the desert until it finally disappeared into the mountains that hid Sedona, where they'd stopped for burgers on the way down.

"Earthquake, earthquake, earthquake," Cherry complained again as she drove past the gawking people and into the parking lot. "Like I said, that's all we'll hear about. Stupid earthquakes." She pulled past the restaurant, impatiently honking at people blocking her way. A row of parked cars faced the town below. Cherry pulled into a slot almost directly across from the lobby's double doors.

"Okay, kid, this is it." She pulled a rhinestone-encrusted brush out of her white handbag and ran it through her platinum blond Jayne Mansfield-style hair - she'd bleached it right after Mansfield died last year with hopes of becoming her replacement. It hadn't happened. She handed the brush to Holly and started reapplying her silvery-pink lipstick while Holly ran the bristles through her own honey-colored hair, using her hand to make it flip up around her shoulders the way Samantha on *Bewitched* did, fluffed her bangs and handed it back. Cherry reached out and straightened the collar of her blue checked shirt. "You'll do. Let's go."

They got out of the car and while Cherry adjusted her tight pink capris and centered the white cropped peasant blouse on her shoulders, Holly paused, looking between the bushes and trees to see the town and valley below. A couple of men stood close by, staring and pointing. Holly followed their fingers and saw a plume of smoke rising from several old buildings clustered together near the end of the main road. She could hear sirens and spotted a fire engine. It looked like a big red ant.

"Looks like Dick's Roadhouse is burning," said the man in the baseball cap.

"Damn shame," said the one in the cowboy hat. "I'll bet the quake cracked a gas line. He shoulda replaced that sonofabitch years ago."

"Hope it don't take out his neighbors."

"Probably will," the baseball guy observed. "Well, the Shrimp Shack is wood, it'll go for sure, but the Tool Shed is cement. She'll stand unless the fireboys don't know their asses from holes in the ground."

Holly fought off a giggle.

"The Shrimp Shed is no big loss," said the cowboy. "I got food poisoning last time I ate there."

"Come on, kid," Cherry said.

The two men looked up and, as usual, both of them grinned at Holly's mother. The Stetson and baseball cap were tipped. "Ladies," drawled the cowboy.

Cherry smiled, then nudged Holly toward the lobby door. She walked quickly, knowing that if she glanced back, the men would be staring at Cherry's rear end. They always did.

As they approached the glass doors of the Brimstone Grand, a creaky rumble startled Holly. A dozen feet down, a cream-colored garage door was being opened, but instead of being pushed up, a man in blue coveralls was rolling it sideways. Within, an engine roared to life and then the long hood of a deep violet car nosed out. It was old-fashioned but shiny-new, its chrome details glinting in the sun. Behind the wheel was a uniformed driver, eyes hidden behind dark glasses, mouth set in a grim line.

"Wow," Holly said. "What kind of car is that?"

"It's your grandmother's Rolls." Cherry blew a bubble then sucked the gum back in her mouth. "It's from the thirties, really old. Just like her."

The driver pulled the car away from the building and away from all the other vehicles, then got out and walked to the rear where he lit a cigarette then stood, legs slightly apart, posture perfect. *He's guarding it.*

"It doesn't look like a Rolls Royce," Holly observed. Except for the big rectangular grill and a glass hood ornament in the shape of a lady, it really didn't. It was long and rounded, like a race car, but weirder. After the windshield, the top of the car fell into a long slash a lot like the new Mustang Shelby or a Barracuda, but sloped all the way down to the wheels instead of cutting off for the trunk like modern cars.

"Can I go ask the man about it?"

"Holly, you're a girl. You're not supposed to think about cars," Cherry said. "It's time to stop being a tomboy and grow up. Let the boys worry about cars. Come on." She grabbed the handle to one entry door and pulled. "Let's go in and get this over with."

Reluctantly, Holly looked at the purple car - *the best color ever!* - and tried waving at the man. He didn't wave back, but did give her a slight nod.

"Come on, kid." Cherry held the door open.

3

NEW FRIENDS

Meredith Granger, manager of the Brimstone Grand, had chosen to remain behind the reception desk rather than retreat to the outdoors after the quake, but she'd sent her desk clerk, Peggy Moran, and the maids outside with the guests. Her husband, Michael, in charge of maintenance and just about everything else that didn't concern managing guests and staff, was inside as well, along with Whitey Sykes and Gilbert Perez, who were checking pipes and walls for cracks and other hazards. His other man, Rowdy, was outside checking the garages and looking for exterior earthquake damage.

Not that anyone expected to find anything. The Grand was poured concrete, solid, built to stand up in a town that once shook with mine blasting on a daily basis. A few framed pictures had tilted and ceiling fans swayed. Postcards on the desk slipped from their stack. That was it. The quake was minor. In truth, the lack of quakes in recent years was the most disturbing aspect and Meredith hoped that didn't mean more were on the way. The lobby bells jangled, followed by the unmistakable sound of heels clicking.

"Welcome to the Brimstone Grand," she said as the bleached

BRIMSTONE

blonde approached. The woman looked like an escapee from a beach party movie.

"Yeah, thanks." The blonde popped her gum.

A little girl about her own daughter's age arrived, her eyes immediately landing on the ancient elevator at the rear of the lobby. She made a beeline for it, stopping at the sign that gave its history. Her golden hair fell around her shoulders in lustrous waves and Meredith was suddenly sure she'd be the object of her mother's jealousy within a few years.

"Keep your hands to yourself," the blonde ordered, then turned to Meredith. She took off her big white-rimmed sunglasses revealing a moderately pretty face coated with expertly done makeup - but way too much of it. She blinked her false eyelashes at Meredith, displaying Carnaby Street-blue eyeshadow that went perfectly with her mod pearly lipstick. "We're expected."

"Do you have a reservation?"

The blonde laughed, a sound too harsh to be pretty. "Honey, I have a million reservations."

Meredith waited.

"I'm joking."

"Yes, I know. What name is your reservation under?"

"Devine."

Meredith's brows raised. *Can this be...*

"I'm your boss' daughter, Cherry Devine." She hooked a thumb toward the elevator, where the little girl studied old photographs on the wall. "And that's her granddaughter."

"It's so nice to have you with us. I hear you'll be staying for an unspecified amount of time."

"Yeah, I'm waiting on an acting job and we'll leave as soon as my agent calls, but I thought I'd bring the kid out here to get to know her granny." She affected a Marilyn Monroe pout. "You know, a little vacation from Hollywood. It can just be so exhausting." She sighed.

Meredith didn't know what to say, but was saved when the switchboard buzzed. She glanced back - it was Miss Delilah. "Excuse me just one moment."

Upon return, she told the blonde, "Your mother has requested that you join her in her penthouse immediately."

Cherry Devine fluffed her hair. "She wants everything ASAP." She laughed bitterly, then coughed. "But I'm sure you know that, don't you? We'll go see her - but meanwhile, get our rooms ready. *Two* of them."

"Miss Devine," Meredith said, "I'm sorry, but she was very specific. She only wants to see *you* right now. Your daughter can stay here with me while you visit."

"You hear that, Holly?" called Cherry.

The girl nodded, her attention fixed on a photograph of the Grand from its days as a hospital.

"Fine," Cherry said. "So how do I work that elevator, anyways? It looks like it's a hundred years old."

"It was installed in 1922," the little girl called. "That makes it-"

"Yeah, yeah." She looked at Meredith and rolled her eyes. "My little math whiz. She likes *cars*, too. I don't know where I went wrong."

Meredith ignored her comments. "Normally, you could take the elevator, but right now it's closed for inspection. You'll have to take the stairs. You'll find them in the alcove, to the right and left of the elevator. Take the right ones. They'll lead you straight to Miss Delilah's penthouse."

"Jesus Christ."

"They're not steep."

"Do I look like I can't walk up some ever-loving stairs? I don't care about that."

"I'm sorry?"

"Mothers," Cherry said, her smile a pale slash. "They just love giving orders, don't they?"

Before Meredith could find an answer, Cherry ordered her daughter to stay put and headed into the stairwell.

CHERRY DEVINE ALMOST ALWAYS EMBARRASSED HOLLY: THAT WAS why she'd gone directly to the elevator to check out all the placards about Brimstone while her mother did her thing. Cherry always tried to impress people by talking about being an actress and it made Holly want to hide.

But now she turned around and the moment she laid eyes on the woman behind the desk, she liked her. The lady had wheat-colored hair, dark blue eyes, and used hardly any makeup, at least compared to Cherry. She wore an empire-waisted dress that was maroon with tiny gray-green paisleys and a white Peter Pan collar and cuffs.

The lady smiled at her. "I'm Meredith, the manager. So you're Holly Devine. I've been looking forward to meeting you. Your grandmother told me you were coming."

"Holly *Tremayne*," she corrected. "I have my dad's last name."

"Holly Tremayne," Meredith repeated. "Like *Johnny Tremain*, the movie."

Holly smiled. "And the book. I love that book, but I love *Call of the Wild* more."

"Jack London's a wonderful writer," Meredith said. "What else do you like to read?"

"H. Rider Haggard, Mark Twain, Ray Bradbury, Nathaniel Hawthorne. I love *The House of the Seven Gables*. He hooked me on ghost stories!"

"Alice Pyncheon," Meredith said, "is one of my favorite ghosts."

"Mine too."

Meredith pulled a book out from under the desk. It was *The Return of the King* by J.R.R. Tolkien. "I'm almost done with *The Lord of the Rings* - I sure hate to see it end."

Holly had borrowed it from the library last spring. "I loved the trilogy! I just started *The Haunting of Hill House* by Shirley Jackson."

"Really?" Meredith looked surprised. "Your mom doesn't think you're too young for it?"

"She lets me read whatever I want. She doesn't care."

"Have you seen the movie?"

"Part of it. It was scary and I loved it. I want to see the whole thing after I read the book."

"It plays on TV now and then." Meredith leaned forward. "That's a really scary book. It gave me nightmares."

"You read it?" Holly liked Meredith even more.

"I did." She paused. "I have to tell you, Holly, this old hotel can be kind of creaky and groany, especially at night. A lot of people claim it's haunted."

"I've heard that." Holly tried to sound serious and sober, but the prospect of a ghost or two made her want to jump up and down.

Meredith studied her a long moment. "I've seen and heard a couple of odd things myself, but I can't say for sure. It's not scary here, but that book you're reading - well, it fired up my imagination and kind of spooked me for a while when I was covering the desk at night."

"I hope my room is haunted," Holly blurted. "I want to meet a ghost."

"You're a brave girl." Meredith smiled. "Holly, perhaps tonight you should read something fun like *The Wind in the Willows* or *The Hobbit* instead of a scary book. Just for the first night."

"It's okay, I'm not scared of anything."

Meredith laughed. "I can see that." The phone rang. "Excuse me just a moment, Holly."

"Sure." While Meredith was talking, Holly walked around the gift shop that filled the front lobby.

They had all kinds of good stuff including T-shirts and sweatshirts that advertised the hotel and the town. She looked through them and found a blue T-shirt with a black silhouette of the hotel and the words, "I spent the night in Delilah Devine's Brimstone Grand!"

"All done, Holly."

Holly returned to the desk and just as she was about to ask what kind of nightmares Shirley Jackson's book gave her, the door opened with a jingle of bells and a girl about her own age with hair the color of stardust came in. "Mom!" she said to Meredith.

"Becky, I want you to meet someone." Meredith came out from behind the desk. "Becky, this is Holly Tremayne. She's going to be staying here for a while. Holly, this is my daughter, Becky Granger."

"Hi," Becky said. She wore dark blue shorts and a white T-shirt with a faded picture of Davy Jones on it.

"Hi," said Holly. "It's too bad they cancelled *The Monkees*. I liked them, too."

"I wrote protest letters, but it didn't help," Becky said. "Who's your favorite?"

"Davy, I guess, but I like them all." Holly wasn't really all that into the TV show, but she liked the music.

"What's your favorite song?"

"*Valleri*. What's yours?"

This one Holly could answer honestly. "*Pleasant Valley Sunday* and *Last Train to Clarksville*."

"Coffee-flavored kisses," Becky said.

"Ew!" Both of them giggled as Becky's mom went back behind the counter. "What's your very favorite song of all?" Holly asked.

"Besides anything by *The Monkees*? I like *Ode to Billie Joe*. I always wonder what they threw off that bridge."

"Me too. But I like *White Rabbit* more than anything." Holly paused as Meredith's switchboard buzzed. "You know what song I hate?"

"No, what?"

"*Honey* by Bobby Goldsboro. It's just creepy."

"I *know*! I hate it, too." Becky paused. "Hey, do you want to come over to my house? We live right next door. We could listen to records and-"

"Holly?" Meredith came over and leaned on the counter. "Your grandmother wants to see you."

"Okay."

"But we were going to go listen to music," Becky said.

"I'm afraid that'll have to wait." Meredith turned to Holly. "Just go up the stairs, all the way to the fifth floor, and ring the doorbell. You can't miss it."

"I could show her-" Becky began.

"You can stay here and dust for me, okay?"

"Do I have to?"

"Yes, afraid so." Meredith smiled. "After that, you can go back to the playground if you want. If her mom says yes, I bet Holly would love to join you."

"I would. She will-"

"Go on up before your grandmother rings again, Holly."

✿ 4 ✿

MISS DELILAH

Holly took her time walking up the staircase to the fifth floor, not because it was tiring - the steps turned and had lots of landings - but because she was nervous. Except for leaving her friends and school behind, she had looked forward to coming to Brimstone and living in a grand hotel, but Cherry had said so many scary things about her grandmother that Holly worried some of them might be true. But her worry mostly stemmed from memories of the tall woman dressed in black with a small black feathered hat with a veil that hid most of her face. She'd carried an unlit cigarette in a long ebony holder that made Holly think of Cruella de Vil.

When Holly arrived on the fifth floor, it wasn't like the others - they all had halls dotted with numbered doorways and potted plants running their lengths. The fifth floor was sort of a big foyer with a door that said 'Miss Devine' instead of a number - and a little way down a second door instead of an exterior hallway. It said, "Staff Entrance."

Holly knocked on the 'Miss Devine' door and tried not to bite her lip too much. The door opened and instead of her grandmother, a plump dark-haired maid dressed in a black and white uniform smiled at her. "You must be Miss Holly."

"I am."

"I'm Frieda."

The maid let her pass then closed the door. "Follow me. Miss Delilah is waiting for you."

The long entry hall was so big that the bright crystal chandelier did little to dispel the gloom because dark venous wallpaper and matching maroon carpet soaked up most of the light. Gold framed photographs of Delilah Devine punctuated the redness, all black and white glamour photos from her days in the movies. *When she was a star.* It was like walking through a theater lobby.

After Frieda pulled a gold tassel a red velvet curtain opened - *it really is a theater!* The room beyond was lined with tall windows covered with ivory lace panels bordered by dark red velvet drapes. "This way." The maid gestured. Holly stepped through.

The next room - a reception room or something - was really big. Dark wood floors gleamed between Oriental rugs. Beside Holly was a Rococo bench, its carved legs covered in gold cherubs and white and gold leaves, the seat upholstered in red brocade. She reached out to touch it, but Frieda made a soft sound in her throat.

They passed by several coat racks, ornate chairs, and a dark curlicue-legged side table holding a silver tray, pitcher, and glasses, and entered the main area - a gigantic living room.

Delilah Devine sat on a white satin settee that was as prim and elegant as its occupant. The long black folds of her skirt spilled onto the crimson and black Oriental rug. With a graceful, slender hand she gestured Holly to a matching chair, her fingers sparkling with a dazzle of diamonds and rubies.

Holly approached, staring hard. Startling sapphire eyes and scarlet lips highlighted a porcelain face that was patrician yet much too young to belong to a grandmother. Like a black slash in the deep red room, Delilah Devine sat so straight it couldn't have been comfortable. "Hello, Holly. Do sit."

No part of her moved when she spoke except for her lips, and even they seemed eerily motionless. Hers was not the voice of an older woman; she sounded the same as she did in the movies she'd starred in decades ago. Holly sat, her eyes taking in the shadowed room; it was lit almost entirely by afternoon sun filtering through the amber sheers.

More heavy crimson drapes framed the windows of the long, long room, and if they'd been drawn, the room would have been black, but for the soft amber glow by old-fashioned table lamps with fringed shades. Her grandmother, even seated, even without a net veil, was still as imposing as when Holly had been five. She sat under a hanging lamp held by a plaster and gilt Cupid mounted above the couch. The shade was red velvet and the pale pinkish light reminded Holly of stage lighting - showing off Delilah Devine perfectly, flowing gently over her head and shoulders. She looked so beautiful, so mysterious - Holly was riveted. "Well, Holly? Do we not answer our elders? I said hello."

"I'm sorry, uh, Grandmother. I've just never seen a house like this."

"Miss Delilah."

"What?" Holly looked up.

"Call me Miss Delilah. Everyone does. Do not say 'grandmother' - it doesn't suit my image."

"Yes, okay. Um, Miss Delilah."

"And don't say 'um' - no one likes a stutterer."

"Okay."

"Do you like it?" Delilah remained statue-still.

In the background, Cherry coughed so softly that Holly knew she was trying not to interrupt. *Or be noticed.* "Do I like what, Miss Delilah?"

Delilah Devine's rich laugh - the one she'd heard in her movies - filled the room. It sounded warm - and a little scary. "My penthouse, Holly. Do you like it?"

"Very much. It kind of looks like a theater when you come in."

Delilah smiled thinly.

"Thank you. I brought all of my most treasured possessions with me when I moved here. You're welcome to look, but never to touch."

"Thank you." Holly was at a loss for words. She suddenly understood her mother a little better - Delilah was very imposing and a little scary.

"Before I let you and your mother explore your rooms, we must go over a few simple ground rules." Delilah paused. "Rules are important, don't you think?"

"Yes, they're very important."

"Good girl. I wish your mother had understood that so readily." She threw a glance over Holly's head. Following it, she saw Cherry sitting in a corner like a school kid being punished. Delilah fixed her gaze back on Holly. It was easy to see the fire in her grandmother's eyes. Her eyes were the same blue as Holly's and her found-cousin, Adeline, but there was no gold in them. Delilah cleared her throat. "Perhaps you can attend a summer session of charm school, young lady. Would you care for that?"

"I- I don't know."

"You don't even know what charm school is, do you?"

Holly shook her head to be polite. She knew what it was but didn't want to go.

"You'll learn to speak and walk like a lady. You learn how to dress and how to dance. It's very nice."

Holly wanted to look at her mother, but didn't dare. She could hear the venom underscoring Delilah's words and knew it was directed at Cherry. *No wonder she didn't want to come here.*

"What do you enjoy doing in your free time, Holly?"

"I like to read and I like to ride my bike." She'd had to leave her beloved bike behind because Cherry had been afraid it would scratch the Falcon.

"Anything else?"

"I really like cars. Is that purple Rolls your car, Miss Delilah?"

Her grandmother smiled. "Yes, that's my Phantom III Aero Coupe. The studio gave it to me after the success of *Violet Morne*." At the mention of the movie, Delilah folded her hands carefully together on her lap. It was the first time they'd moved since Holly sat down. "The phantom's color is, appropriately, Night Violet." She doused the smile. "But cars are hardly an appropriate interest for a young lady. What else do you like?"

"I like music."

"The classics?"

"Um-"

"You like the long hairs, then?"

Holly grinned. "Yes." She was surprised - she hadn't expected Delilah to like the Beatles or the Stones.

"Very good. At least you're not totally lacking in a musical education. What do you want to be when you grow up, Holly? What are your plans?"

"Maybe an astronaut or a secret agent, but probably a dolphin scientist or forest ranger. Or maybe an adventurer like Thor Heyerdahl."

Delilah sniffed. "You're young. You have plenty of time to grow out of those tomboyish notions. You're an attractive girl. Let me see you. Stand up and come to me."

Holly did as she was told. Delilah studied her.

"You take after my beloved sister, Carrie," Delilah said at last.

"I have a great-aunt?" Holly asked.

"No. She died when she was just sixteen."

"I'm sorry."

Delilah didn't speak for a long moment. "You have the same coloring. Your hair is gorgeous. I do hope it doesn't turn dark and drab. It usually does."

She looked so sad that Holly babbled, trying to fill the silence. "Did you ever meet my father? He was a famous photographer. His pictures of the Amazon and Machu Picchu were in *Life Magazine*." His pictures of Mt. Everest were published there, too, but that was too sad to mention. He'd died on the mountain two years ago and though his camera was brought back by his friends, they'd had to leave his body up there in the snow. *Don't think about it!*

"Sit down, Holly." Delilah's voice softened. "Yes, I met him. He was a good man and your mother was wrong to leave him."

"I-" Cherry said from her detention chair.

"I was not addressing you, Charlotte. Do mind your manners."

Charlotte? Charlotte? Charlotte is stuck in Delilah's web! The thought destroyed Holly's momentary sadness; it nearly made her giggle. She wouldn't use her real name either if it were Charlotte. Holly had no idea until now. It was ugly and made her think of Bette Davis with blood on her white ball gown, holding a hatchet behind her back. *Hush, Hush, Sweet Charlotte,* her mind began crooning.

There was a mechanical *click* and chimes rang from a massive walnut grandfather clock in a corner near Cherry's chair. *Charlotte's chair.* Holly made herself stay solemn.

"Sit down, Holly."

Holly returned to her seat.

"Now, as I explained to your mother, as long as you're under my roof, I expect you both to join me for dinner once a week. I will choose the night. We will dine here or downstairs in the restaurant. Do you have any objections to that arrangement, Holly?"

"No." Holly was only surprised they weren't going to have dinner together every night.

"Good. At dinner, I expect you to wear a nice dress and comb your hair. Don't wear what you have on now. Do you understand?"

"Yes." She wasn't too happy about that - she didn't really like dresses because you had to change out of them before you could climb on the monkey bars.

"You will each have your own room on the fourth floor and while the maids will change the beds and do the vacuuming and so forth once per week, I expect you to keep your own rooms clean. Is that a problem for you?"

Holly smiled her happiness. "No. I always cleaned the apartment and cooked dinner in Van Nuys."

Delilah's eyebrow arched. "Why am I not surprised to hear that?" She shook her head sadly in Cherry's direction. "That girl could never keep anything neat. Holly, while you are here, you are *not* to clean your mother's room for her. She must clean it herself. That is a law you will live by, both of you."

Nodding, Holly heard Cherry groan and wished she hadn't said anything. Her mother was going to be mad.

"Your rooms each contain a kitchenette. There's a sink, a few dishes, a hot plate, and a small refrigerator. You can use those or you can take your meals in the restaurant. Our staff has their own dining room and you're welcome to join them. They're expecting you." Delilah's voice rose. "Liquor, Charlotte, is *not* provided."

"Thank you, Miss Delilah." Holly spoke before Cherry could say something nasty. "That sounds great." Not having to make PB&Js or heat TV dinners or *SpaghettiOs* would be wonderful. Here, she'd get to eat *real* food.

"Now," Delilah said. "Am I forgetting anything?"

Holly waited.

"I suppose not. Oh, yes. You do need a source of income, I assume, so Holly, I'd like you to water the plants in the lobby and in the hall-ways of the first through fourth floors several times a week. It's very dry here and they need it. Does that suit you?"

"Yes! I'd like that." *Now I have an excuse to explore! Maybe I'll see the ghosts!*

"Excellent. I've already explained your mother's job to her, and there's no need to go into that with you." Outside, a hawk made a lone-some call. Delilah glanced at a window, then turned back to Holly. "Do not disturb the guests, no yelling or running, or any of that nonsense. Is that clear?"

It was hard to see the soaring hawk through the amber sheers. "Yes. Don't worry. I'll be good."

Delilah eyed her. "I suspect you will. I do hope Charlotte will also be good. Now, have you met my manager, Meredith Granger, yet?"

"Yes, she's nice." Holly smiled.

"You and Charlotte go see her now. She'll see to it that you have your keys and that your bags are brought upstairs." Delilah rose in a hush of expensive black crepe. "There will be no switching rooms. Remember that, Charlotte. Now, if you'll both excuse me, I have drinks with the Commodore in half an hour. She retrieved a silver bell from the side table and rang it. Frieda appeared instantly. "Yes, Miss Delilah?"

"Please see my guests out."

DELILAH DEVINE WAITED UNTIL SHE HEARD HER DAUGHTER AND

granddaughter leave, then walked the length of the vast living room, passing several conversation areas - clutches of settees and chairs, each with their own accent tables and lamps, past a grandfather clock, and the dark alcove where Charlotte had waited. She'd had many of the walls removed on the fifth floor when she moved in because she loved open big spaces where she could see everything. She hated feeling trapped.

She passed a heavy-legged game table, mahogany inlaid with ivory and ebony squares and, finally, the billiards table with its burgundy felt and heavily ornamented Georgian legs. She trailed her hand over the felt; she'd bought the table in 1937, as well as many of the other pieces that filled her home. She acquired her Aero Coupe that same year, after *Violet Morne*, the movie that had transfixed the world and made her a household name and would have earned her an Oscar - if the shenanigans of that *other* actress hadn't swayed the vote.

She'd been just twenty-five years old then, and beautiful. Charlotte was an adorable toddler in those days, coddled by Delilah when she had the time and always by her nanny and her daddy, Clifton Danvers, at least until the selfish bastard ran off with Millicent McKensy in 1939. *Slutty little nobody.* Delilah took solace in the fact that Millicent never made it out of the starlet phase. The studio dropped her like a hot potato after Clifton put a bun in her unbetrothed oven. Before long, Clifton's career began fading along with his good looks - because, after all, he'd never been much of an actor.

Just like his daughter. Charlotte had turned into an even bigger disappointment than Clifton. She took after him in every way from her mud-colored hair and husky-blue eyes - so pale people either loved them or recoiled - to her preoccupation with sex. And the fact that she'd chosen to use - and tarnish - Delilah's own surname was something that couldn't be forgiven. Delilah had paid Max, her loyal driver, to endure one of her daughter's vile movies and report back to her. The girl was shameless.

Delilah entered her bathroom, all gold gilt and marble. When she had inherited the derelict hospital, she'd immediately begun renovations on the first four floors to serve as a hotel. But on the fifth - her penthouse - she had the workmen tear out all the tiny hospital rooms.

She loathed confined spaces almost to the point of phobia - and so had her living quarters made spacious and open. She'd had them build in a few other rooms, of course. The kitchen, laundry, guest rooms, study, a formal dining room, a music room. Her private bathroom was as big as a typical master bedroom and her bedroom was the size of a studio apartment.

Now she looked at the gold-plated swan-shaped faucets and hand-painted sinks, the matching claw foot tub, toilet, and bidet. The porcelain was painted in the manner of Monet, allowing her to be surrounded by water lilies whenever she bathed. She, Max, and Vera had removed all the detailing and fixtures she loved in her mansion in Beverly Hills before the mortgage holder could repossess it after the bad investments had killed her stock portfolio. *Bastards.* Out here, in the wildly uncivilized southwest, she was easily able to find new marble for the bathroom counters and floors, all five of them, at a very reasonable price.

She brushed her hair - still dark with only a little help from a bottle - then removed her makeup and washed her face. After that, she opened a jar of *Visage Ravissant* and inhaled the scent of orange blossoms and honey, before massaging it into her skin.

As she did each day, she forced herself to examine her face for new signs of aging. She'd never had work done - too many of her friends had ended up chasing youth with a scalpel until they turned into monstrosities. Delilah refused to do such a thing, but aging had brought about the end of good leading roles. When she began being cast as a mother or aunt to the younger leading ladies - *before I even turned thirty-five!* - she let her contracts run out. She couldn't face aging in public.

Hollywood treated any woman over thirty-five as a has-been, and Delilah refused to be such a thing. It was better to retire from film. She had continued working on the stage - a much more forgiving venue - for many years, but eventually got tired of fans staring at her; it felt like they were counting the lines in her face while she signed their autograph books. It got to the point that she couldn't shop or dine out in Manhattan for fear of being recognized. She'd never liked that, but as she advanced into her forties, it became intolerable.

Deep inside, she felt she'd somehow failed by aging; she demanded perfection from herself. Eventually she retired from the stage and moved to Beverly Hills where she took up life as a recluse. There, she had her staff go shopping for her, had chefs brought in from famous restaurants to cook in her kitchen, and lived quietly with her long-time servants, Max and Vera, and a few others.

It was a good life until the money began drying up. She had to go back to work, taking roles in Universal horror films and other B movies. It was humiliating even though she acquired a new and enthusiastic set of fans. In the movies, she looked good, but she dreaded the studio asking her to make public appearances or do television interviews.

Even so, those trashy movies had paid the bills and kept her in her mansion, at least until her idiot financial manager, Leon Penske, had convinced her to make a series of bad investments. It was a very good thing that her inheritance had come along when it did because it not only saved her from the public humiliation of losing her home, but provided this wonderful place to live, far from Hollywood and the fans. After Leon turned coward and blew his brains out, she didn't try to hire another advisor. Instead, she consulted with Victor Campion, an old friend who'd lawyered for one of the studios back in the day. The Commodore, as everyone called him, had never steered her wrong; and if they occasionally indulged in a bit of romance - as they had since her first days as a divorcee - he was a consummate gentleman. He never told. She treasured him. He retired to Sedona shortly after she had moved to Brimstone. It was convenient for both of them.

And here in Brimstone she didn't need much income to live well - her decision - encouraged by Victor - to turn the first four floors of the massive old hospital into a hotel was one of the best she'd ever made. It gave her enough income to live as she desired; the only thing she didn't like was the fact that the fans had found her - *I never should have named the restaurant after myself.* The fans weren't just tourists, unfortunately - Brimstone was acutely aware that she was a native and they were forever trying to get her to appear at town functions, act in their little theater, or be the guest of honor at parades and tiny conventions. She countered all of it by avoiding conducting business in Brimstone.

She reapplied her eyeshadow, mascara, and lipstick. Even at fifty-six, her skin remained relatively smooth, relatively flawless. And she needed no foundation, nothing but a light dusting of translucent powder, though if she went out by day, she always wore a little feathered cap and veil to soften gravity's torture.

5

THE BELLHOP

"This is all for me?" Holly looked at Meredith, who had left the desk in her assistant's care in order to bring Holly and her mother to their rooms. First, she had opened Cherry's room on the other side of the hall. It was nice, with a bed, a table and two chairs, a tiny kitchen, and a window that looked out on the mountainside not more than five feet away. Then, leaving Cherry, she had taken Holly across the hall and unlocked room 429.

"This is all yours, Holly. Your grandmother has given you one of the nicest little rooms we have - and she said that I should tell you that if your mother tries to switch with you, to say no and to immediately let her know." She smiled. "Or let me know, if that's easier."

"Okay." Holly loved the room. It had the same furnishings and kitchenette as Cherry's, but big triplet windows looked out over Brimstone, the desert, and the northern mountains. There was a glass-paneled door with a crystal knob next to the windows. Holly glanced at Meredith.

"Go ahead, open it."

Holly did - and stepped out onto a long balcony that ran the length of the building. In front of each room was a little wooden table with a pair of matching chairs. "Wow! How come I get this and Cherry doesn't?"

Meredith shook her head. "I don't know, but Miss Delilah was very specific. I'm sure there's a good reason."

Holly wondered what would happen if Cherry came to her room and saw the balcony. She could close the drapes over the windows. But the door ... "Um, is there any way I can cover the door so you can't see the balcony? Like drapes or something?"

Meredith considered, then nodded. "That's a good idea. I'll measure the door and cut down some extra window drapes to fit it. It's pretty easy. Do you like to sew?"

"I don't know how."

"This evening, we'll make you a drape. How's that?"

"Really?"

"Really. What are you doing for dinner tonight?"

"Nothing. My grandmother, I mean Miss Delilah, said I could eat with the employees."

"What about your mother?"

"She won't care. She likes to go out to eat."

"Maybe she wants to take you out to eat."

Holly laughed. "That'd be a first."

Meredith smiled gently. "Do you think she'd let you come to dinner at our house - it's almost right next door? You could meet the rest of our brood and you and I can hit the sewing machine after that."

"Cherry won't care. She was hardly ever home in LA. She let me do whatever I wanted."

"Really? So, what did you do?"

"I made my dinner and did my homework and read or watched TV. Sometimes I spent the night at a friend's house. It was okay."

Meredith hugged her. Just like that, and Holly, for probably the first time in her whole life, hugged back, and didn't want to stop.

"Come on, let's go get your mom and we'll go downstairs and bring up some of your luggage. Or all of it if the elevator has been cleared. How's that?"

"Great!"

✠

"WHY, YOU'RE JUST A LITTLE SQUIRT, AREN'T CHA?" ARTHUR MEEKS said to the girl as he hefted her mother's massive bags out of the Falcon's trunk. Although the bellhop was six feet tall and no scarecrow, lifting the blonde's luggage was a real chore. "You bring your anvil collection, Miss Devine?"

The bitch couldn't have heard him, but her sudden laugh jeered into his ears. She looked to be making eyes at Jared-Bob Benderson, the pretty delivery boy in a white Stetson who was climbing back in the Gower Pharmacy Metro. *Too bad, lady, you ain't his type.*

Arthur swung out a small bag as heavy as three bowling balls and plunked it on the luggage rack. He'd have known exactly who this woman was the moment he laid eyes on her even if Meredith hadn't said her name before she sent him out. The blonde with delusions of Marilyn Monroe was Delilah Devine's daughter, who grew up to be a porn star - and while he admired the body, he didn't much like the baggage that came with it. He chuckled at his pun. *There's luggage and there's luggage!*

Arthur was good at pegging people. After a dozen years as a bellhop all over town - the last several here at the Brimstone Grand - he was a real expert. Cherry Devine might have a great rack and an ass that could shoot sunshine - Lord knew he'd seen it often enough at the X-E Lady Theater downtown - but she was a bitch.

Again, he looked at the little girl watching him load the cart and wondered if she knew what her mother did for a living. *Don't look like it, but you never know, nosireebob.* He pulled another bag - one printed with stars and moons and adorned with a *U.S.S. Enterprise* sticker - that had to belong to the kid. He wondered if she'd grow up to be a slut like her mommy or a queen douchebag like her granny. The girl had just the beginnings of tiny boobs, nothing but buds really. He gave his desert-dry lips a little lick and wondered if she'd grow melons like her mother's. He hoped not; Arthur liked a girlish figure more than a zaftig one.

He grabbed another bag - it obviously held a big hair dryer. It slipped from his hands and even though he caught it before it touched the ground, Cherry Devine swore at him. "Watch what you're doing, or I'll have you fired."

"I've seen your movies," Arthur muttered.

"What did you say?"

He looked her in the eye. "I've seen your movies."

"I don't give out autographs. Or samples."

"Wasn't going to ask." He glanced at the little girl, then back at Mom. "You've been in a lot of them. I think I first saw you in *Fire Hose Gals*," what, in 1958, was it?"

She glared at him. "If you're trying to earn a tip, here it is: stop yapping and do your job."

She'd already given him a headache; next the broad would give him a hernia. "Sorry, Miss Devine." He hoisted another case bearing a *Star Trek* decal from the trunk and turned his gaze on the little girl. "So, is your rock collection in this bag?"

"Those are my books." Her voice was stern.

He smiled at her, long and slow. "Meant no offense."

Cherry snapped her gum. "You're sure weak for a guy your size. What are you, five-ten?"

"I'm six feet," he retorted, wishing he dared ask if she was fucking a Harlem Globetrotter. *The bitch.* "And I ain't weak."

"Just get done. I've got places to go."

"People to meet."

"Right." She popped her gum.

"So, are you retiring up here?" He made his voice light and harmless. "Like your mother?"

"Don't I look a little young to be retiring?"

Not with your clothes off, baby. "Sorry, you just have so much luggage that I thought–"

"You aren't paid to think, bellboy." Cherry Devine unlocked the rear passenger door. "When you're done there, we've got a lot of clothes on the backseat for you to take upstairs."

"Yes, ma'am." His smile could have eaten a mountain of shit.

The porn star made a satisfied sound and waited for him to shut the empty trunk. She locked it. "We'll meet you inside," she said as she strutted away.

"Miss," he called after her. "I can only bring up a couple of the smaller cases right now. The rest have to wait until Mike Granger okays the elevator. The-"

"Quake, I know," she finished. "The fucking earthquake. Well, get it inside and put it where nobody will steal anything. Bring up those three red suitcases and the blue one for my daughter. That will get us through until evening."

"Yes, ma'am."

"I expect them all to be delivered tonight even if you have to carry every single bag up the stairs yourself. My mother pays you to do that, so that's what you'll do."

He nodded, happy he got off work at six. Steve Cross would have to play slave for the bitch.

HOLLY DIDN'T LIKE THE WAY ARTHUR MEEKS' EYES CRAWLED ALL over her so she trailed behind him and Cherry as he dragged the luggage cart over the gravel parking lot to the lobby. He was having a hard time because it was so overloaded. Holly would have volunteered to help him if he hadn't been so creepy. He wore a uniform with gold epaulets, gold buttons, and a little round hat kind of like Jerry Lewis in *The Bellboy*. Thin colorless hair had escaped it and whickered like wheat on the warm breeze. He was icky.

When they entered the lobby, Holly went straight to Meredith at the desk. The woman smiled. "Did you ask your mom about coming over tonight?"

"Yes, it's fine."

"Good. I'll be done here in just a few minutes, and as soon as Steve arrives, we can leave."

Holly nodded then glanced at the creepy bellhop who had pulled Cherry's three red cases and her blue one off the cart. "Please leave my suitcase there," she told him "I'll get it myself later."

The bellhop grinned and smacked his wide rubbery lips. "Whatever you say, little miss." He set her case in an alcove by a room just behind the front desk. He looked at her and licked his lips.

Cherry didn't notice; she was too busy hurrying Meeks along. "You be polite, Holly," she called over her shoulder. "And don't wear out your welcome. Be back here at a reasonable hour. Before midnight."

"I will."

Meeks waited for Cherry at the stairwell. She glanced at him. "Go on ahead, I'll catch up in a minute." She returned to the desk. "Um, Meredith, right?"

"Right."

"Is there any nightlife around here?"

"What kind of nightlife?"

"A place where I can get a drink and a burger. Hear some music, maybe dance."

"Well, yes. There are several places, though none of them are terribly reputable."

"I don't care about that. What do you have for me?"

Holly cringed, slowly moving away from her mother.

"There's Darkside Johnnie's, right in the center of town, on Main. You'll recognize it by the big green neon sign and all the motorcycles parked out front."

Cherry's eyes lit up. "A biker bar?"

"Yes. One of the nicer ones, I hear." Meredith smiled wanly. "Almost all the bars around here are full of bikers. Probably a quarter of the town's population is bikers."

"You don't say." Cherry smiled. "I do enjoy a man who knows how to ride a hawg."

Arthur Meeks grinned. His chin had a cleft but it was underslung and something about that, combined with his broad flat upper lip and the limp dishwater hair gave Holly the creeps. Cringing, she slipped into the souvenir area and examined some salt and pepper shakers shaped like miners and donkeys, cowboys and cacti.

"Darkside Johnnie's has live music and dancing. I can't guarantee you it's every night though."

"Thanks. I'll check it out after I shower and put on my dancing shoes." Cherry turned to leave, but the entry door jingled as a tall blond man dressed in black came in.

He was handsome and Holly tried not to stare, but Cherry practically tore off his clothes with her eyes. "Steve," Meredith said. "You're here in the nick of time."

He grinned and let himself through the registration desk's gate. His golden hair was probably long - Holly thought there might be a pony-tail hidden under his black turtleneck. He had sideburns sort of like Mike Nesmith of the Monkees, but smaller, so they didn't look hippie-sized. Holly thought he was absolutely gorgeous. She saw Cherry looking at his hair and sideburns, too, and wondered if she thought he was a hippie. Probably not; she was wetting her lips and looking at him like he was dinner. Holly felt a pang of something unpleasant, but hadn't a clue what it was.

"Merry Meredith," he said in a soft, pleasant voice. "How are things tonight? Did the quake do any damage?"

"I don't think so. Michael hasn't given the go ahead to use the elevator yet, but I suspect he will any minute now."

Steve nodded. "He's a cautious guy. That's cool."

"It is. Steve, I'd like to introduce you to our new guests. They'll be staying for a while-"

"Just until my agent calls with a new job." Cherry wet her lips again and squirmed to make her boobs look bigger as she put her hand across the desk. "Cherry Devine. You work for my mother," she informed the handsome man.

"Steven Cross," he said, giving her hand the briefest of shakes. "I'm the night man."

"I'll just bet you are." Cherry spoke in Monroe tones.

He looked confused.

"And over here," Meredith nodded toward Holly, "we have Holly Tremayne, Miss Delilah's granddaughter."

Steve smiled at her, a big winning grin, and the skin crinkled around his eyes in the most pleasing way possible. Holly's tummy did a little squiggle as she approached him.

"Hello, Holly," he said, extending his hand. "I'm happy to meet you. I'm here all night, so if there's anything you need, or if you have any questions, just ring the front desk."

Holly blushed but didn't giggle. Instead, she shook his hand solemnly. It was warm and dry and she hoped hers was, too. She could see he was way too old for her - he was probably at least twenty-five or even thirty. "Hi, Steve."

Her mother looked annoyed.

He opened his mouth to say something but the ding and whoosh of the elevator interrupted. "Mike cleared the elevator?"

"Looks like," Meredith said.

"It's about time!" Cherry turned toward the elevator but stopped cold as the door opened and Delilah Devine and a man in a white captain's hat exited. Without showing herself, Holly watched as her grandmother whisked the handsome white-haired man - *the Commodore* - past Cherry without a word or a glance. Delilah wore a silvery veil attached to a small cap of matching feathers, and her dress was a knee-length silver-gray boat neck with a cigarette skirt and a silver belt. Her high heels were silver, too. They turned down the hall that led to the restaurant.

Meredith was on the phone. "Mike, did you okay the elevator?" She paused. "Okay, great. See you at home." She turned to Holly. "Ready?"

"Ready!"

6

HORSES, HORSES, AND MORE HORSES

The Grangers' home, a multi-level adobe, stood hidden at the top of a curving cobblestone driveway. Only the glowing amber windows of the upper floors were visible above the trees until they arrived at the courtyard. There, all the lights gleamed welcome. "It's beautiful," Holly said.

"We like it." Meredith opened the door.

When she stepped inside, Holly held her breath. It was an old house, Meredith explained as she showed her around, almost as old as the hotel, and the head surgeon had lived there back when it was the Clementine Hospital.

Despite its age, the home seemed modern, with some of the rooms a step or two up or down from the others. The walls were painted in the palest shade of peach and in the cheery kitchen, cobalt blue tile wrapped the counters, with Mexican tiles painted with yellow and orange flowers punctuating the blue sea of tile. It was all so perfect and brilliant that Holly vowed to herself that her own kitchen would look the same someday. "This is the most beautiful room I've ever seen," she said, committing everything to memory.

"Glad you like it." A huge orange fluff ball of a cat trilled and leapt from a kitchen chair. He came right up to Holly and rubbed against

49

her legs, purring. "That's Fluffy," Meredith said. "He's asking you to pet him."

"Hi, Fluffy!" Enchanted, Holly scratched him behind his ears. He trilled again.

"Fluffy, you can beg more pets later." Meredith smiled. "Come on, let's find Becky." A moment later they were upstairs in a wide hall hung with brilliant wildflower paintings, reds, oranges, yellows offset with blues. Meredith knocked on one of the doors. "Becky, Holly's here."

In an instant, Becky opened the door. "Want to see my horse collection?"

"Sure." Holly entered Becky's room. There was an oriole window that looked out over the town and desert. The view was a lot like the one Holly had from her own balcony, but better because the oriole had a built-in bench and books lined the sill. "I could sit there and read all day and night. This is so nice."

"Dinner's in half an hour." Meredith Granger shut the door gently behind her.

Holly was busy looking at the books. There were some *Nancy Drews*, *Little Women*, *Anne of Green Gables,* and *The Hobbit.*

"You can borrow any you want," Becky said, coming up beside her. "I've read all of them."

"Thanks. I'm going to start *The Haunting of Hill House* tonight. Do you like ghost stories?"

Becky looked thoughtful. "I get scared pretty easy. I even had nightmares after we saw *The Ghost and Mr. Chicken*. Did you see that?"

Holly nodded. "That was so fun! I loved the organ that played by itself." She noticed the model of a dappled gray stallion Becky held. "He's pretty."

Becky thrust the horse into Holly's hands. "I got him for my birthday last month. I want a real horse just like him. My dad says I can have one when I'm old enough to get a job to pay the stable rent." She gestured at a wall behind her. "There's the rest of my collection. Don't you just love horses?"

"They're nice." Holly checked out the models. There were palominos and chestnuts and pintos and appaloosas - probably at least thirty different horses on narrow shelves mounted on the wall. Holly liked horses okay, but Becky, like most of her California friends, was insane for them. Holly wanted a Mustang with tires rather than one with hooves. She knew she was a little weird, but didn't care.

Suddenly, the door burst open and a tow-headed little boy yelled "BOO!" at the top of his lungs.

"Todd! Get out of here!" Becky cried.

"Boo!" the boy yelled again, then he noticed Holly and looked away, possessed by shyness.

"You can't come in here, Todd." Becky stalked toward him. "Get out or I'll tell Mom."

The boy shrieked and raced out of the room. Becky closed the door. "Little brothers are horrible. So are big brothers. Do you have brothers or sisters?"

Holly shook her head. "No. I always wished I had a sister, though."

"Me, too." Becky smiled. "We can be sisters."

"Okay."

By the time Meredith called them for dinner, Holly knew every name of every horse and had been introduced to more models of Barbies and Kens than she'd ever seen.

And she wasn't so sure she wanted a sister.

7

ARTHUR MEEKS

In his four years at the Brimstone Grand, Arthur Meeks had drilled discreet holes in a number of walls separating the rooms. They hid behind pictures, in patterned wallpaper, and other places that were hard to spot. Now, off duty, the doorman stood in Room 424 and removed a painting of the desert at sunset done by some local yokel who had more ambition than talent. The Queen Douchebag called it 'supporting the arts.' Arthur called it supporting crap. He set the painting on the bed in the empty room then pressed his eye to the peephole.

Cherry Devine was in 426's shower - he couldn't see her but he could hear her singing *Thank Heaven for Little Girls*. She was crooning in a breathy Monroe fashion.

It was working for Arthur; he liked all girls, but the younger the better was his motto, yessireebob.

He wished he could see her as she sang, watch the hot water spanking her bottom and drizzle down her face, caressing her breasts, kissing her belly, splashing all over her cooch and legs. He wondered how she washed that cooch of hers. With a rough cloth or did she slip the bar of soap right up in there or maybe just use her fingers to get every last bit clean?

Or maybe she's a dirty girl ...

He shivered, refusing to touch himself. That was for later. The faucets squeaked off and he held his breath, hoping she wouldn't dress in the bathroom.

He watched, pressed to the wall for several minutes, then she entered the bedroom, wearing a short white terry robe that swatted her asscheeks without hiding them. *Bend over, bend over, bend over!*

And she did.

The carpet didn't match the drapes, not by a long shot, but seeing that dark bush peek out from behind that sweet ass as she bent over her suitcase brought Methuselah roaring to life. He thumped against the wall, but Cherry Devine didn't hear him - she was singing to herself again as she pulled tiny rose-red bikini bottoms up her thighs.

Panties in place, she dropped the robe and when she finally turned around he saw those double Ds sway as she moved. He remembered them well from the stag films at the X-E Lady. They were still full and heavy, though now they hung a lot lower than they had when she was in *Fire Hose Gals* years ago - but then his own balls got splashed by toilet water when he dropped his business these days. Father Time was kind to no man. Or woman.

Cherry put on a matching red push-up bra that made her melons jut so far out you could eat dinner on them. *Looking good, little lady. Looking good.* Methuselah throbbed.

Crossing to the dresser, she came so close to the peephole that he dared not blink or even breathe. She started putting on makeup, a lot of it, lining her eyes with black mascara and shading the lids with light blue shadow. Finally, she added false eyelashes, applied pink blush, then lipstick so pale it sparkled like snow. It looked cheap and whorey, and he liked it.

Finally, she walked away from the dresser, giving him the perfect view. She shimmied into a glittery red top with long sleeves and a low neck, then fastened a black velvet choker decorated with a red cherry around her throat. A pair of glossy black capris sheathed her legs. Then she stepped into black heels so tall that most gals couldn't walk in them, but she moved like a champ, without a waver. *Just like a pro, yessireebob!*

She stood in front of the full-length mirror turning this way and that, then put a finger to her lips and kissed it then moved it down to her ass, touched it and made a sizzle sound. "You've still got what it takes," she told her mirror image.

Indeed, she did. Arthur Meeks waited for her to leave, replaced the painting, then counted to one fifty before letting himself out of the room. The floor was quiet. He looked across the hall at 429, where the little girl was staying. He knew she'd gone off to Meredith's place for the evening and that there was no spyhole between rooms 429 and 427. At least not yet – but there would be. Pussy that young needed watching.

8

DINNER

"How long are you going to be staying?" Greg Granger asked between forks of spaghetti.

Greg had medium brown hair, dark blue eyes, dimples, and was going to be a freshman at Brimstone High School in September. He was fourteen and really cute.

"I don't know," Holly said as her cheeks heated up. "Cherry - that's my mom - says it's just until she gets a call from her agent about a movie, but she hasn't had a call in months. I hope we get to stay here a really long time. I love it."

"I hope you stay forever and ever!" Becky said.

"What movies is your mom in?" Greg asked. "I go to the movies all the time. Maybe I've seen her."

Mike Granger choked a little, took a big drink of water, then cleared his throat. "I doubt you've seen her, son. I think she makes documentaries." He winked conspiratorially at Holly.

"Yes," she said. "Those. I haven't seen any either. Uh, she says they're boring."

"Any plans tomorrow, Holly?" Meredith asked.

"I don't think so."

"Maybe Becky can introduce you to some of the other kids. Or you two could go into town and have a look around."

"We could go to the Uncle Sheldon's stables and go horseback riding!" Becky chirped.

"Let's give Holly a chance to get acclimated first," Meredith countered.

"Okay. We can do whatever you want tomorrow, Holly. If you want to go horseback riding ..."

"Maybe in a few days?" Holly had never even been on a horse and it sounded like fun, but she really wanted to see the town. "I'd like to go downtown. And I want to go by the Humble Station."

"Sure. We can get sodas there. Did you bring your bike?"

"We had to leave it behind, but Cherry said we'd get one here when she has time."

"You can use mine," Meredith said. "I never ride it anymore."

"Are you sure?" Holly asked, surprised.

"I'm positive, sweetie. It's been gathering dust in the garage for years."

"Maybe Greg can clean it up and check the tires in the morning?" Mike Granger said. "That okay, son?"

"Sure." The boy spoke around a mouthful of garlic bread.

Holly felt like a frog who'd just been kissed. "You're so nice to me." Tears of happiness threatened but she refused to let them spill.

"We only need bikes when we use the road, like for going to the Humble Station," Becky said. "Mostly, we go downtown on foot. There's a shortcut."

"It all sounds nice." Holly looked around the table. Meredith and Michael Granger sat at either end. Little Todd was next to his mother, and she, Becky, and Greg took up the middle. The dining room was just off the kitchen, and it was so warm and cozy and the food so incredible and the Grangers so nice, that she felt like she'd walked into a fairy tale. Or a TV show where everybody was happy and normal. She liked it a lot.

"It's really fast going down but not so fast coming back up," Becky was saying.

"You have to get used to the climb," Greg added. "But it's easy."

"I'm sorry? Where is the shortcut?"

"The path starts near the playground. There are even stairs when you get close to Main Street. It only takes ten or fifteen minutes to get there."

"Wow! That sounds great."

"But it'll probably take a lot longer for you to come back up the first few times," Greg added. "The air is thin because we're a mile up - and it's a steep climb. But you'll get used to it."

Holly loved to run and figured it wouldn't be too bad.

"There's a haunted house a little way down, not too far from the trail," Greg said. "They found a body in there a couple years ago."

"Greg!" Meredith said. "Knock it off. No one found any bodies."

"But-"

"Greg," said his father. "Those rumors have been circulating since your grandpa was a boy." He looked at Holly. "There *is* an old wreck of a not-haunted house but don't go near it. You'll break your neck."

"So, there weren't any bodies?" Holly asked, disappointed. "No murders?"

"No," Meredith said. "It's just an old house that should've been torn down years ago. It's dangerous because it's falling apart. That's all. More salad, anyone?"

"There's this old rocking chair in there," Greg said. "It rocks by itself."

"Greg-" began Meredith.

"Really?" Holly asked. "Did you see it?"

Greg shook his head too quickly. "Nah. I just heard about it is all."

"That rocking chair must be pretty old by now," Meredith said. "Didn't your grandfather tell you the same story, Mike?"

"Sure did. That and the one about the Brimstone Beast."

Holly grinned. "I love folklore. Adeline Chance, at the Humble Station, gave me a book about Brimstone folklore and the Beast is in it."

Mike Granger cleared his throat. "The copper miners told stories about it - kind of like the tommyknocker stories the Cornish miners brought to the Pennsylvania coal mines, but the Brimstone Beast originally comes from a local Indian legend. It's a fun story."

At that moment, it felt like an invisible giant pushed the table up with his knees, a single big *bump* that made the dishes rattle. Holly found herself hanging onto her plate and looking at the Grangers. Todd was oblivious but Becky's eyes were wide. So were Greg's, but then he saw her looking at him and he put on an unconcerned smile. Their parents looked alert.

"Aftershock," Mike Granger said.

"If it happens again, under the table, all of you." Meredith's voice was steel.

They waited, half empty plates untouched. One minute, two. Nothing happened. Greg started eating. Everyone else followed suit.

"Did the Brimstone Beast cause earthquakes?" Holly asked, half-smiling. So far, she kind of liked quakes, thinking they were like E-ticket rides at Disneyland.

"They blamed everything on the Beast," Greg said. "But the Beast is just a fairy tale."

"They used the stories to scare children into minding their parents." Meredith smiled. "I bet the Indians did, too."

"The Brimstone Beast is quite a fairytale," added Mr. Granger. "And not a nice one, unless you like your fairies big, dark, and deadly. The legend goes back centuries. Maybe even a thousand years or more if those petroglyphs up in the ancient Puebloan ruins are being read correctly."

"I want to see the petroglyphs," Holly said. "I love history!"

Becky rolled her eyes. "There's just a bunch of lines and squiggles up there."

"Only if you don't know how to read them," Greg said.

9

TICKET TO RIDE

Darkside Johnnie's was a roadhouse in every sense of the word. When Cherry pulled up to the low-slung building way out on Main, she had to cruise the red Falcon past three dozen motorcycles before she found a place to park.

Johnnie's was done up Western-style so it looked like a gigantic false-front miner's shack turned into a saloon. It belonged on a movie set, except for the green neon sign that read, "Darkside Johnnie's." Above the name a neon cowboy waved his hat from atop a bucking bronco. *What a dive.*

Cherry grabbed her black macramé handbag, checked to make sure her smokes, lighter, gum, lipstick, and a couple of condoms were tucked in alongside her wallet, then got out and locked up the Falcon, checking all the doors and the trunk. You couldn't be too careful in a piece-of-shit place like Brimstone. At the last minute, she shucked her jacket and left it in the car. It was black leather, made just for her, and she didn't need to lose it to some light-fingered bimbo while she was taking a piss. And, as nice as it looked, you couldn't show off the goods in a jacket.

Country music twanged as she moved between the building and the bikes. The windows were blacked out so you couldn't see what was going on inside, but behind the music she picked up the sound of drunken men having a good time. That was a good sign. On her right, motorcycles gleamed. There were a few dirt bikes mixed in, too. Or maybe just dirty bikes. *Who fucking knows?*

She approached the entry doors - they had big X-shaped barn door crosses on them. Two guys, one in a black Stetson, were holding up the wall. The cowboy tipped his hat without taking it off. "Evening, ma'am. How you doin' tonight?" His eyes crawled up her body and came to rest on her tits.

The other guy, in a red ball cap and dirty jeans - he looked like a mechanic - just smoked and stared. It didn't bother her; she was used to creeps like him.

"Real good if this place doesn't water the drinks."

"It sure don't, ma'am," Cowboy replied. "And we have the good stuff." He pulled a door open wide for her. The music amplified and the smell of smoke and beer roiled out into the night.

"Cover charge?" she asked, batting her lashes at the cowboy.

"No, ma'am, no cover for the ladies." His eyes roamed her body as she drew near. "Are you a local? You look familiar."

"I have that effect." Cherry headed into the bar.

It was pretty much one big room with a bar on a long wall, and a little stage on the short one. Cherry stood among tables that ended at the big dance floor in front of the stage. Half a dozen couples hung on each other, slow-dancing. *Oh, brother. This place is one big backcountry shithole.*

The band was dressed in jeans, cowboy hats, and fringed leather jackets. Only the bass player had long hippie hair - the other four had Elvis-style 'dos and that was a good sign that they might be able to play something besides the twangy country shit that was always about some guy and his horse and the girl that threw them out. She hated that crap - it all sounded the same. She wondered if they could play *Heartbreak Hotel*.

They finished the horsey love song then plowed into more country with *The Legend of Bonnie and Clyde*, which had been a big deal a few months back. Cherry didn't care for it - it wasn't the movie theme by a long shot. Too horsey-sounding.

She headed to the bar and ordered a gin rickey, then surveyed the room. Men hugged the bar on either side of her, leering at her cleavage under the shiny red pullover clinging to her breasts like a drowning sailor to a buoy. Half looked like they couldn't afford to buy her a drink. The other half looked like assholes. And they all needed showers.

The tables - there must have been thirty of them - were half filled, some with couples, most with two to six good old boys sharing pitchers of beer. So far, the cowboy she met outside looked like the best stud available. But he wasn't all that interesting, probably just a beer-swilling local who kept himself up.

Nursing her drink, she made her way toward the band. She sipped and waited until the latest number died down - another song about a man done in by a bad horse and saved by a good woman, or something like that - and then caught the eye of the lead guitarist, who looked barely old enough to drink. He had brown eyes and dimples and a bulge in his blue jeans. He played the last chord, took off his Stetson to reveal his Elvis 'do in its full glory, then bent down.

She gave him a good look at her boobs. "Do you take requests?"

"I'll take anything you want to give me, darlin'."

"Can you do *Heartbreak Hotel*?"

"Just a sec." He huddled with his bandmates, who all looked her way. She smiled at them.

"Well?" she asked as he returned.

"You've got it if I can buy you a drink when we break."

She batted her lashes. "What's your name?"

"Kevin."

"Well, Kevin, you can buy me a drink." Slowly, she licked her lips. His eyes bulged and as he stood erect she saw that his pants did, too. *Young guys. Fastest guns in the west, but they can shoot off again in ten minutes.*

Grinning, he tipped his Stetson at her then rejoined the band. A moment later, they began a pretty fair rendition of the song. She tossed back the last of her drink and swayed to the music until someone tapped her shoulder. "Care to dance, miss?"

She turned and looked at a running-to-fat but still handsome man in his late thirties. He wore a blue Hawaiian shirt covered with pineapples, a pair of jeans, and he didn't smell bad, if you were partial to Old Spice. Burst blood vessels edged his nose and pinked his cheeks, but he wasn't drunk, so maybe it was just the blond complexion giving him that look. She never bothered with drunks unless they were wealthy - they couldn't keep it up.

She glanced at Kevin Guitar. He was watching, so she accepted the invitation to dance, making sure to sway her hips and jut her breasts at every opportunity. The song ended but Hawaiian Shirt didn't let go. She waited to see what would happen.

"Excuse me," Kevin said as he jumped off the low stage right next to them. "I promised this lady a drink."

Hawaiian Shirt watched as Kevin Guitar took her arm, led her to the bar, ordered her another gin rickey and a martini for himself. They sat in the shadows at a table for two and when Kevin offered her his olive, she suckled and licked it until he groaned aloud and his hand disappeared below the table to push down a raging boner. He looked flustered and horny. "I wish I'd ordered extra olives."

Cherry just blew him a kiss.

❧ 10 ❧

SETTLING IN

After dinner, when everyone else piled into the den to watch *Bewitched* and *That Girl*, Meredith took Holly upstairs to a small room containing a daybed, a chair, an ironing board, dress model, and a sewing machine. Fluffy leapt from the daybed to Holly's lap and gave a purry meow. She petted him until his purr filled the room and together, they watched Meredith measure, cut, and stitch the beige drape that would hang over the glass door in Holly's new room.

"Meredith?"

"Yes?" Meredith folded the finished drape.

"I saw a missing poster for a little girl. It looked old. Did she ever show up?"

"No, I'm afraid not. Several girls have gone missing over the last few years." Meredith paused. "It hasn't happened for a while, but be careful, okay? If you go to the playground, go with friends."

"Okay."

"It's almost ten. Let's go back to your room and see if this drape fits."

Moments later, Holly and Meredith, the drape in a grocery sack, returned to the Brimstone Grand. Handsome Steven Cross nodded to them from behind the registration desk.

"How's everything?" Meredith asked.

"Picture perfect. That little jolt a couple hours ago didn't affect a thing."

"Good. Is Miss Delilah back yet?"

"No- but here she comes now." Steve nodded at the alcove that led to the restaurant.

Delilah, still on the arm of the Commodore, stood staring down at them. She nodded at Holly then looked at Meredith and her brown bag. "What have you there?"

"A drape for the glass door in Holly's room," she said. "It'll give her more privacy. Holly helped me stitch it up after dinner."

"How domestic of you, Holly." Delilah raised an eyebrow. "It's an excellent thought, but don't all of the balcony doors already have Venetian blinds on them?"

Holly spoke up. "I don't want Cherry to see the balcony door, Miss Delilah. She'd feel bad that she doesn't have one, too."

"As I said, there will be no switching rooms. If she tries, you tell me."

Holly nodded. "I just don't want her to feel bad."

"You're a very thoughtful young lady. Are you coming up?"

"In a few minutes," Holly said.

Delilah nodded. "Is your mother home yet?"

"I- probably."

Her grandmother arched an eyebrow, nodded, then she and the white-haired man stepped into the elevator.

"Steve?" Holly asked as soon as they disappeared. "Is my mom back?"

"I haven't seen her."

"Good," Holly said. "Meredith, would it take long to hang the drape?"

"Five minutes, tops."

"Can we do it now?"

"Of course."

Meredith led her to the old elevator and pushed a button. Inside, it was like a little parlor. The walls were papered with an old-fashioned floral print and there were small framed photos of old-time Brimstone on them. A petite wooden table in one corner held a vase of flowers. Meredith set the bag down and pulled a brass accordion door closed, pushed "4" and stood back. The main door slowly closed and up they went.

"I love this ancient elevator!" Holly said. "I've seen them in movies."

"It's the same one the hospital used. It's over fifty years old."

"Wow. That's old. Maybe even older than my grandmother."

Meredith laughed. "Don't let her hear you say that!" She paused. "This elevator is supposed to be haunted."

"Really?"

"Really. A caretaker lost his life under it a long time ago and they say he rides it up and down to this day."

"So, he might be in here with us right now?" Holly tried not to sound too hopeful.

Again, Meredith laughed. "Maybe. We always say he's riding when the elevator runs by itself."

"By itself?"

"Well, since the accordion door has to be closed for it to run, it might be live people playing tricks, but we sometimes hear it running - even though it's not."

"Like a ghost train. But a ghost elevator?"

"I suppose you could say that." A ding announced their arrival at the fourth floor. The main doors slid open.

Holly carefully opened the accordion door, stepped out and waited for Meredith. "Will I hear it? The ghost elevator?"

"I daresay you might. The ghost is supposed to be friendly but none of us has ever run into him - I doubt he even exists, so don't let it give you nightmares. I shouldn't tell you such stories this time of night."

"It's fine! I love ghost stories. They never give me nightmares."

They approached 429 and Holly extracted her key. "I have *real* nightmares," she said as the door swung open.

"Real? What do you mean?"

Holly closed the door behind them. "Nightmares about real people. They're a lot scarier than ghosts."

ARTHUR MEEKS LIVED IN AN UNRENOVATED ROOM ON THE FOURTH floor. It was small - it had served as a storage room and staff toilet back in the days of the Clementine Hospital. It had one little window right up against the back of the mountain. He'd dragged an old iron hospital bed in, and added a decent used mattress and box springs that he'd bought after getting permission to live in the room in exchange for ten bucks a month rent and a promise to pull overtime whenever things got busy. It was elevator-adjacent so he heard the comings and goings of the guests whether he wanted to or not.

He resented paying anything for the piece of shit room, but he had to live somewhere and you could say guest-watching was his hobby, so he hadn't complained. You really got to know people if you saw their comings and goings, studied their body language, and listened to what they said and how they said it. An hour earlier, Meredith Granger and the Queen Douchebag's granddaughter - Little Miss Fancy Pants - had come upstairs. Meredith was a real looker with a great rack - he wished she'd show it off more and wear shorter skirts, but she was too high and mighty to slut it up. He'd watched as she disappeared down the hall with the girl then reappeared a few minutes later and went back downstairs.

Now, half an hour before midnight, he heard the drunken couple before the elevator doors even opened. Peering out the peephole, he saw the porno actress and a guy in a cowboy hat pass by, hanging all over each other. He waited until he heard her door slam shut then took his skeleton key and trotted to 426 - the room next door to Cherry Devine's - let himself in and put his eye to the spyhole.

She'd picked up a lanky dark-haired guy in jeans and a cowboy hat. She'd already shucked his shirt and boots - and now she stripped the Levis off him like the pro she was. Giggling, she pulled down his shorts then gave his johnson a yank before pushing him onto the bed, still wearing his hat and black socks.

Total porno move.

She did a striptease for him, kicking off her shoes so hard one thunked against the wall near his spyhole. Methuselah jerked to life, as Cherry slowly stripped off the bra, playing peek-a-boo with one boob then the other, then twirled the garment by its strap before letting it fly across the room. Arthur let Methuselah rub against the wallpaper.

Finally, she peeled off her bikini panties, turning to give him a fine view of her ass and bush. She was so close he picked up a whiff of poontang.

Arthur watched it all, until the guy - and Methuselah - splooged. The couple fell back on the bed and Arthur was about to return to his room, when the cowboy - replacing his hat - stood up and approached the dresser. Arthur couldn't see what he was doing, but he could smell the marijuana as he rolled up a joint. He lit it then went back to the bed. "Toke?" he asked Cherry Devine.

She took a big hit, held it, then blew it in his face. "Nice," she said. "Got anything stronger?"

MEREDITH HAD TOLD HER THE HIGH DESERT NIGHTS WERE COOL, even in summer, and she hadn't lied. Holly's bed was big and comfy with a soft mattress and clean sheets the color of pale butter. She folded back the flowered quilt and one of the blankets, but after twenty minutes, tugged them back up.

After Meredith left, Holly opened all the drapes and windows and turned the slats of the Venetian blinds so that she could let the breeze in and see out without others looking in if they happened to stroll by on the long balcony. From her bed, she could spot a few lights down on Main Street between the branches of the trees dancing in the breeze, and lights here and there dotting the hills. Beyond the town were the bright white and yellow lights of the cement plant in Lewisdale, a town just a few miles north.

Brimstone was as quiet as a tomb, so quiet that she could make out sounds she'd never hear at home, even the occasional *whoosh* of a car going by out on the highway far below. Now and then a snatch of boisterous voices drifted up from town, but so soft that if not for the pervasive silence, she'd never have noticed them. A horn honked, and an engine revved as a car took off down on Main Street. Then, more silence. Now, propped up in bed with four extra pillows she'd found in the closet, Holly looked around the room. She'd put her clothes in the dresser and set her books in a bookcase built into a wall near the kitchenette. Her prized possession - a Hummel Friar Tuck bank her father had sent her from Germany when she was five - took center stage on the dresser. It made her smile. Peter Tremayne had died when she was six and Friar Tuck was all she had of him. "I miss you, Daddy." She blew a kiss at the little monk then snuggled down happily with a small stack of reading material - *The Haunting of Hill House* and the booklets Adeline Chance had given her. She didn't know what to look at first.

She finally chose *The History of Brimstone* and began reading about the mining town's origins. The local natives had mined copper here hundreds of years - at least - before the white man came. There were petroglyphs in the ancient cave dwellings up on Brimstone Peak that indicated they had worshipped a spirit who guarded the copper. When white miners had come, they embraced the copper-guarding spirit, calling it the Brimstone Beast and blaming it for accidents, earthquakes, and disasters.

Intrigued, Holly read a few more pages. In the silence, she heard the elevator ding halfway down the hall, then voices: Cherry and a man. They were drunk. *What else is new?*

Holly turned back to the book but couldn't concentrate. Her mother's laughter and speech pattern didn't vary as she struggled to open the door across the hall; as usual, she was doing Marilyn Monroe. Holly wished she'd knock it off. It was embarrassing. The guy with her seemed to like it though - men always liked it. Holly sighed, turned off the light, and buried her head under a pillow, drowning out the laughter.

11

DARKNESS RISING

I n her dream, Adeline Chance looked into two burning red pits sparking with blue. There was no face, so they weren't really eyes, but they seemed to stare back at her. The Beast appeared to be a spirit of darkness, a shadowy elemental demon that sought entrance into the physical realm, but Adeline - and Ike - knew what it really was. She had helped set its master - and it, in the process - to slumber when she was barely more than a girl.

But now it was awake. *Adeline.* She heard the low voice grumble, felt it scratching at the edge of her mind. *Adeline.*

After all these years, after nearly a lifetime, he was calling her again, scenting the air. Hungry.

"Addie! Wake up!"

Adeline stumbled out of the Beast's sinuous mind, opening her eyes to Isaac's dear, seamed face, lit by moonlight. "It's awake. He's awake."

"No, Addie, you're awake. You had a nightmare. You kicked me, girl!"

"No, *it's* awake, Ike. The Beast. *He* has woken up." She sat up, pushed stray gray hairs away from her face.

"You don't think maybe that quake just gave you the jibber-jabbers?"

She turned on the bedside lamp. "I wish it were the jibber-jabbers, Isaac. I really do." She sniffed the air. "Do you smell it?"

"Smell what?"

"Sulfur."

"No, I don't smell anything but nighttime."

Adeline saw fear in his eyes, but he would only deny it as he tried to comfort her, so she rose and donned her robe and slippers.

"Where're you going?"

"Outside. I want to take a look."

"Addie, it's cold. How about I make you some warm milk? It'll help you sleep."

She shot him a look.

"Sorry. It's been so long since anything's happened. Since we were newlyweds. It's hard to feature it."

She watched him pull on his own robe and slippers. "I'm glad to have your company. Ike."

They'd been kids together, then sweethearts who'd married straight out of high school. Not long after that, she and Carrie had put the Beast to sleep, ending his reign of terror over Brimstone. She knew that deep down, Ike remembered and believed. She loved him even more now than she had back when they'd shyly said their I do's. "Come on, then, Ike." She started out of the bedroom, then called back, "Best leave the shotgun behind. Won't do a bit of good."

HOLLY WANDERED IN A DANK, DARK BUILDING. IT WAS OLD AND OFF-kilter, with sagging stairs and cracks in the walls. Dark lumps - bodies - lay scattered throughout the corridors, but she barely noticed them. There were many doors, some shut, some hanging open on darkness. All were rimmed in a cold blue glow, and veins of molten red ran along the edges of the corridor. The dry air smelled of matches; the odor cloyed in her nostrils. She knew she was dreaming but she couldn't stop it, couldn't force herself to wake up. She was strangling on sulfurous fumes.

There was something in the long hallway with her, something

darker than the shadows, impossible to see except for occasional crackles of red and blue electricity, but she knew it was there - and it knew *she* was there. It was trying to seep into her mind; she felt it like a scratching in her brain.

Then a rumbling voice. *"Hello, Holly. I'm your friend."*

Suddenly, something jumped onto the foot of her bed, jarring her toward wakefulness. Small and determined, it padded up next to her then walked onto her chest even as the thing in the blue-scaped corridor approached, red dragon's eyes sparking blue. Terrified, Holly tried to push the small thing off herself, but her arms wouldn't move; she was still dreaming and the dark thing was nearly on her.

"I'm your friend," it cajoled in its itching cavernous voice. *"Come with me."*

Wake up! she told herself, *Wake up! You're dreaming! It's a dream. Nothing's real! Wake up! Wake up!* But she remained paralyzed in a terrified half-sleep.

Then the thing on her chest meowed and licked her nose with a sandpaper tongue. A small cool paw patted her cheek.

And Holly came bolt upright, wide awake, her hand fumbling for the bedside lamp, eager to see the cat that had helped her escape the nightmare.

"Kitty, kitty?" She looked under the bed, in the bathroom, and even inside the closet - but there was no cat. Sighing, she got a drink then climbed back into bed. Tomorrow, she'd ask Meredith if there was a hotel cat. Hoping so, she smiled as she turned off the light and curled up on her side. Nightmares were nothing new to her, nor was being aware that she was dreaming - that was something she'd thought everybody did until other kids told her different. She cuddled into her pillow, enjoying the quiet of the room, thinking about how much she'd love a cat of her own, a cat like Fluffy. She relaxed until she picked up the faintest scent of sulfur - then the nightmare clawed into the edges of her memory as if something dark was waiting for her.

She was about to turn her light back on to read the nightmare away when she distinctly felt the cat jump onto the bed again. She stayed very still knowing the kitty must have hidden herself in the shadows when she'd looked for it. *Maybe it's a stray who needs a home.* After a time, the feline came closer, then nestled right up against her side and began to purr.

"Nice kitty," Holly murmured. She fell asleep before she could reach down and pet the cat.

Isaac and Adeline Chance's neat single-story river stone house was just up the road from the Humble Station. Ike had built it himself, stone by stone; his wedding present to Addie fifty years ago. They had raised their children here and still had Thanksgiving and Christmas with them when they came with their own children - there were even great-grandchildren now. It was a wonderful house, cozy and warm on cold nights, cool and breezy in summer, and although the quake this afternoon had knocked down a few dishes and tilted some framed photographs, the river stone house was too sturdy to allow for any real damage. It cradled Adeline and Isaac Chance, keeping them safe from earthquakes and bad weather and, perhaps, other things.

Adeline heard Isaac coming up behind her in the living room. "Can't you smell it, Ike? The sulfur?"

"I'm sorry, no."

"Let's see what it's like outside." She unlocked the heavy wooden door and stepped onto the broad covered porch without turning on the porch light. Isaac joined her.

Not a leaf stirred, nor a blade of grass. The high desert air held a breezy chill and all Adeline could smell now was juniper and sage. No bird sang to the full moon, no rabbit or ground squirrel stirred.

"Too quiet," Ike murmured. "Hope that quake today wasn't a precursor to something bigger."

"I hope not." Adeline sniffed. "At least the sulfur stink is gone."

"I was thinking - maybe that quake broke something underground, maybe it opened a mining pit that still had some gas or burning ore in it."

The slight quaver in Ike's voice made her uneasy. "Maybe it did at that," she allowed. "But Ike, the Beast is awake, too. I feel him." She shivered. "I feel him like I did when I was a girl. Before ..."

Ike rested his hands on her shoulders. "Addie, girl, I think we're too old to be of any interest to the Beast, even if he is awake. Let's go back to bed."

She nodded and they locked themselves in their cozy house, and moments later, they sat sipping warm milk at the kitchen table. She stared at the familiar red and white checked oilcloth cover. "It's been a very long time. I was hoping that *he* had gone."

"You've got something on your mind, Addie."

"I do." She looked up at her husband. "It's that little girl we met today, Holly."

"Sweet little thing. She sure did put me in mind of your cousin Carrie."

"She did at that." Adeline tried to keep her voice from shaking; no sense stirring up old memories in the middle of the night. "And she has the sight. Just like me. Just like Carrie did. And our grandfather."

Ike slopped his milk. "Henry Hank Barrow. I hoped I'd never say that name again." "Carrie was a lovely girl. Tragic."

"My best friend. Carrie gave her life to save mine. And her little sister's." Adeline looked at Ike. "I'd hoped that Holly's presence wouldn't start it all up again. But, Ike, I'm afraid it already has. It - *he* - knows she's here."

Ike put his hand over Addie's. "Let's get some sleep. No sense worrying tonight. And maybe you're wrong. After all, it's been half a century since anything's happened."

AGAIN, HOLLY WANDERED THE FIRST FLOOR OF THE DERELICT building. It was lit by moonlight that entered through broken windows edged in the same cobalt glow as the doorways. She peered out a shattered window and saw a few faint lights near a reddish glow far below. *That's Brimstone?*

Turning, she continued, refusing to look closely at the sprawled bodies littered on the floor, keeping her eyes on the stuttered path cast by moonlit windows. The corridor turned and twisted as she walked, her hand trailing along the cold cement walls. She knew she was downstairs. She came to an intersecting hallway and saw a heavy planked door hanging open on one hinge. She saw deep claw marks etched into it, saw a rusted padlock, broken. A staircase dusted with cobwebs disappeared into darkness relieved only by a dim red glow somewhere below. *Something got out. Something escaped.* This she knew with all her heart.

Then, came the scratchy sensation in her brain again. She caught a glimpse of ruby eyes dancing with cobalt sparks. They came closer and a hollow voice as old as time rumbled through her head.

"Holly. Come to me, child."

The building began to shake.

"Earthquake," Holly whispered as she came awake. She welcomed the tremors, lying still and calm in her bed until they ended. They were so much better than the dream of the old building and the thing that called to her and tried to get inside her mind.

Then she heard purring and sensed a small body next to hers as she fell back asleep.

IN HER GRAND ROCOCO BED, IN HER EVEN GRANDER ROCOCO bedroom, Delilah Devine gasped and sat up, fumbling for the lamp. She'd been dreaming her favorite dream - she was accepting the Oscar for *Violet Morne* - then the earth was shaking. And this wasn't a dream. The whole room, along with the bed, moved again, jerking down and sideways. It was brief but stronger than the earlier quake. Delilah pulled on her robe and rushed to the dining room, where she crawled under the massive oak table and curled up like a fetus, trembling, hugging herself, and wishing she hadn't sent the Commodore home.

CHERRY DEVINE AND KEVIN GUITAR, IN THE MIDST OF A THREE a.m. grope-fest, fell out of bed. "Holy cow!" the man cried. "You made the earth move!"

"I have that effect." Cherry knew it was just another quake, but was happy to take the credit.

"It's late as hell. I better get home to the wife before she discovers I'm missing."

"Wife?" Cherry turned on the lamp.

"Yeah, is that a problem?" Kevin pulled on his Levis.

"No. You got kids?"

"Two of the finest little rugrats in town."

"*Those* are problems." Cherry rose, naked, and handed Kevin his hat. "See you around."

He had his shirt and socks on, but had stopped dressing, his eyes taking in her curves. "I could stay a little longer."

"No." She handed him his boots.

"Yes ma'am." He stood. "What've you got against kids?"

"Nothing." She opened the door. "But I don't fuck men with kids."

"Ah, come on. Didn't you have a good time?"

"I did. Now go home." She prodded him out the door, locked it, and fell back into bed.

☧

"EVENING," MICHAEL GRANGER SAID TO THE GUY IN THE COWBOY hat coming out of the Brimstone Grand as he walked in. The cowboy nodded and headed straight for a blue Chevy pickup. He tore out of the lot, tires spewing gravel. "Jerk," Mike said no rancor.

"Thought I'd be seeing you." Steven Cross picked up a pile of postcards that had spilled off the desk. "Quite an aftershock."

"Sure was. Who's that guy that just left?"

"Cherry Devine's date. Plays guitar over at Darkside Johnnie's. He's been here before." Steve grinned. "He's a real slut."

Mike hoped Holly hadn't seen the guy. "Anything break?"

"Not that I know of."

"Good." Mike glanced at the elevator. "Anybody use it since the quake?"

"No. The cowboy took the stairs."

The switchboard buzzed. "Excuse me a minute." He plugged in, said, "Desk," listened then hung up. Turning back to Mike, he said, "That's the second phantom call from 329 tonight."

"Guess the ghost didn't like the quake." Mike looked at his watch. "Three a.m. I've gotta be back here at six. I'm just going to put out-of-order signs on the elevator landings and go back to bed."

"Go home and get some sleep," Steve told him. "I'll do it."

"You're a peach, you know that?"

"I am."

"Thanks, man. See you in the morning."

12

DONKEYS AND OTHER BEASTS OF BURDEN

Holly awoke to sunlight streaming through the slats of the ivory Venetian blinds, and for a moment, she didn't know where she was. Her bed was in the wrong place, the curtains were the wrong color. Then her mind cleared and she remembered: *The Brimstone Grand!*

She remembered that the cat had come back and slept with her, but there was no sign of it now. Eagerly, she got out of bed and searched everywhere, calling *kitty, kitty, kitty.* But there was no cat. *I guess maybe it was a dream, after all.*

But a good dream, not like the nightmares full of dark hallways bathed in flame-blue and etched with red pulsing veins. The eyes glowing in the darkness, coming at her; the voice scraping through her brain. In the nightmare, she'd run. "Something got loose," she murmured. Holly strained now to recall more even as those images began to fade.

She rose and stretched, recalling the day's plan to check out the town with Becky Granger. Dreams forgotten, Holly dressed in blue shorts, her favorite polka dot tank top, and her worn-out tennis shoes. After pulling her hair into a ponytail, she opened the French door and walked out on the balcony. The morning breeze, still cool, felt good. A few people were sitting in chairs outside their rooms but thankfully, they were far away.

It was sunny and quiet at eight in the morning. Holly leaned on the black wrought iron railing and stared out at Brimstone. The center of town lay at the bottom of the surrounding hills. Narrow roads, a few asphalt, most unpaved, ribboned up and down and back and forth among buildings large and small dotting the hillsides. A huge pit from back when strip mining was in full swing lay just west of the main part of town and she could see houses and a church edging it.

Leaning as far as she could over the railing, Holly squinted almost due west and spotted the big wooden cross she'd seen yesterday on the way up. *That has to be that cemetery!* She hoped Becky liked cemeteries half as much as she liked horses.

Closing her eyes, Holly enjoyed the morning breeze's kiss on her cheek and let the high desert speak to her. Birds called, another car went by out on the highway, and somewhere below, a donkey brayed. It was like living in the Wild West. She smiled to herself and turned around to peer up at the hotel, then felt a dizzying wave of recognition. *This is the building from my nightmares!*

Though the dreams had been all but forgotten, her stomach dipped like she was riding a roller coaster and she forced herself to turn, to look back down toward town. She tried to see the Humble Station where her newfound cousin, Adeline, was probably just opening for business. She couldn't - there were too many bushes and trees cutting off her view of the road.

Stomach growling, Holly went back inside and opened the round-shouldered refrigerator in her kitchenette. It was chilled but empty. Holly closed the drapes, grabbed her key and tiptoed out of the room, not wanting Cherry to hear her.

As she approached the elevator, the unnumbered door across from it opened and that yucky bellhop from yesterday came out, dressed in a blue uniform. He had a puffy oval face with bags under his washed-out eyes and a big hawk nose like that actor from *Dr. Strangelove.*

"Hello, Miss Devine." He tipped his cap to reveal lank colorless hair that needed combing. He wet his flat rubbery lips and smiled.

"I'm Miss *Tremayne*, not Devine." She caught a glimpse of an unmade bed in the room behind him. Stale tobacco smells wafted out like bad breath. *He must live there.*

"Miss *Tremayne*, then," he corrected as he joined her at the elevator. "I would think you'd rather use Devine." This time his smile revealed little corn kernel teeth.

Holly ignored him, staring instead at his name tag. It said "Arthur Meeks."

The elevator dinged and they stepped inside. Meeks pulled the brass accordion door shut then pressed a button to close the main door. They began moving. "Why don't you like Devine? Do you think it's a funny name?"

"No." She finally looked at him. His eyes were moving up and down again, like he was examining her. She didn't like it, not one bit. "It's not a funny name, but it's an actress name to me, perfect for Miss Delilah and my mother. I don't want to be an actress."

The elevator opened in the lobby foyer and Meeks put his hand on the accordion door handle but didn't open it. "What *do* you want to be when you grow up, Miss Tremayne? Or may I call you Holly?"

She wanted to be a forest ranger or a painter or a sculptor, maybe all three. She wanted to be a race car driver, a dolphin scientist, an author, and maybe an astronaut, too. She looked him in the eye. "Miss Tremayne. And I want to be a police officer so I can put bad guys in jail."

He chuckled and wheezed. "A little girl who wants to be a cop? They'll make you a meter maid."

"Not me. I'm going to be a real cop and arrest bad guys." *Like you.* She made herself stare at him so that he would stop looking at her and it finally worked. He opened the gate and gave a little bow. "Ladies first."

She tore out of the elevator and went straight to the desk. "Hi, Meredith!"

"Hey there. How'd the drape work out?"

"You can't even tell there's a door in the room. Thanks for helping me!"

"You're very welcome. Did you sleep well?"

Holly nodded. "I think there was a cat in my room, though. I heard meows and then she jumped on my bed, and licked my nose, but she must have gotten out again because I looked everywhere. Does a cat live here? Or maybe she needs a home ..."

Meredith smiled. "Holly, I believe you've met Miss Annie Patches! She's a ghost kitty who's supposed to haunt the fourth floor. She's very nice. Sometimes our guests hear her."

"Did she die here?"

"She lived a long life here and I guess she decided to stay on after she passed. The story is that she's a little calico that belonged to a live-in nurse back when this place was a hospital. She probably lived in your room or the one next to it. And don't worry, Miss Annie Patches is sweet and harmless."

"A *ghost* cat?" Holly tried to look calm, but she wanted to jump for joy.

"Yes. I believe some of our maids have even encountered her."

"I hope she decides to stay with me."

"Well, it sure sounds like she likes you - nobody's ever reported getting a kitty kiss from her before. And I'm glad *you* like her!" Meredith paused. "Did you start your scary novel last night?"

"No. I was looking at a book about Brimstone and I fell asleep."

Meredith nodded. "Have you seen your mom this morning?"

"I heard her come in really late, so I don't think she'll be down for a while. She hates mornings." Holly basked in Meredith's gentle smile.

"Arthur?" Meredith said, looking up. "May I help you?"

The bellhop was standing in the foyer arch. "There's no such things as ghost cats." He made an ugly face. "You shouldn't tell a little girl scary stories like that."

"And you shouldn't eavesdrop, Arthur." Meredith gave him a look like he was a school kid in trouble.

Holly looked at him. He was pale. She smiled. "I'm not afraid of ghosts. Are you?"

The bellhop, milk-white, glared at her. "They ain't real. Nothing to be scared of. Ghost cat. If I saw it, I'd stomp it."

Holly watched him, realizing the man was terrified of something.

"Is there anything else, Arthur?" Meredith asked.

His eyes darted. "Got any bags to take upstairs?"

"No, no one has checked in yet this morning. Perhaps you could polish the luggage carts if you have no other duties right now. They're covered with fingerprints."

"I'll get to it after I make my rounds." He winked at Holly. She ignored him.

Meredith raised an eyebrow, but nodded. Arthur Meeks returned to the elevator. As soon as it began rising, she said, "Arthur is peculiar."

Holly nodded. "I feel like I should feel sorry for him - my mother gave him a really hard time - but, well, I don't like him. Not a bit. I don't like anybody who'd hurt a cat. Even a ghost cat."

"I know. There's just something about him. Best to keep your distance, Holly."

"I will." She hesitated. "But it's okay to be alone with Steve, right?"

Meredith laughed. "Yes. If you can't sleep and want to come down here and talk, I know he'd enjoy that. He's fond of history and ghost stories, just like you." She paused. "So, are you on your way to see Becky?"

"Pretty soon, but I want some breakfast first. There's nothing in my refrigerator yet."

"I'll pick you up some basics this afternoon, but meanwhile, you can either go help yourself to milk and cereal at my house or you can go to the restaurant and eat in the employee lunch room. It's nice. Oh, here comes Peg."

The stocky middle-aged woman with tortoiseshell teacher's glasses riding her nose and her hair in a stiff black beehive, opened the front door, bringing with her the powdery scent of old lady perfume and stale tobacco.

"Peg Moran, this is Holly Tremayne, Miss Delilah's granddaughter. You two didn't quite get a chance to meet yesterday what with the earthquake and all. Peg's our assistant manager."

"Hi Miss Moran," Holly said, wondering just how many tiny paisleys were printed on the woman's dress.

"Call me Peg. We're informal around here, aren't we, Meredith?"

"We are."

"How do you like it here so far, Holly?"

"I like it a lot, I think."

"Holly hasn't had a chance to see much yet," Meredith explained.

"Oh, you have so many fun places to visit. They have donkey rides over at Sheldon's Ghost Town. Becky just loves that, doesn't she, Meredith?"

"Yes, she does."

"Do you like to ride?" asked Peg.

"Horses? No, I never have."

"If you go to Sheldon's with Becky, she's going to insist on riding."

"How much does it cost? Miss Delilah is giving me a job, but I won't have any money for things like that until she pays me."

"You don't need to worry," Meredith assured her. "Becky's their unofficial donkey groomer so she and her friends ride for free."

"Really?" Holly felt a lot better. She'd saved twenty dollars over six months - all tucked away in her Friar Tuck bank - by cleaning a neighbor's apartment in Van Nuys, and she didn't want to let a penny of it go until she had a new source of income. Cherry would give her a quarter or fifty cents if she had it, but she rarely did. "I think it would be fun to ride a donkey sometime." She looked from Meredith to Peg. "But I really want to see the cemetery!" She paused. "It's where the big cross is, right?"

Peg chuckled. "Yes, but whyever would you want to go to a cemetery, young lady?"

"I love them. I like to read the gravestones and make up stories about the people. It's fun."

"You sound like a budding writer." Meredith smiled. "It's the old miners' cemetery. There won't be much to read - most of the stones are pretty worn down - but it's pretty scenic in a spooky sort of way." She paused. "You'll have to work hard to talk Becky into going."

"Going where?" Becky Granger asked as she came through the door.

"I want to see the cemetery, do you? And that haunted house your brother talked about." *Oops.* Holly glanced at Meredith and Peg, and quickly added, "Just the outside. I know it's too dangerous to go inside."

Becky's hair was in two long blond pigtails and she curled the end of one around her finger. "Eww, no, it's too creepy."

"Maybe Sheldon will let you ride the donkeys up there on a quiet day," Meredith said.

"Really?" Becky seemed interested.

"Probably, though it's plenty close to just walk."

Becky looked worried.

"I'll go by myself," Holly said. "I don't mind. My mom used to drop me off at Hollywood Memorial Park sometimes, just to walk around. There are a lot of movie stars buried there, like Rudolph Valentino and Tyrone Power and Jayne Mansfield."

"Jayne Mansfield!" Becky said. "She got her head cut off in a car accident! She's there? You saw her grave?"

Holly nodded. "It's pretty. It's sort of a big heart. There are always lots of flowers on it." Because her mother was so interested in Mansfield, Holly knew the actress hadn't really been decapitated, but decided not to spoil the fun with the truth. Instead, she looked to Meredith. "Are there any famous outlaws buried here?"

"Not that I know of, but you could research it at the library."

"There's a library? That's wonderful! She paused. "But I'm still going to go see the cemetery."

"It's deserted, sweetheart," Meredith said. "I don't think it's a good idea to go there all alone." She glanced at her daughter, then Holly. "It's best to travel in twos. Holly, maybe you and I can take a walk there together if Becky doesn't want to. Or, I bet Steve would be happy to give you a tour."

"I'll go if we can take the donkeys," Becky piped up. She sounded annoyed.

"We'll ask Sheldon." Meredith smiled. "I doubt he'd have a problem with that."

"Okay!" Becky turned to Holly. "Okay, we can go to the cemetery if we ride. Donkeys sense stuff we don't, so if they get spooked, we have to leave. I don't want to see a ghost."

"Sure." Holly said, ignoring the girl's commanding tone. She fully intended to check out the cemetery without a scaredy cat like Becky along - but going on a donkey would be fun, too.

"So, did you feel that earthquake at three a.m.?" Becky asked.

Holly shook her head. "I think so. I don't really remember."

"You're a sound sleeper, Holly" Meredith said. "It woke us all up."

"It wasn't so bad," Becky said. "So, you want to go downtown today?"

"Yes."

"Why don't you two go have cereal at the house?" Meredith smiled. "Greg might have the bike ready for you by the time you're done."

"That's so nice of you. I'll take good care of it."

"I'm glad to see it get some use! Be careful though, Holly. It's really big. I've had it since I was around your age and they used to build them taller back then."

"Thanks. I'll be really careful."

"Good. Now you two run along. Peg and I need to do the books."

THE POUNDING ON CHERRY'S DOOR MATCHED THE RHYTHM OF THE jackhammer grinding her skull. She pulled the covers over her head. "Go away!"

The knocking continued.

"Go away, damn it!"

"Sorry, but I'm here on Miss Delilah's orders." It was a female voice.

What the hell does that old bitch think she's doing? Cherry glanced at the clock. It was barely past eight in the morning. *Obscene!* "Come back at noon. Bring fresh sheets and towels."

"Sorry, Miss Charlotte. Miss Delilah will be angry if I don't deliver this to you."

"Tell the old bitch I wouldn't let you in."

"She told me to use my passkey if you refused."

"Goddamnit! Goddamned old bitch!" Rubbing her forehead, Cherry crawled out of bed. "Holy fuck, it's too early for this shit." She opened the door. The maid was a fortyish Latina in a pink and white uniform. Her dark hair was pulled back in a neat bun and if she lost twenty pounds she might have been pretty. According to the label sewn on her bodice, her name was Elvira.

Cherry looked at the paper bag in the maid's hands. "What's that?"

Elvira didn't answer. She was staring at Cherry, her mouth hanging open.

"What's the matter? Haven't you ever seen a naked woman before?"

Elvira thrust the bag at her. "Miss Delilah wants you to put this on. I'll be back in twenty minutes." She turned to leave.

"What is this?"

"Your uniform. Miss Delilah says I'm to train you for your job." To her credit, she didn't look too happy about it.

"What can *you* train me to do? Scrub toilets?" Cherry's head throbbed and she thought she might throw up. If she did, she'd aim for Elvira's sensible shoes.

"I am the head of housekeeping," the woman said, keeping her eyes on Cherry's face. "You are going to work for me, and yes, I will teach you how to scrub toilets properly."

Cherry stared at her. When her mother said she was going to have a job here, she hadn't dreamed Delilah would humiliate her like this. It was ridiculous. *Fuck you, Delilah. You can't do this to me.*

"See you in twenty minutes. Be ready." Elvira turned and walked away.

"Half an hour." Cherry slammed the door and threw the bag on the bed. An ugly pink dress and white apron fell out. And a lacy cap. "Delilah, if you think this is happening, you are wrong. Dead wrong." She entered the bathroom and turned on the shower. The only thing she'd be scrubbing was her own body - it stunk of sex and the cowboy's cheap aftershave.

❦ 13 ❧

CHERRY, INTERRUPTED

"Thank you, Frieda. That will be all." Delilah Devine tucked into her breakfast. As her personal maid, Frieda had her own fifth floor quarters in Delilah's huge suite. She took good care of her, but as much as she loved Frieda, Delilah still preferred to eat without her hovering. She picked up a crustless triangle of buttered toast and nibbled between sips of orange juice, then plunged her fork into a perfect ball of honeydew. Then cantaloupe, a red grape and a green, saving the pineapple tidbits - fresh, not canned - in her fruit cup for last.

As always - except when the Commodore came for dinner or when Vera joined her for lunch - Delilah sat alone at the long table. It had graced her dining room in Beverly Hills, the wood so dark it was nearly black, the Italian marble inlay - complete with a central fountain that had once burbled merrily - gleaming in the diffuse light. Here, she had entertained Hollywood elite, a few mobsters, and several presidents. It was a table full of memories. She touched the marble veins, hearing once again the music of the live bands that had entertained her guests back in the glory days. Delilah nibbled more toast, sipping coffee between bites.

While she missed the old days, she loved her quiet life here in

Brimstone. Sometimes she felt as if she were living in a museum - all her things had been shipped here from the Beverly Hills mansion. Everything she'd loved and collected over the years graced this penthouse and reminded her of times gone by.

Troubled, she dipped the edge of her toast in coffee. She did not like intrusions and would have turned Charlotte away if it hadn't been for the child. From what she'd seen of her, which was precious little so far, the young girl, with her honey-colored hair and open smile, took after Delilah's beloved sister, Carrie. Carrie had died when Delilah was very young, but she remembered her honeyed hair and the fleck of golden-copper in one bright blue eye.

So much like Carrie. So very much. Delilah shivered and hoped there wouldn't be trouble. When Carrie had died Delilah was devastated. All she remembered was crying and clinging to Carrie's lifeless body while her cousin Adeline tried to pull her away. She wasn't having it. Instead, she pulled up the lid on Carrie's eye, knowing she'd wake up and hug her. But her sister's blue eye was dull, all except for that golden fleck, which still shone and sparkled. Adeline had dragged her away, muffling her cries against her breast. Delilah screamed that Carrie was alive, they couldn't bury her, but no one would listen. Even Adeline hadn't listened.

She hated her for it. To this day, she hated her, and though she couldn't remember what had happened, she knew that Adeline was the reason Carrie had died.

Adeline has the golden fleck, too. And Holly's eyes are full of gold.

Soon after Carrie's death, Delilah's father had sent her to live with Aunt Beatrice in Boston. She always suspected that he'd done it because he hadn't the patience to raise a small girl, but whatever the truth, it had proven to be the best thing that ever happened to her. Even so, she would have traded it all to have Carrie back.

But that was not to be. She grew up back east, never seeing or hearing from her father again. Her only contact was with the executor of his will many years later. Bill Delacorte had inherited the long-closed Clementine Hospital and had left it to her, his only surviving heir, the same year Holly was born.

Delilah sighed, her thoughts returning to the present. She hoped

Charlotte - she of the blue movies - would quickly move back to Hollywood where she could root around amongst her own kind. She was a disgrace and Delilah hoped the job she'd given her - working alongside the maids - would probably drive her away. *And good riddance.*

She'd tried so hard to bring Charlotte up properly, but the girl had been bad from the start. Maybe it was her father. Delilah had married dashing Clifton Danvers in 1931 and the wedding had made headlines. She was still a few years from making it big with *Violet Morne*, but Clifton was already a huge star. He was forty when she married him, a stage and screen actor who had easily made the transition from silent movies to talkies with his Shakespearean voice and craggy good looks. He'd already been married three times when he proposed to Delilah, but she was smitten and didn't think about what that might mean. Within a few years, of course, he'd run off with Millicent McKinsey, a little twist of a starlet he'd met on the set of *Minions of the Castle.*

Delilah hadn't minded anything other than the public humiliation - by then Clifton had become a womanizing drunk, excessive in all things - gambling, spending, fucking, swearing. The man was known as a gentleman, but that was only because Hedda Hopper hadn't seen him behind closed doors.

Charlotte had taken after Clifton in all the wrong ways. Delilah smiled thinly as she wondered what her ex-husband would say if he could see his little girl today. *A chip off the old block, is that what she is, Clifton. She fucks anything that moves, just like you.*

At least, she reflected, Holly seemed nothing like Charlotte. *She's Carrie, back from the dead.* It wasn't just the coloring and the gold in her eyes, but her demeanor as well. She had looked Delilah straight in the eye during their interview yesterday. The girl's audacity had annoyed her, but she was pleased that the child had so much gumption. Holly was a tomboy, to boot, but that could be easily remedied if she were around long enough.

But you don't want her here. She's not your problem.

She heard the doorbell and Frieda bustling to answer it. A moment later, Delilah's assistant, Vera Kotzwinkle, entered followed by Elvira Guerrero, the hotel's head housekeeper. Delilah touched a linen napkin to her lips before rising.

"Miss Delilah," Vera said, "You look wonderful this morning. I take it you slept through the earthquake?"

"No, I didn't, but thank you anyway, dear. Why don't you go straight to the office? We have some correspondence to take care of." She raised her voice. "Frieda, please fetch a pot of coffee to the office. And some of your cinnamon rolls." She turned back to Vera. "I'll join you shortly. By the way, that's a lovely shade of lipstick. What's it called?"

"You like it?" Vera smiled. "It's called Coral Sunset."

"I do. It matches your hair perfectly."

"That was what I was aiming for. I also tried a new facial mask recipe on myself last night. Cucumber, melon, almond, glycerin, a little paraffin. I declare, I think it took a decade off my face. Touch my cheek."

"As if you need to take a decade off, Vera. You have the skin of a young girl." She reached up and ran her fingers over Vera's cheek. "That's your bare skin, isn't it? You're not even wearing foundation?"

Vera smiled. "Yes. Isn't it wonderful? I brought the rest of the mask with me. Would you like me to give you a facial this afternoon?"

"Absolutely." Delilah didn't know what she would do without Vera Kotzwinkle. Vera's skills as her personal secretary and assistant were second only to her abilities as a beautician and stylist. She'd majored in business and minored in theater arts, then had gone to work at Universal where, as a girl of twenty-two, she had done wonders for Delilah's complexion. Delilah had been trying to resign herself to middle age and oblivion when Vera entered her life, but ended up finishing out her contract on a note that, while not high, was at least mildly respectable, which was the best women of a certain age could do in monster movies. When Delilah left, she took Vera with her and they'd been together ever since. "I'll be in shortly, Vera. Perhaps you might touch up my roots while the mask is on this afternoon?"

"Absolutely." Vera, elegant as usual in black pumps, a forest green skirt and a black poor boy sweater, headed for the office.

"Elvira." Delilah approached the head housekeeper who waited near the foyer. "Is there a problem?" She knew there would be and, perversely, it pleased her.

"Yes, Miss Delilah. There's a problem." Elvira looked flustered and more than a little annoyed.

"I take it my daughter is not cooperating?"

"She isn't. I gave her the uniform over an hour ago and she wasn't happy, I can tell you that."

"I imagine she is anything but pleased. How did she behave?"

"She was naked, Miss Delilah. She opened the door stark naked and didn't bother to cover up. I was shocked."

"She likes to shock, Elvira. Being shocking and improper is her forte."

"I was so embarrassed I could barely speak," the maid continued. "But I gave her the uniform and told her what we would be doing. She asked for thirty minutes and I gave her that. When I returned, she didn't answer. After another half hour, I used my passkey, like you said. Miss Delilah, she's gone."

"Gone? Her suitcases, too?" Brief joy was knocked aside by the realization Charlotte may have dumped the child in her lap.

"No, her things are still there. And the uniform - she stuffed it in the toilet."

Delilah sighed, but wasn't surprised. *At least she didn't try to flush it.*

"Very well, Elvira. Please tell Meredith to send Charlotte to me as soon as she reappears."

14

LIES MY MOTHER TOLD ME

After bowls of Corn Chex and bananas, Becky led Holly out to the garage behind the Granger's multi-level house. "Greg?" she yelled. Her brother was working on a bicycle, little Todd watching intently. "Is it fixed yet?"

Greg turned around. His thick brown hair hung in his eyes reminding Holly a little of Dino Danelli, *The Young Rascals'* drummer. Greg was really kind of cute. Most boys had suddenly started looking cute in the last year.

He grinned at her. His brown eyes were the color of Hershey's Kisses. Even the pimple on his chin was cute. "It's not ready. I need to go into town and buy new inner tubes. These're both shot."

"Well, how long will that take?" Becky's voice rang with impatience.

"I have baseball practice in an hour, so I'll pick them up after that." He swiped hair from his eyes. "Maybe two o'clock?"

Holly smiled at him and nodded. "Thanks!"

But Becky's hands were on her hips. "Can't you get them now?"

"Not enough time. Sorry, squirt."

"Don't call me that!"

The boy grinned. "Okay, squirt."

"Knock it off or I'll tell Mom—"

"It's fine," Holly said. "Why don't we walk, Becky? We could see that haunted house. That would be fun!" Holly could see her new-found cousin, Adeline, tomorrow, after she'd read more about the town.

Rising, Greg pulled off his T-shirt, then wiped his face and chest with it. "Make sure you take water bottles. It's hot today! And watch out for snakes."

"Snakes?" Holly asked.

"Yeah, there's a lot of them around here. Just watch where you walk. Stay on the trail. You'll be fine."

Holly didn't like the idea of snakes. "Rattlesnakes?"

Greg nodded. "Yep. Mojave rattlers. They're the most poisonous rattler of all. Do you know what creosote and mesquite look like?"

"I think so."

"You need to be able to recognize them. Snakes hang around them. Becky, you be sure and show her."

"Okay." She turned to Holly, eyes wide. "I almost stepped on one two weeks ago, but I heard it rattle and jumped backwards like ten feet!" She paused. "My dad says to wear jeans and heavy shoes when we hike in the summer. I don't want to even look at that stupid haunted house though. That's creepy boy stuff."

"You don't? Well, that's okay." Holly didn't argue because she really didn't want to hike with Becky where there were rattlers since the girl would probably shriek so much that the snakes would attack them just for fun. "Hey, maybe we could just go check out the cemetery for now. It's really close."

Becky was unimpressed. "If we're not going to town, we'll go to the playground."

Holly remembered the monkey bars. "Yeah, that sounds fun, too."

"Let's go,"

"Hey, wait up," Greg called.

"What?" Becky planted her hands on her hips.

"Stop at the hotel and tell Mom I'll bring Todd over before I leave for practice." He put on a winning smile. "Unless you guys want to watch TV or something. Then he can stay home."

"I'll tell her," Becky called. They began walking. "I *hate* babysitting Todd. He's such a pain."

They walked toward the hotel. "I babysat for my neighbor some-times. She had a two-year-old," Holly said. "It wasn't so bad except for changing diapers. She paid me a dollar an hour."

"I'd sit all the time if I got paid," Becky said.

They entered the hotel parking lot and as they walked past a big white Cadillac, someone called, "Holly!"

"Mom?"

"Call me Cherry!" her mother ordered. "And come here!"

"Where are you? I can't see you."

"I'm behind the Caddy. What, do you think I'm invisible?"

A plume of tobacco smoke assaulted Holly's nose. She gave Becky a half-assed smile, hoping her mother wasn't about to embarrass her even more. "Wait here just a sec, Becky."

"Okay."

Holly slipped between the Cadillac and a beat-up Jeep and found Cherry crouched by the front bumper, right at the edge of the embankment. "You'll fall if you're not careful."

"I need you to get my purse out of my room." She handed Holly a key. "The white one. If you can't get it without anyone seeing, just take out my wallet. Bring it to me, pronto."

"Okay, Cherry. Where's the Falcon?"

"It's parked down there." Cherry nodded toward the embankment. "On the side of the road where nobody can see it."

"Why?"

"Because your grandmother is an old bitch. Go get my stuff."

"Sure. I'll be right back." She turned and trotted back to Becky. "I need to go upstairs and get my mom's purse."

"Hurry up," called Cherry.

"I am! Come on, Becky!" They ran.

A moment later, they were in the lobby.

Meredith was checking in a guest so they slipped past her and entered the elevator. Holly pushed the brass accordion gate closed, pressed "4," and the elevator creaked to life. "It's so cool your mom lets you call her by her first name," Becky babbled. "I don't get to come upstairs normally. Guests only, my mom says."

"The stairs are faster." Holly wasn't in the mood to talk; her stomach was in knots because Cherry wanted her to lie again. Her eyes wanted to cry but she wouldn't allow it; instead she was building a big ball of anger around the stupid tears so they could never escape. Anger at Cherry and anger at herself for doing her mother's bidding. She felt torn apart inside and she hated that feeling more than anything.

They arrived at the fourth floor and Holly opened the gate, quickly looking up and down the hall and hoping that creepy bellhop wasn't lurking around. She was in luck. "Come on!" She trotted down to her mom's room and put the key in the lock as Becky peered over her shoulder.

"I bet your mom has some great clothes and stuff."

"Huh?"

"Because she's a movie star, I mean."

"I don't know, but she really hates people in her room." Holly pulled her own key out of her pocket and handed it to Becky, pointing. "That's my room - 429. Go check out my balcony - you can see the whole town and even the mountains around Sedona from there. I'll get my mom her purse, okay?" No way did she want Becky seeing Cherry's room. You never knew what she'd leave lying around in plain sight.

"Sure!" Becky took off like a shot and was in 429 before Holly even got the door open.

As usual, Cherry's room looked like a tornado had hit. Clothes were tossed everywhere, the bed was a big mess, and an almost-empty bottle of vodka, uncapped, sat on the dresser along with two hotel glasses and a red push-up bra. "Oh, gee, Cherry, really?" Glad she hadn't let Becky in, she snatched a baggie of marijuana off the nightstand then began searching for the white purse. She checked the bathroom - all the towels were soggy and on the floor and the toilet hadn't been flushed; for some reason Cherry always forgot to flush. Holly took care of it then put the lid down and headed out, past the bed, to the kitchenette. The purse was nowhere in sight. Holly's eyes landed on the fridge. She opened it and saw three Hamm's Beers - one of them open, a mostly empty bottle of Boone's Farm Apple Wine, capless, beside it. *Good to the last drop.* Holly's nose wrinkled at the boozy scent. But no purse.

Then she opened the tiny freezer and there it was, the white plastic purse, frozen, right next to another bottle of vodka. She yanked it free from the layer of ice, left the marijuana in its place, then closed the fridge and lit out of the room, taking the stairs to the lobby.

"Holly?" Meredith asked. "Where's the fire?"

"My mom forgot her purse."

"Miss Delilah wants to speak with her. Would you let her know?"

"I will."

"As soon as possible."

"I'll tell her."

"Holly?" Meredith said as Holly opened the door. "Where's Becky?"

"Oh, I forgot. She's in my room. I'll be right back."

Meredith nodded.

First, Holly ran to the Cadillac and found Cherry still crouched at the edge of the embankment, smoking. "Took you long enough," she said as she withdrew a lipstick from the purse.

"I couldn't find it. You left it in the freezer."

Cherry coughed a laugh. "I don't remember doing that. Sorry, kid."

You never remember. "It's okay. Meredith says you need to go see Miss Delilah right away."

"You tell Meredith to tell the old battleax that I'm out on a job interview. I don't know when I'll be back."

"Really? That's great!"

Cherry inspected herself in her compact mirror. "Yeah, it's in Sedona. Tell her it's a modeling job."

"Maybe you should see Miss Delilah first?"

"Nah, just say I'm gone, you couldn't find me."

"But I already told Meredith I was getting your purse."

"Why the hell did you tell her?"

"Because she asked."

"Goddamned busybody."

"Cherry–"

"You go tell Delilah I'm gone."

"But–"

But Cherry wasn't listening. Holding her high-heeled sandals in one hand, her purse in the other, she scooted along the edge of the hill in front of the row of cars until she reached a set of stone steps that led to the road below. Thirty seconds later, Cherry's red Falcon roared off, spewing a cloud of dirt all the way up the hill.

Holly stared after her. "I always get in trouble when I lie for you, Cherry. I'm not doing it again." Coughing on dust, she turned and looked up at the Brimstone Grand. The first thing she saw was Becky standing on the balcony outside her room, waving at her. Holly waved back.

The second thing she saw was Miss Delilah watching her from a fifth floor window almost directly above Becky. She didn't wave, and she wasn't smiling.

"Crap."

"HOLLY?" MEREDITH SAID AS THE GIRL WALKED IN, MOVING SLOW, looking glum. "What's wrong? Did you find your mother?"

She nodded.

"And?"

The girl just stood there looking at her hands. Finally, she mumbled something.

"What, honey? I'm sorry, I didn't understand."

Holly still didn't meet Meredith's eyes. "I said I'm supposed to tell Miss Delilah that Cherry's gone." She looked up now, her face pale and pinched. "That she's got a job interview in Sedona."

"Does she?"

"Maybe, I don't know. She said to say it's a modeling job."

The switchboard buzzed. "Just a minute." Meredith answered it then turned back to Holly, feeling bad for the little girl. "That was Miss Delilah. She wants to see you right away."

Holly nodded. "Okay."

"What are you going to tell her, sweetheart?"

Emotions crossed the girl's face; apprehension, anger, doubt. Lots of doubt. But then she straightened up and looked Meredith square in the eye. "The truth."

"That's always best." Meredith came out from behind the lobby counter and hugged her. "Miss Delilah can be tough, but she's okay. She really is. Don't be afraid of her."

Holly finally broke the hug. "I'm not afraid," she declared, defiance and unshed tears in her eyes. "I'm not afraid of anything."

"I know you're not. You're the bravest girl I've ever met."

"Thanks." Holly mumbled the word and trudged toward the stairs, head down, shoulders slumped.

As soon as she was out of earshot, Meredith rang Holly's room and told Becky to come downstairs, that she needed her to babysit Todd, and that she and Holly could play tomorrow. Then she wiped away a tear of her own. *Poor little thing.* Having your own mother ask you to lie had to be something from the seventh circle of Hell.'

CHERRY DOWNSHIFTED THE FALCON AS SHE PASSED THE HUMBLE Station and took the last steep incline to Main Street. Darkside Johnnie's was closed. *So much for a little hair of the dog.* She sighed. Of course, a lot of regular businesses weren't open - it wasn't even nine yet. Her head ached and she was out of aspirin. "Damned one-horse towns."

Finally, she spotted a hole-in-the-wall grocery store among the tall buildings looming along the narrow street. "Brimstone Market," she read as she pulled to the curb. "Such imagination, but if you have aspirin and beer, I'll forgive you for being boring."

She adjusted the little red triangle scarf over her platinum hair and brushed her hands over her white blouse - the low-cut one with little red hearts all over it - and red pencil skirt. She'd chosen the outfit because it not only showed off her legs and boobs, but it made her look younger than her thirty-five years. She got carded whenever she wore the ensemble.

Inside the narrow market, a balding bespeckled man behind the checkout counter stared at her, taking her in from stem to stern as she picked up a handbasket. "Aspirin?" she asked.

She waited while he put his eyes back in their sockets.

"Aisle three." The look on his face was one of unadulterated lust.

She saw that a lot in backwards places like this. The guy was probably married to a fishwife and cried into his pillow at night. *Typical.* Cherry gave him a shiteater and headed for the aspirin. Putting it in her basket, she saw the coolers on the back wall and grabbed a couple bottles of Schlitz before heading up to the cash register. Another customer, a stern older woman built like Maggie in *Jiggs & Maggie* stared at her from above reading glasses.

"You're a teacher, aren't 'cha." Cherry spoke in an attempt to be friendly.

The woman looked her up and down, her eyes stopping on Cherry's cleavage. "Why would you say that?"

"You've got those teacher's glasses on a string around your neck," Cherry said. "And you're dressed like a teacher. You remind me of my fifth grade teacher, Mrs. Tarmack." She chuckled. "That woman had a stick up her butt, let me tell you-" She grinned under the woman's withering gaze. "But she was a great teacher. She had a dress just like the one you're wearing."

"Is that so."

Cherry glanced at the items the clerk was ringing up, trying to find something to say that would turn off the woman's glare. "Those look like great apples. An apple a day keeps the doctor away." For some reason - probably because the woman looked like Mrs. Tarmack, who was the meanest, ugliest teacher she'd ever had - Cherry felt like a little kid. She couldn't stop talking. The old bag made her nervous. "And Preparation H. Man, I can relate. I've had some nasty 'rhoids myself. I told my director that I get hazard pay when a job gives me 'rhoids."

The woman's eyes widened, then narrowed. "What is it you do for a living?" she huffed.

"I'm in pictures," Cherry said. "Movies."

The register rang and the woman paid without answering, then strutted out of the store. Cherry moved up and set her basket on the counter, adding a pack of Juicy Fruit and Hostess Twinkies to her haul. "Man," she said to the bald guy whose name tag read 'Billy.' "Something crawled up her ass and died."

He rang up her purchases, goggling at her through Coke-bottle lenses, and waited while she pulled out a couple of crumpled ones. "You're new around here?"

"Yeah, why?"

"That was Mrs. Stuffenphepper, the mayor's wife."

Cherry cackled as Billy handed her change. His hand lingered. She let it. "Really?"

Billy grinned, showing tombstone dentures. "Old Brunhilde is going to be giving him an earful about you tonight!"

Cherry chortled.

"I thought I recognized you when you came in," Bald Billy said. "You're in the movies?"

"Sure am, sweetie."

"Firehose Gals." You had dark hair, but that was you, wasn't it?"

"That was a long time ago. And you remembered!"

"I was over to the X-E Lady Theater not two weeks ago. It was a double feature. *Florence of Labia* and *Who's Afraid of Virginia's Muff.* You're Cherry Devine!"

"In the flesh."

"I dream about those babies every night." He stared at her breasts.

"That's so sweet."

Billy glanced around, making sure no customers were near then reached under the counter and brought out a copy of *Popular Mechanics.* "Can you give me your autograph?"

"Sure, sweetie." She was eyeing the array of liquor bottles behind him, thinking of offering to give him more than her John Hancock for a bottle of the good stuff, but decided to wait and see if she got the job up in Sedona first.

He opened the magazine, revealing a 1962 copy of *Playboy.* She'd recognize it anywhere - she hadn't made centerfold, but she was in it. She waited while he opened to her pictures. "Could you make it out to Brimstone Billy?"

"Sure." She took his pen and wrote, "To Brimstone Billy, Love and Kisses, Cherry Devine." She put the magazine to her lips and kissed her signature.

Just then a busty middle-aged woman walked in and Billy, blushing as red as the hearts on her shirt, hid the magazine. "Thanks, Miss Devine. Morning Mrs. Garrett." He nodded at the red-headed lady who was so freckled that even the sunbaked shelf of a bosom peeking over the top of her sundress, had freckles.

"Morning, Billy," she said, and disappeared up aisle four.

"Edna's a nice lady. She has a sense of humor, you know."

"That's nice," said Cherry. "I'll see you around, Billy."

"Miss Devine?"

"Call me Cherry."

"Are you any relation to Delilah Devine, up there at the Grand?"

"I'm her granddaughter," she said.

"I like her movies, too," he said. "But not like I like yours."

Cherry blew him a kiss and left. She didn't want to be late for the casting call. She'd rather be in the movies than cleaning toilets any day of the week.

"DO YOU THINK YOU'RE IN TROUBLE, YOUNG LADY?"

Holly stared at her grandmother, who once again sat beneath the flattering pink cherub lamp. Delilah Devine intimidated her more than anyone she'd ever met in her life. It was the way she sat, her posture so perfect, her clothes immaculate, as if they wouldn't dare wrinkle - and the way her face and eyes stayed so calm and still so you couldn't guess what she was thinking.

"I *feel* like I'm in trouble, Miss Delilah."

"Should you be in trouble, Holly?"

"No." She spoke softly, then looked up at her grandmother and said, "No! I haven't done anything wrong."

"Then why do you feel as if you have?"

"I don't. I just feel like you're mad at me."

"I am not angry with you. Why would you think that I am?"

Holly, angry at Cherry, furious with her, made her own back ramrod straight, and used her anger to fuel her courage. "Miss Delilah, you know why. You know exactly why."

Delilah didn't say a word. Instead she rang the little silver bell and the maid appeared. "Tea, please, Frieda. For two."

Frieda bustled off, then her grandmother gestured to a chair. "Holly, sit down." Delilah seated herself. "I suspect your mother has put you in a very awkward position."

Holly sat and lowered eyes that burned with tears. "You have, too."

"Excuse me?"

"Sorry."

"No, don't be sorry, Holly. Never say you're sorry if you aren't. Just speak up. I couldn't hear you. You mustn't mumble."

Screwing up all her courage, Holly peered at Delilah from beneath her brow. "I said you did, too."

Delilah studied her another excruciating moment, then nodded. Her posture relaxed the tiniest bit as she leaned forward. "Look at me, Holly."

She did.

"You're right. I *have* put you in an awkward position, and I apologize for doing so."

Holly was stunned. "Thank you."

Frieda returned with a tea service like in the movies. She set the ornate silver tray on the coffee table between them. It held a fancy silver teapot, matching bowl of sugar cubes, tiny tongs, a pitcher of cream and two china cups and saucers painted with pink roses and ribbons.

"Do you like tea, Holly?" Delilah asked.

"I do."

"You may have milk if you prefer."

"Tea, please."

"Please pour, Frieda."

She poured and added two sugars and a dollop of cream to one, which she set before Delilah.

"Cream and sugar, Miss Holly?" Frieda asked.

"Yes, please. The same as Miss Delilah."

Frieda smiled, poured, then took her leave.

They sipped in silence, Holly growing more and more uncomfortable until she blurted, "Your teacups are really pretty."

"Thank you. They were hand-painted in Japan, especially for me. A gift from a director, a very long time ago. See the initials in the heart?"

Holly set her cup down carefully, afraid of dropping it. It rattled against the saucer. "That's very nice."

"Don't you care for your tea?"

"It's good. I–"

"What's bothering you? Spit it out, girl."

"I don't want to break it."

Delilah laughed. "They're only cups. You don't need to worry so much."

"I've just never touched anything so nice before. It's so thin."

"That's why I only have three left. The rest broke over the years."

"I don't want to break–"

"I rarely need more than two cups, Holly. We're safe if you break one. Now drink up."

She did, trying not to make any sipping sounds.

"Holly, how has your life been so far? What do you like to do?"

"It's okay." She shrugged. "I mostly just go to school and to the park and the library."

Frieda returned with a plate of lacy cookies dusted in confectioner's sugar and placed it on the table.

"Have a cookie. They're lemon. Frieda makes them herself. She's very talented." Holly took a cookie and dipped it in her tea.

"Thank you." She let the cookie melt on her tongue, trying not to stare at her grandmother. "This is the best cookie I've ever tasted."

"I daresay I know what you do at the library, but what do you do at the park?"

"I like the monkey bars." She finished the cookie. "Especially horizontal bars. I love to hang upside down by my knees."

Delilah raised a delicate brow. "Hang upside down?"

"I'm good at it. And I like to twirl around. You know, on one knee."

"So, you're something of a gymnast." Delilah refilled their tea cups and fixed Holly's cream and sugar just like her own. "Have all the cookies you'd like." She took another.

Holly considered Delilah's words. "I never thought of that. That I could be a gymnast."

"Well, that would be an odd profession. Have you had tap dancing or ballet lessons?"

Holly shook her head. "Some of my friends took tap, and I asked because it looked like fun, but Cherry couldn't afford it." She took another cookie. "We have to be careful with money most of the time."

"Most of the time?"

"Sometimes we have money, and Cherry takes me to Hamburger Hamlet to celebrate. Last year she got paid right before school started and she even bought me a new dress."

"*A* new dress?"

"From J.C. Penney's. Brand new."

"Where does she normally get your school clothes?"

"Thrift stores."

"You're wearing *used* clothing?"

Delilah looked horrified and Holly's face went hot.

"What you're wearing now - except for those terrible dirty tennis shoes - looks nice. Are your shorts and shirt used?"

"Yes." Humiliation filled her, making it hard to talk. "But lots of stuff at Goodwill is practically brand new. This shirt still had a price tag on it so it really was new."

Delilah nodded. "Does your mother buy her clothes at Goodwill, too?"

"She's an actress, so she needs new clothes."

"I see. Before school starts, we're going into town to buy you new clothes."

"Before school starts? Will I be here that long?" As embarrassed as she was, she hoped so.

"I think it's possible. Do you understand why you are here?"

"Because my mom is waiting for a call from her manager."

"I see. Holly, do you know what kind of movies your mother makes?"

"Not exactly. She doesn't let me watch them."

"Well, that's something, at least." Delilah leaned closer. "Do you know why you can't watch them?"

"They're for grown-ups."

"So are my movies and you've seen them, haven't you?"

"A couple. I got to spend the night at my friend Stacy's house and *Violet Morne* was on the Million Dollar Movie so we watched it. It was really good!"

"Thank you, dear. But your mother hasn't shown you any of my movies?"

"I don't think so. Are they on TV very much?"

"Yes, fairly regularly."

"I want to see them all." Holly looked her in the eye. "You're so beautiful, Miss Delilah. I wish I looked just like you."

"That's very kind of you."

"But you are. You are the most beautiful lady I've ever seen."

"Perhaps when I was younger."

"Cherry says you're old-"

Delilah's smile disappeared and her eyes went cold. "Little girls should learn to mind their tongues."

"I mean, you don't look old to me at all. You're beautiful. I'm sorry."

Delilah didn't answer, but rang the bell, summoning Frieda.

"Yes, Miss Delilah?"

"I would like you to show Holly where the watering can is and teach her how to water the plants."

"Yes, ma'am." Frieda smiled at Holly. "Come with me. We'll start with the lobby."

Holly rose and looked back at Delilah. "I'm sorry." She was close to tears.

"Holly, do you have any other shoes?" Her voice remained chilly.

Holly shook her head. "No."

"Very well, there's no time like the present. This afternoon, Max will drive us into town and we'll get you some. Those are filthy and obviously too small for you. They'll cripple your feet."

"You don't have to-"

"Yes, I do. You are my relation and you must look the part." She looked Holly up and down. "Do you have a dress?"

"The one from Penney's."

"Wear that, and brush your hair and wash your face. If I'm going to be seen with you in public, then you must look nice. Be back here at two o'clock."

"Thank you, Miss Delilah."

Delilah nodded. "And Holly? I want you to remember something."

She waited.

"I will never ask you to lie for me. I promise you that. And in return, I want you to make me a promise."

Holly waited.

"Never let anyone - including your mother - make you lie for them."

"I promise."

Delilah looked harsh, but Holly adored her for what she said. She wasn't anything like what Cherry had claimed. She was strict and old-fashioned but she was like an M&M - sweet under that hard coating. Holly knew it.

She ran up to her grandmother and kissed her on the cheek before Delilah could move.

"Holly!" Delilah began.

But Holly had already made her escape and awaited Frieda beyond the foyer's red velvet drapes.

15

TAKING CARE OF BUSINESS

alf an hour later, Holly began her new job watering the plants in the public areas of the Brimstone Grand. And she loved it.

Frieda had shown her where, on each floor, a big aluminum watering can was stowed in a sink room adjacent to Housekeeping's walk-in storage room, where tiny soaps and shampoo bottles, and clean towels and blankets, were stored. The sink room itself contained a deep sink, a bucket and mop, brooms, dustpans, and lots of cleansers in addition to the watering can.

Starting in the lobby, she watered the myriad plants, amazed at how many there were. She had to use the stepladder for the hanging ones - Meredith offered to do those for her, but she wanted to do them herself. Meredith and Peg applauded when she was done and to be honest, Holly was pretty proud of herself - she hadn't spilled a drop.

After finishing the first floor, she moved to the second floor. It looked a lot like the fourth floor. Since the Brimstone Grand had been a hospital, the halls were wide and potted plants lined both sides, some hanging, some on antique tables and bureaus. A dozen big ones - leafy philodendrons and other plants Holly planned to look up and identify - lived in large floor planters and grew tall and lush on stakes and trellises. She was amazed at how plants blended into the decor.

She moved to the third floor and everything was the same except for different colors of paint and wallpaper. It took her twenty minutes to finish there, then she took the elevator to her own floor - the fourth.

Stepping out, she decided to take a quick break to use the toilet and get a drink but when she looked toward her room at the far end of the hall, she saw her door was open. She peered from behind the plants and after a moment, saw the creepy old bellhop, Arthur Meeks, stick his head out of her room and stare her way. *He must've heard the elevator.*

She stepped back inside and pulled the brass gate closed, praying he wouldn't see her. She waited one beat, two, but didn't hear Meeks coming, so she peeked out once more - and saw him entering the room next to hers.

Maybe he went in my room by mistake.

But she knew better.

Once Meeks shut the door, Holly, key in hand, trotted to 429, quietly let herself in, and did the inner locks - a deadbolt and a chain. Looking around, she noticed two things; a painting across from her dresser was on the floor leaning against the wall instead of hanging, and a couple of her dresser drawers weren't quite shut. *Maybe I forgot to close them? No.* The lower drawer contained her pants and shorts; she pushed it closed with her knee. The other drawer was the long narrow top one where she kept her underwear. She started to push it closed then noticed that her best pink panties, the ones embroidered with seed pearls, weren't folded up anymore. They were spread out on top of the drawer. And they looked damp.

She knew she hadn't left them like that; she took good care of her clothes. In the bathroom, she filled the sink and put them in to soak, then checked the rest of the drawers. Nothing seemed out of place, but she was sure someone had been going through her things. Her Friar Tuck bank looked like it had been moved, too. It had to be Arthur Meeks. The thought made her stomach twist.

She heard a noise. It came from the wall, from right where the painting was supposed to hang. It was a creaky, grinding sound. For an instant, she almost panicked because she knew the bellhop was in the next room, but she forced herself to stand still and listen. After a couple minutes the sound became an insistent buzz. Then the silver tip of a drill bit poked through the wall. She ran into her bathroom and grabbed her hairspray, then returned as the buzzing sound continued.

The hole was getting bigger. It was hard to see because it was smack dab in the middle of a dark red rose in the wallpaper. Shaking the hairspray, she moved in close, standing just to the side. *He put it where nobody'd see it!* She looked down at the painting. It showed the edge of the balcony - the curved black wrought iron framing the town below on a stormy day. It was detailed and dark and there was a dark spot on it - someone had cut a small circle right in the middle of the painting. *He's making a peephole!*

The hole in the wall was almost half an inch in diameter now and she almost phoned Meredith, then decided not to because she was too angry. As the drill bit withdrew from the hole, she removed the hairspray cap.

He's there! In the quiet, it was easy to hear him breathing right against the wall. Pretending she was a spy like Napoleon Solo on *The Man from U.N.C.L.E.,* she flattened herself against the wallpaper right next to the hole, counted to three, then slammed the nozzle against it and sprayed.

Arthur Meeks screamed like a little girl. She kept spraying until she heard him open the door and run down the hall. Far away, a door slammed.

"I hope you go blind, you pervert!" Holly grinned, proud of herself. It had gone even better than the time she shoveled dog poop into a week-old newspaper and put it outside to teach Mr. Fromper next door to stop stealing their paper. Quickly she wrote on a piece of hotel stationery: "If you ever do that again I'll have you fired."

Giggling, fighting back near-hysteria, she went to the next room and slid the note under the door. When he came back to clean up, he'd find it. And that would be a lot more fun than telling on him. *He'll learn a lesson about messing with me!*

After locking her door again, she mixed sheets of toilet paper and toothpaste together to make spackle, and shoved the glop into the hole, then hung the picture over it. It would do until she could fix it for real. And the hole in the wall was exactly where the hole in the painting was. Proof that the pervert had intended to spy on her.

She washed her hands and got a drink of water then unlocked the door, thrilled at how scared Arthur Meeks would be when he found the note.

Suddenly nervous, she peeked into the hallway. *He might come after me,* she thought, then told herself he wouldn't dare - if he did, she really would tell on him. *And he knows it!* After she hung the *Do Not Disturb* sign on the doorknob, she made sure she had her key, then shut the door behind her.

She hadn't finished taking care of the plants. Resisting the urge to tiptoe, she unlocked the sink room and filled the can then went down to the other end of the long corridor and began watering. When she was halfway back to the elevator - and Arthur Meeks' room - she saw his door open. The man peered out. Screwing up her courage, she smiled at him. His right eye was swollen and red. Like a turtle, he pulled his slimy head back into his shell of a room. She even heard the door lock.

Holly, stomach filled with butterflies, smiled again. "Gotcha, you creep!"

AFTER A LIGHT LUNCH WITH VERA KOTZWINKLE, DELILAH GAVE her assistant the rest of the day off then called down to the garage to tell Max to get the car ready for a trip to Sedona. Max sounded happy behind his perfect calm. He took the Rolls out regularly, but she so rarely accompanied him that it was a bit of an event when they went anywhere together.

In the bedroom, she opened her closet and laid out a lavender skirt and an antique white silk blouse trimmed with long lacy ruffles and a faux ascot. She set out a matching lavender tam with a pale veil, and her white pumps. She checked her watch - it was an hour before they were to leave.

She entered the music room - it was separate from the vast open living area. English hunt tapestries adorned the walls and the pale gray-green carpet whispered softly beneath her feet. There were two pianos in the room, but this one was her pride and joy - a Steinway baby grand that she'd bought in 1935. When she moved to Brimstone, they'd used a crane to hoist it in through the garden room at the east end of her penthouse.

She sat down and opened the keyboard cover, ran her fingers lightly over the ivories. The only flaw was a cracked white "e" near the top of the keyboard. Charlotte had hit it with a hammer as she stared her mother right in the eye, lower lip stuck out, face red with an incipient tantrum. The girl did not want piano lessons; she wanted to play the flute.

She did not get piano *or* flute lessons. Furious, Delilah banned the girl from all music lessons because of the damaged key. Even now, as she touched the ruined ivory, the old anger filled her. Some things were difficult to let go.

Violet Morne had nearly won an Oscar, just like she had, but they were up against *The Great Zeigfeld* and its lead, Luise Rainer, who was so unappreciative of the honor that she left acting only a few years later. *Who could compete with a musical like that?* Delilah picked out a few notes of *A Pretty Girl is Like a Melody* from *Zeigfeld*, sighed, then put both hands on the keyboard and began playing the dark, lush theme from *Violet Morne*. It was so beautiful that any other year it would have won best musical score. So, too, would she have walked away with the Oscar if not for *Zeigfeld* and Hollywood politics. *A pity*.

She lost herself in the melody, the demanding chords, the tinkling minor notes, the lush rills and progressions, the brilliant intermezzos. Delilah was only a moderately talented pianist, but *Violet Morne* was one piece she could play flawlessly. She loved it; she had always loved it.

A tear of joy escaped as her fingers glided over the keys. The music soothed her, made her feel young again, and gave her hope. It always had. She'd had an affair with Guy Lamont, the composer, and he had lain her against this very Steinway, ravishing her with kisses, asking her to leave Clifton and run away with him. After Clifton took up with Millicent McKensy, she wished she had. But Guy killed himself - death by alcohol - in 1942. Sometimes she wondered if he might have lived if she'd gone with him.

She played and played, thinking of nothing but the music, and was surprised when, during a pause, she heard Frieda. "Miss Delilah?"

She stood in the open doorway, Holly beside her wearing a blue dress that would have been appropriate if it had been two sizes larger. As it was, the girl was bursting out of it.

"That music is beautiful!" Holly said. "I've heard it before."

"*Violet Morne*," Delilah told her, starting to rise.

"Wait," Holly cried. She very nearly ran to the piano. "Would you play some more? I want to watch your hands!"

Delilah stared up at the girl, surprised by the passion in her eyes. "Have you had music lessons?"

"No. Cherry can't-"

"Afford them," Delilah finished, looking at the cracked high e.

Holly nodded. "I asked for them but she says they aren't worth the money and I don't need them."

Delilah played a quick intermezzo from the movie then looked from the key Charlotte had tried to destroy to Holly. "I daresay I'm not surprised. She hasn't taught you much of anything, has she?"

Holly hesitated. "I can iron and do the laundry and cook and clean."

"That's all your mother has taught you?"

"And to vacuum and sew buttons on. She showed me when I was really little."

"And I'd imagine you're much better at all those things than she is."

Holly looked at her hands. "I guess so."

"Did you enjoy your first day on the job, watering the plants?"

"I loved it!"

"Good. Frieda tells me you did a very good job. I'm going to pay you three dollars a week for watering three days a week."

Holly's eyes widened. "That's too much-"

"It's my decision, not yours."

"I didn't mean-"

"I understood what you meant. It's my decision and it shall stand. If you are willing to water all the plants here in my penthouse twice a week, too, I'll pay you two dollars more. Five dollars a week. How does that sound?"

"It sounds wonderful!"

"Very good." Delilah eyed her. She hadn't been going to allow Holly to water the penthouse plants, but after Frieda's glowing report - and the girl's obvious lack of social skills - she decided that it might be wise to have her around more and instruct her in deportment and hygiene. And music, if only to spite Charlotte. She reached out and pressed the cracked key. "Your mother did this when she was ten years old."

"Why?"

"Because I wanted her to take piano lessons. She disagreed."

"Why wouldn't she-"

"I don't know. Holly, would you like to have piano lessons?"

For a moment, Delilah thought the girl might faint. Her face paled and bright pink spots appeared on her cheeks.

"Are you serious?"

"I wouldn't offer if I weren't. Don't you know that by now?"

Holly's eyes sparkled with tears, but she wiped them away before any could fall. "I would *love* piano lessons!"

"Very good. We'll locate a teacher-"

"Please, Miss Delilah, will you teach me?"

Delilah started to laugh, then looked at the girl's face, saw real hope and desire. And knew how angry it would make Charlotte. "Very well. I'll order a beginning book for you and as soon as it arrives, you shall have your first lesson." She snatched Holly's hands. "Show me your fingers."

Holly did.

"We'll buy you a manicure set in town. If you're going to play my piano, your hands must be pristine."

The girl nodded, her eyes on the broken key. "Can I ask you a question?"

"May."

"May I ask you a question?"

"Go ahead."

"Why didn't you get the key fixed?"

Delilah looked into her eyes, searching for something she couldn't quite define, finding it, nonetheless. "I don't know, Holly. But I think I'll ask Vera to call the piano tuner first thing Monday. He's wanted to repair that key since his first visit." She smiled. "It's his lucky day, isn't it?"

Holly nodded, eyes sparkling, lips smiling, and she reminded Delilah painfully of her beloved sister Carrie. Her death had broken Delilah's heart.

"Miss Delilah? Are you okay?"

Delilah rose. "I'm fine, but you need to excuse me while I change clothes for our shopping trip." She raised her voice. "Frieda?"

Her maid appeared in the doorway.

"Please tell Max we will join him in ten minutes."

🏵 16 🏵

CHERRY'S PIE AND OTHER
DELIGHTS

Cherry wished Delilah had a place in Sedona instead of Brimstone. Brimstone was a historical wreck of a town that clung tenaciously to old, ugly hillsides. Sedona, though, was something else. Nothing like the big city, of course - a little too cowboy - but the huge red rocks and mesas were dotted with forest and the main drag had some ritzy shops and restaurants.

Plus, westerns - big ones - had been filmed around the town for years. *The Rounders, The Comanchero, 3:10 to Yuma,* and a shitfest more had been shot there. It wasn't a bad place for an actress, and it occurred to her that branching out into legit movies might be something to consider - *either that, or getting my boobs done.* They were sagging enough now that they were costing her jobs. She was having to do double-dips and three-ways to get work and it was getting really old. Her butt was losing its tone from all the hammering - she hated that when she farted, it just whistled nowadays.

But you do what you gotta do. She'd made the audition and was fortunate because they were looking for girls to shoot immediately for some shorts that would be put together into a complete movie. There weren't too many actresses there and most of them, though younger, were strung-out and hollow-eyed.

The director instantly recognized her from *The Good, the Bad, and the Sexy* and hired her on the spot. He even gave her a card for a plastic surgeon good with silicone and told her he'd give her her own movie if she'd get her boobs lifted. As it was, she was naked within the hour, being plowed by three guys, all mediocre in the face and body department, except for the black stud with the biggest Afro she'd ever seen. She'd never been with a black guy before and he turned her on something fierce. Later, she suggested going out for drinks, but he was into men and turned her down. *What a waste.*

The young director, Peter Hoden, wasn't a really big deal yet - she thought he might be someday since he had balls as big as Nebraska - but he was local and gave her an open invitation to act in his 8mm shorts. After she got to know him better, she told herself, maybe he'd ask her out.

Now, with plenty of money in her pocket - she'd been paid cash for the movie and the photo spread - she entered a compact department store that looked like it belonged on Rodeo Drive. New clothes, shoes, and makeup were all in order.

Screw you, Delilah. I'm not cleaning your toilets! I'll pay you rent until I find a place here.

HOLLY WAS SURE THAT THE DRIVE TO SEDONA IN DELILAH'S VIOLET 1937 Phantom III Aero Coupe would prove to be one of the most wondrous things that would happen in her entire life. The driver, Max, wore a black suit and cap and was just about the most elegant man Holly had ever laid eyes on, and the sleek Rolls was the most luxurious car she'd ever seen, let alone ridden in. Outside, it was all purple - her favorite color - with swaths of gleaming chrome, and a fastback sort of like a Mustang Shelby, except that it swooped all the way down to the tires. A pale Lalique glass figure of a kneeling lady with her arms held high, appeared to tilt backward with wind and velocity on the hood. Inside, the dashboard was shining burled wood and the seats, pale gray leather. She sat in back with her grandmother, sinking into the softest cushions ever. Despite the bumpy roads, the ride was comfortable and once they hit the highway, it felt like they were riding the big puffy clouds in the blue, blue sky.

In Sedona, Max pulled onto a downtown street lined with shops and restaurants and let them out. Delilah, who had spoken very little on the forty-mile trip, merely said, "Come along," and led Holly into the first of several small, expensive-looking clothing stores.

The first thing Delilah did was find her a new outfit, a sunny white sailor dress with navy piping and stars on the collar. She had her try it on, then told the clerk Holly would be wearing it and to throw out Holly's too-small dress. Holly was shocked but thrilled.

Then came more clothes; dresses, shirts, shorts, pants, socks, even underwear and a light jacket.

Next, they went in a shoe store and Holly came out with new tennis shoes - two pair; one for hiking and playing, the other for indoors - as well as white sandals, and shiny patent leather Mary Janes. She'd never even imagined having so many shoes. In another shop, Delilah got her a pair of fuzzy slippers, lavender pajamas with dainty flowers embroidered on the collar - she'd always worn T-shirts to bed - and a fuzzy purple chenille robe that was nicer than Cherry's. Delilah didn't ask what colors she wanted, but that didn't matter because Holly loved purple as much as her grandmother did.

As they shopped, Delilah talked a little more, telling her about the clothes she'd worn as a girl living in Boston. After that, they went in a beauty shop and had manicures. Holly loved the clear polish on her nails and hoped someday to have color like Delilah's. Her grandmother's nails looked sheathed in crimson glass.

When they came out of the salon Max was there, leaning against the Phantom. Holly glanced at Delilah in surprise and her grandmother smiled. "I always get my hair or nails done last, Holly. Max knows to bring the car around." Then she added, "Next time, we'll have our hair done."

"Next time?" Holly asked as they approached the car.

"Yes. You can't go around looking like a poor relation while you're visiting."

Poor relation. Instantly, Holly thought of Adeline, but knew better than to bring her up. Instead, she said, "Thank you, Miss Delilah. I love all my new things."

"You're welc-"

Cherry walked out of a dress shop a few doors down, her arms full of shopping bags. A tall man followed her, also bearing bags. Cherry looked up and down the street and her mouth dropped open when she saw them. She said something to the man and the two walked briskly in the opposite direction. A moment later, a black Chevy Malibu peeled out.

"I see Charlotte has found herself a sugar-daddy."

Holly answered without thinking. "She always goes shopping when she gets a job. That man is probably an actor or something."

Delilah looked down at her and sighed. "That girl never could hold onto a red penny. Come, Holly, let's get back to Brimstone."

Max put their bags in the trunk then helped them into the car.

When they were most of the way back, Delilah asked, "Holly, do you like root beer floats?"

"I love them!"

"Max?"

"Yes, Miss Delilah?"

"When we get back to Brimstone, pull over at Gower's Drugs on Main." She looked at Holly. "There's nothing better than something cold after a long day shopping, is there?"

Holly had never had a long day shopping before, but she nodded. She couldn't imagine it wasn't true.

"THAT OLD BAG OF BONES!" CHERRY DEVINE LIT A CIGARETTE WHILE Rod Stone, one of her co-stars, drove her back to her car.

"What's wrong?"

"What's wrong is my damned mother is a bitch!"

"She is? What? Why?" He looked eager for dirt.

"Didn't you see them, with those shopping bags? Delilah's been spending money on *my* kid. She's stealing her from me! She's *buying* her."

"You have a daughter?" Rod grinned. "With a figure like that?"

Cherry, pissed that she'd slipped up and said she had a kid, batted her lashes. "Thanks. She's my step kid - her father skipped out and left me to raise her." It was a lie she often told and it always worked. "Anyway, my mother is a total cunt."

"Cherry Devine," Rod mused. "She isn't Delilah Devine, is she? That old movie star?"

"Yeah, and she still thinks she's as big as shit on a hot tin roof." Cherry lit a smoke. "But she's washed up. Has been for years. That's why she's out here in the boonies. To hide her wrinkles."

"*Violet Morne*," Rod said. "That was her. I saw that. It was pretty good."

"Why don't you just shut the fuck up?" Cherry said it with a smile, so he'd think she was joking.

"Or what?"

"Or I won't go back to your motel with you." She batted her lashes. "Our chemistry-"

"Is great," Rod finished. "I knew a chick a couple years ago who would only screw on camera. She really got hot being watched, but never touched a dick otherwise."

Cherry laughed. "What'd she do? Eat pussy?"

"Nope, only fucked on camera. She dried up like a raisin as soon the director yelled cut."

"She still making movies?"

"No, she went down to Mexico on a shoot. Got herself murdered."

"Too bad." Cherry grabbed her purse as they pulled up beside the Falcon. "So, you wanna get something to eat, Rod? I could eat a horse. That was quite a workout, today." She winked at him.

"Pete Hoden's a hell of a director. He makes us work hard. I'm starving, too."

She nodded and got out. "Let's drop my car at your motel and go for dinner and drinks. Lots of drinks."

"You're on. Maybe we can bring a bottle back to the room, too."

"Sure. Say, you married?"

"Does that matter?"

"No, just wondered."

"I'm single."
"Got any kids?"
"Does that matter?"
"Yeah, it does. Got any?"
"Not a single one."
Cherry unlocked her car. "Good. I'll follow you."

❧ 17 ❧

AT GOWER'S DRUGS

The massive soda fountain in Gower's Drugs gleamed silver behind the shining counter as Delilah and Holly sat on tufted green stools. A cute teenage boy wearing a white apron and a matching garrison cap set at a jaunty angle on his sandy brown hair approached. "May I help you ladies?" He smiled, his blue eyes lighting first on Delilah, then on Holly. His name tag - embroidered red on his white apron - said "Eddie."

"Two root beer floats, please, young man," Delilah said. "And make sure the glasses are well frosted first. We don't mind waiting."

"Yes, ma'am!" He winked at Holly and her stomach filled with butterflies. Then, Eddie turned and Holly saw he had a short neat ponytail hanging over his collar. *He's a hippie!* She had never gotten to meet one before, and he sure didn't look gross and dirty like Cherry always said they were.

"He's got a ponytail," she told her grandmother.

"So he does. It's nice that Ben doesn't make him cut it off to work here."

Holly looked at Delilah, wonder in her eyes. "You don't hate it?"

Delilah chuckled. "Why should I? Fashions change, you know."

"Really? But it means he's a hippie."

"My dear girl." Delilah caught her in her gaze. "He's clean, polite, and holding down a job. His eyes are clear. Obviously, if he *is* a hippie, he's not the sort of hippie you're thinking of." She studied Holly. "What do you know about hippies, anyway?"

She hesitated. "Cherry says they're dirty and diseased."

"I'm sure that's true of some. But I think your mother is simply intimidated by the younger generation; she doesn't fit in with them and she's uncomfortable with her age." Delilah laughed. "I doubt she'll ever understand that one cannot halt time."

"What?"

An elderly man, wearing an apron and white pointed cap like Eddie's appeared, his gaunt face turning into an embroidery of pleasant wrinkles when he saw them. "Why Miss Devine, I haven't seen you in ... well, I don't know how long - since the Fourth of July parade in '66. You haven't aged a day."

Delilah smiled through her veil. "You're a liar, Ben Gower."

"Why Miss Devine-"

She laughed. "Delilah. And I adore you for it."

"And who's this little lady?" He turned his old blue eyes on Holly and stared hard at her before glancing back at Delilah. "I must say, she reminds me of your sister, Carrie."

"The spitting image," Delilah responded. "This is Holly, my granddaughter."

"Ah, no funning me, Delilah. You're not old enough to have a granddaughter. Holly must be your youngest girl." He put out his hand. "I'm charmed to make your acquaintance, little lady."

Holly shook it. "Pleased to meet you, Mr.-"

"Ben, honey. Just Ben."

"Ben." Holly wanted to ask him how old he was but knew it wouldn't be polite.

"What will it be today, ladies?"

"Your assistant already took our order," Delilah said.

"Very good. You know, Delilah, Holly also takes after Adeline Chance, too. "She has that same golden fleck as Carrie and Adeline." He studied her. "Why, little lady, you have gold dust in *both* your eyes, don't you! Isn't that something!" He paused. "Delilah? Is something wrong?"

Delilah was studying her gloved hands. "Sore subject, Ben. Let's change it, shall we?"

He didn't miss a beat "Did you hear about the ruckus at the last town council meeting?"

"No, I haven't, Ben. Enlighten me."

"Well, it seems Billy Capstone - you know, Brimstone Billy from the market - thinks he'd make a better mayor than Tom Stuffenphepper. Seems he had a bunch of supporters in the audience, so Tom's wife corralled a group of her husband's voters and brought them along, too."

Delilah chuckled.

"Edna Garrett," Ben continued, "told me they nearly came to blows, right there in the meeting room of the Baptist church. Pastor Johnson broke it up by invoking his heavenly Boss, but it wasn't easy and he got a black eye for it." Ben looked up. "Well, there's my number one employee!"

Eddie placed a paper doily in front of Delilah, set a tall root beer float on it, then did the same for Holly. He drew two long-handled silver spoons and two straws from his apron pocket and set them on their napkins. "Ladies, may I get you anything else?"

"This is perfect, young man," Delilah said. "Thank you."

"Thank you, Eddie," echoed Holly, all eyes.

"Good lad," muttered Ben Gower as Eddie left to serve new customers at the far end of the counter. "I'm going to miss young Mr. Fortune when he goes back to school in September. At least he'll still be working after school and weekends. Best worker - and the youngest - I've ever had. And you, Holly. Will you be attending school here this fall?"

Without glancing at her grandmother, Holly said, "I hope so!" as quickly as she dared. Delilah might be a little stiff, but she was liking her more and more - she was way more open-minded than Cherry *and* she appreciated nice cars. She didn't want to go back to Van Nuys, to keeping her mother's crappy apartment clean and listening to Cherry and her boyfriends making noise and drinking at all hours. "Never again."

"What's that, Holly?" Delilah's spoon was poised above the foamy float. "Never again? What do you mean? You don't like school?"

Ben nodded at them and headed off to serve new customers.

"Oh, no. I didn't mean to say that out loud."

"That may well be, but what *did* you mean?"

Holly looked her in the eye. "I don't ever want to go back to Van Nuys. I love it here."

"You haven't been here long enough to know that."

Holly said nothing. She did know; she knew for sure, but her grandmother wouldn't understand that, and probably didn't want her around anyway.

"Holly, your mother isn't likely to stick around for very long."

"I know." Holly set her spoon down, appetite gone.

"Perhaps when she leaves, you might stay on for a while."

Holly looked up, daring to hope. "Really?"

"If she insists you go with her, I can't do a thing about it."

"But if she says I can stay, you'd let me?"

"Perhaps for a semester. As long as you behave and do well in school."

"I always do well in school," Holly said. "And I behave. Well, mostly."

Delilah chuckled. "Mostly. You're an honest girl. Now, enjoy your float while it's nice and cold."

Holly did and it was the best thing she'd ever tasted. The root beer was sharp and tangy and sweet, and the ice cream, thick and rich.

"How are we doing?" Ben approached when they were nearly finished. "Do you ladies want Eddie to bring you anything else?"

"I've put on five pounds just sitting here, but perhaps Holly would like something more?"

"No thank you. I'm full, too, and I want my mouth to taste like root beer and vanilla for the rest of the day."

"You're welcome back anytime, Holly, with or without your beautiful grandmother." Ben gave Delilah a watery blink. "But I hope you bring her along! She's quite the lady, you know."

"I know."

Holly saw Delilah's blush, even through the thin netting.

✗

BACK IN THE PHANTOM, HOLLY LOOKED AT DELILAH. "CAN I ASK A question?"

"*May* I ask a question."

"May I?"

"You may."

"How old is Ben?"

"Why, he must be pushing eighty by now. He was just a boy when the disaster happened."

"Disaster? What happened?"

"There was some kind of natural disaster. A lot of people died quite horribly. It was before my time."

"Miss Delilah," Max called, revealing a fine British accent. "We need petrol. Do you mind if I stop at the Humble station?"

Delilah sighed. "Please try to remember gasoline sooner next time Max. Yes, stop, but be quick about it."

Holly, full of questions, kept her mouth shut. She couldn't let Delilah find out about her talk with Adeline. Not yet, at least. "Everybody died?" she prompted. "Please tell me what happened." Fuzzy dreams from the night before nibbled at her memory.

"You have a morbid streak, young lady. Do you really want to hear this?"

Holly nodded. "I do."

"Very well. I believe it was around the turn of the century and Ben Gower was about your age. He was working as a delivery boy and was sent to the Clementine Hospital and found everyone dead inside. Doctors, patients, everyone. A gas leak, they thought. My grandfather and father weren't there that day, or they'd have died, too. That's all I know."

The bell dinged as Max pulled up to the pumps. Holly craned her neck to see past Delilah as Ike Chance came out to wait on them. He spoke with Max then filled the car.

"Want those windows washed? Tires, oil, or water checked?" he called as he returned to the driver's door.

"No, thank you," Max said. "I prefer to do those things myself."

"Very well, that will be four dollars and twenty-four cents."

Max counted out the money and handed it over. Then Ike leaned into the long window behind him and smiled at Holly. "Hello, little lady! Are you all recovered from the quake yesterday?"

"Yes." Holly was afraid to say more in front of her grandmother.

His eyes shifted to Delilah. "Miss Delilah. Adeline sends her regards."

Delilah gave a curt nod.

"Well, you folks have a nice evening." Ike tipped his cap and headed back into the station as Max pulled onto the road.

"Holly, have you met that man before? He seemed to know you."

"Yes, Miss Delilah. Yesterday, when Cherry was buying gas. We were there when the earthquake happened."

"Did you meet Mrs. Chance?"

Holly almost lied, then decided that would be a stupid thing to do. "Yes, I did. I was buying us sodas when it happened."

"What did you think of her?"

"She seemed nice." Holly was going to leave it at that, but her mouth had a mind of its own. "She had gold in her eye, too. Like Ben Gower said."

Long seconds passed before Delilah spoke. "It's not unusual. My grandfather and my older sister both had it. You take after Carrie quite a bit. Remind me to show you her picture."

"I'd love that!" Holly screwed up her nerve and put on her most innocent face. "Miss Delilah? Is that lady at the gas station related to us? You know, because of her eye?"

Delilah cleared her throat. "Distantly."

"How?"

"Adeline Chance is a cousin, but she's not a nice person. I must insist you avoid her."

"But ..." Holly let the word trail off. "Okay." As they drove up Hospital Hill, she imagined Ben Gower as a delivery boy walking up to the doors of the Clementine Hospital, maybe with a telegram, or flowers, or medicine, stepping inside, and seeing all the dead people. She flashed on her faded nightmare, not quite knowing why, and wondered if the people were bloody, with their eyes bugging out and their throats slit. Probably not if it was a natural disaster. Then she wondered if there was a fire. "Miss Delilah, you said it was a gas leak? Do you know what happened? Was there an explosion?"

Delilah arched an eyebrow. "Holly, where do you get this morbid streak?"

"I'm just really curious." She gave Delilah her most disarming smile. "I like to investigate stuff. When I grow up, maybe I'll be a detective like *Columbo* or a spy like *The Man from U.N.C.L.E.* Or-" She stopped, realizing she had motor mouth. "Anyway, Miss Delilah, I don't think it's morbid to want to know about history. Do you?"

"I suppose not. It happened years before I was born. As far as I know, there was only a gas leak, no explosion. If you really want to know, you could go to the library." Delilah paused. "Or better, ask Steve Cross. He knows a lot more about the town than I do. Have a chat with him when there aren't any guests around."

She smiled, happy to have an excuse to talk to the handsome night manager. "Yes, Miss Delilah. I sure will."

HOLLY AND DELILAH ENTERED THE HOTEL FROM THE GARAGE, SO she didn't see Meredith before they rode the elevator up to the fourth floor. She'd been glad when Delilah got off with her to help carry her new clothes and shoes, and to see what else she might need in her new room - it meant that she wouldn't be alone if Arthur Meeks was around. But he wasn't. Delilah looked through her kitchen cupboards and refrigerator, nodding and hmm-ing approval of the groceries Meredith had stocked. When Delilah left, Holly watched through the peephole and saw her grandmother let herself into Cherry's room. She only stayed a couple minutes before heading upstairs, looking irritated.

But Holly couldn't help smiling as she turned to look at all the bags and boxes. It was better than any Christmas she'd ever had.

❧ 18 ❧

UNWANTED MEMORIES

B en Gower sat in the pharmacy office sipping a root beer float for the first time in years. The bubbles tickled his old nose and bit his tongue, the same way they had when he was a boy. *Heavenly*, he thought.

"Mr. Gower?" Eddie Fortune stuck his head through the doorway. "Do you want me to close up?"

"Yes, Eddie." He handed him the keys. "Make sure you check the rear door, too, would you?"

"Sure will, Mr. G." Eddie grinned. "How's the float?"

"Absolutely perfect, thanks, son."

"Who was that lady with the little girl? She looked familiar."

"She ought to. She was one of the biggest movie stars of all time in the thirties and forties." He chuckled. Have you seen *Violet Morne?* That's her most famous movie."

"That's *her?*" Eddie's tongue nearly fell out of his mouth. "I love that movie!"

"Delilah Devine," Ben smiled.

"I wonder why she lives here."

"She was born here, my boy. I knew her when she was knee-high to a footstool. Cute little thing with dark curls. She inherited the Brimstone Grand a few years ago. Her granddaddy, Henry Hank Barrow, owned the property originally. He was the chief honcho when it was a hospital, you know."

"A doctor?"

"No, he was the administrator. He told the doctors what they could do and how much they could spend."

"Holy crap, really? My cousin Steve is the night manager there. He didn't tell me he works for *her*! I'm going to ask him about it." Eddie paused. "But why would somebody like Delilah Devine want to come back to this podunk town?"

"Well, this is a pretty nice place to retire to, son. Quiet, friendly."

"But there's nothing to do here. I'm going to explore the world someday."

"I'll just bet you are, Eddie. But finish your education first."

The boy grinned. "I'm going to go to UC Santo Verde in California. My uncle's a professor there and he says he'll pull some strings if necessary, but I don't think he'll have to; I get good grades. And college will keep me out of 'Nam if that nonsense is still going on."

Ben nodded. "You just let me know if you need more study time once school starts and I'll reduce your hours."

"Don't worry about that, Mr. G. I can do both."

Ben smiled. The boy not only had his whole life ahead of him, he had the brains and fortitude to do whatever he wanted. Right now, the kid was still interested in ghosts, UFOs, coffins banging around in Barbados, and all sorts of crazy stuff, but soon enough, he'd probably become a lawyer or something like that - though Ben secretly hoped he'd keep his crazy interests and become a novelist or a reporter. He cleared his throat. "Better get those doors locked before the mayor's wife comes along and asks me to make her another batch of that crazy herbal mixture for her bursitis."

"Right away." Eddie was off like a shot.

Moments later he said goodnight, then took off on his bicycle for his home on the east side of town. Ben, who lived just a flight of stairs above the drug store, slipped on a light jacket - though Brimstone summers were hot, it tended to cool down once the sun set. In his younger days, Ben loved the cold nights, but now the chill made his bones ache. It was hell getting old, he thought, *but it's also hell being young.*

He walked up the street to the Wet Whistle. Inside, he inhaled beer and tobacco smoke, but not too much of the latter. Most of the regulars were old farts who had cut back on tobacco - many had worked the mines and just didn't have the lungs for it anymore. Ben was lucky he'd inherited the drugstore from his dad - otherwise, he might have toiled down there too.

"Ben, how they hanging?" That was Richie Shaw. He only had one good eye, but it was sharp.

"Hanging fine, Richie. Just fine." He bellied up to the bar.

"What'll it be?" Bartender Hedison Keller wiped the counter and put a bowl of beer nuts in front of him. "Bud on tap?"

"I'm in the mood for stronger stuff, Heddy. How about a scotch rocks?"

"You got it." Heddy clinked ice into a glass then poured Johnnie Walker over the cubes. "Hard day?"

"No, pretty good, actually."

"What's with the whisky, then?"

"Drowning some old memories." He sipped. "You know how they pop up when you least expect them?"

"Sure do."

Ben stared up at the photos above the bar, his eyes finding the old shot of the Clementine Hospital at the top of the hill. The hospital was brand new in the photo; it might not have even held any patients yet. There were a few smaller buildings nearby, most long gone now. Ben hadn't set foot up there since that day so long ago ... A day when the hospital was still fairly new, but had occupants - patients, doctors, nurses.

They were all dead.

He shivered, got a refill, then took his drink over to Richie Shaw's table, sitting so the photo was out of sight.

Some things were best forgotten.

❦ 19 ❦

DINING IN

Holly ate dinner in the employee breakroom at Devine's, on the first floor at the hotel's west end. The food really was divine; employees got to eat leftovers and were even allowed to cook extras pans of food like lasagna and scalloped potatoes. She arrived during the dinner rush, so she had no company, but one of the waitresses, Sandy, brought her butternut squash bisque, slices of turkey, potatoes au gratin and a fresh baked apple tart for dessert. She also brought her a bag full of containers. "Miss Delilah said you might like having some food for your own refrigerator."

After thanking Sandy, Holly settled at the table and began reading *The Haunting of Hill House*, a heavy salt shaker holding the paperback open beside her plate. She savored the words as much as the food. *"Hill House, not sane, stood by itself against its hills, holding darkness within ..."*

She wondered if the Brimstone Grand, standing alone against its own hills, was equally insane. She hoped so.

"Well, hello there, little lady."

Crap. Meeks the bellhop sat down directly across from her. She gave him the barest of glances, glad to see his eye was still bloodshot.

"It's nice to have some company at dinner tonight." The man picked up his fork.

He had to know she was the one who sprayed his eye, so the fact he talked to her like nothing had happened gave her a major case of the creeps. She forked the last bite of turkey into her mouth and swallowed. "I'm done."

"Too full for your dessert?" Meeks eyed the apple tart. "Or are you watching your figure?"

She wrapped the treat in a napkin and placed it in the bag Sandy gave her to take upstairs. "I'm saving it for later."

"Miss Devine, you're as standoffish as your grandmother, did you know that?" He gave her a smile that made her skin crawl. Instead of his bellboy uniform, he wore a rust-red button-down shirt that looked freshly pressed, but it didn't help - he was still ugly. Without his uniform cap, light reflected off his colorless hair. His lips were too red for a man, livery and thick under that giant nose, and his eyes were the color of dishwater. He was repulsive.

"Miss *Tremayne.*" Rising, she scooped up her book.

His tray held a slice of turkey and a small scoop of potatoes in addition to a huge bowl of vanilla pudding. He began spooning white glop into his mouth. "What are you reading, Miss *Devine?*"

She could see the pudding behind his liver-lips, oozing over his stumpy little teeth like a bunch of popped pimples. She looked away. "A book."

"I like books. What are you reading?"

She held the book up so he could see the title, then placed it in her bag of leftovers, preparing to leave.

"That's a scary book for a little girl to read."

She didn't reply.

"Did you know the hotel is haunted?"

"Sure."

"There's a ghost on the fourth floor that rattles door knobs. Does that scare you?"

"Nope."

He pointed at his bloodshot eye. "What if I told you a ghost did this to me?"

"I wouldn't believe you." *Why would he even say that?*

"Why not?" His smile was so wide it looked like he was about to unhinge his jaw.

He was messing with her, but she couldn't figure out why, so she didn't answer him, just gathered up her bag and turned toward the door.

"Do you know what kind of movies your mother makes?"

It stopped her cold and made her stomach clench.

"Miss *Devine*?" he asked. "Have you seen your mother's movies?"

She turned and looked him in the eye. "No. I like books."

"You should watch one of her movies. You'd learn a lot." He looked her up and down. "It's a shame. You have just what it takes to follow in your mother's footsteps." His eyes did another slow crawl over her body.

"You better leave me alone." As she spoke, she thought it, hard. *Leave me alone!*

He hesitated, looked flustered, but only for an instant. "You have some crazy eyes, little girl. Did you know that?"

"Leave me alone."

"Why? Don't you want to be friendly?"

"No." She turned and crossed the threshold, then without looking back, said, "You leave me alone or I'll put out your other eye." Her posture straight and tall, she left, his soft laughter trailing behind her.

❦ 20 ❦

THE PAGE OF WANDS

T he setting sun cast reddish-gold light through the penthouse windows as Delilah spread tarot cards in a Celtic cross. She'd represented Holly with the Page of Wands, but as she dealt the hand, she grew alarmed. At the heart of the matter was the Devil - bad influences. That had to be Charlotte. The Page was crossed by the Fool - innocence and new beginnings. Delilah wasn't sure she liked where this was headed. The cards were encouraging her to allow the girl to stay here, escape those bad influences and start a new life. To stay for a little while was one thing, but...

No. I can't allow her to stay indefinitely. I don't need such problems.

Then her subconscious betrayed her.

You were given a new life.

Ignoring the thought, she continued the reading. The basis of the matter of her granddaughter was represented by Temperance reversed. And no wonder; Charlotte had always been excessive and unbalanced. The girl had grown up in her shadow. Had she inherited her ways? At the very least, she must have been influenced by them.

The recent past was the Hermit reversed. Holly had been lonely and isolated. *No surprise there.* She started to move to the next card, then paused, staring at the Hermit, who shone a light into a dark cave.

A flash of memory - sifting dirt - startled her, but it was gone in an instant and she turned the near future card: Death. The image always alarmed Delilah even though she knew it wasn't literal, it spoke of change, of metamorphosis, and surely, that was what Holly was experiencing here in Brimstone. Given her circumstances, it could only be a good thing. Aunt Beatrice Lane, who had given Delilah a second chance, loomed large in her thoughts. *But I will not ... I cannot make that girl my responsibility. It's not the same thing.*

But it was.

Again, Delilah shrugged off the thought, and turned the crowning card. It represented Holly's conscious influences and goals. The Sun. There was no better card. The girl desired happiness and success. *A very good omen, indeed.*

The following card was the Moon, which suggested that Holly's intuition was important, but that she was full of imagination. The next represented how others responded to her and when Delilah turned it, what she saw vexed her: The Hierophant, reversed. Rebelliousness. Perhaps even subterfuge.

Holly's hopes and fears were represented by Justice - clarity and truth. That backed up the spread's other cards - thus far, Holly was basically a good, honest, child despite her upbringing and rebellious nature.

But as Delilah turned the final card to reveal the likely outcome, her fingers trembled. The Magician, reversed. Trickery and illusion. The card, as always, touched a deep fear in Delilah, one she understood no more now than she had as a child. *Danger.*

The combination of cards spoke of danger as well, and with a shiver, she swept her hand over them, swirling and scattering their message.

When she'd turned twelve, Aunt Beatrice taught her to read the tarot. As a girl, it had felt like a game to her, especially since Aunt Beatrice's Spiritualist bent had seemed over-the-top. Delilah had never believed that spirits spoke through the cards, but she had come to understand that they were keys that unlocked her own unconscious thoughts. There definitely was something to the cards.

Beatrice had become her legal guardian when she was barely seven and from her first day in the grand townhouse in Boston, she'd felt like she was Alice down the rabbit hole. Even as she'd grieved for Carrie, she took joy in her new life. Aunt Beatrice might have been a little wacky with her séances and Spiritualist circles, her tarot cards and tea leaves, but she was kind to Delilah and saw to it that she received the best of everything - clothes, music lessons, and schooling. They summered in Europe.

Delilah gathered up the tarot deck, wrapped it in purple silk, and slipped it into a narrow drawer in the writing table. She'd taken to Boston as if she'd been born there and she had loved Beatrice - she'd been a far more loving guardian than Bill Delacorte.

Delilah never missed her father but she missed the town itself; she had few memories of either. She rose and opened the glass balcony doors. Stepping out, she peered down at the twilit town. It had been little more than a mining camp when she'd left, dusty, dirty, and smelling of sulfur. It was still a dusty place, but the acrid yellow fog had disappeared when the last mine closed in the late thirties.

Enjoying the cool evening breeze, Delilah saw golden light already twinkling in the windows of houses and businesses, and headlights moving along Main Street. She heard the call of an owl, the howl of a coyote. *What would I have been if I hadn't gone to live with Aunt Beatrice?* Certainly not an actress, certainly not a lot of things. If she'd stayed, she probably would have become a simple housewife like her cousin Adeline. *Perish the thought! It would have killed me!*

What might Holly become if she goes back to Los Angeles with her mother? A porn star? The girl showed no sign of that now - nor did the cards indicate such a fate - but soon enough her hormones would kick in, and then there was no telling. She might take after her mother. *Or after Carrie. Or even after Adeline.*

She dwelled on Adeline now. The very name angered her. Delilah was only six when Carrie died, but she remembered Adeline, just standing there - *standing where?* - doing nothing. *What was she supposed to be doing?* As always, confusion fogged her memory.

She recalled her sister and Adeline before that, laughing, talking, best friends, thick as thieves. *How could she just stand there while Carrie died?* Though Delilah's few memories of that day were blurred and jumbled, she knew Adeline had somehow failed Carrie. *And me.*

But whatever happened that day was lost to her. All she knew was that somehow, Adeline was the reason Carrie was dead. *And why am I thinking about this now?*

Delilah sighed. *Why, indeed?* Holly was the obvious reason. The girl reminded her so much of Carrie - younger, of course, but it was all there. Since her first audience with the child, she'd been fascinated, even drawn to her, because of it.

She didn't want to be; what she wanted was to have Charlotte and her child out of her hair as quickly as possible. But Holly ... Delilah glanced at the writing desk, thinking of the tarot reading. It hadn't told her much except that it was dangerous to have the girl here - dangerous for Holly - and for Delilah. The cards did not explain. But Delilah, especially after spending the hours in Sedona with her, almost felt as if Holly were Carrie incarnate. That feeling, in itself, was dangerous. And delusional.

Carrie Delacorte had died too young. At sixteen, she'd still been a tomboy, given to dressing in men's trousers and hiking and exploring, more interested in collecting rocks than beaus. Their mother, Myrtle, had died when Delilah was only three; she barely remembered her at all, except for the stories Carrie told about how she saw to it both her daughters wore nice dresses and shoes, and always had their hair combed. After Myrtle died, their father, Bill Delacorte, tried to make Carrie dress like a lady and take care of Delilah and the house - even though they could easily have afforded servants. She had to do the cooking, the cleaning, all of it. And even at age six, Delilah knew Carrie didn't like their father much.

And she didn't like Henry Hank Barrow, their grandfather, at all.

"He's a bad man, Delilah. A very bad man. You stay away from him, you hear?"

Delilah gasped. She'd heard Carrie's voice as clearly as if her sister had been standing behind her. Gripping the wrought iron railing, she realized that what she thought she heard was actually a *real* memory, a true memory, undoubtedly sparked by Holly's presence. Details followed - joy at seeing Carrie come through a door; running into her big sister's arms. There were tears on Carrie's cheeks as she hugged Delilah close. *What's wrong, Carrie?* she'd asked. Her sister, in a long pink dress that was freshly ripped at the bodice, hadn't answered, but knelt down and took her hands, staring fiercely into her eyes with her own brilliant blue ones. Delilah's gaze fixed on the golden fleck. It was pulsing. *"He's a bad man, Delilah. A very bad man."*

Stars had begun to dot the cobalt sky. She heard a car approaching the hotel long before she saw it. Delilah watched, waiting, wondering if Charlotte had finally returned. But, no. They were guests, a family in the maroon Rambler station wagon. They parked, then a couple and two children emerged, laughing and talking as they headed into the lobby.

Delilah forgot them. *Our grandfather had a pocket watch.* Another memory, long buried. She remembered the grandfather holding it up, dangling it before her. It was gold, ornately engraved with a peculiar symbol - An X with a triple-armed cross with tiny rubies set into the short middle ones and sort of a triangle with an upside-down cross at the bottom. At the top were his initials, H.H.B., and just above an infinity sign was something in Latin. He taught her what it said - *Infurnam Aeris*. It was the symbol of the secret club Henry Hank belonged to, and to this day she had no idea what *Infurnam Aeris* meant. Back then she'd thought it was a Christmas ornament he kept in his pocket.

More than the pocket watch, though, she remembered Henry Hank Barrow's eyes. Despite being the same bright sapphire as Carrie's and Adeline's, with the same gold fleck, they seemed darker ... and somehow frightening. And his golden spot was more of a stain, dark and disturbing. Or perhaps it seemed that way because his bushy salt and pepper eyebrows were always drawn down, bookmarking the deep vertical lines that made him look like he was frowning.

While Carrie's death had affected her deeply, the grandfather's was a bare blip on a radar screen. Delilah had never been close to him. He was a businessman, chilly and unapproachable, disinterested in the foibles of little girls.

Carrie hated him.

"He's a bad man, Delilah. Stay away from him."

Her sister's voice returned, confounding her, making her wonder what else she'd forgotten about her childhood in Brimstone. Most likely there were many things - after all, she was very young when she'd been sent to Boston. That had been so exciting that everything else - except a few warm memories of Carrie - had fallen away. After a time, Delilah had even claimed to be born there.

I wanted to forget Brimstone. And it was no wonder.

But how did Carrie die?

There'd been an accident. Suddenly, she remembered running, and darkness, then dirt sifting onto her head and face, stinging her eyes. And screaming, far away. A swinging lantern had revealed something - *but what?* - and then eyes, dragon's eyes, flaming cobalt and copper-red, staring into her soul.

Dear God. Dizzy, Delilah gripped the balcony rail. She'd seen those eyes in her nightmares for years after that. Seen them and run from them. *How could I have forgotten?* Aunt Beatrice had held and soothed her when she awoke at night screaming.

Grandfather called himself the Brimstone Beast.

The thought, unbidden and unwanted, shocked her.

The balcony began to tremble; she felt it beneath her feet and in the railing. Her head swam. She clung to the rail as the shaking strengthened. *Another earthquake!*

"THE BRIMSTONE BEAST," HOLLY READ AS SHE SAT AT THE LITTLE round table in her room, *"is at the heart of Brimstone's folklore. The tale dates back hundreds, if not thousands, of years. The people who lived here long ago told tales of the Beast."*

Holly grabbed an apple out of the blue bowl in the center of the table, polished the red fruit on her shirt, then took a bite. Chewing, she returned to the folklore book.

"The legend goes that they once lived deep in the earth but were driven to leave by an evil shaman. They tunneled up and found the sun. The shaman - in the form of a serpent - chased them, wanting to claim the sun for himself.

"As the last of the Desert People climbed into the sunlight, the Hellfire

Serpent was close behind. Just in time, a good shaman closed the hole, trapping the evil creature inside the earth. There it died and became the Hellfire Spirit.

"The native people continued to fear the spirit of the serpent and attributed earthquakes to its attempts to come to the surface. But after a while, the earth quieted and the local inhabitants felt they were finally safe, saying the evil spirit had fallen asleep. After that, when the occasional minor quake hit, they attributed it to the serpent rolling over in its sleep.

"After a time, the natives began digging for copper and made tools and jewelry out of the pliable metal. You can see some of these items at the Desert Museum in Lewisdale.

"Many years passed and the mining pits and trenches grew deep. According to legend, that's when the trouble began once more. The story goes that the native peoples dug too close to the Hellfire Spirit and it woke up with a roar that shook the earth so violently that all the miners suffocated in a great landslide. Many other members of the tribe - those anywhere near the mining pits - lost their lives as well.

"The few who lived to tell the tale refused to work in the mine again, and the native peoples moved away from the Brimstone region, gradually mixing with other tribes. The tale of the evil Hellfire Spirit was then taken up by white miners and became the legend of the Brimstone Beast."

As Holly reached for her apple, it rolled across the table, and the small television on the chest of drawers across the room began rattling. She felt vibrations beneath her feet and the hanging lamp in the middle of the room began swaying.

Earthquake! A big one! Feeling the rumble beneath her feet, Holly ran to the balcony door. As the rumbling became a roar, she stepped outside.

Everything seemed to be rolling in slow motion as she looked out over the town. Lights on the north side of Brimstone suddenly winked out. Then Main Street went dark as the ground calmed.

Another sudden jolt, so strong that Holly hung on to the rail to stay on her feet. The lights to the west extinguished.

Then the hotel went dark. And silent.

Breathing hard, more excited than afraid, Holly went back inside, shut the door and opened the blinds and drapes to let the scant moonlight into the room. It wasn't enough; she dug her flashlight out and turned it on. It had new batteries and let her see that lots of books and the painting over the peephole was now face down on the floor. "Wow," she breathed, relieved to see her Friar Tuck bank hadn't fallen. The cobalt bowl of apples lay cracked, under the table, scarlet fruit everywhere. It reminded her of something, but what, Holly didn't know.

Grabbing her room key, she stepped into the pitch-dark hallway and glanced toward the elevator just as the bellhop's door opened. Her light glanced off his broad forehead.

"Hello?" he called. "Who's that?"

No way! She turned the light toward the stairs at the end of the hall and ran, aware that Meeks was somewhere behind her, calling for her to wait. At the stairwell, she paused, torn between going up to her grandmother's penthouse and heading downstairs.

"Holly Devine? Is that you?" Meeks was closer.

She took the stairs two at a time, racing up to her grandmother's floor, sure he wouldn't dare follow.

She reached Miss Delilah's and rang the bell, then pounded on the door. She pressed the bell again as more little trembles vibrated into her feet.

"Miss Delilah!" she yelled.

At last, she heard noises inside; chain-locks being undone, a deadbolt turning. Then Frieda, in a housedress and slippers, and carrying a candle in a hurricane glass, opened the door. "Miss Holly! Are you all right?"

"Yes. Did you feel the earthquakes?"

"I did. I think everyone did."

"Can I see my gr - Miss Delilah?" Holly made a move to step inside, but Frieda blocked the way.

"She's not seeing anyone right now, honey." Frieda's face looked ominous in the flickering candlelight.

"Is she okay?"

"She's fine, don't you worry."

"Why can't I see her?"

Frieda bent close and spoke very softly. "Miss Delilah is busy right now. Why don't you come back in the morning? I'll tell her you stopped by and asked after her."

"But–"

Frieda began to close the door.

Holly pulled the desperation card, letting her voice pitch higher. "But my mom isn't here so I'm all alone and it's dark!"

"You have a nice flashlight, *mija*. Why don't you go down to the lobby and see Steve? I bet he'd love some company right now!"

"But–"

"I'm sorry. I have orders from Miss Delilah. You need to go back to your room or down to the lobby." She paused, her face full of understanding. "I think that's best. But take the stairs, not the elevator."

The door closed.

🦋 21 🦋

GHOST IN THE MACHINE

The quake seemed to be over. Steven Cross, barely functional flashlight in hand, had just put a CLOSED sign on the elevator and was about to head to the utility room to start the generator when he saw the light bobbing down the stairwell. "Who's there?" he called, expecting it would be a guest coming to find out what was wrong. *Earthquake, sir. We have them every night for your pleasure, and twice on Thursdays.*

"It's me, Holly." She shined the light under her chin.

"Hey, what are you doing here?"

"Frieda said you might like company."

"I'd especially like yours, Holly. Frieda's pretty smart." He knew what it meant though - the girl had gone to her grandmother's door and been turned away. Delilah Devine hated earthquakes almost as much as she hated being seen while frightened. "Bring your light. You can help me start the generator."

"Okay!"

Holly's smile delighted him and he led her to the copper-sheathed door across the lobby from the registration desk. "Here we go." He turned the key and shined his light on the half-dozen steps that led down into the utility room. "Don't trip."

"Wow! This is great!"

It was a big space and they walked to the far end of the room to a smaller room where the generator was kept. He opened the door, then opened the windows and vents within the room and got to work. Holly held the light just where he needed without even being asked. "We usually use the generator two or three times a year, but it's always been during storms - wind, snow, or thunder. This is the first time we've had to use it after a quake."

"Really? Brimstone sure seems to have a lot of quakes!"

He laughed. "Only since you arrived!"

The generator roared to life and lights bloomed, dim, but a lot better than nothing. Steve double-checked everything then shut the generator room door behind them.

As they began walking back, Holly paused in front of a padlocked wooden door that led to the old basement rooms. It was painted the same dirty-white as the walls and nearly blended with them.

"Where does that go?" she asked.

"A basement - but the door is kept locked. No one's allowed down there." He began walking.

"Why?" Holly caught up.

"Too dangerous."

"Why?"

Steve grinned. "You sure are full of questions. I don't know for sure, but it's in disrepair."

Holly nodded. "Maybe earthquake damage? I read that the natives believed the Brimstone Beast caused earthquakes."

"Indeed, they did." Steve stopped walking. "Some people still believe it. But there's a lot more to it than just the old tales. There are newer ones, too." He grinned. "Still old, but from the days when this building was a hospital."

"Really?"

"Yep." He immediately regretted speaking - Delilah would *not* approve - and he didn't need her to find out he'd been telling tales to her granddaughter. He needed a diversion. "Holly, follow me." He led her past the boiler room toward the elevator shaft.

"Meredith told me you're a ghost story fan."

"I am! I think Miss Annie Patches visited me last night!"

"Some of the maids and guests have reported seeing her," he said.

"I felt her walking on my bed - on me - and I heard her purr, I think. I hope I get to see her!"

"I hope so, too, Holly."

"Do you know any other ghost stories about this hotel?"

"I do."

They wound through a short walkway and arrived at the elevator shaft. Steve craned his neck, leaning into it, and pointed. "That's the bottom of the elevator. It's way up there, stopped on the fifth floor. See it?"

Holly stepped closer. "Yes."

Steve spoke softly. "The hospital had a caretaker, a nice old man named Jack Purdy. He started working at the hospital not long after it opened. In fact, your great-great-grandfather, Henry Hank Barrow, probably hired him himself," Steve added. "Jack did a fine job and stayed on. He maybe drank a little too much now and then, but he was a good guy. And he took really good care of the elevator - and everything else in this building that was mechanical. He loved machinery. In 1917, they replaced the original elevator with a brand new one - the one you've ridden in. It was state of the art - and Jack loved it and took very good care of it."

"What happened?"

"Well, Holly, Jack was murdered." Steve pointed at the floor where the elevator would land. "Right there."

"Under the elevator? He was squished?"

Steve nodded. "Just his head. Rumor is that he owed someone money and they knocked him out, put his head under there, and had someone ride down and crush his skull." He paused. "The elevator doesn't actually touch the floor, but his murderer - and the accomplice who almost assuredly worked here - put a wooden crate under it to hold his head up high enough to crush it." Steve decided not to tell Holly that it was likely that the murderer was Henry Hank Barrow himself. The old man was known to hate gambling and had a reputation for accusing his employees of theft.

Holly dragged her eyes from the murder spot. "Was it bloody?"

"I think it was probably pretty bad."

"Are there bloodstains?" She looked eager.

"Probably on the crate, but that's long gone." He grinned. "Disappointed?"

"Maybe a little." She studied the floor so intently that he knew she was hoping to spot a stain, no matter how tiny.

"They say Jack's still here."

"He is?"

"Well, he could be. Sometimes we hear the elevator going up and down all by itself. There's no one inside the car, so we just say it's Jack."

"Have you heard it?"

"I have, maybe half a dozen times since I've worked here. But there's no way to make that old Otis elevator run without both doors closed." He shook his head. "It's pretty mysterious."

"Did you ever see it move by itself?"

Steve grinned. "Just once. The other night when I heard it start up from the fourth floor. It came down to the lobby and the outer door opened, but I didn't hear anyone open the folding gate - so I walked over to see what was going on. I thought maybe kids were horsing around." He paused. "But the cage was secure across the doorway and the elevator was empty. It was kind of creepy."

"Wow!"

"And you know what?"

"What?"

"Before your grandmother came and renovated the building, the Clementine Hospital was closed for more than a quarter of a century. There wasn't any electricity - just like tonight - and it was locked up tight - and still, people heard the elevator - and some even said they saw lights flash as it passed by different floors."

"Oh, I want to see that so bad!"

Steve was amazed that Holly wasn't spooked by the story. He stepped closer and lowered his voice. "Once, I even heard the elevator when the place was boarded up, years before Miss Delilah came."

"Tell me!"

"Well, I was fourteen and a bunch of us guys decided to camp out up here by the empty building. We stole some beers from my dad and brought them up. I'd only had a sip when I heard the elevator. We all heard it. It was going up and down. I could hear that and the bells as it stopped at the different floors."

"Wow, that's so cool! What'd you do?"

Steve laughed. "We ran!"

Holly grinned. "That must've been pretty scary."

"It was."

"Have you ever seen Jack Purdy? Is he scary, like with a crushed head and stuff?"

Steve shook his head. "No one's ever seen him. Sometimes things move around in the lobby and we say Jack did it - but he probably doesn't even exist. It's probably just a story."

"Were his killers ever caught?" Holly asked as they took the stairs up to the copper door.

"No. His death remains a mystery." Steve held the door open for Holly then locked it behind them.

She stared at the silent elevator. It was coming down. "I guess the power's back on?"

Steve scratched his head. "The power isn't on yet - see how dim the lobby lights still are? - and the generator doesn't power the elevator."

"But it's coming . . ." Holly glanced at him, eyes wide.

The lobby light came on as the elevator touched down. Steve stepped forward and laid a hand on Holly's shoulder. Despite saying there was nothing to fear, Steve felt almost as shook up as he did that night when he'd camped out with the guys.

Holly stayed put, eyes glued to the elevator as the doors slid open to reveal nothing but darkness behind the firmly shut brass accordion gate.

Chill air and the faint odor of alcohol wafted from the compartment. It wasn't whisky, but a sharp, sterile tang. "Smell that?" Steve asked.

She nodded just as the accordion gate shivered, as if someone was waiting impatiently for it to open. "Rubbing alcohol."

"Yeah."

The gate shivered and rattled again, so softly it might have been a breeze.

Suddenly, Holly stiffened under his hand.

"What's wrong?"

"Don't you see her?"

"See *her*?"

"She's right there in the elevator. She's looking at us. I think she wants us to open the gate."

Her? Goosebumps prickling up, Steve stared into the darkness. "I don't see anyone, Holly."

"You don't?"

"No. Not a soul." The lobby seemed to be chilling, as if the elevator car were a refrigerator with an open door. "Maybe it's Jack Purdy." His words sounded lame.

"No! It's a woman. A nurse, I think. She's wearing an old-time black dress with a white apron and a little red cross." Holly crossed her arms, hugging herself as she glanced at Steve. "She looks kinda mean. I don't think we should open the gate."

"I don't either." He hesitated, peering into the chill darkness, seeing nothing. "Is she still there?"

"Yes."

"Holly," he said softly, "we're going to turn away and go sit behind the desk. She doesn't sound nice and I've read that paying attention to a ghost can feed it. I don't know if that's true, but we'd better ignore her." He pressed Holly's shoulder and she took the hint.

Hidden behind the tall lobby desk, they sat in two chairs by the elderly switchboard. No elevator lights blinked; it was completely dark except for the dim glow of the overhead lights. The lobby was cold but he could still smell the rubbing alcohol. A hospital scent, he realized. Holly shivered and stared up at the countertop, no doubt waiting for the phantom nurse to peer down at them. *Brave kid.* Steve kept his eyes lowered.

All at once, the elevator came to life. Gears engaged. Steve and Holly stood up, staring as the doors shut on darkness and the elevator began to rise. It ascended for a few seconds then the sounds faded and the elevator landing lights dimmed to nothing as if it had all been an illusion. Even the chill was gone.

"Steve? Can I ask you a weird question?"

"The weirder the better." He spoke lightly, not wanting Holly to know how unnerved he was.

"Okay, well ... Where do you think the elevator went?"

"That's a good question."

"I mean, the way it just sort of faded away, it seemed like a ghost elevator. You know, like a ghost train? But different."

"That's a good theory, Holly. And it makes sense since the elevator has no power right now. If it happens again, I'll see if I can touch it to see if it's really there." He grabbed a couple of root beers out of a cooler under the desk, uncapped them and handed one to her.

"Thanks. That lady," Holly said. "I wish you'd seen her, too."

"So do I." He rose. "Wait here for just one minute, Holly, will you?"

"Sure."

He raced back to the copper-clad door, entered the utility room and trotted to the elevator shaft. Peering up, he saw that the elevator remained moored on the penthouse level. Satisfied, he returned to Holly and told her she was right about it being a ghost elevator.

"I want to show you something." He pulled a large photo album from a shelf beneath the ancient switchboard and laid it on a low desktop between their chairs.

The switchboard rang. "Hang on." He turned to answer it, then stared. It was room 329.

"Aren't you going to answer it?"

"Come here." He crooked his finger then held up the headset between them. He hit the switch. "Lobby. May I help you?"

They heard nothing, not even static.

Holly looked at him as he broke the connection. "You waited too long. They hung up."

"There's no one in there."

Holly's eyes widened. "It's haunted?"

"I think so."

"Have you ever gone inside?"

He nodded. "There's never anything there, but it's always kind of chilly. Guests don't like it. They have nightmares, and a few have reported hearing voices."

"Can I answer if it rings again?"

Steve grinned. "Absolutely. Now, I want you to look at some photographs."

Holly scooted closer and watched as he carefully opened the old book.

"These are early shots of the hospital," he explained as he turned the first pages.

"I'd love to look at all the pictures."

"You can whenever you want, but right now, I want to show you some people." He turned pages until he came to faded photos and portraits from the days of the hospital. "Check these out, Holly. See if anyone looks familiar."

Holly turned a few pages, examining the photos, then looked up at him from beneath her brows. "Is my great-great-grandfather in here?"

"Yes."

"Which one is he?"

"Here." Steve turned a couple more pages and stopped. The glowering portrait of Henry Hank Barrow took up an entire page. The man was middle-aged in the portrait, his dark hair only salted at the temples. "That's him."

"He doesn't look very friendly."

"Back in those days, it was the fashion to glare at the camera. You had to sit for a long time without moving to have your portrait done. Maybe it put people in bad moods, though from what I understand Henry Hank Barrow always looked angry."

"I think he was mean for real." Holly spoke with certainty.

Steve shifted, uncomfortable; it wasn't his place to put down Henry Hank to his great-great-granddaughter. "Well, he was a hardcore businessman and they can be pretty mean." He turned the page.

"That's her!" Holly pointed at the woman standing beside a line of nurses like a drill sergeant. Her dark hair was parted in the middle and pulled severely back.

"That's Pearl Abbott, the head nurse in Henry Hank's day. They were ... friends." Goosebumps rose as Steve studied the photo. Everything about Pearl Abbott was so severe that even her hourglass figure and white pinafore apron couldn't soften her looks. "She does look kind of mean. It's said she ruled the nurses with an iron hand."

"She saw me," Holly whispered, still staring at the photo.

"I wouldn't worry about her - she's just a ghost." He paused. "And you're the first to ever see the elevator ghost - at least now we know who it is."

"I know." Holly turned more pages. "But she saw me, and that's kind of creepy."

"Why?"

"Because I've seen ghosts before and they never saw me. There was this little girl I used to see at the park sometimes, but she never saw me; it was like she looked right through me. She was there, but she was sort of like a movie or something, you know? That nurse *really* saw me."

"Well, Holly, maybe it just seemed like she did because her eyes were looking in your direction. Could that be it?"

"Maybe, but I don't think so."

They sat there, sipping their root beers and looking at photos until the electricity came back on. Steve tried to lose himself by telling Holly some of the history of the hospital, but he couldn't quite get past the fact that the girl had identified Pearl Abbott, R.N., Henry Hank Barrow's lover, and companion - a woman who understood poison and was likely behind many deaths, including Henry Hank's wife, and Delilah's mother.

22

THE DAY THEY DIED

Ben Gower, unable to sleep after the quake, sat in darkness at the writing desk in his apartment above the drugstore. From here, he had a perfect view of Main Street, but there was little to see. The power outage had gone on for some time now and the dim glow of candlelight and oil lamps flickered softly in a few of the homes and businesses. A generator noisily chugged over at the glassblower's where Sid was undoubtedly sweeping up broken trinkets. Otherwise Brimstone's main street remained utterly dark.

The drugstore hadn't suffered much in the quake - it was nothing he and Eddie couldn't straighten up in the morning, but the power had been off long enough now that Ben was worried about the ice cream; although tightly packed in the freezers, it would start melting before morning. If the power didn't come back on in the next few minutes, he'd go back downstairs and start his own generator. Ben raised his reluctant gaze to Hospital Hill where the Brimstone Grand, a crouching gargoyle, surveyed the town through a few dim eyes. Only the fifth floor, where Delilah lived, was well lit. She must have turned on every lamp she could. Ben hoped for her sake that her generator wouldn't run out of gas before dawn. He recalled that even as a little girl, Delilah wasn't fond of the dark. Carrie had told him. *Carrie. So long ago.*

Can't risk melting my inventory. But as Ben made to rise, streetlights jittered to life outside and the turquoise case glass desk lamp glowed. Relieved, he settled back down. Then his gaze returned to the former hospital high on the hill.

He shivered. The last time he'd visited the Clementine Hospital, he'd been ten years old, working as a delivery boy for his father and grandfather, owners of Gower's Pharmacy and the Brimstone Telegraph Company back at the turn of the century. He was a newly-minted, very proud delivery boy. He wore a uniform his mother had made him that was modeled on the Western Union uniforms that bicycle delivery boys wore back then, and rode a new bicycle his parents had given him in honor of his first job.

He was barely big enough to ride the tall bike and, back then, all the roads were dirt or gravel, but ride he did, delivering telegrams and drugs and other purchases to people all over Brimstone. Now, Ben closed his eyes, remembering the good times, how proud he was in his navy uniform, riding his bike - and rarely falling. Back then, Brimstone was yellow-skied and a little wild, at least on Saturday nights. He delivered to mining company executives, to churches, shops, and private homes. He delivered to the busy red light district, to ladies in fancy robes who smelled of powder and perfume. And he'd regularly delivered to the Clementine Hospital.

He'd liked cycling up to the building, even though it was so hot in the summer that he'd get off and push the bike up the steep dirt road. From the outside, the building looked much as it did now. Inside, it smelled clean like rubbing alcohol and the nurses wore starched pinafores over blue and white striped dresses with puffy mutton chop sleeves and high collars. Their white mob caps were charmingly ruffled. He remembered watching them in their long dresses, gliding through the halls with their trim hourglass figures accentuated by the way the big bows of the pinafores lay over their behinds. They always smiled at him and his first awareness of the gentler sex came courtesy of those nurses.

And then, one day, everything changed.

It was early on a March morning in 1900. He'd been tasked with hand-delivering a telegram to Henry Hank Barrow himself. The hospital's chief administrator inspired fear in all children and many adults, and Ben was nervous but doing his best to hide it. It didn't help that on his way up, a riderless horse came barreling down the road, barely missing him. And when he arrived, he noticed all the horses - saddled and those pulling carriages - were uneasy. They stood at hitching posts, ears swiveling, some pawing the ground, others snorting with heads held high, nostrils flared, eyes darting. Patting his pocket to make sure the telegram was safe, Ben swallowed and entered the hospital lobby.

It was as silent as a tomb; no one was in sight, not a doctor, nor a nurse, or even a patient. Curious, but not alarmed, Ben went to the nurse's station and dinged the service bell.

No one came.

"Hello?" he called. "Is anyone here?"

Silence. Silence so thick that goosebumps traveled up his neck and arms. Ben circled the nurses' station, going to the side gate, thinking he could leave the telegram on the desk inside.

That was when he saw the nurse. She was sprawled face down on the floor, her blue and white dress rucked up to her knees, her mob cap and a clipboard beside her. Ben stared. "Ma'am? Are- are you all right?"

She's on the floor. She's not all right! He opened the gate and went to her. He touched her hand; it was warm. "Ma'am?"

She didn't respond. Ben shot to his feet and ran out of the station, past the elevator and into the main corridor of the hospital yelling, "Help! I need help!"

The words died on his lips. He saw more nurses collapsed on the floor, and doctors, too. A patient in a maroon robe sat slumped in a wheelchair, his face hidden, a nurse sprawled behind him. She was on her back, eyes open, mouth slack, a thin drool of blood at one corner. A single drop suspended from her lips plopped to the floor as Ben stood frozen in shock.

He yelled - *no, I screamed!* - and as he ran for the doors he imagined he heard faint rumbling laughter coming from all around him. He'd raced out and, blinded by terror, made for his bicycle.

But a hand clamped onto his arm like an iron pressing into his flesh.

"What's the hurry, boy?" He looked up into the eyes of Henry Hank Barrow. His dark suit and arched black eyebrows accentuated the unreal blue of his eyes and the gold stain in the left one seemed to throb. Though Barrow's lips smiled, his eyes did not. Beside him was Pinching Pearl Abbott, the head nurse, in her black dress and white apron with the little red cross pinned above her bosom. She was the one holding his arm, her nails stabbing into it so hard now that it felt like knives. Her charcoal eyes glittered as she smiled down at him.

He'd never seen her smile before and he never wanted to again.

"T-Telegram, sir." He yanked the envelope from his pocket and thrust it into Barrow's hands, staring at the man's big gold ring. A smooth, round lapis, bluer than blue, was set into it and in that was embedded a strange copper symbol tipped with tiny brilliant rubies.

"Let the boy go, Pearl," he rumbled then before turning his awful gaze back on Ben. "Off with you, boy!"

He mounted the bike, wobbling, nearly falling as he began pedaling. Barrow's laugh - and Pinching Pearl's cackle - followed him.

When he arrived back at the pharmacy's telegraph office, his father smiled and rose from his desk. Then his smile faltered. "What's wrong, son? You look like you've seen a ghost."

Ben shook his head. "It was worse than that." He told his father what he'd seen, and then Dad called Grandfather in and had him tell the story again. After that, Dad went to fetch the sheriff and Doc Peyton.

When his father returned, hours later, he barely spoke, but he hugged Ben close. Later that night, he overheard him telling his mother what had happened. "They were dead, Maude, all of them, on every floor. Doctors, nurses, patients, everyone. And not a mark on them. Doc Peyton is baffled. He thinks maybe they all suffocated."

"John, that's horrible. Was it a gas leak?"

"Likely. He's not sure of anything except that there were no survivors. I think maybe Ben was real lucky he didn't get there any earlier than he did." His father's voice cracked. "Maude, even the babies in the nursery were dead. And their mothers."

Ben's mother gasped. A few moments later, she came into his room and he pretended to be asleep as she bent and kissed him, one hot tear splashing his cheek. At last, she wiped it away and left the room, closing the door softly behind her.

Everyone in town had been baffled. Everyone who'd been in the hospital, including the head surgeon, the chief of staff, and most of the hospital board died that day. But many lived - a good number of the staff had been off duty.

That incident, Ben reflected, like the other, smaller ones that happened over the next decade or two, was quickly forgotten. *Hushed and covered up is more like it.* Or maybe people just didn't want to think about such things. He never knew and rarely wondered, except after one of the damnable nightmares he'd suffered for evermore.

And in all the years that followed, Ben Gower never set foot inside Clementine Hospital again.

🜲 23 🜲

2 A.M

After helping Steve put out-of-order signs on the elevator landings, Holly had reluctantly returned to her room. There she picked up the cracked cobalt bowl and the red apples, and straightened the crooked paintings. It was after two a.m. when she finished. She'd rarely been up so late and she loved it.

Now, cozy in her new robe, she leaned against the balcony railing and stared down at the sleeping town. Beyond Brimstone, the lights of the Lewisdale Cement Plant glittered. It looked like a lit-up Tinker Toys tower.

The chill night wind kissed her face and blew strands of hair across her eyes as she thought about the ghostly nurse in the elevator. Holly *knew* the spirit was aware of her. When she'd locked eyes with her, it was everything Holly could do not to turn and run - but she hadn't because no way did she want Steve to think she was a coward. *No way! And I'm not! I'm not afraid of ghosts, or anything else!*

But Pearl Abbott had given her the creeps. Big time.

"You feel better, Missy Delilah?" Frieda Mendez adjusted

the shawl over her employer's shoulders. "More chamomile tea?" She'd found Delilah clinging to the balcony in abject terror after the quake and coaxed her in, then made her rest in her rocking chair, knowing the movement would soothe her. The power had been out and even though Frieda opened the drapes to let in the moonlight, it had been too dark and her mistress hadn't been able to stop trembling until Frieda lit every oil lamp and candle in the penthouse. Even then, Miss Delilah hadn't spoken until the generator started. Now the power was back on, but Delilah still wasn't herself. "Missy Delilah?"

"I'm fine, thank you, Frieda. No more tea, but perhaps a dollop of sherry will help me sleep."

Frieda fetched the sherry and a glass.

Delilah sipped. "That's better. Have you heard anything about the earthquake? Is everyone here all right?"

"As far as I know. Steve said there was no damage. And Miss Holly came to ask after you shortly after it happened."

Delilah looked up. "Was she frightened?"

"I don't think so. You know how kids are."

"They all think they're immortal." Delilah held out her glass. "Just a tot more. Holly seems especially fearless, don't you think?"

Frieda poured. "She does."

"She reminds me so much of my sister, Carrie. She was fearless, too. Carrie was my hero." Delilah pulled the shawl closer around her.

As soon as the lights came back up, Arthur Meeks left his room to prowl the fourth floor. There were only a handful of guests tonight in the entire hotel and the lights were off in almost all their rooms, but he paused at several, giving the door knobs a quick turn - guests would think it was the ghost rattling their doors. It amused him.

Not like that goddamned ghost cat. That didn't amuse him at all; it terrified him. *Little Miss Fancy Pants probably made that up.* Arthur shivered. He hated all cats, including made-up ones. His mother's voice razored through his memory. *"The lion will come and eat you if you don't be quiet and go to sleep, Arthur!"* In the dark, her black cat sounded as big as a lion as it stalked up and down the hall outside his bedroom. *You ugly old bitch and your ugly old cat!*

He shook off the memory as he saw the light glowing beneath the little girl's door. Her mama's room was dark, but that was just dandy; the daughter interested him more. He let himself into the room adjacent to 429 and examined the new peephole he'd drilled, but Little Miss Fancypants had shoved something inside it; he couldn't see a damned thing. Anger blossomed; his eye still hurt. *Little slut.* He didn't dare try to unblock it now; the girl might hear him and he sure as hell didn't need her tattling to the Queen Douchebag.

Annoyed, Arthur Meeks turned to leave the room and saw a piece of paper on the floor. *She'd* left it for him; it was a threat to tell on him. He sniffed the paper, folded and pocketed it, and smiled as he let himself out of the room. *You'll get yours, little miss, oh yes, you will.* Without a glance back he took the stairs down to the second floor where a young couple slept. He had a peephole into their room, too, and if they were still up, he might see something good. The woman was a real looker.

24

THE DRAGON

When sleep finally took Holly it was fitful at best. She dreamed of the old hospital again and this time it was shaking loose from its foundation and rising higher and higher into the night sky, pushed by some gigantic angry thing beneath it.

Then suddenly she's in her room, standing on the balcony's threshold, watching thin clouds skitter across the moon as if they're being chased. She stares down at the lights of Brimstone, far, far below - so far, it's almost like seeing the town from an airplane. She is terrified.

Then a whoosh! Something flies past her, something huge. Wind whips as the creature turns and comes around again. It's a dragon, its body blotting out the stars behind it. Black scales rimmed in cobalt fire gleam in the moonlight as it spits coppery red fire into the sky.

With a roar, it flies at her. She stands paralyzed as it halts at the balcony railing and turns its head to study her. Its great black-blue wings are alive with tiny licks of red flame. Holly stares into one great eye - copper edged with sapphire, with a pupil sparking crimson from a fire deep within. She feels an itch in her brain.

"Holly. Come ride the Beast."

The voice echoes through her mind, deep, rumbling. Friendly.

Charming.

Slowly, the dragon's huge eye blinks.

Holly steps across the threshold onto the balcony.

"That's right. Come closer. We'll fly."

The voice vibrates through her body, scratching at her mind. Apprehensive, curious, intrigued, she takes another step.

"Come, child. We'll fly. We'll fly forever on the wings of the Beast, you and I."

A thousand thoughts collide in her head. The voice seems friendly and the dragon, nice, and for a moment she wants to climb on its back and soar through the sky. But it reminds her of something. Something fearful. What, she can't recall, but it prickles in the back of her mind and won't go away.

"Come, girl. It's time to fly."

Suddenly, she hears the robot's voice from Lost in Space, *loud and clear:* "Danger, Will Robinson!"

Holly takes a step back.

And runs into an icy wall. Freezing hands clamp onto her shoulders. Holly twists, sees the ghost from the elevator, Pearl Abbott, sees the grim face, the chill hate in those charcoal eyes. The nurse pushes her toward the rail easily despite Holly's resistance. One, step.

Two.

Three.

"Hurry, girl. Onto the Beast." *The male voice rumbles through her body, tingling in her brain, electrifying every nerve ending.*

Pearl Abbott pushes.

Holly trips, falls to her knees. "NO!" *She rolls away from Pearl Abbott and scrambles to her feet, trying to dodge her, but the woman's claw-like hands dig into her shoulders and yank her off the ground, Holly twists and kicks and flails but the ghost pushes her toward the dragon.*

Yellow smoke that smells of matches puffs from its nostrils. A long forked tongue slithers across reptilian lips.

"NO!" *Holly kicks and thrashes, but Pearl Abbott's icy fingers only dig more deeply into her arms. They feel like knives.*

"Time to ride the Beast." *The rumbling voice sounds angry now and the dragon's copper eye pulses and the veins of blue throb.* "Get on!"

Pearl Abbott lifts Holly as if she were a feather and holds her out over the balcony railing, pressing her to the dragon's shining black scales.

"NO!"

But the nurse pays no heed; Holly fights, clinging to the railing, to Pearl Abbott herself. "NO!"

Holly sees her own tears run over the dragon's scales as the voice comes again, tearing into her brain. "Holly, we will ride the Beast together, you and I."

"NO! NO! NO!"

Suddenly something thumped her chest, hard, and she came awake in darkness. The thing on her chest came closer, purring, and a rough tongue licked the tip of her nose. Trembling, she opened her eyes and just made out pale green ones staring back at her. Another lick. A purr.

And then the cat was gone. Vanished.

Sitting up, Holly turned on the lamp. "Annie Patches?"

A distant, faint, *meow.*

"Thank you, Annie! Thank you!"

Rising, Holly closed and locked the windows then stared out the glass door. The black railing was there, the twinkling stars, too. But no dragon, no voice, no Pearl Abbott - yet the room was icy cold, too cold for a summer night. And she could still smell matches.

After checking all the locks, Holly made sure the painting was still blocking the peephole, then made herself a cup of tea with milk and sugar. She took it to the little round table and warmed her hands on the mug as she sipped. She didn't know if she could sleep any more tonight. The dream had been too real.

So real that her arms hurt where Pearl Abbott had grabbed her. She reached up and touched her bicep, surprised at the increased pain since it had only been a dream. Her skin felt icy cold. *That's weird.* She stood up and went into the bathroom, unbuttoned her pajama top and slipped it off.

Holly gasped. Both upper arms were marked with fresh bruises - deep red fingerprints already purpling, and there were tiny crescent-shaped scratches, spotted with blood, where the phantom fingernails had dug into her arms.

"It wasn't a dream," she told her reflection. "It wasn't a dream."

And she knew the shape of the Brimstone Beast now; it was a dragon.

Trembling, she left the bathroom and dressed in jeans, a tank top, and a long-sleeved cotton shirt over it to hide the bruises.

Holly had had nightmares before, plenty of them, and she was usually pretty good at realizing she was having a bad dream and making herself wake up. It was a trick she'd taught herself. But it hadn't worked tonight; she hadn't even realized she was in a dream. *Only it wasn't a dream.*

Dreams didn't leave bruises.

Sitting at the dinette table, she sipped her tea and thought about going back downstairs to talk to Steve, but knew even he wouldn't understand that she'd had more than a nightmare. Sighing, she looked at the books scattered on the table. The ones Adeline had given her about the town and the Brimstone Beast were the ones that she knew she should read, but she couldn't, not now. Too much had happened; she'd seen Pearl Abbott's ghost in the elevator - and it had seen her. And then the dream that wasn't a dream, the dream that left bruises and bored into her brain. She couldn't concentrate. Crossing to the bureau where the TV rested, she opened the top drawer and pulled out a spiral bound notepad and a pencil. Back at the table, she began to write down everything that had happened. Writing always made her feel better.

STEVE CROSS SPENT THE LAST HOURS BEFORE DAWN POURING through the old scrapbooks and photo albums stored behind the registration desk. He was trying to find out more about the ghost Holly had seen in the elevator, but he found nothing new about Pearl Abbott. He wasn't surprised; he'd poured over these albums many times before.

He thought about going down into the basement; he'd actually been down there twice on nights when boredom and solitude had overwhelmed him. He hadn't lied to Holly about the dangers. There were no lights, just cobwebs, broken stair railings, and a cold that seemed preternatural. He'd only remained there long enough to see tables and shelves lining one wall - there were books, stacks of them, murky bottles and jars, antique medical equipment - he'd recognized a microscope and a Bunsen burner. Those things were all against the wall about twenty feet from the staircase. He'd seen a desk and chairs, and a lectern, all draped in dust and cobwebs. Left of the stairs, his flashlight barely picked up shadowed crates and sheeted furniture. The darkness was all but impenetrable. *Preternatural.*

He knew from studying blueprints that the basement extended a long way into the darkness, perhaps forty feet, but he had never explored further. For one thing, it was forbidden to go down there and he didn't want to lose his job. For another, it had bad vibes. Very bad.

But right now, he was tempted to return just long enough to haul up a box of books and papers in the hopes of finding more information about Pearl Abbott and Henry Hank, and his cult, *Infurnam Aeris.*

It has to have something to do with the Brimstone Beast. Barrow, although an administrator, not a medical man, had been something of a mad scientist by all accounts, and was rumored to have kept a lab in the basement. He was involved in the occult arts and considered himself a magician or sorcerer of some stripe; he admitted to being the high priest of *Infurnam Aeris.* Pearl was his priestess. Accounts varied, but it all came down to a couple of basic facts: H. H. Barrow was a control freak, a freak-freak, and almost assuredly a little bit mad. *Or a lot.* It all depended on which stories you believed.

Dawn wasn't far off as Steve studied the copper-clad door. The most intriguing story about Henry Hank concerned the Beast. By all accounts, Barrow had been known as the Brimstone Beast, a name he chose for himself and encouraged. Steve had found a passage in an old book that said Barrow actually tried to bring the creature of folklore to life to do his bidding. And that made perfect sense since Barrow was into sorcery.

Steve stretched and yawned. Holly's interest in Brimstone history had piqued his own. His gaze returned to the copper door; he would not visit the basement tonight. But soon, he promised himself. Very soon.

ADELINE CHANCE STOOD ON HER FRONT PORCH WATCHING THE

first rays of sun breach the red rock mountains to the northeast. The sky had lightened, but the stars were still out. Everything looked the same as it had the day, the week, the month, even the year before.

But something was different.

It wasn't a sight or a sound. It was a feeling, a sensation that set her teeth on edge and made her skin prickle. Her nose wrinkled at the faint odor of sulfur, there and gone in a fraction of a second.

But she knew it wasn't her imagination. "Lord, but I wish it was," she told the salmon sky.

Turning her gaze up to Brimstone Peak, she could just see the bulk of the hotel jutting from the mountainside. Lights burned on the top floor, and she thought of Delilah hiding from the darkness, and of Carrie, her cousin and best friend, dead these many years.

But most of all, she thought of Delilah's little granddaughter, Holly, up there in that building full of terrible secrets. *Stay safe, Holly. Stay safe.*

The screen door squeaked; Ike came out and handed her a cup of steaming, fragrant coffee. She took it gratefully, let it warm her hands. "Thank you, dear."

"Mighty fine sunrise."

"Mm-hmm." She couldn't get her mind off Holly.

"What's the matter, Addie? Those quakes got you all riled up?"

"No. That little girl has the *Beast* riled up." She looked into Ike's dear, seamed face. "Holly needs to leave before things get worse."

"Honey, all that happened so long ago. Don't you think it's possible we're just having a few quakes? That it's coincidence? After all, we're overdue."

She took his hand and squeezed it. "You know better, Ike. There are no coincidences."

He squeezed back. "Well, hardly any. I guess I just don't want to believe that it's waking up. We're too old for this."

"We are."

25

MORNING MATTERS

There had been no more shaking, not so much as a tiny aftershock, and Holly had stayed at the table, writing about the elevator ghost, the dragon dream, and meeting her grandmother, when she'd finally gotten sleepy. At ten a.m., she awoke with a start and lifted her head from the table. She put the notebook in the bureau drawer, hiding it under a crossword puzzle magazine and a treasured copy of National Geographic that contained photos that her father had taken in Iceland.

She brushed her teeth and combed her hair into a ponytail, happy she'd suffered no more dreams. Everything seemed better by light of day, at least until she slid off her long-sleeved shirt to check the bruises on her arms; they were deep purple-red and tender, a grim reminder that some dreams were more real than others.

Holly put the shirt back on, resolving not to think about it. She turned her mind to safe things like watering the plants and the merits of hanging out with Becky versus going down to see Adeline by herself.

Ready for the day, she stepped into the empty hallway and knocked on Cherry's door. There was no reply; if her mother had returned, she was still asleep.

Holly started toward the elevator then remembered Pearl Abbott, and turned back and took the stairs. In the lobby, Meredith was dealing with a guest, so she slipped by and stepped out into the hot sun, shading her eyes as she checked the parking lot for the red Falcon - it wasn't there.

Neither relieved nor disappointed, Holly walked to the edge of the mostly-empty lot and peered out over the Brimstone Valley. Everything looked so bright and fresh and clear; she had never imagined air could smell so good; at home, you couldn't even see the skyscrapers in downtown L.A. half the time because of the smog.

I never want to go back. She glanced at the hotel, and remembered last night. *Or do I?*

"Holly!" Becky Granger's voice carried on the warm breeze as the girl waved and trotted to join her. "Did you feel the earthquake last night? Some of my horses fell down! What happened in your room?"

"Not much."

"Want to go to the park?" She hooked a thumb toward the playground down the street.

"Sure."

"Miss Delilah, there's a call for you."

Delilah glanced at the phone on the writing desk. "Who is it?"

"Miss Meredith said it's your daughter."

"Oh? Very well, thank you, Frieda. Would you fetch me a cup of tea? Darjeeling?"

"Of course."

Delilah watched Frieda disappear toward the kitchen then stared at the phone, loathe to take the call; when Charlotte phoned, it was always because she wanted something. With a sigh, she lifted the receiver and heard Frieda hang up instantly. "Yes, Charlotte?"

"I got a job in Sedona! Modeling."

"That was yesterday, Charlotte. Did it require you to spend the night?" Her voice was calm and even, but inside, Delilah seethed. Her daughter had defied her and wouldn't even acknowledge it.

"Yes, I had to spend the night. I have work for a whole week here. Isn't that exciting? I'll be able to pay you rent. If you want me to."

"Are you telling me you're staying in Sedona this week?"

"Yeah, that's why I'm calling."

"What else do you want, Charlotte?"

"Could you tell Holly I'll be gone a few days?"

"Why can't you tell her yourself?"

"I was going to, but that Meredith person said she isn't there. Could you tell her for me?"

Delilah paused, but Charlotte said nothing else. "Don't you want to know where your child is?"

"Sure. Is she having fun?"

"She's gone on a rock-climbing campout with the Boy Scouts. They're going to catch and kill rattlesnakes for dinner."

"Holly sure is good at making friends, isn't she?"

"Did you hear what I said?"

"Sure, she's on a camp-out."

Delilah stood, biting back rage. "You think of no one but yourself, Charlotte, not even your own child! You brought her here without any clothing that fits, dumped her, and then took off to go on a shopping spree for *yourself* with some disease-ridden actor. And you think it's just fine for her to camp with Boy Scouts. I don't understand you, Charlotte. Sometimes I think you were born without a soul."

"Look, will you just tell her? 'Cause I can ask that Meredith person to tell her if you won't." Charlotte paused, screwing her voice into the old whiny tone that made Delilah cringe. "I thought you'd be happy I got a real job so I can pay you your stupid rent without having to scrub a damned toilet!"

"You are incapable of taking responsibility. You are incapable of love, even for your own daughter."

"Like *you* love me! Like you ever loved me!" Charlotte pitched her voice up to tantrum tones. "You never loved me! Never!"

"I will see to Holly until you return, Charlotte." Delilah spoke calmly, refusing to indulge in the fury she felt; it would do no good.

"You always hated me! How dare you say I'm a bad mother!"

"I didn't say that, Charlotte. You did. Good bye." And she hung up, without even slamming down the phone.

"Missy Delilah?" Frieda hovered in the archway holding a silver tray. "Your tea?"

"Yes, thank you, Frieda. Just leave it here."

Frieda set the tray on the desk and nodded at a second tea cup. "Miss Vera has arrived."

"Send her in, please."

Vera Kotzwinkle appeared momentarily and came to sit beside Delilah at the desk.

"Tea?" Delilah nodded at the steaming cup.

"Don't mind if I do. What are we doing today?" Vera paused, tilting her head. Her auburn hair rode her shoulders in a *That Girl* flip. "What's wrong?"

"Charlotte."

"What now?" Vera had been with Delilah long enough to have witnessed plenty of Charlotte's antics.

Delilah told her. In detail.

"There's something wrong with Charlotte, if you don't mind my saying."

"You know I don't mind."

"I don't think she'd recognize love if it bit her on the butt. In fact, I don't think she's capable of it."

"I've wondered about that myself." Delilah rubbed a knot in her neck. "I don't know how I went so wrong."

Vera shook her head. "Don't even think that. You were a great mother."

"I was always working."

"Sure, you worked a lot, but you always made time for Charlotte. Always." Vera laid her hand over Delilah's. "I saw how hard you tried, but Charlotte was ... difficult."

Delilah nodded. "She was a chip off her father."

"I'm glad he was out of the picture before we met."

"So am I, dear. So am I. Clifton was a real piece of work. Just like Charlotte." She shook her head. "The man left me for a starlet who was little more than a child. Now I'm afraid Charlotte has left me *with* her child. Vera, I don't want her child."

"She's your granddaughter."

"That may be, but I can't keep her."

"First of all," Vera said in her all-business voice, "Charlotte said she'd be back in a few days. That doesn't sound like she's dumping the girl on your doorstep to me. She's got a job, she'll be back for her daughter."

Delilah couldn't think of a thing to say; the image of Aunt Beatrice loomed large in her mind.

"Second of all," Vera continued, "to quote the bard, 'Methinks you doth protest too much.'"

"I don't know what you mean."

"Yes, you do."

Delilah sighed impatiently. "Enough of this nonsense. Let's get to work. They've invited me to some sort of awards ceremony celebrating fifty years of Universal monsters. I'd like you to decline for me with as much grace as possible."

"I think you should go."

"Nonsense. The last thing I want to be remembered for are those horror films."

"But they've brought you so many fans." Vera smiled. "You're a scream queen whether you like it or not. And we met at Universal."

"You're the only thing I want to keep from that time, my dear. I prefer to remember the career I had before I passed the age of thirty-five. *Violet Morne, Crandall Street, Fording Fenway, Murder Confidential* - those were films I took pride in. The Universal movies were all I could get once the dew was off the lily. They only paid the bills and I do *not* want to be celebrated for them."

"Okay, but I still think you should be proud of them. Delilah, do you even look at all the mail you get from the Universal fans?"

"No, I don't. That's what I pay you to do."

"Yes, boss lady."

THE PLAYGROUND WAS ALL THAT REMAINED OF AN ELEMENTARY school that had been rebuilt down the hill many years ago and Holly liked it despite the heat and the lack of trees and grass. There weren't any other kids there, but there were two jungle gyms, both impressively big and tall, a lot of monkey bars - her favorite thing - and a couple of old metal merry-go-rounds that despite being creaky, traveled at breakneck speed when you got them going. There were two towering metal slides that were too hot to ride in the midday sun unless you wore long pants, several teeter-totters that would crack you in the crotch if your partner got off too fast, horizontal bars, hanging rings, and a couple of sun-bleached and cracking horses on springs.

Holly had tried out everything but the butt-burning slide and was now on a swing,

Becky sat on the one beside her, as talkative as ever. "So, my mom is going to ask Miss Delilah if you can spend the night tomorrow and then go camping with us for the weekend."

"Huh." Holly pumped her legs, swinging higher. She wished Meredith and Becky had invited her before seeking permission from her grandmother. It wasn't that she didn't want to go - camping sounded like fun - but she liked to make up her own mind about things. If Miss Delilah said yes, she pretty much had to go. She swung higher, dreading a night in Becky's room with all those horses and Barbie dolls. *But camping will make it worth it, right?*

"You're going to go too high and fly over the top!" Becky cried as Holly pumped her legs and positioned her body to attain the most lift.

"I want to!"

"You want to? My Aunt Pam did that once and broke her arm. And Mom says she got a concussion and was never right in the head after that." Becky giggled. "She wouldn't wear underwear anymore!"

"Really?"

"That's what my mom said."

"I promise I won't stop wearing underwear if I swing over the top."

"I can't watch." Becky stopped her swing and trotted over to a bleached-out spring-horse and climbed on, rocking hard and calling the horse "Snowflake."

Holly kept swinging. Each time she reached the top she saw more of the old cross in the cemetery at the far end of the road. She'd forgotten all about it until she spotted it, but now, she wanted to go check it out.

The sun burned in the sky, started hurting her eyes and she realized it probably was well after noon by now. She squinted, watching a couple of boys lean against a jungle gym and peer out over the valley. Wondering who they were, Holly let the swing gradually glide to a stop before jumping off.

It was really hot, so she pulled off her long-sleeved shirt, wiped sweat from her forehead with it, then tied it around her waist before walking over to Becky, who was still riding the pale horse.

"Hey."

Becky stopped rocking. "What?"

"Who are those guys on the monkey bars?"

Becky shadowed her eyes with her hand. "Um, Keith and Tommy. They're in my class." She grinned. "So they'll be in yours, too, if you stay. They're okay for boys."

"Cool. Think they'd want to go check out that old cemetery?"

Becky frowned. "I don't want to go there."

"Why?"

"It's a *cemetery*. Who wants to hang out in a cemetery?"

"I do." Holly grinned. "They're very historical and I love history. I want to see it, don't you?"

"No. But I'll introduce you and you can ask them. But it would be way more fun to go back to my house and play horses and Barbie. Want to? We have air conditioning and-" Becky stared at Holly. "What happened?"

"Huh?"

"Your arm." She dismounted the spring-horse and took Holly's arm, turning it. "How did you get those bruises?"

Crap. Holly had forgotten them. "No big deal."

"And they're on both arms!" Becky's eyes widened. "They're finger-prints! Who grabbed you? Your mom?"

"Of course not."

"Well somebody did!"

Holly couldn't think of anything to say except the truth. "A ghost."

"That's not funny!"

Holly smiled just a little. "Sorry. I don't know how I got them. I guess in the earthquake."

"Do they hurt?" Becky poked one.

"No," Holly lied as she rubbed her arm. "It's just dirt. I think it's coming off."

Becky looked skeptical but stopped staring. "So, do you have a Barbie?"

"No."

"Your mom never got you a Barbie?" Becky looked aghast.

"Oh, she did. A couple of them. I gave them to a friend last year."

"Why? Why would you do that?"

"I just wasn't into Barbies and my friend liked them." In truth she'd only given one to Debby. The other one was sacrificed after Holly read about the French Revolution and how they'd beheaded Marie Antoinette. She'd built her own guillotine, dressed the blond pony-tailed Barbie in her fancy black evening gown and poured red paint on her neck and dress and held an execution. The guillotine hadn't actually worked, but bloody Barbie/Marie on a balsa wood guillotine had looked great on her bookcase until Cherry made her throw it out. She'd also told her not to tell anyone what she'd done, and Holly figured that was good advice, especially when it came to Becky.

"How can you not like Barbies?"

"They're okay, but they're all about clothes and dating. I like other stuff. Outdoor stuff and reading and exploring."

"Horses, right?"

"Sure. And monkey bars and hiking."

"Well, we could go play with my horses. Or we could do each other's hair. I want to go in. It's too hot today. So, do you want to?"

"Maybe tomorrow, okay?" Holly smiled. "Could you introduce me to those guys?"

"Sure."

MEREDITH LOOKED UP WHEN BECKY CAME RUSHING INTO THE LOBBY of the Grand. "Hi honey, where's Holly?"

"I think she and Keith Hala were going to the cemetery to look around."

"Keith's a nice boy. I'm glad she didn't go alone."

"There's something wrong with Holly, Mom."

Meredith saw real concern on her daughter's face. "Come behind the desk and sit with me a minute."

The girl sat, looking like she was about to burst. Meredith smiled to herself - Becky often looked that way.

"Now, tell me what's wrong with Holly." She pushed pale hair from her daughter's face.

"She doesn't like Barbies! She gave hers away!"

"That doesn't mean there's anything wrong with her, Becky. Not all girls like dolls as much as you do."

"But - Barbies!"

"Holly is a little old for her age."

"What do you mean?"

"Sweetheart, I think Holly has had to act grown up for a long time."

"Why?"

Because she has a lousy mother. "Well, her mother has to work to support them, so Holly hasn't had a lot of time to play because she had to cook and keep their apartment clean."

Becky nodded. "But her mom got her Barbies. She said. Why wouldn't she like them?"

"Different people like different things. I think Holly really likes books, for instance."

"And ghosts! I bet that's why she wanted to go to the stupid cemetery. To see ghosts."

"Maybe. She does like ghost stories. And history, too. There's plenty of history in cemeteries."

Becky nodded. "She said that, too. But mostly, she likes ghosts. She even said all those bruises on her arms were from ghosts."

"What bruises?"

"She had big purple fingerprints on her arms. She said a ghost did it."

"I'm sure she was just joking. Honey, what did the bruises look like?"

"Fingerprints. Just like fingerprints. Like somebody had yanked her arms. And I told her that and then she said she didn't know how they got there and maybe they were dirt and would wash off."

What's going on here? Meredith felt real concern now.

"Mom? Can I have Fruit Loops for lunch?"

"No, you may not. There's a chicken sandwich for you in the refrigerator."

26

KEITH HALA

I t took almost fifteen minutes for Holly and Keith Hala, a slender nimble boy only an inch taller than Holly, to hike to the cemetery and check out the tall wooden cross. After that, they'd wandered among graves marked by mounds of rocks or rusted iron crosses and stones so weathered that they couldn't read the names. There was a small mausoleum in the distance and they were going to explore that after they cooled off a little.

Now, sitting in the scant shade cast by a parched old cottonwood twenty feet from the wooden cross, they sucked on strips of prickly pear cactus Keith had cut for them. "Next time," he said, "let's bring water."

"For sure. But this is good. How'd you know to do this?"

"Grandpa taught me." Keith's brown eyes sparkled. "He says the tribe we come from has always eaten it and know how to make it taste really good. Sometimes my mom cooks the fruit. It's pretty tasty."

"You're a real Indian? That's so exciting!" Holly was bursting with questions.

Keith grinned again.

"Do you live on a reservation?"

"No. My great-grandfather did when he was a kid, but he moved to

Brimstone and opened an ironworks shop. It's called Hala Metalworks and my grandfather runs it now."

"What does he make? Like horseshoes?"

"Sometimes. He makes all sorts of stuff, and fancy fences and things. My dad worked for him until he died."

"I'm sorry. My dad died, too."

"Mine died in a car accident," Keith told her. "How did yours die?"

"He was a photographer and was shooting pictures on Mt. Everest. He fell." She paused. "If you die on Everest, you never come home, my mom said. You stay there."

Keith nodded somberly. "I live with my mom and my grandfather down there." He pointed toward town. "Where do you live?"

"The Brimstone Grand." She pointed at the structure, barely visible at the other end of the road.

"Are you just visiting?"

"No, I mean I hope not. My grandmother lives there and my mom says we're just staying with her until she gets a new job in California." Holly leaned forward. "I hope she doesn't get one. I want to stay here."

Keith's eyes widened. "Why would you want to stay here?"

Holly shrugged. "It smells good. I like it - there's no smog - not like in Van Nuys. I have my own room and my own refrigerator and Miss Delilah is going to give me piano lessons."

"Miss Delilah." Keith's eyes widened. "Is Delilah Devine your grandmother?"

Holly nodded. "She was a movie star."

"I know, but if Miss Delilah is your grandmother, your ancestor is H.H. Barrow. My grandfather says he tried to bring the Brimstone Beast to life a long time ago!"

"What?" Holly's belly filled with ice as the nightmare crashed back into her mind.

"The miners called it the Brimstone Beast, but it's way older. Like really, really old and sleeps inside the earth. Your ancestor woke it up once. Grandpa was talking about it last night. He says it's awake again."

"What? Why does he think it's awake?" Holly felt excited and a little worried.

"The earthquakes. He says the Brimstone Beast makes the earth shake when it wakes up or turns over in its sleep."

Holly tried to sound casual. "Does your grandfather believe it?"

"I don't think so. He just likes storie- Hey!" He grabbed his arm.

The rock that hit Keith tumbled toward Holly. It was ragged and sharp, the size of a lemon. She looked up. Two older kids were approaching, one tall and lanky with carrot-colored hair and an ugly little nose. The short one had dark hair and weasel-eyes.

"Crap," Keith muttered. "That's Shawn and Tony."

"Who are they?"

"Eighth graders. Bullies."

Tony lobbed another rock, just missing Keith.

"Hey, knock it off!" Holly cried as she and Keith scrambled to their feet.

"Dirty Injun!" yelled Shawn. "Why don't you go back to India where you belong!"

Holly stared in disbelief as the pair of bullies approached. Shawn had weird little scrunchy blue eyes and his toady kept glancing at him for direction. He wasn't getting much.

"Your daddy died 'cuz he was a drunk!" the tall one taunted. "A drunk Injun!"

"Yeah," yelled the minion. "Your daddy's a drunk! Why don't you go back where you belong?"

Tony threw another rock, smaller, and this one hit Holly on the knee. It hurt. "Ow! Cut it out you stupid bullies!"

"You can't pick on her!" Keith ran at them, plowing straight into the red-haired one, knocked him over, and tried to pummel him.

The dark-haired minion stared at Holly. "Slut girl wants to make out with the Indian." He made a kissing noise. "Why don't you make out with me, instead?"

Holly stared. She'd never, not once, been in a fight. She'd come close once or twice but always - *always* - stopped fights with words, not actions. Right now, she had no words. She just wanted to beat the snot out of the kid.

Keith yelped as Shawn rolled him over, sat on his chest, and began punching him.

"Slut girl!" The short one stepped closer, leering like an idiot.

Fury spilled into Holly's blood. Her body stiffened and her vision, always clear, became even clearer, more intense, almost magnified. She stared past Tony even as he stepped in front of her to block her way.

He grabbed her arm. "Slut girl, gimme a kiss."

"Get out of here." The words came out low and hard, full of disinterest. She barely registered the boy's open-mouthed stare before he turned and ran.

She stalked up behind Shawn and grabbed a handful of his orange clown hair, then yanked his head backward. His arm, poised for a blow, fell as he stared at her.

She glared at his ugly frightened bully face. "You leave us alone!"

Holly had always been able to sway people. Even if Cherry hadn't pointed it out a million times, she knew it. But this was different - she could see he was afraid of her. She let go of the ginger hair. "Get up."

Without a word, the bully rose, but wouldn't meet her eyes.

"Apologize to Keith."

"I'm sorry," he mumbled.

Keith, rubbing his jaw, scrambled to his feet, his eyes on Holly, staring. But all her attention remained on the rusty-headed bully with the squinty eyes and squished nose. She could see every speck of dirt on his shirt and in his hair. Every speck, and she'd never felt so angry in her life. "Look at me."

Slowly, the terrified eyes met hers. He was trembling.

"Don't you *ever* bother us again."

The boy nodded as a wet stain spread on the front of his pants.

"Get out of here," she ordered. "Never come back."

Shawn took off like a shot.

Suddenly, Holly felt like jelly. She wobbled, dizzy, then Keith's arm was around her. "Are you okay?"

"I don't know."

He helped her back to the shady spot and they sat down. Her legs went from trembly to weighing tons. "I don't know what happened. I was just so mad!"

Keith handed her a fresh piece of prickly pear. "Have some."

"They were afraid of me. I don't know why."

"You don't know? You really don't?"

She shook her head.

"What do you know?"

"I got really, really mad when that Shawn guy started whaling on you. He's older and a foot taller than you. I was thinking what a little coward he was and I was so mad that it was like everything changed. It was like I was looking at him under a microscope or something."

"Did you do that to Tony, too?"

"I barely noticed him. He took off running when I got mad at Shawn."

"So, have you ever been mad like that, before?"

"Never. Never ever. I don't know what came over me." She stared into Keith's eyes. "I really don't."

"Holly?"

"Yeah?"

"When you were mad, your eyes turned gold. I saw them change. They turned from blue to gold."

"Really?" Holly had a hard time believing it. "I know I have little gold flecks in my eyes, but my eyes are blue."

"Yeah, well, they changed. They got really bright and well, the gold throbbed or something."

Holly nodded. "Okay, so all I know is that I can see 20/20, but I saw even better when I got mad."

"You said like a microscope?"

"Yeah. Kinda like that." She hesitated. "Keith, did you feel afraid of me at all?"

"No, but I knew you weren't mad at me." He chuckled. "You made Shawn wet his pants!"

She smiled, feeling better. "I guess I did. Isn't that crazy, though?"

"You have a super power, like Superman or something." He grinned. "Wonder Woman."

"It was a little scary. What if it happens again?"

"I think you need to meet my grandfather."

27

NEWS OF THE DAY

Ben Gower handed Brunhilde Stuffenphepper a white pharmacy bag. "Do you have any questions, Mrs. S?"

"Of course not, Mr. Gower! You've filled this prescription a hundred times." Brunhilde huffed like a bum with a can of gasoline. "What do you take me for, a fool?"

"I have to ask. It's my job, you know."

The mayor's wife huffed again and marched her tightly girdled bulk toward the drugstore's exit.

That woman's not happy unless she's complaining. Ben remembered when she was a little girl coming in to buy Double Bubble and peppermint sticks. She'd tried to return half-eaten candy and chewed gum on a number of occasions, for reasons ranging from a lack of flavor to strange allergic reactions. *Some people never change.* Brunhilde was examining a rack of newspapers and magazines by the front door, her face pruned with disapproval. She clucked her tongue, looked up and caught Ben watching her.

"That Richard Nixon needs to shave!" she announced, then whipped around and pushed on the door at the same moment as someone outside tried to enter. As the cacophony of bells subsided, whoever was outside stepped back and pulled the door open for her.

"Hello, Mrs. Stuffenphepper." Steve Cross tipped an invisible hat.

Brunhilde looked him up and down. "Gosh darned hippie. Get your gosh darned hair out of your eyes and maybe you won't smack right into people!"

"You have a nice day, Mrs. S." Steve let the door close behind Brunhilde then gave Ben a grin. "She's in a mood."

"That woman was born angry."

"I wonder how her husband stands her." Steve leaned against the counter.

"I'd like to be a fly on the wall in their bedroom." Ben shook his head. "On second thought, maybe I wouldn't." He glanced over his shoulder. "Eddie's straightening up the stockroom. Did you want to see him?"

"I came to see you."

"Well, then, what can I do you for?"

"I need batteries for my flashlight. Four Cs will do it."

Ben turned and picked up a pack, set it on the counter. "Got caught in the power outage?"

"I did."

"How was it up at the hotel?"

"Not too bad. We have a big generator."

"I noticed a lot of lights on up there."

Steve nodded.

"How did Delilah weather things? She never did like the dark. Or earthquakes."

"Not too well, I guess. I didn't see her, but her granddaughter came down after Delilah refused to let her in."

Ben nodded. "Dee's a fine woman but even as a little girl she could never stand to let anyone see her frightened."

Steve grinned. "You remember her?"

"Indeed I do." He smiled, caught in a memory. "She was just a little thing, cute as a bug. Her big sister and her cousin Addie used to bring her down for ice cream now and then." He shook his head. "Carrie was a beauty. I first started noticing her when she was about fifteen, ten years my junior, and I fell in love with her the summer before she died." He smiled. "She brought Dee down almost every day that last summer and while the little girl had ice cream, Carrie and I would talk and talk. I think maybe she liked me, too."

"I'll just bet she did."

"I was waiting for her to turn sixteen so I could ask her out. She did, but she didn't come down that week, or ever again. I never saw her again, except for the funeral." He roughly wiped away a tear before it could escape.

"You've never told me that story before. Thanks for sharing, Ben."

"Guess it was your lucky day. You keep it mum."

"I will."

"Can I get you anything else?"

"Pack of Juicy Fruit." Steve took it from the display and placed it next to the batteries. "What was Miss Delilah like back then?"

"All sunshine and pigtails, but she changed after her sister died. She became somber. Sad. And afraid. Wouldn't speak a word. When her daddy sent her to that aunt back east, I thought it was a real good thing." Ben smiled wistfully. "And I guess it was. Look at her now."

Steve nodded. "She's a lovely woman, and a good boss. Ben?"

"What?"

"Okay, may I ask..." He hesitated.

"Spit it out."

"I know you were a delivery boy back in the day."

"I was."

"You must've met a lot of people."

"Indeed I did. For better and worse."

Steve leaned closer and looked him in the eye. "Pearl Abbott. The head nurse up at the Clementine Hospital. Did you ever meet her?"

Gooseflesh tickled Ben's neck. "I did. Horrible woman. Met her a number of times and always came away with a bruised arm. We called her Pinching Pearl."

"She pinched?"

"Sure did. Did it to anyone who was unlucky enough to be near her and couldn't defend themselves. Kids, patients. The woman would grab your arm in that iron grip of hers and stare at you with those beady little black eyes, just waiting for you to whimper. I refused, and more than once, I came home with her fingerprints embedded in my arm or shoulder." He shook his head. "That was one mean woman. So why are you asking about her?"

"It'll sound crazy."

"Mr. Gower?" Eddie came out from the stockroom. "We're almost out of toilet paper. Should I order- hey, Steve!"

"Hey, Eddie."

"Put in the usual order, Eddie. We can't have the citizens of Brimstone running out of necessities."

"Okay." Eddie looked from his cousin to Ben. "What's up?"

"Just buying some batteries."

"Who's Pearl Abbott?"

"I don't pay you to eavesdrop, Eddie." Ben tried to sound stern.

"I didn't mean to. Who is she?"

"She was the head nurse at the hospital a long time ago. Now, scoot."

Reluctantly, Eddie turned to leave, then paused. "Is she one of the ghosts at the hotel?"

"Why do you ask?"

Eddie shrugged. "I like ghost stories. She is, isn't she?"

"Sorry, I've never heard a thing about her haunting the hotel."

"Get back to work, Eddie," Ben ordered.

They waited until the boy left, then Ben said, "What happened?"

Steve leaned in. "I told you that Holly came down after the earthquake last night."

"I recall."

"She's like Eddie - loves ghost stories. I told her how we hear the elevator move by itself sometimes and that it's rumored it's the ghost of Jack Purdy."

"I recall that story," Ben said. "So, what happened last night?"

"Well, the elevator moved. But it didn't; it happened while the power was out."

"Scare her much?"

"No, she loved it."

"Good."

"But then, the cab door opened. We both saw that - but Holly saw more. She saw a woman inside the cab. Described her. Ben, she saw Pearl Abbott. She picked her out of a photo album after that."

More goosebumps. "Maybe she's heard stories about Pinching Pearl."

"I wasn't lying to Eddie when I said there are no stories about Pearl Abbott haunting the hotel. And Holly hasn't been here long enough to hear any."

"True." Ben nodded. "Holly was here with her grandmother the other day. She looked just like Carrie at that age. Right down to her eyes."

"You mean the gold flecks?"

"The blue and the gold. Same piercing blue." He paused. "When the light hit Holly's eyes, you could see more gold shimmering in both of them. A lot more than I've ever seen before."

"More than Carrie?"

Ben's voice darkened. "And her great-great-granddaddy."

"It's inherited. I get it."

"Adeline Chance has them, too."

"She's Carrie and Delilah's cousin."

"I know."

"What's the point?"

"Well, those eyes are special. Rumor was Carrie and Addie had certain talents because of them, that maybe they could see things others couldn't."

Steve considered. "Maybe."

Ben rubbed his chin. "Henry Hank dabbled in the dark arts and rumor was that he could *do* things. And he had that secret society of his."

"That's why he called himself the Brimstone Beast," Steve said. "Delusions of power."

"I hope they were delusions." Ben's voice was still, somber.

"Do you believe Carrie and Addie could see or do things?"

"Well, I'm not clear on that. It wasn't much talked about." Ben paused and looked Steve square in the eye. "But Addie once told me she can see ghosts. You might ask her about that."

28

LESSONS

Breathless, Holly made it to Miss Delilah's penthouse with thirty seconds to spare. She'd sprinted back from the cemetery at quarter of four, used a washcloth to wipe off her face and arms, then slipped into clean clothes - a white skirt and purple short-sleeved blouse that her grandmother had bought her in Sedona.

Now she sat at the tall upright piano; her grandmother was going to give her an "unofficial" lesson while they waited for a music primer to show up in the mail, and Holly was excited. Carved art nouveau flowers twined along its edges and the music board was a hand-carved work of art, too beautiful to cover up with a music book. The walls of the music room were covered in leafy floral tapestries and a harp rested in a corner, a harp seat upholstered in purple velvet beside it. A small white marble table with two ebony chairs rested halfway across the room. Under the window was a chaise lounge upholstered in the same deep purple as the harp seat. Several leather club chairs clustered together in a corner. The place of honor belonged to a baby grand that Holly instinctively knew not to touch.

"Good afternoon, Holly. You were very nearly late." Miss Delilah stepped into the room. She wore a simple navy dress with small gold earrings. Reading glasses on a golden chain dangled around her neck. "Were you aware of that?"

"I'm sorry, but I did get here on the dot. I wasn't late."

"It's never wise to cut things so close. I want you to remember that in the future."

"I will."

Delilah nodded. "Stand up, child. I want to look you over."

Holly rose, fighting back an urge to rebel against being ordered around. *It's just how she is. She's a movie star, so she orders everybody around.*

"Um-hmm. Turn around."

Holly obliged and felt Miss Delilah lightly tug her ponytail. "Your hair is dusty, Holly."

"I'm sorry. I didn't have time to brush it."

"This needs washing, not just brushing." Delilah picked something from her hair then touched her shoulder to turn her back around. She held up a twig. "Is this your new hair ornament?"

Holly saw a slight - very slight - smile on her grandmother's face and smiled back. "It's the latest thing."

Delilah tried to look stern, but failed. Slipping the twig into a pocket, she let her face relax. "Let's have a look at your hands."

Oh crap! She'd forgotten all about cleaning her nails. She held them out for inspection, palms up.

"Very good. Now turn them over."

Reluctantly, she obeyed.

"There's dirt under your nails."

"Not much."

"Any dirt is unacceptable. Don't ever show up with dirty nails again." Delilah took her hands and held them closer. "That's red dust under your nails. Holly? Where were you and what have you been doing?"

"I was at the cemetery."

"And what were you doing there of all things? Digging graves?"

Making a bully pee his pants. "Just looking around. I like history."

"Well, you won't find much of it there - and you shouldn't go there alone."

"I wasn't alone."

"Becky Granger reported that you went there with a boy." Delilah's eyebrow rose. "Is that true?"

Tattletale. "Yes. Becky wouldn't go and Keith Hala wanted to."

Delilah nodded, looking thoughtful. "I know his grandfather, Abner. He's done some very nice ironwork for us. I suppose that's all right." She paused to point at a half-hidden door. "There's a bathroom. You can wash your hands there."

Holly started to rise.

"One more thing."

Holly turned. "What?"

"How did you get those?"

She was looking at her arms. Holly had forgotten the bruises when she'd dressed and a couple poked out from under the short sleeves of her shirt. "Uh, I don't know."

"Push your sleeve up higher so I can see."

Stomach knotting, Holly obliged. Delilah took her arm gently, turning it this way and that, careful not to touch the tender purple marks. "How did you get these, Holly?"

"The earthquake, I guess."

Delilah gently rolled Holly's sleeve back down. "Sit." She nodded at the piano bench.

Holly sat and Delilah joined her. "Tell the truth, Holly."

Holly couldn't tell the truth; Delilah would never believe her, not in a billion years. She shook her head. "I really don't know."

"Holly, did your mother do this to you?"

"No."

Delilah nodded. "They're too fresh, or I'd think you were covering for her. So, who did?"

Holly felt hot tears trying to fill her eyes and fought them down. "I woke up this morning and they were just there. That's why I think it was the earthquake."

"Those are fingerprints, Holly. Don't think me foolish enough to not know that."

One traitorous tear slid down her cheek. She wiped it roughly away. Holly wanted to tell her grandmother about Pearl Abbott and the dream, but she didn't dare. She'd think she was lying or crazy. "I don't know, Miss Delilah."

"Someone did this to you. You're covering up for them."

"I'm not."

Her grandmother's strict expression dissolved as a second tear escaped. Delilah wiped it away then pulled Holly to her breast, held her there, stroking her hair. "I won't let anything bad happen to you, Holly."

Despite her fear, Holly fell into her grandmother's arms, tears flowing freely. She tried to stop them, but couldn't. And it wasn't because she didn't dare tell her a ghost had done it. It was because no one had ever held her so close before. No one.

🜸 29 🜸

DINNER AT DEVINE'S

It was their first weekly dinner together and Holly sat across from her grandmother at the hotel restaurant. Devine's was the fanciest, most beautiful restaurant she'd ever been in, about a million times nicer than even the Hamburger Hamlet back in Los Angeles.

They sat in a booth by a window where they could see the lights of Brimstone twinkling between wind-whipped trees. The lighting in Devine's was soft - each table sat beneath its own milk glass art deco pendant lamp and a sea of red hurricane glasses flickered like fireflies throughout the dining room. Holly watched the candle flame on their table as it threw light and shadows over the salt and pepper shakers. She touched the napkin in her lap to make sure it hadn't fallen; like the tablecloth, it was linen, and so nice Holly didn't want to get it dirty.

Delilah cut a dainty bite of prime rib, dipped it in horseradish sauce. "How's your steak?"

Holly swallowed. "It's the best steak I've ever had."

"And how many steaks have you had, Holly?"

Her cheeks heated. "Just this one." She forked another piece. "Cherry says you have to be grown-up to appreciate steak."

Delilah's brow rose. "And is she correct?"

"No. She's wrong. This is *so* much better than hamburger!"

Delilah laughed. "I'm glad you like it."

"Thank you, Miss Delilah." Holly tried a bite of broccoli. She'd never tasted it fresh before and was surprised she liked it.

"Holly, I was very impressed with you today." Delilah sipped red wine. "You said you've never had a piano lesson before, but you seem to know a little about music. You can read notes. Did you teach yourself?"

"I took band for a semester last year, but Cherry couldn't afford to pay rent on the clarinet anymore, so I had to quit."

"That's a shame. I'm going to order a beginning piano book - something with melodies in it in addition to the primer - and as soon as it arrives we'll continue your lessons for as long as you're here."

Holly felt tears prickle her eyes again, and looked down at her plate. "I hope I never have to go back to Van Nuys," she told her steak.

Silence, and then Delilah patted her hand. "We'll see."

Holly looked up, hopeful. "What?"

"As I told you, if your mother wants to take you back to California, I can't stop her. But she might be willing to let you stay a little while if ..."

Holly watched Delilah. She was gazing at the window, lost in thought. "If what?"

Delilah looked at her, but her eyes weren't soft. Holly saw something that looked like determination.

"If you're here long enough for school to begin in the fall, perhaps I can persuade your mother to allow you to stay for the school year."

"Really?"

Don't tell her such things! Delilah knew herself well and her behavior around Holly was atypical. Leading the girl to believe she might be able to stay on was not only inconsiderate, it was foolish. Delilah didn't care to take on the responsibility of a child.

Her granddaughter was staring at her with those big blue eyes that glittered so like Carrie's had. They were filled with hope and expectation. *No, I won't be swayed.* Delilah turned her voice brusque. "I shouldn't suggest such things, Holly, not without talking to your mother first. I have no idea what or how she thinks." She sipped water from a crystal goblet. "And I have to think about the burden it would be on me to act as your guardian, if she did agree. It's not an easy decision."

"It's okay. I understand." Holly pushed a piece of potato around on her plate, then ventured, "I know how Cherry thinks."

"Enlighten me." Delilah was genuinely curious.

Holly looked up. Light reflected on the tiny motes of gold suspended in her blue irises. "She mostly thinks about making a movie that will make her famous like you. It's sort of like she's jealous or something." Holly raised questioning brows. "Do you know what I mean?"

Delilah studied the girl. She was mature beyond her years; Charlotte had robbed her of her childhood. "How old are you, Holly?"

"I just turned eleven. I start sixth grade in September."

Delilah considered. The little girl showed no outward signs of adolescence yet, but perhaps it didn't matter. Perhaps it was for the best. "I think you're old enough to understand something about your mother and her movies."

Holly nodded.

"Your mother doesn't make the same kind of movies that I did." Delilah looked into those fathomless eyes. "She makes what are called 'adult films.' Have you heard that term before?"

Holly nodded. You mean like *The Pawnbroker*?"

"No, dear." Delilah hid her shock that Holly knew of the movie. "*The Pawnbroker* is a legitimate film that has a little nudity in it. Adult films are almost entirely ... nude. There's ... a lot of hugging and kissing."

Holly nodded somberly. "I figured that's why she doesn't want me to see her movies. Sometimes, I overhear her say things on the phone to Larry."

"Larry?"

"Larry Zimmer. He's her agent."

"And what have you overheard?"

Holly shrugged, embarrassed. "Just stuff about kissing and things."

"Things?"

Holly blushed fiercely. "Um."

Delilah patted her hand. "Tell me, Holly. I need to know what you know. I promise I won't be mad."

"Okay, well. I heard her telling Larry she didn't want to take it up her ass."

Delilah swallowed her shock. "Do you know what that meant?"

"Not exactly, but it sounds gross." Holly paused, searched Delilah's eyes. "I don't want to know."

"You're right, Holly. It is gross, and you don't need to know." She forced a tight smile. "*I* don't care to know. The thing is, adult films are always gross." She hesitated. "But I must commend your mother for keeping you in the dark as well as she has." Delilah meant it. At least Charlotte was making some effort to protect her daughter.

"Does she make adult films because she can't make regular films?"

Delilah answered carefully. "It's very difficult to break into legitimate cinema. My guess is your mother started making those adult films because she needed money." Delilah paused. "Once you get a reputation for making adult films, no one in legitimate cinema will hire you."

Holly nodded, staring at her plate.

Delilah heard herself say, "It's not good for a little girl to spend time around the people your mother works with."

Holly looked up now, her eyes sparkling like a clear blue creek full of gold dust. "So it would be good to be here, away from those people, right Miss Delilah? I don't think Cherry would mind at all, except when she has to do dishes or vacuum."

Delilah realized the girl wasn't looking for sympathy, but simply stating facts.

How do I say no? Aunt Beatrice Lane's kind face filled her mind. "We'll see, Holly. We'll see. Now, eat up."

Holly's appetite returned and between bites she first chattered about movies and books, then went on in detail about the Brimstone history lesson that Steve had given her, enthusiastically and graphically reciting the story of the death of the caretaker who had his head crushed beneath the elevator so long ago.

Delilah couldn't help smiling. "Why do you like such gruesome stories, Holly?"

"It's history." She studied Delilah. "But Steve says nobody has ever seen Jack Purdy's ghost. Have you?"

"No, I haven't."

"I think maybe it's a different ghost," Holly said.

"Why do you think it isn't Jack Purdy?"

Holly looked lost in thought. "I don't know." Finally, a smile crept to her lips. "But you know what?"

"What?"

"I think I've been visited by Miss Annie Patches."

Delilah smiled at the girl's answer, but suspected she was hiding something. "Our resident feline ghost. Tell me."

"She woke me from a nightmare by walking on me. I heard her purr, too. Later I saw her eyes. They're gold."

Delilah smiled. "It sounds to me as if you've met a delightful spirit."

"You believe me?" Holly seemed surprised.

"I've heard stories about the ghost cat so many times that I think there's something to it." She called the waiter over and ordered Darjeeling tea for both of them. "If I were you, I'd be very happy this is the ghost who decided to visit."

"I am. I hope she comes back lots. I love cats." Holly paused. "Have you ever seen a ghost here, Miss Delilah?"

She hesitated. "I've experienced a few odd things since I moved in. I've heard the elevator moving when it's still. One night, I heard what sounded like footsteps walk right by me when no one was there, and once, I even saw a pen just float off the registration desk right in front of my eyes." She smiled. "But no, I've never actually *seen* a ghost. My big sister, Carrie, told me she could see ghosts."

"And you believed her?'

Delilah had been so young that she wasn't sure what she believed, but wanted Holly to continue talking. "Yes, I did. Tell me, Holly, what else did you see?"

"Last night, after the earthquake, when I was in the lobby, we heard the elevator come down. Only it didn't really - it was just like you said.

Steve said it couldn't work because the power was out, but we heard it - and it opened. Did you see it open?"

"No, I didn't. Go on, Holly."

"That's when I saw a ghost in the elevator - but it wasn't Jack Purdy."

"So that's why you don't believe he's the elevator ghost?"

"Yes. But Steve didn't see her at all."

"Her?"

"A mean-looking woman in an old-time black dress and apron with a red cross pinned on it."

A drop of fear trickled down Delilah's spine, but she didn't know why. "What did she do?"

"She stared at me. I know that sounds weird, but it's never happened before."

"What hasn't happened before, Holly? I don't understand."

"Staring. The other ghosts I've seen didn't see me. Not at all. They were like pictures."

"How many have you seen?"

"Just a couple. This little girl on the swing at the park a few times and once I saw an old man sitting on a bench at the bus stop near our apartment. He looked like he was reading a book. I asked him what it was, but he didn't answer, so I touched his arm - he wasn't really there at all. He faded away."

The girl spoke so matter-of-factly that Delilah thought maybe she really had seen these things. *Like Carrie. Stranger things have happened.* "Those are the only ghosts you've seen?"

Holly nodded. "Until last night. That mean woman ghost could see me and it was really creepy. I've never been scared like that before. I sure was glad when the elevator went back upstairs." A small smile. "I mean the ghost elevator went upstairs, because the real one hadn't really come down in the first place. Steve checked."

"Could you see where it went?"

Holly shook her head. "No, it kind of faded away after a couple seconds. You can ask Steve. He saw that part, too."

"But he didn't see the ghost?"

"No."

"Holly, maybe you imagined it. After all, it was a pretty scary night, what with the earthquake."

She hesitated. "I don't think so, Miss Delilah. I described her to Steve and we looked through the photo albums and we found her."

"You did?" Another unexplainable pinch of fear.

A somber nod. "Her name was Pearl Abbott and she was the head nurse. In the picture, she was with Henry Hank Barrow. Steve says he was your grandfather and my great-great-grandfather? Miss Delilah? Are you okay?"

A tall woman with a ramrod straight back and black hair pulled back so severely that it tugged her skin too tight over her cheekbones. A woman in black with beetle-black eyes who always stood next to Grandfather and stared through me. The memory shot into her mind as if it had always been there. *How did I forget her? How?*

"Miss Delilah?" Holly's worried eyes bored into hers.

Delilah took a deep breath and looked at Holly. "I think I remember her."

"You knew her?"

"I was very small, much younger than you, but I remember seeing her with my grandfather." She paused. "Your great-great-grandfather. I don't remember anything about her except that she terrified me even more than he did." She forced a smile. "That was probably just because of the way she looked. I'll bet she was a nice lady. She just needed to smile more."

Holly's somber eyes questioned every word and then she stated flatly, "She wasn't nice."

"Holly, dear, I'm not questioning that you saw her ghost, but I doubt she was looking at you. She had piercing eyes - that's what I remember most. It just *felt* like she was staring at you, don't you think?"

Holly contemplated the idea. "Maybe."

But Delilah knew she was unconvinced.

"Has anyone ever said they've seen her before?" her granddaughter asked. "I mean, is Pearl Abbott one of the ghosts they tell stories about?"

"No," Delilah said gratefully. "I've never heard or read about her ghost being seen here." She paused. "I think, Holly, that your eyes might be special. That's what my sister told me about hers. She said she could see ghosts because of the gold in her eye. And-" She cut the comment off as she remembered her grandfather's eyes.

"And what?" Holly prompted as the waiter set their teacups down.

There's no sense lying about it. "Your great-great-grandfather. He had similar eyes."

"Did he see ghosts, too?"

"I don't know, Holly. I only know that he ran the hospital and that he wasn't a nice man."

"Miss Delilah? Do people see *his* ghost?"

"I don't think so." She hesitated, then spoke firmly. "But enough about ghosts. Holly, Meredith asked me if I thought you'd like to go camping with her family this weekend. They're leaving very early, so you'd have to spend tomorrow night at their house."

"What did you say?"

"I said I'd ask you if you want to go camping."

"You didn't just tell her yes or no?"

"Of course not. If you want to, you may, but it's up to you."

Holly beamed. "Then I think I'd like to-"

Almost imperceptibly, the pendant lamp above their table began to sway. Then Delilah saw her tea tremble as if someone had tossed a pebble into a vast lake. Putting her hands on the table, she felt the vibrations beginning. Across from her, Holly's eyes went wide.

Suddenly, the earth gave a hard sideways jolt and, dimly, Delilah was aware of the silverware and dishes jittering on the table, of diners' voices lifting in surprise. The lamp swayed hard now, casting shadows Alfred Hitchcock would approve. "Under the table, Holly! Now!"

Delilah slipped below the small table, saw Holly safely in front of her, and then everything went dark.

THERE HAD ONLY BEEN THE ONE BIG SHAKE, BUT HER GRANDMOTHER was out cold. "Miss Delilah?" Holly held her grandmother's hands under the table, rubbing them. "Miss Delilah?"

Delilah's eyelids fluttered.

A waiter lifted the linen tablecloth and peered at Holly and Delilah. "I'll call an ambulance."

"No, she's okay."

"She needs a doctor, young lady. Here. Let me help her."

Miss Delilah's terrified eyes opened and stared into Holly's. She squeezed her hands tighter. "It's okay," Holly whispered. "It's over." The waiter was joined by another and now both reached for Delilah.

"No!" Holly glared at the pair of them, suddenly furious because they didn't understand and wouldn't listen. "Leave us alone! No doctors! Just go clear out the restaurant!" The order tumbled from her lips as she remembered Steve Cross talking about how you shut things down after an earthquake. "Go!" she ordered. Part of her couldn't believe she'd said it, but she knew it was right. Knew beyond all doubt.

Everything was crystal clear now, from her vision to her knowledge of what to do. She felt the blaze in her eyes as she stared at the waiters.

"Yes, okay," one said. The other nodded. And they both disappeared.

"Holly," began Delilah.

"It's okay, Gram. It's over."

Miss Delilah nodded.

They waited there beneath the table until Holly heard the last guests leaving, then she said, "Let's go. Everyone's gone."

Miss Delilah nodded and they rose together. Her grandmother brushed herself off, adjusted her skirt and jacket, and raised her head proudly, as if nothing had happened. Holly saw waiters and waitresses watching and looked at them all, willing the blaze in her eyes to return, thinking at them, *Look away!*

And they did. They all did.

✤ 30 ✤

THE BASEMENT

Startled by the sudden quake, Steve Cross rose, tense, ready for more, but the postcard rack on the desk didn't twitch and the ceiling fan in the center of the lobby barely jittered now.

Hoping the shake was just an aftershock, but concerned because it didn't feel that way, he came around the desk just as the elevator dinged. As the outer doors slid open, he was ready to assure the passenger that everything was fine. And it was; the lights hadn't so much as flickered.

The cab was lit, but no one came out. "Everything okay?" he called, laying his hand on the handle of the folding gate. He yanked it back: the handle was freezing cold. But this was no phantom elevator. He peered into the cab, seeing the old-fashioned floral wallpaper and the little corner table with its vase of flowers.

But something else was within, something cold. Before he could move aside, he felt it ooze onto him like thick dark water. He stepped back as it began to envelop his hands, his arms, his legs. Fingers aching from the chill, he pulled out of its path and followed the cold mass as it moved, staying three feet back to keep from shivering. He could almost see it - it shimmered like heat on a desert highway as it glided slowly from the deep alcove, and into the lobby. Finally, it arrived at the copper door, and then moved through it, leaving a sheen of frost on the metal. As it vanished, Steve stepped closer. The air was no longer chilled but the copper door emanated preternatural cold.

"What the–" Steve stepped back, unwilling to follow that pillar of cold behind the copper door. Instead, he returned to the elevator and peered inside. It was empty and when he touched the metal grate, he found it cool, no longer frigid.

He closed the outer doors and used the key switch to shut the elevator down; it wouldn't be going anywhere until Mike Granger cleared it.

After a nervous glance at the copper-clad door, Steve returned to the safety of the desk, and checked the old-fashioned switchboard. The hotel was almost empty tonight and the board was blessedly dark. He rang the penthouse and was pleased to hear Delilah and Holly had returned from dinner safely. Frieda told him Delilah had taken a tranquilizer and gone to bed. He wondered if Holly had remained with her, but didn't ask.

Grabbing the short stack of out-of-order signs, he trotted upstairs and placed one at each elevator landing. He was back in less than five minutes.

He thought about Holly, who had seen an actual apparition. What she'd described was something far more interesting than his encounter with a roaming cold spot. He smiled to himself - he had always wanted to experience the supernatural beyond mere elevator sounds or phantom footsteps, and now, with the moving cold spot, he had. *I should be grateful! Instead, I'm wishing I'd seen something, like Holly did. Ridiculous.* He rose and rounded the desk. If Eddie, his ghost-loving cousin were here - they'd already be investigating the backroom.

What? Am I afraid to go in alone? Steve rose and crossed to the copper door. His hand shook the tiniest bit as he unlocked it, but he opened it, stepped inside, and left the door ajar in case any guests phoned down or entered the lobby.

Switching on the lights, he saw that everything looked just as it had when he'd done his rounds a few hours ago. Following his usual route, he walked past the boiler, then to the elevator shaft - he couldn't see in the pit since the cab was on the lobby floor. Finally, he returned to the front and walked to the generator room, checked the lock, then began his return to the lobby.

Halfway there, he stopped. The copper door that he'd left ajar was closed.

He'd paused beside the forbidden entrance to the basement, and now he saw that the big padlock was undone and the basement door hung open a bare inch, the darkness beyond bleeding onto the cement floor.

"What the-?"

Steve knew beyond a doubt that the basement door had been locked earlier. It was always locked, and he would have noticed if it hadn't been - you couldn't miss it. *But no one's been in here.* Tentatively, he pulled on it. Silently, smoothly, it yawned open. He could see the cement stairs disappearing into the dark. Taking one step down, he reached in, feeling for the light switch, wondering if the bulb worked.

Something cold clutched his ankle. Something so cold it burned.

Steve looked down, saw nothing, but it felt like a hand - an icy one with an iron grip. Panicked, he instinctively braced his palms against the doorjambs and yanked his leg up - but whatever grasped his ankle held on tight.

Then it yanked.

Steve fought for balance, lost, and fell backward, light exploding behind his eyes as the back of his head smacked against the threshold. "Son of a bitch!" Scuttling, he pulled himself back, off the stairs and threshold, and finally the thing - *the hand!* - let go. Steve jumped to his feet, slammed the door, and breathing hard, put the padlock through the hasp and jammed it home.

HOLLY HAD BEEN DISAPPOINTED THAT DELILAH DIDN'T WANT TO talk after they left the restaurant. Instead, they'd taken the stairs and Delilah had seen her to her room. She'd hoped to be invited up but since the quake, her grandmother had become distant and polite; Holly knew she was frightened.

After exchanging her dress for jeans and a hot pink T-Shirt printed with swoopy psychedelic letters reading "Frodo Lives," Holly spent the next hour in her room curled up reading *The History of Brimstone*, the other booklet Adeline Chance had given her. Even though the facts were interesting, it was a pretty boring read - all dates and dryness, just like the history books in school. She drowsed off, only to wake when she heard someone knock.

"Who is it?"

No one replied. *Maybe I dreamed it.* She got up and crossed to the door, standing on tiptoes to peer out the peephole. She couldn't see anyone, so she cautiously opened the door and looked up and down the hall. There wasn't a soul in sight.

She consulted her wristwatch; it was after eleven. Things would be quiet downstairs now, so she grabbed her key, put the Do Not Disturb sign on the knob and headed out. She didn't know if the elevator was running or not, but either way, she didn't want to ride. Between Arthur Meeks' room being opposite it and the ghost she'd seen last night, she doubted she'd ever ride it again.

Trotting downstairs, she entered the lobby, giving the elevator alcove one defiant glance as she passed it. She approached the registration desk. "Steve?"

He wasn't there so she wandered into the souvenir area in front of the desk and was looking through the selection of books and postcards when she heard pounding and Steve's muffled voice call, "Hello?"

She crossed to the glass entry doors - they were unlocked - but there was no sign of him. The pounding came again and this time, she tracked it to the copper door. The knob jiggled. "Steve?"

"Holly!"

"Are you okay?"

"Yeah. I think the door is stuck. Can you open it?"

She grasped the knob. It opened easily. She stared at Steve, at the smudges of dirt and dust on his clothes and face. "What happened?"

"Crazy stuff. Holly, you know how we talked about the basement door and how it's always locked?"

She nodded.

"It was open."

"I didn't-"

"I know you didn't." He attempted a grin. "But I wish you had."

He stepped into the lobby and shut the copper door, then reopened it several times. It worked smoothly. "I left this door open when I went in. It closed while I was in there, which happens sometimes, but it's never stuck before. Not until now." He shook his head. "Weird."

She looked him up and down. "But what happened to *you?*"

Locking the door, he turned to Holly. "The truth is, I'm not sure, but I'm lucky I didn't break my neck." He paused. "Hold down the fort for me for just a minute? I need to wash up."

"Sure." Holly watched him leave - he was limping a little - then went to the lobby entrance and opened one of the doors. The warm scent of sage wafted on the breeze.

AFTER WASHING UP, STEVE SAW HOLLY STANDING IN THE OPEN doorway looking out at Brimstone's night sky. He grabbed a couple sodas from the cooler and approached, trying not to limp. "I could use some fresh air myself."

When she turned, her smile betrayed worry. He gave her a grin and opened the door wider then flipped down the doorstop to keep it that way. "Nice night. Soda?"

"Thanks! Are you limping?"

"Yeah."

"What happened?"

"That's what I'd like to know. Let's sit down." He nodded at two curlicued iron chairs outside the lobby.

They settled down and Steve took a pull on his soda before crossing his sore leg over his lap. He pulled up the cuff on his cords while Holly watched. "Did you trip in the backroom?"

"Something like that." He pulled down his sock. "Wow."

She gasped when she saw the dark bruises. She reached over and lightly touched the skin between the purple-red marks. "Your leg is freezing! Look how white the skin is around the bruises!"

BRIMSTONE

Steve gave her a sick smile. "It felt like a Frost Giant grabbed my ankle."

"Look." Holly pushed up the sleeve of her blouse and pointed at similar bruises on her arm. "This happened last night."

"What in the world?" Steve stared at the dark bruises. "They're the same. Holly, do you know how it happened?"

"I dreamed that Pearl Abbott grabbed me. But now I don't think it was a regular dream. I don't know what would have happened if I hadn't woken up." Holly paused. "My arms were super cold after she touched me. There are fingerprints all over my shoulders and arms. Just like your ankle. So, what happened?"

"Crazy stuff," he said. "I don't know. When I saw the basement door was open, I was afraid someone had broken in so I stepped down onto the top step to turn on the light. And something - like a really strong ice-cold hand - grabbed my ankle and yanked. If I hadn't been hanging on to the doorjambs, it would've pulled me downstairs."

"I'm glad you're okay." Holly continued to stare at his bruised ankle. "It was her."

A long pause. "Pearl Abbott."

Steve rolled his pant leg down. "I guess so." He tried to smile. "I doubt there are two ghosts here with hands that cold, huh?" He shivered, remembering Ben Gower's stories. *Pinching Pearl. My God, she's really haunting this place.*

She smiled back. "You didn't hear the elevator again or anything, did you? I mean before you found the basement door open?"

Steve would never feed stories like this to an ordinary child, but this girl was anything but. "Yeah, I heard it. I don't know for sure if it was the real elevator or the ghostly one, but the real one opened. I thought a guest had come down and I went to meet it, but the cab was empty and the accordion gate was closed." He paused. "And freezing cold. Way colder than what we felt last night."

"Did you see anything?"

"No, but I felt *something.* Have you ever heard of cold spots?"

"Yes. I read about them in Hans Holzer's books. Did you-?"

"Feel one?" Steve took a swig of soda and wished it were something

203

harder. "I did. It was big, maybe the size of a human, I'm not sure. And it was more than cold. It made my hands ache where it touched me."

"Cold spots and ghosts are supposed to go together," Holly said.

He nodded. "So I've heard. "Had you felt any before you came here?"

"A little. Not like what you're talking about. Like the little girl at the park I saw sometimes, it was always a little cool where she was, but that's all." She paused. "Tonight at dinner, I asked Miss Delilah if she's ever seen the ghost of Jack Purdy and she said no, but that her sister Carrie could see ghosts. And she said my eyes are like Carrie's - and my great-great-grandfather's."

Steve blinked at her. "And?"

"What I mean is, maybe if I'd been here tonight, I'd have seen Pearl Abbott because my eyes are weird."

He nodded. "You know who else has eyes like yours?"

She nodded, smiling. "Adeline Chance. I know she's my cousin but I promised not to say anything in front of Delilah. You can't either."

Steve chuckled. "Cross my heart."

"I'm going to go see her tomorrow and ask if she's ever seen anything here."

"I think that might be really interesting."

Holly nodded. "She gave me some books about Brimstone. I read the history one last night. The one about folklore and the Brimstone Beast was better." She drank from her bottle of soda, then blew into the lip, checking the tone. "It's like playing clarinet, but easier."

Steve grinned and blew a note on his. It was deeper than Holly's. "So, what do you know about the Beast?"

"Well, it was this Indian legend..."

"True," Steve said. "But your great-great-grandfather claimed *he* was the Brimstone Beast."

"Why?"

"Henry Hank Barrow wanted people to think of him as a magician. A dangerous wizard. He formed *Infurnam Aeris*. It was something like a club - like the Masons - but much darker. He was the high priest. It's said that Pearl Abbott was his high priestess."

"So, he was sort of like Saruman in *Lord of the Rings?*"

Steve considered. "No, more like *The Wizard of Oz*."

Holly laughed. "You mean he was a fake?"

"Well, I've never met a *real* wizard, have you?"

"No, but I guess anything's possible, right?"

"Right." Steve finished his soda. "I'd be very interested in hearing what Adeline can tell you about your special eyes." He looked straight into them and saw the sparkles. "Maybe it's true."

"Maybe." Holly sipped. "Steve, Miss Delilah said she remembered Pearl Abbott from when she was little and that she was afraid of her - and of my great-great-grandfather."

"I'm not surprised. They weren't very nice people." He paused. "You've met my cousin, Eddie, I believe? He works at Gower's Drugs."

"Yes. Miss Delilah took me there for a root beer float."

"Well, his boss, Mr. Gower, told me something about Pearl Abbott today. She was known as Pinching Pearl."

"Really?" Holly's eyes widened.

"Ben's old enough that he remembers a lot about your great-great-grandfather and the old hospital. And Pearl. It might be fun to talk to him about it sometime. I can ask Eddie to see if he's willing."

Holly nodded. "I'd like that."

"I did some reading today and there was a rumor that Pearl Abbott killed some of the patients - ones who weren't getting well, and some crazy ones. And there were rumors that *Infurnam Aeris* occasionally sacrificed babies born in the hospital. Though that's probably nonsense."

"I guess. *Infurnam* what?"

"*Infurnam Aeris*. It means something to the effect of 'Copper Hell.' They wore funny robes and held secret meetings."

"What for?"

"Well, that's hard to say since it was a secret group." Steve wished he hadn't brought it up - Miss Delilah would not approve - but what was done was done. "They probably tried to make themselves rich or influence people at the hospital or maybe win elections." In all honesty, he thought all those things were likely true, but that *Infurnam Aeris* boiled down to Henry Hank's lust for power and greed. He'd gathered that sex was a major aspect of their rituals and beneath that black dress, Pearl Abbott wasn't the prude she'd have people believe.

He looked at Holly. "Let's go in. I want to show you something."

A MOMENT LATER, HOLLY FOLLOWED STEVE INTO AN OPEN ROOM just behind the lobby desk. She hadn't noticed it before because it was partially hidden behind parked luggage carts.

"The hotel lobby used to be the lobby of the Clementine Hospital and the main nurses' station was where our front desk is now. And this," he said gesturing around the room, "was H.H. Barrow's private office." The walls were white tile and the room held tables, luggage racks, a couple of cabinets, coat racks, and umbrella stands. "Now it houses the hotel safe, guest luggage, and anything else that needs temporary storage."

Holly walked up to an ornate safe built into the wall between two tables. It was polished black, trimmed in gold. She ran her fingers over the shining enamel finish. "Wow, that's really old."

"It is. It was your great-great-grandfather's safe. And your great-grandfather's after that." He crossed to another wall. "But this is what I want you to see."

It was a framed painting of the hotel. Holly raised her eyebrows.

Steve lifted the painting off its hook and laid it on the table, revealing an ornate tile mosaic. *"Infurnam Aeris,"* he said.

Holly stared. It depicted a coppery-gold X with three narrow bars crossing it horizontally against a black background that glowed cobalt near the symbol. The central bar was shorter and broader than the other two and each end glowed with a ruby gem. A narrow bar at the bottom of the X created a triangle and an inverted cross hung from it. Above the symbol were the words, *INFURNAM AERIS.*

"That's weird looking," Holly said. The symbol gave her the creeps though she didn't understand why.

Steve traced the X and cross bars with his finger. "This is the alchemical symbol for copper." He outlined the triangle and cross at the bottom. "That's the symbol for sulfur - or brimstone, which is associated with the devil. Hence, 'Copper Hell.'"

Holly nodded. "What about the rubies on the middle arm?"

"Those were supposed to symbolize the eyes of the Brimstone Beast." He rubbed his chin. "I suspect in this case that the Beast was Henry Hank himself. You know, as in 'his eyes are always watching. 'But I could be wrong - Holly, are you okay?"

She stepped back, putting distance between herself and the symbol as the dragon dream came rushing back. The glowing copper-red eyes. Staring at her.

"I've seen it before. The Beast is a dragon, isn't it?"

"It's a serpent in native art, so yes, I guess a dragon is a good description. Holly, where did you see it?"

"In my dreams."

31

A NEW DAY

"How are you feeling?"

Delilah, reclining on her velvet chaise lounge in her darkened bedroom, removed the cold cloth from her aching head and smiled thinly at Vera Kotzwinkle. "A bit better."

"Would you like anything? Another compress? Tea?"

"Tea would be lovely." Delilah sat up. "Have you already taken care of the fan mail?"

"No. Not by a longshot. Several more theaters are doing Universal revivals. Your popularity is soaring these days."

"I wish they'd revive something other than those dreadful monster movies."

"At least they remember you." Vera paused. "In October, Maisie Hart is going to appear at a monster movie convention in Phoenix. I know you'd like to see her - and I haven't RSVP'd on your invitation yet. Are you sure you don't want to go?"

"I'm certain. Though find Maisie's address. Perhaps we can ask her here for a visit."

Vera nodded. "That sounds lovely. I really liked her."

"She could have been more than a scream queen if she hadn't gotten typecast so young. The tea?"

"Coming right up."

Vera left and Delilah stood, adjusted the tie on her long lavender dressing gown, then sat at the vanity. She hadn't seen Maisie in years. The woman had taught Delilah the ins and outs of starring in monster movies. She'd even coached her in the creation of her signature scream - the one that had made her a star in the genre.

As she brushed her hair, Delilah realized the headache really was lifting now. It had begun right after that embarrassing fainting spell in the restaurant. At least no one but Holly had seemed to notice. She could tell the girl had questions but she couldn't face them last night. Nor could she today.

Her head began to throb again. She didn't need another relationship with a child. *I tried so hard the first time and look how badly that turned out.*

Delilah looked in the mirror and told herself, "I can't keep her here. I won't."

"You won't what?"

Delilah turned to Vera. "I didn't hear you come in."

Vera set the tea tray on the coffee table and waited for Delilah to join her. "I'm as quiet as a mouse. So, who won't you keep? Cherry? Can't say I blame you."

"Not Charlotte." Delilah sipped. "Her daughter."

"Your granddaughter." Vera spoke firmly.

"Her daughter. I don't wish to become a grandparent."

Vera raised an eyebrow. "I have news for you, boss-lady. You already are. And your granddaughter is a charming kid. Smart as a whip, too." She paused. "So, what's up? Did Holly ask if she could stay on?"

"She's hinting." Delilah looked at her hands. "And I'm afraid that, in a weak moment, I implied it might be possible, at least for a little while." She shook her head. "I don't know what I was thinking." Looking up at Vera, she added, "She just looks so much like Carrie."

"I wish I could've met your sister."

"So do I."

Vera stirred a lump of sugar into her tea. "Did you feel the quake last night?"

"Very much so," Delilah admitted. "It was awful and Holly was with me. We were in the restaurant just finishing dinner when it struck."

Vera looked her in the eye. "Did you pass out?"

"Don't I always?"

"I'm so sorry. What happened?"

"Fortunately, no one noticed. We'd already hidden under the table and the waitstaff was too busy escorting the diners out to look our way."

"But Holly noticed. Right?" Vera wouldn't look away.

Delilah nodded curtly. "I opened my eyes and the girl was staring at me with all this ... concern. Sympathy. It was humiliating."

"Nonsense. It wasn't humiliating. You have such a hang-up about looking perfect every minute of every day."

"It's expected of someone like me. You know that, Vera."

"I do, of course I do. But not when it comes to me or Frieda. And now your granddaughter. So she's seen you faint. Get over it. I haven't seen that much of her yet, but it's already obvious to me that she loves you, Dee."

Delilah barked a laugh. "Love? Good God, Vera, you sound like a starry-eyed teenager. You can't just suddenly love someone. It doesn't happen that way except in the movies. I've met the girl exactly once before when she was half the age she is now. I'm a stranger to her."

"I'll say it again. She loves you."

"She sees me as an opportunity."

"An opportunity? What do you mean?"

"An opportunity to stop living in a one room apartment with her no-account mother. To have her own room and not have to listen to - well, whatever it is she overhears when Charlotte drags home her boyfriends."

Vera reached out and touched Delilah's hand. "Makes sense. And there's nothing wrong with wanting to get out of a bad situation. Speaking of which, you've never told me about *your* life here as a child. What was that like?"

"I barely recall it. I was six when I was sent to live with my aunt in Boston."

"But you remember your sister."

"A little."

"What about your mother?"

"She died when I was three. I have a vague memory of a dark-haired lady who smelled good lifting me up and singing to me. That's about it."

"What about your father? Did he die right after you lost your sister? Is that how you went to live with your aunt?"

"Oh, heavens, no. He shipped me off to Aunt Beatrice's weeks after Carrie passed. I never saw him again. When he died, he left me this place. That's the only nice thing he ever did for me." She paused. "Besides send me to Boston."

"Did your aunt love you? Did you love her?"

Delilah smiled. "You've always been good at distracting me, Vera."

"Well?"

"My aunt was very proper and strict, but she was good to me and she loved me. I loved her, too."

"Well, that's something. What about your father? When he sent you away, you must have been devastated."

"Vera, stop playing shrink. I'm sorry to disappoint you, but I don't remember much, but I do know I was anything but devastated."

"What was he like, your dad?"

"He was ... a hard man." Memories flooded. Bill Delacorte forcing her to stand straighter at her grandfather's funeral. His eyes boring into hers like knives, his breath smelling of whiskey. And Carrie's words. *"He's a bad man, Delilah! A bad man!"*

But she meant Grandfather, didn't she? It was all a blur. "Vera, stop grilling me. I can't recall much about him, but I don't think I liked him very much. I most certainly didn't love him."

Vera nodded. "Okay, but I don't think you're seeing yourself clearly in this situation with Holly."

"That's quite enough, Vera."

"Okay. Okay. But, Dee, just look to your own past and I think you'll understand your feelings better." Vera rose, smoothed her skirt. "I'd better get back on that fan mail."

"Indeed. And I need to get dressed. The day is slipping away."

Delilah waited until Vera returned to her office, then took her tea out on the balcony overlooking the Brimstone Valley. Below, she saw the oldest Granger boy parking a bicycle at the close edge of the parking lot. A moment later Holly came out with Meredith. She could hear the girl's clear voice thanking mother and son before she climbed on the bike and started pedaling down the road, legs pumping, ponytail flying.

Delilah sat down with her tea. What she'd seen last night after the quake disturbed her and it was something she couldn't tell Vera. She couldn't tell anyone.

She remembered how the gold mark in her older sister's right eye seemed to shimmer and pulse when Carrie was upset, but Delilah had long assumed the image was a product of her imagination - but last night, while recovering from her faint, she saw Holly's blue eyes become swirling gold pools when the girl told the waiters not to call an ambulance, and to go away.

"Nonsense. I must have imagined it."

❦ 32 ❦

SECRETS

The Humble Station came into view after only a few short minutes and Holly, already sweating, parked her bike by the newspaper rack. After patting her pocket to make sure her change was still there, she opened the door to a jangling of tiny bells.

"Holly! How are you, dear?" Adeline Chance, feather duster in hand, smiled.

"I'm fine. I've been reading the Brimstone books you gave me."

Adeline smiled and opened the soda pop cooler. "It's so hot this morning that I think I'll have a ginger ale. Care to join me?"

Holly dug a dime out of her pocket. "A Dr. Pepper, please."

The old lady pulled the bottle out and snapped the lid off in the opener, quick as a wink. "Here you go." She waved the money away. "You're my guest." She extracted a ginger ale, opened it and took a long pull. "Mmm, good. Holly, come sit with me behind the register."

"I'M GLAD YOU CAME TO VISIT. I'VE BEEN THINKING ABOUT YOU." Adeline sipped her soda and smiled at the little girl beside her. "Tell me, what do you think of the hotel?"

"It's pretty interesting." Holly stared up at her with those bright blue eyes. The gold fleck, the fleck that was so much like her own and Carrie Delacorte's, was what had originally drawn her attention, but now she marveled at the tiny sparkles throughout Holly's irises.

"Interesting?" Addie asked. "When I say something is 'interesting' the way you just did, it usually means I don't much care for it."

"The hotel - I'm not sure about it yet. I mean, on one hand, I *love* it! I have my own room and Miss Delilah pays me five dollars a week to water all the plants." Finally, Holly smiled.

"That's a well-paying job!"

"And there are nice people there like Meredith and Steve."

"I'm acquainted with them both. Lovely folks."

Holly nodded. "Miss Delilah's going to give me piano lessons. And she took me to Sedona and bought me new clothes. I really like her but I'm not sure if she likes me. Sometimes, I think she does, but other times, not so much. She said she might ask if I could stay on and go to school here if Cherry goes back to Van Nuys, but then she pretended she didn't say it."

"She runs a little hot and cold, doesn't she?" Adeline patted Holly's hand.

The girl nodded. "Like last night, we had dinner at the restaurant and it was so great! And then the earthquake happened and she fainted and then would barely talk to me."

"She fainted?"

Holly nodded. "We got under the table and then she fainted. For less than a minute. A waiter wanted to call an ambulance, and I said no." She shook her head, bafflement evident. "I don't know why I did that exactly." Holly's eyes searched Adeline's.

"I think you probably just sensed it was the best thing to do."

"Maybe. Anyway, Miss Delilah woke up before I said no. And then..." Her words trailed off.

"And then?"

"Well, another waiter came and they said they were going to help Miss Delilah out from under the table and I said no again." Bafflement flitted across her face. "I knew I could help her..." She gazed at the slowly-circling ceiling fan.

"And?" Adeline finally prompted.

"That's all."

"No, it's not." She smiled gently.

Holly studied her. "How do you know there's more?"

"The gold fleck in our eyes, Holly. It helps us with things like that."

Holly looked relieved. "The waiters kept staring so I told them to go away and not look at us while we left. And I thought it really hard at them, too."

"What happened?"

"They did."

"Do you think you made them do that?"

"I don't know. Maybe."

Holly launched into a hurried story about a pair of playground bullies who'd picked on Abner Hala's grandson, Keith. "I got really mad," she finished, "and I told them to go away, and they did. Then Keith asked me if I'd ever gotten that mad before and I didn't think so. And you know what Keith told me?"

"What, honey?"

"He told me my eyes turned gold! Like bright gold! Just for a minute."

Adeline managed not to gasp. She and Carrie had, at Henry Hank Barrow's insistence, learned to push people, but it took years and barely worked. The old man had frightened them into doing it.

Holly, oblivious, continued talking. "So, anyway, last night when I thought at those waiters to go away, I made myself mad at them before I told them not to look at Miss Delilah. That's how I did it, I think."

"Holly, did your grandmother see your eyes?"

"Probably." She hesitated. "Do you think she's mad at me?"

"No, honey, I think maybe you startled her. Maybe even scared her a little."

Holly looked worried. "She won't want me if I scare her."

"That's not true, Holly. It's not you that scares Delilah. It's complicated, but your grandmother went through something horrible when she was young - much younger than you are now. Nobody knows everything about what happened the day her sister and grandfather died - I was there and I don't know everything. The point is, she lost her sister, whom she loved dearly, and she was frightened out of her wits. She wouldn't speak after Carrie died. Not a word. A few months later, her father sent her to Boston to live with her aunt."

"It seems mean that he'd send her away."

"Holly, we have an awful lot to talk about, but I'll tell you two things right now. I grew up with Carrie, and you look exactly like her; I'm sure your grandmother has noticed that - it probably troubles her as much as it delights her."

Holly nodded. "She told me I look like Carrie. I think she really loved her. What's the other thing?"

Adeline leaned closer. "It's simply that Delilah's father wasn't a nice man. Oh, nothing like her grandfather, Henry Hank Barrow - that man was downright evil - but Bill Delacorte wasn't terribly pleasant. Leaving here was the best thing that ever happened to your grandmother." She paused. "She might never have spoken again if she hadn't gone to live with her aunt. I wrote to Aunt Beatrice regularly in the early days to find out how Dee was doing." She smiled fondly. "Before Carrie's death, your grandmother used to tag along with Carrie and me on adventures - we'd hike up Mt. Brimstone to look at the petroglyphs or go pick wildflowers. She was such a sweet little thing."

Holly smiled. "It's hard to picture my grandmother as a little girl. She's so ... grown-up."

Nodding, Adeline rose. "Wait there a moment. I have something to show you."

She went into the back office and picked the copper-framed photo off the desk. It showed herself, Carrie, and little Dee, taken in town not a month before the tragedy. She brought it back and handed it to Holly, then sat down, watching the girl's face.

"Which one is you?" was her first question.

Adeline chuckled. "I'm the tall one."

Holly smiled. "And so this is Carrie? And I look like her? Really?"

"Right now, you look like her at age eleven. She's just shy of sixteen in the photo - and I guarantee you, you'll look just like her. If the photo was in color, I think you'd see it yourself."

"She's pretty. So are you." Holly glanced up. "Delilah is so cute."

"She was. She was a dark-haired beauty."

"When did Delilah start talking again?"

"About six months after going to live with Aunt Beatrice. Up until then, she was as somber and silent as a judge, but Beatrice said that once she got her words back, she became quite a chatterbox. She said it was as if she'd flipped a switch."

"Did Miss Delilah remember what happened to her?"

Adeline shook her head. "No. It was Beatrice's opinion that she began talking again after she'd buried the memories so deeply that they were lost to her. I think she's right."

"Why doesn't she like you, I mean, if she can't remember anything?"

"She blames me for Carrie's death, but I seriously doubt she knows why. I certainly don't know."

"Were you there when she died?"

"I was."

"How did she die?"

"I'll tell you what I know one day, but not right now." Adeline smiled gently. "We need to talk about our eyes today."

"Okay. Miss Delilah told me that Carrie said she could see ghosts."

Adeline was suddenly full of questions of her own.

"Could she?" Holly asked.

"Yes, she could. So can I. I'm surprised Dee remembers - and would tell you so."

"I think she remembers because Carrie told her she could."

"I see. And why do you think she told *you*?"

"Because I asked."

Adeline nodded patiently. Getting anything out of this little girl took work. "What exactly did you ask your grandmother?"

"If she'd ever seen Jack Purdy. She said no."

"The elevator ghost. Did you see him, Holly?"

"No." The girl drew the word out.

"But?" prompted Adeline.

"I saw a different ghost in the elevator. Steve was with me but he couldn't see it."

"He doesn't have your eyes, sweetheart. What did you see?"

"*Who*. Steve got out an old picture album and she was in it. Do you know who Pearl Abbott was?"

A wave of dizziness swept over Adeline. *Pinching Pearl.* Unbidden, the name filled her memory.

"Are you going to faint?" Holly peered at her.

"No, dear. I'm just surprised. I haven't heard of anyone seeing her since ... well, since she died. All the kids were afraid of her." She finished her ginger ale. "Now tell me about Pearl Abbott. What did *you* see?"

"She had a long black old-fashioned dress, and a white apron with a little red cross pin and she was really mean looking. I've seen ghosts before and they never scared me. She did."

"Why?"

"Because she *saw* me. She stared at me. The other ghosts never saw me. They were just there, in their own worlds, but Pearl Abbott was in *my* world."

"Stay away from her." Adeline didn't want to say it, but she had to. "Stay far away. She's dangerous."

"I already thought so because I saw her in a dream before that."

"You did? Tell me about it."

"There was like a dragon, a big blue and black one with fiery eyes and a man's voice was telling me to ride it with him. He knew my name. It was right outside the balcony of my room. I didn't want to so I started to go back inside and she grabbed me from behind really hard and tried to make me get on. Adeline, are you okay?"

The world swam.

"I'm fine. Go on, Holly. What happened next?"

"I got away. I mean I woke up. The ghost cat at the hotel, Miss Annie Patches, she jumped on the bed and licked my face and I woke up." Holly's eyes darted, searching Adeline's. "I know that sounds stupid."

"No, it doesn't." Adeline smiled faintly. "So you've met Miss Annie."

"She's come to see me every night. Well, maybe not last night. I don't remember."

"I've heard about Miss Annie for a very long time. You're lucky. She's looking out for you. She's your familiar."

"Really?"

"Really." Adeline smiled. "I'm glad she's chosen to visit you. I think that's wonderful."

Holly returned the smile. "Me, too. I think she saved me."

"Saved you from the nightmare? Most certainly."

"More than that." Holly peeled off the shirt she wore over her tank top. "I'm not sure it *was* a nightmare." She turned, showing Adeline the bruises - still dark and angry but the red had faded a little.

With effort, Addie kept her voice steady. "Pearl Abbott did this to you? In your dream?"

"Yes."

"Holly, this-"

"It happened to Steve, too. Last night, he followed a big cold spot from the elevator into the backroom and the basement door was open. Something grabbed his leg and tried to pull him down the stairs. He has the same bruises as me."

Fighting off another round of vertigo, Adeline shook her head. "My Lord."

"Adeline? Why is Pearl Abbott hurting people?"

"Pinching Pearl - what she did in life, she does in death. She was a sadist." Adeline paused. "Holly, honey, you need to leave Brimstone. It's not safe for you there."

"I don't want to go back to Van Nuys."

"I know. But you shouldn't be sleeping at that hotel."

"I'm going to sleep over at Becky Granger's house tonight and then I'm going camping with them for a few days."

"That's a good idea. But when you come back you still shouldn't sleep in that hotel."

"Why?"

"Because *they* want you. A long time ago, they wanted Carrie. And they wanted me."

"They?"

"Pearl Abbott and Henry Hank Barrow."

"Why?"

"Because of our eyes. Holly, you have abilities you don't even understand yet. Henry Hank had eyes like ours, too, and he used the gifts that came with them for evil. But he didn't have as much gold as Carrie, or me. And, Holly, honey, you have more than all of us put together. You aren't safe here." She hesitated, hating that she was telling a child all this. But she had to. "Holly, the dragon you saw, that *was* the Brimstone Beast. That was your great-great-grandfather."

"THE VOICE CALLED IT THE BEAST," HOLLY SAID. "BUT IT'S AN Indian legend, so how could it be my great-great-grandfather?"

"Yes, it's a very old legend. Henry Hank perverted the story to his own use. At first, he did it just to impress people. Later, he used it to further his power and feed his greed."

"*Infurnam Aeris*." Holly said.

"How do you know about that?"

"Steve showed me the tile picture in the room behind the lobby."

Adeline nodded. "Henry Hank was schooled in the dark arts and used his knowledge to make himself one with what everyone called the Brimstone Beast. It's a thought form - sort of a mental creation that can be powerful enough to interact with other people if the creator really wants." Adeline bent close, eye to eye. "Holly, that is why you must leave. He's strong enough to show you the thought form, to communicate with you."

More intrigued than frightened, Holly looked up at Adeline. "You saw the dragon?"

"A very long time ago Carrie and I both dreamed of it. And once, on the day she died, we saw it."

"How did Carrie die?"

"All in good time. First, we need to discuss your powers."

"My powers?"

"The ones that come with your eyes. Like how you made those boys leave Keith Hala alone. And made the waiters go away."

"I was mad when that happened."

Adeline nodded. "So you said, but what did you feel like while you were doing it?"

"Mad."

"What else?"

"Well..." Holly thought. "Nothing except that I could see really clear, sort of like things are magnified. I just see a ton of details or something. It's hard to describe."

"I've experienced that same thing in a minor way."

"Like in a movie where the camera zooms up on something important for a minute and everything else gets blurry?"

Adeline nodded. "I understand. Now, Holly, can you show me show me how your eyes turn gold?"

She smiled. "No. I'm not mad."

"Were you actually mad at those waiters when you spoke to them?"

"Yeah, well, no, not exactly. I just really wanted them to go away and not look at Miss Delilah."

"Okay, well, I think that means you've already learned a little about how to use your gift." Adeline smiled. "Tell me, sweetheart, do you usually get whatever you want?"

"No, Cherry doesn't have much money or anything, so I don't think about buying stuff. That'd make me sad."

"How about when you want to watch a TV show and your mom doesn't?"

Suddenly, Holly understood. "Yes! My mom hates that I watch *Dark Shadows* after school if she's home, but I really, really love it and it's like she says no once but I keep thinking about how much I want to watch it and then she tells me it's okay. But she's not very strict, so, I think she just gives in easy."

"Hmm. Holly, let's try something. You go over to the candy display and concentrate on something you'd really like. Don't tell me, just think about it. I'm going to turn my back. Go ahead."

"Well, okay." Holly walked around the counter and looked over all the candy. Her favorite was there. She thought, *I want a Jolly Rancher Apple Stix* as hard as she could.

"I think I know," Adeline said. "But keep thinking it, don't stop. Think very hard."

"Okay." As Holly concentrated, she became aware of every detail – the tiny bubbles and ripples in the green stick of candy, of how it must have flowed and hardened before it got cut and wrapped.

Adeline stood up suddenly and reached across the counter, picked up a Jolly Rancher and stared into Holly's eyes.

"That's right!" Holly said.

"Keep thinking about it." Adeline reached out and touched Holly's chin, lifted it and stared into her eyes for what seemed like forever. "Holly, you're amazing."

The back door opened and Ike Chance entered the store. "Well, goodness, what are you two up to?"

Adeline glanced back then looked at Holly again. "See if you can get Ike to pick you out another candy bar."

"If you really want me to."

"I do." Adeline turned to her husband. "Look at Holly's eyes when I tell you too, Ike."

He joined his wife, with a grin for Holly. "I never ask why, I just obey."

Holly smiled then looked over the candy. Next to Apple Stix, her favorite candy was Mounds Bars. She concentrated until her vision seemed to magnify.

"Look now, Ike," Adeline ordered.

Ike gasped. "Lord Almighty!"

"What?" Holly asked.

"Keep thinking, sweetheart."

Holly obeyed as Adeline pulled her purse from under the counter and dug out a compact. She flipped it open, turned it toward Holly. "Think hard and look!"

Holly saw her own eyes swirling with so much gold that she could barely see the blue. Suddenly dizzy, she grabbed the counter and blinked, then stared into the mirror again. Still, they were mostly gold. Finally, she rubbed her eyes and looked once more. The gold was almost gone, save for the flecks that always showed.

"Holly," Ike said, handing her the Mounds Bar. "You've earned this."

"And this." Adeline pushed the Apple Stix toward her.

"I don't understand." Holly looked at the fleck of gold in Adeline's eye. "Can you do that?"

"Not that I know of," Adeline told her.

"When Addie's all fired up, that little gold beauty mark of hers looks like it's pulsing," Ike said.

Adeline nodded. "So did Carrie's."

"What about my great-great-grandfather? Could he do it?"

"Not like that," Adeline said, "but his fleck would get brighter - although I'd call it more of a sulfur-yellow than gold, and only for a second or two." She shivered. "The day Carrie died, we saw it." She paused. "Holly, show Ike your arms."

Holly lifted them, turning to display the marks to Ike.

He bent close. "Somebody really grabbed onto you, young lady. Hurt much?"

Holly shook her head. "Only when it happened."

"Pinching Pearl Abbott did that to her." Adeline's hands went to her hips. "She's back. She got Steve Cross, too." Shooting Ike a look, she added, "Holly saw her. And she saw Henry Hank in the form of the Beast."

"Lord save us all." Ike shook his head.

Holly turned to Adeline. "So, you think Pearl Abbott grabbed Steve, too?"

"Most like, sweetheart, most like."

"They didn't call her Pinching Pearl for nothing," Ike added.

"I thought it might have been my great-great-grandfather."

"It was Pearl. That was the kind of thing that old witch was known for." Ike winked at her. "She was a witch with a capital B, if you get my drift."

"Ike!" Adeline elbowed his ribs. "Enough." She looked at Holly. "But he's right. She was a mean one. Even the patients tried to stay out of her reach."

Ike cleared his throat. "I once saw her lead one of her nurses out of the hospital by the ear. Poor girl was sobbing."

"Holly," Adeline said, all business, "did Steve have any idea about how that basement door got unlocked? Henry Hank's lair was down there and it should have been locked up tight."

223

"No idea."

"Well, someone unlocked it and I doubt it was anyone breathing." Adeline sat down with Holly. "Don't go near that basement door. Don't go in the backroom, either. Promise me."

A shiver traveled down Holly's spine. "I promise. I'm not taking the elevator anymore, either."

"Good." Adeline took a gas station business card from behind the counter and scribbled on the back. "This is our home number, Holly. I want you to call me anytime, day or night, if you see anything or anything happens. Call me even if you have a nightmare. Do you understand?"

Holly nodded, feeling a little annoyed. Adeline was taking everything so seriously that it was starting to seem ridiculous.

"And, Holly?"

"Yes?"

"If you encounter something - anything - that scares you, remember, you have a very great power within you. You can use it, just like you did on those bullies on the playground and the waiters in the restaurant. Just remember, don't be afraid."

Holly stood. "I will."

"Are you going back to the hotel now, sweetheart?"

"I don't know. I was thinking of going down to the drug store."

"If you do, it's very hot out, and we're a mile up, so the air is thinner than you're used to," Ike chimed in. "You might want to walk your bike back up at least part of the way." He winked. "And stop by here. There's a soda with your name on it in the cooler."

Holly smiled up at Ike, then Adeline. "Thank you."

As she left the building, Adeline called after her to be careful. That felt kind of nice.

IKE PUT HIS HANDS ON ADDIE'S SHOULDERS AS SHE STOOD WATCHING Holly biking toward town. "What're you thinking, old girl?"

She faced him. "I'm going to have to speak to Dee about Holly's safety."

Startled, Ike asked, "How are you going to manage that?"

Addie swallowed. "The mountain won't come to Muhammad, so ..."

He didn't even try to hide his surprise. "You swore you'd never go up there again."

"I know." Addie straightened the red bandana in his pocket matter-of-factly, but a fine tremble betrayed her. "It's been a lifetime, Ike, but frankly, I'm more afraid of Delilah Devine than any old ghosts."

LIP CURLING IN ANNOYANCE, ARTHUR MEEKS LOOKED AT THE DO Not Disturb sign on Little Miss Fancy Pants' door. He doubted she was in there, but he couldn't be sure since she'd taken to putting it up whether she was there or not. *Damned little bitch.*

He made it a point to explore every guest room and he especially wanted to explore hers, but the little bitch was cramping his style. Disgusted, he crossed the corridor and used his skeleton key on Cherry Devine's room. Obviously, she still hadn't been back. On a previous expedition, he'd already found her vodka in the freezer and filled his favorite flask with the stuff - he knew from long experience she'd never notice that he'd topped her booze off with water. He'd found a baggie of marijuana in the freezer too, and had taken it to sell in town. What was she going to do? Report it missing? The cheap cunt wasn't that stupid.

He opened her drawers and rifled through her things - he'd already lifted a pair of satiny red panties that smelled like sweaty pussy and he rarely took more than one article of clothing from most females. One was all he needed, after all. Disgusted, he left the room and took the elevator down to the lobby. He'd polish a few carts to keep Meredith from nagging him and get a gander at the register. There were several new guests whose belongings he had yet to visit, and he especially wanted to check out the family in the second floor suite. They had three kids, and two were girls. Mom wasn't too shabby either.

33

STINKEYE

When Holly arrived in downtown Brimstone, she was already dreading the ride back up. It was so hot that damp strands of her ponytail stuck to her neck and the relentless sun was already pinking her arms and legs. But that was nothing compared to her thirst.

She parked her bike in the rack outside Gower's Drugs. The druggist was the person she really wanted to talk to. After double-checking the change in her shorts pocket - there was plenty for a root beer float and a bottle of soda to drink on the way home - she stripped off her outer shirt and dropped it in the bike basket - it was too hot to wear it and she really didn't care about strangers seeing the bruises.

Bells tinkled as she pushed the glass door open. Inside, she shut her eyes and let the refrigerated air fan over her body.

When she opened them, Eddie Fortune, in a white cap and apron, was leaning on a broom watching her, a big grin on his face. "You're sunburned."

She felt herself blush and hoped the burn hid it. "Hi, Eddie." His blue-gray eyes, the sweep of his brown hair across his forehead, and the dimples when he smiled made her feel funny, like she'd just stepped off a roller coaster.

"Can I help you?" Another heart-stopping grin. "Or are you just here to cool down?"

"Yes, I mean, I want to buy a root beer float."

"Mr. Gower is at the soda fountain. He'll make you a big one." Eddie paused. "You were here the other day."

"Right, with my grandmother."

"And your name is . . . Don't tell me. Holly!"

She grinned. "How did you know that?"

"My cousin, Steve."

"I like Steve. He's great."

"He is."

"He says you know even more ghost stories than he does."

Eddie's gaze intensified. "He said that?" A wide grin.

"He did."

"Ha! So, he finally admits it. I collect ghost stories. And UFO stories and stories about cryptozoology."

"Crypto-what?"

"Weird animals, like the abominable snowman. Come on." He began walking toward the soda fountain. "You know about the abominable snowman?"

"A little. It's very interesting. All of it." She climbed onto a red stool and he spun her toward the counter.

"Mr. G? Customer for you!" Eddie called then went back to sweeping the aisles.

The old man came out from behind the cash register at the far end of the counter and gave her a smile. "What'll it be, young lady? Another root beer float?"

Holly was surprised. "Another?"

"Once you've had one, you have to have another." He smiled. "Root beer floats are the secret of my success."

"Yes, please."

"Coming right up." Gower scooped ice cream into a silver cup. "How's your grandmother today?"

"Fine."

"Glad to hear it." Slowly he added root beer, careful not to let it foam too much. "Here you go, little lady. Holly, isn't it?"

"Thank you." She couldn't believe he remembered her name, too.

"You're very welcome. You put me in mind of Delilah's big sister, Carrie, may she rest in peace."

Holly sipped the creamy, fizzy perfection. "Miss Delilah told me that, too. Thank you."

"You're welcome." He hesitated then stared at her with somber eyes. "Those are some serious bruises you've got on your arms."

Holly tasted the ice cream. "Steve Cross says you knew Pearl Abbott a long time ago."

He nodded. "And he told *me* you had a run-in with her."

Ben Gower glanced around the drug store then, satisfied, turned back to Holly and spoke softly. He nodded at the bruises. "Pinching Pearl did that to me on more than one occasion."

"When?"

"When she was among the living, back when I was a delivery boy." He leaned against the counter, hands folded. "Steve came by asking about Pearl. Says you saw her in the elevator."

Holly nodded. "And I had a dream and she grabbed me in it. I woke up with bruises."

"I've never heard of a dream leaving you with bruises. Leastwise as long as you don't fall out of bed or sleepwalk."

"Me, neither."

"Um-" Eddie appeared from behind a display of suntan lotion.

Ben looked at him. "Couldn't help overhearing, son?" He gave Holly a grave look. "The boy has big ears."

"May I say something?" Eddie asked.

"That's up to Holly." Ben gave him a warning look.

Holly turned to Eddie. "Yes. I want to hear."

Eddie cleared his throat. "There are lots of theories about being bruised - or bitten - in dreams. Depending on what you believe in, the answer varies from demons to hysteria, but it all boils down to the same thing. Something is attacking you while you're sleeping."

"Eddie-" Ben began.

"It's okay." Holly looked from Eddie to Ben. "Adeline Chance says I shouldn't sleep at the hotel because they want me."

"They?" asked Eddie.

"Pearl Abbott and my great-great-grandfather. Because of my eyes. She says they want my power."

Eddie looked confused, but Ben nodded. "Addie and Carrie had eyes like young Holly here, and they saw ghosts. They'd come in for a soda - just like you, Holly - and sometimes they talked about seeing a phantom orderly who pushed a cart with a bad wheel. Oh, and a cat. They saw a calico cat."

Holly smiled. "Miss Annie Patches. She woke me up when Pearl Abbott was hurting my arms. Adeline says Annie's my familiar."

"If that's what she says, it's no doubt true. Listen to her."

"I will."

The doorbells jangled and a heavy-set lady in a black and white polka dot dress walked in, fanning herself. "Ben? Ben Gower? Where are you? I need my water pills!"

"Coming, Mrs. Stuffenphepper." Ben smiled at Holly and went to greet the Polka Dot Lady.

Spooning ice cream into her mouth, Holly watched him lead the woman to the drug counter. Her dress reminded her of a bedspread Cherry hung around her bed for privacy when she had a boyfriend over.

The entry bells jangled again and Keith Hala walked in. Holly waved. "Keith! Over here."

Grinning, the boy joined her and ordered a strawberry ice cream cone when Eddie showed up a few seconds later. "I told my grandfather about you. About what you did. He wants to meet you."

Eddie gave Holly a look and spoke in mock parental tones. "What did you do?"

Holly blushed again. "Nothing."

"Nothing?" Keith said. "Nothing?" He looked at Eddie. "She made Tony Pimbrough wet his pants!"

Keith and Holly both giggled as the Polka Dot Lady glared at them.

Eddie looked from Keith to Holly in amazement. "Really? You did that?"

Keith nodded. "She really did. Swear to God."

"They were picking on us at the playground," Holly said quickly.

"Those two butt-breaths were picking on you? They were in my grade until they got held back twice. Stupid bullies. Nobody but cowards picks on little kids."

Holly felt hurt.

"What did you do, Holly?" Eddie asked.

"Nothing. I just told them to get lost."

"She gave them the stinkeye, too," Keith bragged. "Big time."

"I'll be back." Eddie reluctantly left to wait on a new customer, a little man with a cleft chin so deep that Holly thought there were probably pirates hiding in it.

"That's the Baptist preacher, Reverend Swallows. He's kind of a jerk." Keith finished his ice cream. "You want to go back to the playground? I'll bet Shawn and Tony aren't there today."

"Sure. But I rode down on my bike. Do you have one?"

"Yeah, but it's too hot for that and it's like a mile out of the way. If we hike up the trail it's not very far at all."

"Can I walk the bike up?"

Keith thought. "No, probably not. Hey, Eddie?"

The young man paused on his way to the soda fountain. "What?"

"Do you think Mr. Gower would be okay with Holly storing her bike here until later?"

"Sure."

"I can't," said Holly. "It's not mine. I borrowed it from Meredith Granger."

"It's too hot to ride up," Keith told Eddie. "And I want to show her the shortcut."

"Steve comes by every day before going to the hotel," Eddie said. "He has a pickup. He can bring the bike up."

"But—"

"Keith's right," Eddie said. "It's too hot. Take the trail. It has shade and Meredith won't mind." He pulled a phone up from under the counter. "You can call and ask if you want."

Holly decided that was a very good idea.

THE STEPS BEGAN AT AN ANCIENT RETAINING WALL NEAR THE TOP OF Main Street, not too far from the Humble Station, and though tall and steep at first, they were easy to climb. Soon they transformed into a series of broad switchbacks, part wood, part earth, part stone. It was surprisingly shady, lined with shrubs, flowers, and trees, and Holly thought taking it was a great idea, at least until Keith yanked her back just before she stepped on a rattlesnake sunning itself on a stone.

After that, she kept her eyes on the trail until low green shrubbery studded with white flowers crisscrossed a ten-foot portion of the path. "Wow. Look at the morning glories."

Keith halted. "Those aren't morning glories."

Holly bent, looking at the trumpet-shaped flowers. "Really?"

"That's jimson weed," Keith told her. "It's poisonous. My grandfather said never to touch it. Sometimes shamans used to use it to have visions, but it was dangerous even for them."

"I wonder why it's growing right here." She raised her half-empty can of Coca Cola to her lips. It tasted good even though it was warm now.

"You want to see something cool?" Keith asked.

"What?"

He pointed at a narrow trail half hidden in weeds. "If we go just a ways, we can see the haunted house. Do you want to?"

Holly hesitated only a fraction of a second. "The place with the rocking chair?"

Keith nodded. "Yeah, it's pretty spooky in there."

"Okay. That sounds great."

They turned onto the narrow path, Keith in the lead. As they passed more jimson weed, Holly pushed her bangs off her forehead and wondered if they'd see any ghosts. As nervous as she'd become about seeing them at the hotel, this was different. It was exciting. Fun.

Less than five minutes later, the trail ended in a wide spot. Everything green fell away, even the jimson weed. A ramshackle old house stood in a clearing. Everything around it was dead.

"There it is." Keith spoke softly, as if he didn't want to be overheard.

Holly nodded. "Wow."

It was a ruin, a dilapidated mess, for sure, and bigger than Holly had expected. Way bigger. Two gnarled old trees, dead, leafless skeletons, framed the tall building. The house itself was covered in parched, faded clapboard, once orangish, maybe the color of rust, and the corrugated tin roof shone dull gray in the hot sun. Holly stepped closer, looking at the broad but broken wooden stairs that led to a covered veranda. Pale blue paint hung in curls from the porch ceiling. The curlicued columns that held up the porch roof were oddly ornate for a house with a tin roof.

The windows were half-broken victims of boys and rocks and revealed nothing but gray twilight on the first floor. Suddenly, something pale moved in one window. Holly jumped, then realized it was just an old piece of curtain waving in the summer breeze.

Keith watched her. "Well, what do you think?"

"I don't see any ghosts yet." With a quick grin, she walked to one side of the house, then the other, where she stared at a tall cement staircase that stood at least six inches from the wall and led to an upstairs door. "That's weird."

"For sure. Let's check it out!" Keith started up the freestanding steps, hand lightly skimming the old iron railing. Holly followed. When she was even with a first floor window, she bent and peered in. From here she could see turquoise paint on the walls of the front room. Though peeling and stained, it gleamed bright where stray sunbeams hit it and somehow that made the house even creepier. Beyond that, she saw a dark doorway at the far end of the room. She craned her neck, but couldn't spot a rocking chair.

Taking the stairs, she joined Keith, who stood looking in a small window beside the second floor door. "See anything?"

Keith jumped and nearly lost his footing. Holly grabbed his arm. Both looked down. Up here, the stairs were at least a foot from the house. They looked at each other, breathing hard.

"You scared me!" Keith dragged his eyes up to Holly's.

"I'm sorry. I didn't mean to!"

"It's okay. Look inside." He pointed at the window.

It wasn't broken and layers of grime stuck to it, but Keith had rubbed a spot clean enough that you could just see in. Holly, mindful of the foot of daylight between the stairs and the house, tried to make out what was beyond the haze on the inside of the glass. Sunlight pierced holes in the tin roof like bullets, spotlighting the dark floor and grimy turquoise walls. "It's a hallway."

"Yeah. See the doors?"

"I do." The doors, once white, were all neatly closed. "Do you think there's anything in the rooms?"

Keith giggled. "Maybe piles of dead bodies?"

Holly snorted. "All chopped up in pieces!"

"My grandfather says this was a boarding house for nurses for a while, but they moved out."

"I wonder what happened."

"Maybe they were murdered!" Keith suggested.

Holly nodded. "Maybe they're still there, in their rooms." A million ghost stories swirled into her brain and she loved them all. "Keith, this is so much fun! Back in California, my girlfriend and I would walk around the neighborhood and I'd tell her ghost stories about the houses and people we saw. But she didn't really like them. She got scared, you know?"

"I like getting scared." Keith peered in the window with her. "It's fun."

"I know."

Keith looked at her. "Have you ever been scared for real?"

She nearly said no, but the scare was too recent, too personal, to deny. "Yeah."

"By a ghost?"

Somberly, she nodded.

"Tell me."

She glanced in the murky window. "Not right now. I want to have fun here. You want to go in?"

"Upstairs?"

"Sure." Holly tried the knob, and to her surprise, it turned. "Have you ever been upstairs?"

"No. Just downstairs, just for a minute. It's a lot spookier inside." He hesitated as Holly pushed the creaky door open. "Maybe we shouldn't go in up here."

"Why?" Holly almost teased him about being scared, but he didn't look afraid. He looked like he was thinking.

"Because these old buildings have lots of rotten wood, especially if the roof leaks - and this one does. My grandpa says never to go upstairs in ruins like this because you're likely to get killed. He says never to go in here downstairs either, because it has a basement and the floor can break through."

Holly peered in, saw no sign of broken floors, and it made her want to go in all the more. "What if we watch where we walk?"

Keith considered. "Well, maybe if we're really careful."

"Let's just go in for a minute. We'll come back out if it's too dangerous."

"Well ... I guess."

"I bet nobody's been up here for a million years. We'll be the first. There might be all kinds of neat things in there!"

"Okay, but you follow me, and step where I step. I've explored stuff with my grandpa before, and he showed me how."

"Okay. You lead."

The inside of the old house smelled like dry wood and dust. A sickly sweet scent that made Holly's nose twitch hung behind the other odors as they trod lightly on the creaking wood, staying near the walls. Long creases of black edged the floor moldings and patches of mold stained the walls where rain had come in. Holly stepped away from Keith as they neared a door on the other side of the hall.

"No, don't walk in the middle!" he ordered.

"I want to see what's inside."

"The floor is really bad; can't you hear it creaking? It's worse in the middle."

"But–"

"There's a door on this side coming up. We'll open that one."

Knowing he was right, she moved back behind him. They halted at the door and Keith turned the knob. The door creaked open and they gasped. There was a huge hole in the ceiling in the middle of the room and the wooden floor was littered with plaster. Beyond that, in the far corner, stood the shadowy form of a woman. A headless woman.

"Holy crap," Keith whispered. "Do you see that?"

"Uh huh." Holly stared at the figure, but it didn't move or resolve into a person. She stared harder, willing her eyes to super-see like they had when she practiced with Adeline. After a moment, her vision strengthened. "It's not a ghost. It's a dress form."

"A what?"

"It's a model you use when you're sewing clothes." She stepped over the threshold, but Keith yanked her back by the arm.

"The floor is ruined. You'd fall through it."

"Yeah, okay." She stopped concentrating - she didn't want Keith to stare at her eyes - and contented herself with looking around the room. It was the same ugly turquoise and the sickly sweet smell was strong. She wrinkled her nose.

"It's rotting wood," Keith explained. "Come on."

She pulled the door closed and followed Keith along the hall. There was one more door and when they opened it, the room was small and simple and held nothing of interest. They moved until they arrived at the stairs.

"Wow!" Holly touched the nearest bannister, ran her hand over the cherry finish. Dust came away on her fingers, but the rail was smooth, shining, and perfect. "It looks almost new."

Keith nodded. "It does."

They peered into the dim main room below - the gray light entered mainly through the windows. It was just enough to see the planked floor and the bottoms of the bannisters - she even saw a single shredded curtain on the front window.

They looked at each other. "Is the rocking chair down there?"

Keith nodded.

"Want to go down?" Holly's eyes were getting used to the darkness and she could now see an old pendulum clock hanging on the wall, the hands stopped at twenty of four, like a frowning slash of a mouth.

"The stairs aren't safe." Keith said. Thoughtfully, he reached out and gripped the bannister, shook it. It didn't budge.

Holly watched him. "That looks safe."

"I dunno." He tested it again. "Maybe."

"Let's. I've always wanted to slide down the stairs."

After a long pause, Keith spoke. "Okay, but do exactly as I do. Step where I step. And wait until I'm all the way down and say it's okay."

Holly nodded as Keith took a cautious step closer, tested the bannister once more, then threw his leg over the rail and looked up at Holly. "Ride 'em cowboy!" he cried and slid down to the first floor.

Holly waited, watching as he dismounted. "Okay, come on down."

"Thanks for dusting it for me!" She settled onto the rail and raised her arms like she was on a roller coaster until Keith ordered her to hang on tight.

She slid down the steep rail and as she cleared into the first floor, the atmosphere changed. "It's chilly down here," she whispered.

"It always is," he whispered back.

"How many times have you been here?"

"A few. It's creepy, huh?"

"Yeah. Where's the rocking chair?"

"I don't know. It was in here before."

Except for the old wooden clock, there was nothing in the room but a moldering braided rug near a window. There were ugly dark stains about five feet up on one turquoise wall and on the floor beneath it.

"Blood stains," Keith said softly.

"Really?"

"They look like bloodstains, don't they? They're really old."

Holly took a step toward the stained wall, cautiously testing each board as Keith had. Finally, she stood before the stain. It really might've been blood, the way it was all in one spot except for small spatters on either side. It had run to the floor and puddled there. A foot out from the wall was another, bigger stain.

Keith joined her and she pointed to the wall stain. "If somebody got murdered, that's where he was standing when they blew his brains out." She pointed at the floor. "And that's where he fell."

"You think?"

"If it's blood."

"Yeah." Now Keith pointed. "The kitchen is back there. Come on."

The kitchen was empty save for an old rusted farm sink hanging at an angle on the wall. The cracked yellow tile looked bleached and pitted and there were traces of linoleum still clinging to the wood plank floor. The room was bright and hot with sunlight streaming in through broken-out windows. You could see places where cabinets had hung, but it wasn't very interesting. There was a door at the far end. "Basement?"

"Probably."

She looked away - basements were officially on her too-creepy list now. "Let's go see the other rooms now."

"Sure."

Returning to the living room was a shock. In the shadowy room, it felt so cold that she wished she had a sweater. And then she remembered the cold at the hotel elevator, the chill fingers stabbing her arms, and how freezing cold Steve's ankle was where he'd been grabbed. "Keith?"

"Yeah?"

She scanned the room but saw nothing unusual. "It's too cold in here. It feels weird."

"I know."

"It shouldn't be this cold. It's like a hundred degrees outside!"

"Yeah, it's weird. But it's okay, it's always cold in here. It must be because it's haunted."

"But I don't see any ghosts."

"Neither do I." Keith hesitated. "Have you ever seen one?"

"Yes." She told him what her grandmother said about Carrie's and her eyes, then added, "Adeline Chance up at the Humble Station can see them, too. She's my cousin and we all have special eyes. We see ghosts. I don't see any here, but sometimes it's cold like this when they're around, you know? And when it's this cold, it's not nice."

"Why didn't you tell me before?"

"Well, you were already freaked from my eyes when I got mad at the bullies."

"Yeah, I guess, but I thought it was really neat." He lowered his soft voice to a bare whisper. "It's okay I told my grandpa, right?"

"About the playground thing? Sure. Just don't tell any kids or anything. When school starts, if I get to stay, I don't want to be called a weirdo or anything."

"I'll never tell, cross my heart." He took a deep breath. "Grandpa told me you could probably see ghosts, like Adeline. He knew you were kin. But he said I couldn't say anything unless you did."

Holly rubbed her goosebump-covered arms, her eyes on the dark doorway on the other side of the room. "Did you want me to see if there are any ghosts in there?"

"Well, yeah, sort of."

"Okay." She nodded at the dark doorway. "Do you know what's in there?"

"Just another empty room." He paused. "You want to see if the rocking chair's in there now?"

"Yeah."

The short hall beyond the dark door led to three more doorways. Sunlight streamed in the one in the rear - it was next to the kitchen, she realized. She started to step that way, but Keith stopped her, pointing - the floor was splintered and sodden, broken through. The room straight ahead, also doorless, lay in shadows, but after a moment, she was able to see into it. "Look!" she whispered.

The rocking chair sat in the center of the empty room.

"Somebody must've moved it."

It felt even colder here and there was a darkness in one corner that seemed to waver. She stared at it, then at the other corners, almost sure there was something different - something darker - about this one.

"You want to go in?"

Holly gave the barest shake of her head. "I don't think so."

"Do you see a ghost?"

"Maybe."

"Where?"

She nodded her head toward the dark corner beyond the rocking chair. "It might be my imagination."

He stared for a moment. "I don't see anything."

As he spoke, a misty column of translucent blackness detached itself from the shadows and glided toward the rocking chair. The chair creaked as it was cloaked in darkness.

And began rocking.

"Holy crap!" Keith whispered, grabbing Holly's hand, tugging it. "Do you see that? It's moving!" His breath frosted.

"I see it." Holly squeezed Keith's hand as the chair rocked harder and harder, all in the space of a few seconds. "We'd better go."

The chair suddenly flipped into the air and hurled toward them. "RUN!" The chair cracked and broke against the door frame as Holly yelled, and the column of darkness glided toward them.

They ran straight to the front door. It wouldn't open, wouldn't even budge. The dark wavering mass hovered nearby, emanating cold and anger. "Stay away from it!" Holly ordered as they checked the front windows - too much sharp pointed glass in both.

"The kitchen!" Keith yelled. "There's no glass in those windows!"

The darkness rushed at them as they ran, and then it was suddenly in front of them, blocking the entrance to the kitchen. "NO!" Holly screamed, grabbing Keith's arm as he ran smack into it. Too late to stop him, she entered it too, pushing him forward.

Time stopped. It felt as if she were a fly stuck in a blob of freezing cold goo. There was no air, no sound, and they moved like they were in Jell-O. She squeezed Keith's hand; he squeezed back, and that was all she needed to fight on. She pushed him with her other hand and heard herself yell, "Run!" It sounded as if she were in a long muffled tunnel.

And suddenly, they pressed through the darkness into the bright, hot kitchen. She pushed Keith at the window and he scrambled through. As she tumbled out behind him she looked up. The darkness hovered in the shadowed doorway, cold and hateful.

"We win!" Holly screeched as she hit the dirt. "We win!"

ADELINE CHANCE HAD PUT ON A SUMMER FLORAL DRESS AND A little lipstick before leaving Ike in charge of the gas station. Now, she pulled her white-over-aqua Rambler into a parking spot in front of the Brimstone Grand and got out. She stared at the lobby doors, fear in her heart. It wasn't Dee that she feared - it was walking into the place where she'd nearly lost her life - and where Carrie had died.

She straightened her dress, brushed off imaginary crumbs. She had nearly worn white gloves and pumps for the visit, but finally decided her nicest shirtwaist and a touch of makeup was enough. She patted her hair and started for the lobby doors, willing her hands not to shake.

It was much cooler in the lobby - the building's cement walls were thick and the ceiling fans whirred away the summer heat.

"May I help you?" someone called from behind a desk hidden by postcard racks.

"Yes, please." Addie walked toward the voice, marveling at how much had changed and how much hadn't. She'd not been in the building since it was converted into a hotel. The colors were brighter, so much happier, and the cold hospital sterility was long gone, hidden behind fresh paint, souvenirs, and the historical photos and art decorating the walls. But the structure hadn't changed. The old elevator still waited dead ahead in its alcove.

The lobby desk came into view on the right. It was a tall new desk, bearing little similarity to the nurses' station of long ago. But as she spied the copper-clad door on the left, Adeline felt chills run down her spine. That hadn't changed one iota.

"Adeline!" Meredith Granger's smile was wide enough to make flowers bloom.

"I don't ever recall you visiting us before!"

"I haven't been here since it was the Clementine Hospital." She approached, her eyes taking in every detail.

"Why not?"

Addie tried to cover her nervousness. "Never any need to, I guess, not after Carrie died. I was caught up in being a wife and mother. And business partner to Ike, of course."

"You didn't have your children at the Clementine?"

I'd sooner have squatted in a field. "No, they were all born at home with the help of a midwife named Daisy. A lovely lady, God rest her soul." She smiled wistfully. "Back then, I thought Daisy had to be a hundred years old, but I'm older now than she was by at least two decades. Perceptions do change, don't they?"

"They do." Meredith gestured around the lobby. "When I was a girl, this place was an empty shell. We were all afraid of it and we told ghost stories to terrify ourselves. I never guessed I'd be working here one day." She shook her head. "If anyone had said so, I would have called them crazy."

"I'm so glad you invited Holly along on your camping trip!" Addie suddenly felt as nervous as a cat. "She is going, isn't she?"

"I believe so." Meredith gave her a curious look. "May I help you with something?"

"Yes. I need to speak with Delilah." Adeline barely kept the tremble out of her voice.

"Is she expecting you?"

"No. This is a surprise visit."

"I'll tell her you're here. Meredith turned to the switchboard and spoke in low tones before swiveling in her chair. "I'm sorry, but her housekeeper says she's busy today."

Addie had expected to be turned down. "Tell her it concerns her granddaughter."

Meredith nodded and this time, the conversation was longer. But when she stood and returned to the desk, she looked puzzled. "I was told to tell you that Miss Delilah can't see you."

"Today?"

"Ever."

"Rubbish." Adeline paused then spoke sweetly. "Meredith, do you suppose you could pick out one of those T-shirts for me? A large. My son-in-law would love it."

"Sure. I'll be right back."

The moment Meredith left the desk, Adeline made for the stairs; Meredith might catch her if she waited for the elevator.

At the fourth landing, she paused to catch her breath then climbed the final steps to Delilah's floor and rang the bell.

A middle-aged Hispanic woman in a pink maid's uniform opened the door and warily looked her up and down.

"I'm here to see Delilah."

"I'm sorry, but Miss Delilah said no."

"I'm her cousin."

"It doesn't matter, she won't see you. I'm very sorry." With a look of understanding, the maid closed the door. The lock snicked.

Adeline turned away from the door but instead of retreating, walked the twenty feet to another door at the end of the short corridor. It bore a small sign that read, Staff Entrance.

Addie tried the knob, found it locked. *Just as well. I don't know what I'd do if it wasn't. Delilah would probably call the constable.*

She left.

"Adeline!" Meredith crooked her finger as Addie tried to pass through the lobby unnoticed.

"Yes?"

"Did you want that T-shirt?"

"I changed my mind. Sorry to put you to the trouble."

"No trouble." Meredith gave her the eye. "I hope you didn't do something that'll get me in trouble."

Addie smiled and shook her head. "No, hon, I didn't."

"Good."

"But not for lack of trying." She leaned against the tall desk and looked into Meredith's eyes. "I really do need to talk with Delilah. I've respected her wish to keep distance between us until now, but ..."

Meredith nodded. "You're worried about Holly?"

"I am."

"Is she in some sort of danger?"

"I believe she may be." Addie searched for the right words. "As for an explanation, well, I'm not sure ..."

"Does it have anything to do with-" Meredith glanced around and lowered her voice to a whisper, "Arthur Meeks?"

"That name is familiar."

"He's the bellhop here. He has a room on Holly's floor."

"Arthur Meeks. Arthur Meeks." An image of an awkward kid with a round head, close-set eyes, a hawk nose, and receding chin came to her. "I believe one of my daughters went to school with him. Strange fellow, carried around a collection of lizard tails in a pencil box and showed it to girls to try to get them to play doctor with him?" Addie made a face. "Quite the ladies' man, hmm?"

Meredith laughed. "That sounds about right."

Addie turned serious. "Is he bothering Holly?"

"She hasn't said so," Meredith confided. "Holly doesn't like him and

I've cautioned her about him. It's just that there were bruises on her arms."

"Yes, the bruises," Addie said. "She showed me."

"I think Arthur may have done it, but she won't tell me, just says she woke up with them. Is he why you're glad she's coming with us?"

"No, and while I can't say it makes me happy to know he's here, I know he's not responsible for the bruises." Adeline hesitated. "The danger to her has to do with ... the nightmares this building seems to cause her."

"Nightmares?"

"Holly is a girl who's very ... sensitive to atmosphere."

"Atmosphere? I don't understand."

"This building has a lot of history and much of it is rather dark. I guess you could say that these old walls hold a lot of emotions. Memories are embedded in them. Holly is sensitive to such things."

"You mean ghosts?"

Addie spoke carefully. "You could say that, I suppose."

Meredith's brows knitted. "Holly seems to be such a ghost story fan. It's hard to believe she'd be frightened."

"She loves ghost *stories*," Adeline explained. "What I'm talking about is a little different. I believe she senses the past; events, and especially, people who weren't, shall we say, so savory. The other night, she picked up on one such memory in a nightmare - the memory of a person - a ghost if you will - and that, I'm almost certain, is what caused the bruises. In the dream, she was grabbed by this ghost and because it was so real to her, the marks appeared."

"They sure did look real."

Forgive me Holly. "The mind is more powerful than we know, and because Holly believed so strongly that someone was grabbing her, the marks appeared. That's what I think happened."

Meredith looked thoughtful. "That's wild - but it makes some sort of sense." The desk phone rang. "Excuse me." She picked it up. "Yes?" After listening a moment, she said, "Oh, yes, Mrs. Chance is leaving now." She winked at Adeline, said, "You're welcome," and hung up.

"Is Delilah worried I'm staging a sit-in?" Addie asked.

"Nothing so exciting." Meredith smiled. "In about five minutes, the garage will open. Max will be driving Miss Delilah down to town. I think she wanted to be sure she wouldn't run into you." Meredith came out from behind the desk and Adeline trailed her to the lobby door. "Where are you parked?"

Addie pointed. "There, just behind that green VW Bus."

"Hmm. That's not visible from the garage. Maybe you should go back to your car and wait for the Rolls to pull out. But I never said that."

"You never did. I thank you, Meredith."

Addie hurried to the Rambler and waited until the Rolls pulled away. After another minute, she followed at a stately pace.

"I DIDN'T *SEE* ANYTHING," KEITH HALA TOLD HOLLY. THEY SAT ON the top bars of the jungle gym at the old playground. Ever since they'd fled the haunted house, all he wanted was to be in the sun, and was relieved that Holly felt the same way. "I mean, I saw the rocking chair - that was amazing! - but I didn't see that black thing you're talking about. I sure did feel that cold, though."

Keith shook his head, remembering how the rocking chair had flown through the air and crashed in the doorway. He could barely believe it. "That cold - it was *so* cold. And I felt like I was drowning when we were trying to run into the kitchen. Cripes, if you hadn't pushed me, I think I *would* have drowned." He smiled at Holly, but what he really wanted to do was hug her. "You saved my life." At least he got that out without sounding like a total dork.

Holly looked at her lap. "Thanks. I didn't save your life. I doubt it can kill people." She looked him in the eye. "I think it wanted to, though."

A chill ran down his spine. "Holly, have you ever seen anything like that before?"

"No, not like that. Before I came here I liked the ghosts I saw." She smiled. "They minded their own business. And they didn't see me."

"But that black thing, it saw us, right?"

She nodded solemnly. "Just like the woman in the elevator saw me. And she was almost as cold as the black cloud."

"Is it the same ghost, do you think?"

"I think if it was, she'd have looked like she did in the elevator to me." Holly paused. "And when she was in my dream and pinched my arms, she still looked the same. Not like a black cloud."

"That's scary. Can I tell my grandfather?"

"You mean tell him what happened in the house?"

"Yeah. He won't be too mad. He'll understand." Keith nodded toward the hotel - from the jungle gym, you could see the top floors. "Is it scary in there at night?"

"Not exactly. I only had that nightmare once and the little ghost kitty woke me up. Adeline told me she's my familiar and protects me."

"My grandpa would call it your spirit animal." He grinned. "I think it's pretty much the same thing."

"I believe it." Holly swung her feet. "It's a little scary downstairs, though. I'm not riding the elevator. Or going in the backroom again."

Keith realized Holly sounded more worried than brave now and he felt bad about that. He put on a big grin. "Hey, Holly, I double dare you to go back in that haunted house tonight. At midnight!"

She looked aghast for a fraction of a second, then grinned back. "You first!"

They both laughed and Keith was pretty sure he might be in love.

34

AN OVERDUE TALK

While Max parked the Phantom, Delilah entered Gower's Drugs. As soon as the refrigerated air hit, she paused to let it fan over her. Outside, it was one hundred and three, but inside the drugstore, it was pure heaven.

She took a handbasket and strolled the beauty row, buying Pond's Cold Cream, several bars of Dove, bobby pins, and emery boards. Then she moved down the notions aisle, choosing a spool of jade green thread to sew a loose button back on a favorite jacket. In the office supply row, she picked up a small packet of envelopes, then paused in front of boxes of pastel stationery sets. One featured a little calico cat at the top of the stationery and a paw print border. Thinking of Holly, Delilah picked it up, started to put it back, then placed it firmly in her basket and continued down the aisle, looking for more things her granddaughter might appreciate.

Remembering her penchant for reading, it was logical to assume the girl might like to write as well, so Delilah added a pack of multicolored Bic pens and a couple of spiral-bound notebooks to her basket. At the end of the long aisle were bookshelves full of magazines and paperbacks. She'd forgotten to bring her reading glasses but easily picked out a *Merriam-Webster Dictionary*, a *Roget's Thesaurus*, and several novels. Holly had mentioned liking something called *Dark Shadows*, so she selected a slender olive novel with that title, a black novel with a huge red orb on the front called *The Martian Chronicles* by Ray Bradbury because Holly said the author was a favorite, and finally, a novel called *Rosemary's Baby*. Delilah couldn't read the print on the back of the book, but thought it might be nice to expose the girl to something that encouraged domesticity. It wasn't that she wanted Holly to grow up having the desire to settle down, it was just that her interests in science fiction and horror were so decidedly boyish that a little family-oriented reading might be good for her. At the last moment, she snagged a thick novel by Anya Seton called *My Theodosia*. It was obviously historical, and that, reflected Delilah, ought to broaden Holly's horizons as well.

She took her purchases to the cash register just as Max entered and sat down on a stool at the soda fountain. The poor man looked half melted in the dark livery he insisted on wearing. She nodded at him, then turned to see Ben Gower smiling at her from behind the counter.

"Hot," he said as he rang up the purchases.

"Indeed, it is. I think I might need a cool drink before going back out to face the elements."

"Your granddaughter was here just a bit ago. She had a float. She's headed back up the hill now with Abner's grandson, Keith. Great kids, both of them."

Delilah nodded. "Yes, they are."

Ben stared at her purchases. "Quite a selection of books."

"Holly's a big reader."

"And a budding writer?" Ben nodded at the reference books and notebooks.

Delilah smiled. "It's only a guess."

"A wise guess. You never know what you might inspire by giving a child such things."

Delilah adored old Ben. She had when she was a little girl, too. He was a tall man who'd seemed ancient to her back then, but he couldn't have been more than twenty-five.

"Penny for your thoughts?"

"I'd like a root beer float. And I'll pay for Max's drink as well."

"One root beer float, coming up." Ben scooped up her bag of purchases, waited for Delilah to sit at the fountain counter, then set the bags beside her.

As she watched him make the float, a memory stirred. She'd come here with Carrie and had strawberry ice cream in a little silver bowl. Carrie always ordered a chocolate malt.

"Here you go." Ben set the frosty glass on a paper doily and put down a long-handled spoon, a straw, and a napkin.

Delilah could feel the sharp, bright bubbles tickle her nose as she dipped the spoon into the float. "Ben, how well do you remember Carrie?"

"Like she was here yesterday. She always ordered an egg cream."

Delilah smiled. "Ben, you're blushing."

"To tell you the truth, I had a crush on her. I was waiting for her to turn sixteen so I could ask her out. My, how she loved egg creams." He silenced, the color draining from his face.

"Egg cream? I thought she always got a chocolate malt."

"No, Dee. You loved strawberry ice cream, plain. Carrie always ordered the egg cream. Addie was the one who craved chocolate malteds."

"Addie?"

"Sure. She and Carrie were inseparable."

"I don't recall that."

Ben nodded. "Those girls were thick as thieves, always laughing and giggling. And they nearly always had you between them. You were so little and cute, holding their hands as if your life depended on it." He sighed. "The boys always stared at them, but Addie'd been steady with Ike Chance since eighth grade and though Carrie would bat her eyelashes and smile, she never settled on one." Ben's eyes were faraway. "I was hoping she'd choose me."

A sudden memory shot into Delilah's head.

Carrie on her bed, holding a pen over a notebook.

"What're you doing, sissy?"

Carrie looks up. "Writing a letter."

"A letter to who?"

"Whom." Carrie smiles. "To Mr. Ben Gower, the young pharmacist at the drugstore. I write lots of letters to him, but I never send them."

Confused, Delilah asks, "Why?"

"If I tell you, you can't tell a soul."

"I won't."

"Cross your heart?"

"And hope to die. Tell me, Carrie."

"I'm going to marry him someday."

"You are?"

"I am, and you'll come live with us and have free strawberry ice cream for the rest of your life. How do you like that?"

Delilah nods. "But he's really old."

"No he's not. I'm ten years older than you and I'm not old."

"You kind of are."

Carrie smiles, sits up, and takes Dee's hands in her own. "He's only eight years older than me."

"That's really old."

They laugh, and Dee asks, "Did he ask you to marry him?"

Carrie shakes her head. "Not yet, but he will. And I'm going to say yes. I've been in love with him since I was thirteen."

"Dee? You all right?" old Ben Gower asked. "Did my confession shock you? I'm sorry if it did."

"Ben, I don't remember much of anything about my childhood here, but you just gave me back a memory. A nice one." She reached out and laid her hand over his. "She loved you. One night I caught her writing you a letter."

"A letter? I never got any letter." The look in his eyes betrayed both hope and worry.

"She never sent it." Delilah squeezed his hand. "But she told me she was going to marry you."

Ben's eyes welled and a tear rolled down his cheeks. He removed his wire-rimmed glasses and roughly wiped it away.

"I never knew, Dee. I only hoped that she might say yes. The three of you came to the drug store at least once a week and Carrie, she often came by even more often for small sundries. I should have realized, but your daddy and granddaddy were such big shots in this town that I didn't hold out much hope." He paused. "Thank you. Thank you for remembering. And for telling me."

"You're very welcome." She stirred her float. "I don't know why I forgot that. Now that I recall it, it's like it was yesterday. I was excited. She said that after you were married she was going to bring me to live with you. I was overjoyed."

"If only," Ben murmured as someone hit the buzzer at the pharmacy counter. "Excuse me a moment."

Less than a minute passed before Ben's young soda jerk approached. He had eyes that would soon drive young girls crazy. "Do you need anything? More napkins? A new straw?"

"I'm just fine, young man." Delilah smiled. "What has you so nervous?"

The boy blushed, looked at his hands briefly, then bravely met her eyes. "Mr. Gower told me who you are, Miss Devine. *Violet Morne* is one of my all-time favorite movies. I think it's better than *Sunset Blvd.*"

"Well, thank you ..."

"Edward. Eddie. I'm Steve Cross' cousin."

"You remind me of him. I'll bet you're a good worker, too."

"I hope so." He glanced down then met her eyes again. "You own the purple Phantom parked out there, right?"

"I do, indeed. The color is called Night Violet. The studio gave it to me in honor of *Violet Morne.*"

"It's beautiful." He hesitated, his cheeks pinking again. "May I ask you a question?"

"Certainly."

"Do you think I could have your autograph, Miss Devine?"

"Of course." She smiled, charmed by the boyish innocence the young man displayed.

Eddie brought out a square paper napkin, then pulled a pen from his apron. He pushed them across the counter and watched as Delilah signed and returned the items to him.

"Thank you, Miss Devine."

"You're welcome, Eddie. Now tell me, young man, what are you planning to do with your life-"

The entrance bells jingled. An instant later, Adeline Chance came into view. The old woman looked toward the pharmacy counter, then the soda fountain, and before Delilah could turn away, Adeline saw her.

"Miss Devine?" Eddie asked. "Do you want anything else?"

"Nothing, thank you." Delilah felt Adeline's presence behind her a few long seconds before the woman spoke. "Delilah." She moved into view, her face a mask of concern.

"Hello, Adeline." The words came out sounding as chill as they felt. "We need to talk."

Delilah didn't look at her. "I believe I made it clear that we have nothing to say to one another."

"It's about Holly," Addie said, trying in vain to get Delilah to meet her gaze. "And it's far more important than any grievances you have against me."

Delilah looked at Eddie, who had backed up. "Max," she called to her driver, who still sat at the counter, reading.

He jumped up and joined her. "Yes, Miss Delilah."

"Max, this is Eddie, Steve's cousin. He greatly admires the Phantom. Tell Ben I've requested Eddie take a fifteen minute break so that you can show him the Rolls, and perhaps take him for a short ride."

"Yes, Miss Delilah." The tall, solemn driver gave Eddie a very small smile. "Come along with me, son."

Speechless, wide-eyed, Eddie nodded and followed Max. Addie watched them speak with Ben, who was between pharmacy customers. Finally, Ben nodded, Eddie took off his apron, and in less than a minute, the pair departed.

Delilah intently studied the melting remains of her root beer float. "What could you possibly tell me about my own granddaughter, Adeline?"

Addie eased onto the stool next to Delilah's. "I believe Holly is in danger. Mortal danger."

"Why do you say that?" Dee still wouldn't look at her.

Addie decided to jump straight in. "The Beast is awake. He and his bitch-queen are both awake."

"Nonsense." Delilah spoke to her ice cream. "Utter nonsense. The Brimstone Beast is just a legend. And what that has to do with Holly, I can't imagine."

Addie screwed up her courage - Delilah could freeze the Sahara if she wanted. "You're probably too young to remember, but our grandfather called himself the Beast."

"You're right, I don't remember. And it sounds like utter nonsense. Explain to me what this has to do with Holly."

"The first earthquake occurred when Holly and her mother stopped for gas at our station. They've continued since. Holly's presence has awakened him."

Delilah turned to Adeline, glaring. "You think an earthquake means Grandfather has risen from the grave? Are you daft?"

"I wish I were. Truly, I do." Addie paused. She didn't want to give away anything Holly had confided, but she had to get Delilah's attention. "Are you aware of Holly's talents?"

"She's seen the hotel's ghost cat, if that's what you're referring to." Delilah's voice hardened. "And how do you know anything about Holly? Has she been to see you?"

"Did you see the bruises on her arms?"

"Of course I saw them. But how do *you* know about them? I expressly forbade her to have anything to do with you, Adeline Chance!"

Ben Gower glanced their way; Delilah's voice had carried. Addie sat straighter and spoke softly. "I have eyes, Delilah. Eyes like Holly's. Eyes like Carrie's. And you need to know that Holly has more talent than all of us combined, including our grandfather." Addie paused. "And it's putting her in great danger."

"Talent? What are you talking about?"

"I think you know."

"How would I know? What did she tell you?"

Despite the angry words, Addie recognized fear in Dee's eyes; the same fear she had seen the day Carrie died. A variation on the truth would protect Holly better than total honesty. "I was taking a walk the other day and ended up at the old playground. A couple of bullies were picking on a nice little boy Holly was talking to. They were obviously about to get physical. I was going to step in but Holly got there first. She was angry and she told them to leave Keith alone. And just like that, they turned tail and ran as if she'd sicced hellhounds on them."

For the first time, Delilah cocked an eyebrow. "I wonder what she said to them."

"It wasn't what she said, Dee. It was her eyes. When she ordered those bullies away, her eyes turned to gold. Solid gold."

Delilah's hard expression disappeared. She looked at Addie now, really looked at her. "I saw her do that, too. In the restaurant, after the quake. She made the waiters look away while we left. Her eyes were gold." Delilah shook her head with something like awe. "That little girl was protecting me. She didn't want them to see my fear. She *knew*." Delilah hesitated. "I don't like earthquakes, Adeline. They frighten me."

Addie resisted the urge to take Dee's hand; she knew the woman wouldn't accept that much sympathy. Instead she said, "I know you hate them, Delilah, and with good reason. Do you remember anything about the day Carrie died?"

For a moment, it looked as if Dee might break down, but then she sucked it up and her voice hardened. "You killed Carrie." Her tone went stone cold. "You killed her."

"No. But if I could have, I would have died in her place. I loved your sister as much as you did. You have to know that."

Delilah just stared at her.

Addie gave Ben Gower, who hovered a dozen feet away now, a slight nod. She wanted him to hear this. "There was an earthquake that day, Dee. A strong one. Your sister and I were trying to stop our grand-father from doing something very, very bad and you helped us. Carrie sent you on a mission. Do you have any memory of that?"

Delilah hesitated, thinking. "Dust. Lots of dust. And noise and ... petroglyphs?" She shook her head. "I don't know. There was a lot of yelling." Delilah straightened her shoulders. "And then Carrie was gone but you got to live." She whispered it. "You got to live."

"I did. And so did you. Neither of us would be here if not for Carrie. She saved us all. You, me, Ben, maybe the entire town."

"She did," Ben murmured, approaching.

Delilah glanced at him. "From what?" she demanded.

"From your grandfather. The Beast." Addie paused. "He's back, Dee. Henry Hank Barrow is back. Pearl Abbott is too - she left those fingerprints on Holly's arms."

Skepticism bloomed fresh on Dee's face. "That's ridi-"

"It's a fact, Delilah," Ben said. "A naked truth. Pinching Pearl left those marks on me more than once."

"Ask Steve about the marks on his ankle," Addie said.

"What?" Delilah looked from Addie to Ben and back again.

"They're back. Henry Hank and Pearl, too." Addie held Delilah's gaze. "And they want Holly."

"Nonse-"

"It's not nonsense, Dee." Ben spoke solemnly.

"It's true," Addie affirmed. "That day - the day Carrie died - the Beast tried to take possession of Carrie and me. He wanted to add whatever small powers we had to his own."

"I see." Delilah's voice was a wall of skepticism.

"In the end, Henry Hank failed. Carrie and I were able to stop him, but at a terrible cost." Addie glanced at Ben, then back to Delilah. "His spirit is still trapped, and that's probably why no one has seen his ghost. But have no doubt; he is awake, and now that Holly is here, he wants to possess her, to destroy her soul and take her body for his own. He wants to *be* her, Delilah. He wants to *be* her."

Delilah's face remained unreadable.

"If Holly leaves Brimstone, the Beast may go back to sleep," Addie continued. "But until she leaves, she shouldn't sleep at the hotel."

"Why?"

"He's there, Dee. He's everywhere. And he's waiting."

ADDIE'S WORDS BROUGHT A MEMORY TO DELILAH, UNBIDDEN, unwanted.

Voices and weird sounds carry up from beyond the basement door of the Clementine Hospital. She opens that door and stares down into yawning dark-ness, terrified of something, but what, she doesn't know. Only the first few steps of the steep cement staircase are visible; the rest are swallowed in forever night, except for a dim amber glow far below at the base of the stairs. It's a lantern, but the dark is so thick that it only illuminates the very bottom steps; it cannot penetrate the surrounding gloom.

She's not supposed to open the basement door, ever, and she's not even supposed to be in the backroom; Carrie says it's too dangerous because of the boiler and the elevator shaft. But she had to come. She dreamed her big sister was calling her. Calling and calling.

Dawn hadn't yet broken when she arrived and sneaked past the nurses' station to slip behind the copper door.

Now she stares into the darkness, listening. Something bad is happening down there. There's scuffling. Glass shatters. She hears an inhuman growl and then her big sister pleads, "No, no, no, no, please! No!"

There's more scuffling, more growling, and Grandfather's voice - the growling voice - yells, "You'll do as you're told, both of you!"

"Get away, old man!" Carrie again, and then Cousin Addie's voice rises in a shrill scream. "Nooooo!" Something crashes. Addie screams again then, abruptly, her voice is cut off.

"Dee, I need you. Dee!" She hears Carrie's voice.

"Carrie!" Dee screams her sister's name, her hand on the stair rail, peering into unutterable darkness.

And then Carrie, hair wild, face streaked with dirt, clothing torn and bloodied, appears in the lamplight and bolts up the stairs. She thrusts a heavy black book into Dee's shaking hands. "Run! Hide it. Hide it where it can't be found! Promise!"

Delilah stares at her sister, paralyzed.

"Dee, take the book. Hide it, and never tell anyone, not anyone, where it is! Promise."

"I promise."

"GO!"

Below, she hears scuffling, then Addie's choking sobs. Grandfather yells obscenities in the dark and then a black hulk hits the lantern below, making it sway and sputter. The hulk starts up the stairs.

"GO!" Carrie screams. She pushed Dee out of the doorway. "GO!"

The door slams shut.

Little Dee runs, hearing her sister's and cousin's screams echoing behind her.

She doesn't know if they're real or not, but she runs and runs and runs, the heavy black book clutched to her chest.

"OH ..." DELILAH'S HEAD SWAM, HER VISION DARKENED, AND THEN she realized Adeline had a supportive arm around her as Ben patted her forehead with a cool cloth.

"Delilah? Are you all right?" Adeline peered at her.

"Should I call the doc?" Ben asked.

Delilah righted herself. "I'm fine. Perfectly fine. Do not call the doctor, Ben. I'm prone to fainting."

Addie studied her. "Like when something surprises you?"

Delilah nodded. "You do know how to choose your words, I'll give you that." She glanced from Adeline to Ben and swallowed her pride. "I'll be honest. When I'm shocked or frightened, my blood pressure drops quickly. That's why I faint easily. It's rather embarrassing." She glanced around - the store was quiet, no one was watching. "Thank you for keeping me from falling, Adeline. I'm fine now."

Adeline nodded and returned to her stool.

"What was it, Dee?" Ben asked gently. "A shock or a scare?"

"Both. A memory. Addie, you and Carrie were in the basement of the hospital. I heard you. I heard Grandfather. There was shouting and screaming. I was terrified."

Adeline bent closer, and the gold fleck in her eye seemed to pulse. "You heard us?"

Delilah nodded. "I'd heard Carrie's voice calling me in my head - that's why I came in in the first place. And then Carrie ran up the stairs, gave me the book, and slammed the door in my face. I never saw her alive again."

"I'd imagine that's why you thought I killed her," Adeline said somberly.

"I'm sorry, Addie." Delilah paused. "I was very young."

"Indeed."

"There's something else. Carrie gave me a big black book and told me to hide it where it could never be found."

Adeline gasped and Delilah could see, beyond doubt, that the gold fleck really was throbbing; it wasn't her imagination.

"The book!" Adeline searched her face.

"You know what I'm talking about?" Delilah asked, surprised.

"I spent years trying to find it. I searched the basement, his offices - I searched everywhere. When the hospital closed down a few years later, Ike and I prowled that place at least once a week, looking for that book. It contains the formula that will put Henry Hank Barrow to rest forever. Do you know where it is?"

Delilah shook her head. "I have no idea. None at all."

"Well, Dee, it's in there somewhere." Adeline tapped her own temple. "You've hidden the memory away."

"Yes. I don't consciously recall anything about a book, but what you say rings true."

Adeline put her hand over Delilah's. For the first time, she didn't want to pull away. "We have to help you remember, Dee. If we can find it, Holly will be safe."

35

SLEEPOVER

olly arrived at the Granger home in time for fried chicken and fresh corn on the cob. During dinner, all talk was about their campout in Oak Creek Canyon. They were leaving at dawn and planned on fishing, hiking, and swimming. They'd cook over a campfire and sleep in tents.

After dinner, they watched *Tarzan* and Holly's favorite, *Star Trek*. She'd hoped to stay up longer, but Meredith insisted the whole family go to bed early so, reluctantly, she grabbed her knapsack and followed Becky upstairs.

Trudging behind her, Holly hoped the girl would stop talking soon. She'd never stopped chattering all evening, mostly about horses and Barbie dolls and what fun they'd have playing with those things on the campout. No way was Holly going to waste a second playing with dolls when she could be hiking and exploring, but kept her mouth shut.

Becky shrilled as she opened the door to her room, "I'm so glad you're sleeping over!"

Holly didn't answer. In addition to the wall full of horses, the room was furnished with a cotton-candy-pink carpet, matching walls, fluffy white curtains, and twin beds with peppermint-striped spreads and mounds of stuffed animals. There was a record player and albums by the Beach Boys, the Monkees, the Rascals, and even the *Magical Mystery Tour* album. On the wall was a framed portrait of Jesus, as well as posters of the Monkees clowning around and The Beatles in *Sergeant Pepper* finery.

"Put your bag on the bed by the window. I hate being by the window," Becky prattled. "I'm afraid someone's going to look at me."

On the second floor? Holly was happy to take the window.

"Okay, don't take all day, I want to show you something." Becky, hands on hips, tapped her foot beside her open closet door. "Come here."

"Wow, you have a lot of toys," Holly said as she peered inside the huge closet. There was a built-in cubby that held not only a dozen board games, but an ugly orange and aqua Barbie sports car, a Daktari Jungle Set, and a tea set, white with tiny pink roses. Beside the cubby sat three big black vinyl Barbie Doll fashion cases that Becky opened to reveal four Barbies, a Midge, two Kens and a Skipper, and more clothes for all of them than Holly could believe.

"What do you think?" Becky burbled. "I'm getting a Dream Kitchen for my birthday, and a Rickey so Skipper has a friend, and an Allan so Midge can get married and-"

Holly spaced out. She didn't like the pastel pink room; she loved purple, cobalt, and ruby red. And she hadn't liked dolls since she was eight. She wouldn't tell Becky, but Barbies, especially the blond ones, made her think of stale cigarette smoke clinging to her mother's hair when she came home late at night. In Holly's head, Barbie had alcohol on her breath and giggled the same high-pitched way Cherry did when she was trying to get something from a boyfriend. Barbie was what Holly *didn't* want to be when she grew up, and the fact that almost every girl she knew loved Barbie Dolls was why Holly preferred to hang out with boys. They were easier to get along with, easier to understand.

Right now, she wished she was camping out and roasting marshmal-lows over a fire with Keith. Or talking history with Steve Cross. Or Adeline Chance. Or having a root beer float made by Eddie Fortune and listening to him tell her about, well, anything he wanted to tell her about. *Eddie's really cute.*

"Holly? Are you listening?"

"Sorry?"

"Did you hear anything I said?"

"Sure. Your doll collection is really nice."

"Thanks, but did you hear what I said about how I want to marry Davy Jones and have three babies?"

"Yes, sure."

"Who do *you* want to marry?"

"Uh, I don't know."

"Well, you can't have Davy, he's mine. So, who?"

Holly shrugged. "Little Joe on Bonanza?"

"He's cute. You want to play Barbies now? They could go horseback riding." She started to rummage in her closet.

Holly figured Becky would throw some kind of fit if she didn't play along. "I have an idea for a game. Maybe a Barbie and a Ken could be horse thieves." Holly held back a snicker at the look on Becky's face.

"Huh?"

"And the other Barbies and Ken could be the posse who catches them."

"I don't get it."

Holly smiled. She couldn't help it. "Never mind. I just thought of it because of Little Joe."

"Tell me more!"

"Never mind. You wouldn't like it."

Becky was in her face, all excited. "Tell me!"

"Well, I was just thinking ..." Holly drew the words out. "The posse could catch Barbie and Ken and hang them. String them up. You know, like in the old days." She lowered her voice. "I bet they hung horse thieves right here in Brimstone."

Becky's eyes went wide. "You - you want to *kill* Barbie and Ken?"

"I told you you wouldn't like it."

Becky hesitated. "Then what?"

"Well, then they could leave them hanging for Skipper and Midge to find so they won't be tempted to steal horses. And they could bury them. And then ..." Holly shook her head. "No, never mind. It's too much."

"Tell me!" Becky demanded.

"Well, okay. Then the ghosts of the bad Barbie and Ken can come back and haunt them!" Holly tilted her head sideways and stuck her tongue out. "They'd look like this." She laughed.

But Becky shook her head. "No, that's too scary"

"Okay." Again she wished she were somewhere else. Keith would've laughed or at least rolled his eyes.

Becky's eyes lit up. "I know! We could have a horseback wedding for them! A double wedding. I have two bridal gowns." Her eyes lit up. "And we can take them all with us camping tomorrow! It can be their honeymoon!"

"Oh, shoot," Holly said.

"What?"

"I need to go back to the hotel. I forgot something." She stood up and headed for the door.

"What'd you forget?"

"My toothbrush."

"My mom has extras for guests. I'll get you one in a minute."

Drat. Holly glanced at her watch. It was almost ten. Steve would be on duty and she really wanted to tell him what happened at the abandoned house before she went camping. Plus, her need to get out of playing with Barbie Dolls was almost overwhelming. "No, I have a special toothbrush I have to use. I need to go get it."

"Special? What's wrong with your teeth?"

"Nothing."

"Then why do you need a special toothbrush?"

Holly wanted to smack Becky. "Because the dentist said so."

"Why?"

She counted silently to three. "I don't know. I didn't ask. He just said so." She went to the door.

"I'll go with you."

Holly thought about trying her luck at using her newfound eye-power to make Becky decide to stay home, but it didn't seem like a very nice thing to do. *And what if she sees my eyes turn gold?* No, that was definitely a bad idea. Instead, she said, "I thought you didn't like going outside when it's dark."

Becky paused only an instant. "Alone. I'll be with you and we can run."

Well, it was worth a try. "Okay." At least it would kill enough time that she wouldn't get stuck playing Barbies before bed.

They tiptoed past Todd's room - he was fast asleep. Holly paused. "Becky, why are we sneaking? Your mom won't care if we go out for a minute."

"It's more fun." She put a finger to her lips then they crept downstairs, past the family room where Meredith and Michael were talking quietly, then Becky led them to the kitchen door.

A moment later, they stepped out into the warm, humid night. A sickle moon hung overhead, highlighting the thick blanket of stars that Holly had never seen in Van Nuys. She stared up, picking out the Big Dipper and Jupiter before Becky tugged her sleeve. "Come on. Let's go!"

They walked down the long curving cobblestone driveway. It smelled of night-blooming jasmine and mesquite, and of coming rain. After a couple minutes, they finally arrived at the gravel road. The pale gray gravel looked silvery-white in the thin moonlight and the hotel was a great dark hulk dotted with gleaming amber eyes. Holly scanned the windows and balconies of the fifth floor. Delilah wasn't watching. "Let's go." She started walking, her tennis shoes crunching gravel.

"Go faster," Becky urged. "It's spooky out here."

Holly couldn't imagine how the other girl could call this spooky, but she walked a little faster, but refused to run, no matter how scared Becky claimed to be.

She opened a lobby door and headed for the desk, Becky beside her. As she passed the copper-clad door, Steve's voice rang out. "Good evening. Welcome to the Brimstone Grand."

He stood up and smiled at them. "Oh, hi, guys. Becky, your mom just called. She said that next time you sneak out, you should be quieter. And if you're not back in twenty minutes, she's coming to get you."

"I told you to stay home," Holly said as Becky blushed.

"So what's up?" Steve leaned on the tall desk.

"Holly forgot her toothbrush," Becky volunteered.

The way Becky looked at him, Holly figured he was running neck and neck with Davy Jones for the job of husband.

"Holly," he said, "I brought the bike up from the drugstore. It's parked in the garage."

"Thanks!"

Becky gave her a curious look. "You rode downtown today?"

Holly nodded. "Yeah, but it was too hot to ride back up, so Keith Hala offered to show me the trail. Your mom was cool with me leaving the bike with Eddie at the drugstore, so I did."

"Keith Hala?" Becky's eyes got big. "You went with Keith? What'd you do?"

None of your beeswax! Holly was annoyed, but didn't want to show it. "He was at the drugstore so we walked up the trail to the playground." She would never tell Becky more than that - Keith's grandfather might be okay about the haunted house, but no way would she risk Meredith finding out.

Becky grinned. "Do you like *Keith?* I mean, aren't you taller than him?"

Holly rolled her eyes.

"Holly and Keith, sitting in a tree, K-I-S-S-I-N-G. First comes love then comes mar-"

Steve tapped his watch. "Tick tock, Becky. Tick tock."

Becky looked put-upon. "Come on. Let's go get your toothbrush." She tugged Holly toward the elevator.

"Take the stairs," Steve called.

Holly threw him a grateful smile.

"Why do we have to take the stairs?" Becky whined.

"The elevator's acting up."

"There's no sign on it."

Steve came around the desk and stuck an Out of Order sign on the door. "There is now." He grinned like the Cheshire Cat.

Becky looked annoyed. "Sheesh, I never get to ride the elevator!"

"Your time will come, Becky." Steve tapped his watch. "Better get going."

"Come on." Holly headed for the stairs.

"I'll wait here." Becky stared longingly at the elevator.

"Be right back." Relieved, Holly trotted to the fourth floor. As she put the key in the lock, Cherry's door opened. Holly whirled, expecting to see her mother. Instead, she found herself staring into the ratty little eyes of the creepy bellhop. Surprise etched his features and he reminded Holly of Leroy, the caretaker in *The Bad Seed*, as he rapidly stuffed something lacy and black into his pants pocket.

Suddenly furious, Holly glared at him. "You put those back. Right now." She stepped toward him.

He backed into Cherry's room, his eyes trying to dart but they were trapped in Holly's gaze. He stumbled against the foot of the bed as she advanced, caught his balance, then continued backing up. He stopped at the dresser.

"Put them back," Holly ordered. "Right where you got them." Rage filled her as she watched the bellhop simper. Rage and disgust. Her eyes zoomed in on a drop of spittle that hung from his lower lip and when it fell, Holly followed it until it dropped to the floor. As her eyes came back up, she saw a wet stain spread over the front of his gray pants. Disgust beyond any she'd ever known filled her and as Meeks put her mother's underwear away and shut the drawer, Holly's vision went crystal clear and she knew for certain her eyes had turned gold.

He should be scared!

She smiled as he tried to shrink away from her. "You're never coming in this room again, understand?"

He nodded, as meek as his name.

"And you're never, ever going in my room." Fire flowed in her veins. "Repeat it."

"I'm never going in your room." He sounded like a robot.

Holly remained in the doorway, imprisoning him. "If you ever do, or if you peep on me or if you even look at me, I'm telling my grandmother and you'll be fired. Understand?"

He nodded.

Holly backed up, her microscopic vision taking in every eyelash, every pore, every blackhead and trace of pale stubble on the man's face. His eyes were the color of dishwater and his upper lip was an ugly liver-colored caterpillar under his gigantic nose. She saw armpit sweat beginning to stain his jacket.

"Go back to your room and stay there until it's time to go to work."

She made room for him to pass and with his head down, arms flat at his sides, the big man sped into the hallway. She watched until the door of his room slammed and the lock turned.

"Holly?" Steve was on the landing. "Is everything okay?"

She nodded and, keeping her eyes on the carpet, walked toward him.

"Did something happen?"

"Where's Becky?" she countered.

"I put her in charge of the front desk."

"Good idea." The anger was filtering away, but her heart was still drumming like Ringo Starr. He knew about her eyes, so she looked up at him.

"Wow. I thought your eyes were more blue than gold."

"They change. Adeline explained it to me."

"Okay, makes sense."

She adored him for not pressing. She didn't want to tell him anything about what had just happened, didn't want to have to answer questions about the bellhop, not Steve's questions, not Delilah's, not anybody's. Not now. She manufactured a self-deprecating smile. "It was stupid. When I started to open my door, I thought I heard a noise and freaked out."

"Do you want me to check?"

"Yes, I'd like that." Her eyes had to look normal before facing Becky and she wanted to talk to Steve anyway; it was the perfect solution. She unlocked the door and stood back as he pushed it open.

Flipping on the light, he glanced in the bathroom then crossed to the balcony door, opened the blinds and peered out. "There's a couple sitting outside the room two doors down. Do you think that was what you heard?"

Relief filled her. "That had to be it. Gee, I feel like a real baby."

"Don't feel like that," Steve said. "It pays to be cautious."

"Steve, can I tell you a secret? You can't tell my grandmother or Meredith or anyone else."

He zippered his mouth with his finger then crossed his heart.

"Today, Keith Hala and I went in that old haunted house on the trail."

"It's a spooky place. Dangerous. You have to watch where you walk-"

"Oh, I know. Keith was super-careful. But that's not important." She caught his gaze. "We, well, *I* saw something. A black fog, sort of like a column, like six or seven feet tall."

"It didn't look like anyone? Like Pearl Abbott or-?"

She shook her head. "It didn't look like anybody at all, but I think it was some kind of ghost. It chased us and it was super-cold. Colder than Pearl. We got stuck inside it when it blocked the door to the kitchen. It was like walking through Jell-O. Before that, it was in a bedroom. The old rocking chair was in there, too, not in the living room like Keith thought. It made the chair rock and then threw it so hard that it broke into pieces against the doorframe. Then it chased us. It was *so* cold."

"Keith didn't see it?"

"He saw the chair moving, and he felt the cold. He said he felt like he was drowning when we were stuck inside the black cloud-thing. That's how I felt, too. He's going to tell his grandfather what happened."

Steve nodded. "Good idea. Abner's a great guy. He knows a lot. I hope you'll tell me what he says."

"I will. Maybe he'll know more about the house."

"Well, if Abner doesn't, I bet we can dig up some information somewhere. Ben Gower might remember something. Maybe even Adeline." He glanced at his watch. "We'd better go. I'll call Meredith and tell her I held you girls up telling stories."

"Thanks." They still stood staring down at the twinkling town lights. "At any rate let's get back downstairs before Becky has to check somebody in."

"Okay."

They turned and that's when the dresser mirror caught Holly's eye. "Steve! Look!"

He did.

There, in the middle of the mirror, smeared in red, was the symbol

"*Infurnam Aeris.*" Steve looked at Holly. "I wish you'd tell me you drew that as a joke."

"Me, too."

"Any idea who might have put it there, Holly?"

"Maybe it was my great-great-grandfather." She said it with a lightness she didn't feel.

Steve shook his head. "I can't think of anyone who'd do this. Hang on a minute." He disappeared into the bathroom, returned with a damp hand towel. After wiping the symbol off the mirror, he turned the white towel over, then over again. There was nothing on it, not a stain, not a mark. He sniffed it, then looked at Holly. "I don't get it. Where'd the red go? If you hadn't seen it, too, I'd think I imagined it."

"It was real," she said, trying to sound brave. "Just like our bruises."

"Yeah, I guess so. Come on, let's get downstairs before Becky comes looking for us." He paused. "I wouldn't say anything to her about this."

"No way," Holly agreed as they locked the room behind them.

UNEASY, STEVE INSISTED ON WALKING THE GIRLS TO THE GRANGER home. When he started back, he noticed the storm clouds beginning to roll in from the east. Rain would be nice, he thought as he returned to the quiet lobby, where he sat back in his desk chair, fingers steepled, lost in thought. Whatever had happened in Holly's room, it was as unnatural as the bruises they both bore; as unnatural as the bitter cold he'd experienced the other night.

The Brimstone Grand had always fascinated him; he loved its history, its ghost stories. He loved the fact that he's seen and heard the impossible within its walls on more than one occasion. All those experiences, spooky or not, had been benign. The resident ghosts had ranged from the switchboard-calling spirit in 329, to the invisible orderly with the squeaky cart who roamed the halls upstairs, to Miss Annie Patches, the ghost cat who was hanging out with Holly. There was supposedly a phantom that knocked on doors, but Steve wasn't sure he believed that one really existed.

However, he had to admit that the basement had a decidedly creepy vibe - as basements often do. But it had been safely locked and nearly forgotten.

Until now.

Until Holly had come.

He rose and went in the back office to make a pot of coffee. Waiting for it to perc, he stared at the painting that covered the *Infurnam Aeris* symbol tiled into the wall, trying to come to terms with the idea that Holly's presence had awakened dark things slumbering in the walls of the old hospital.

ARTHUR MEEKS CLOSED HIS *NAUGHTY LITTLE GIRLS* BEAVER magazine and tucked Methuselah back in his pants. Entering his dinky bathroom, he rinsed his hands then dried them on a dirty white towel - the fucking maids refused to change his towels and the Queen Douchebag was on their side. That meant that Arthur wasn't just the Grand's only full time bellman, he had to be his own maid, changing his sheets and doing his own damned laundry. It wasn't fair. The Queen Douchebag had told him he could pay a maid five bucks a week directly for the service. Fucking five bucks! That was highway robbery, so every now and then he threw his towels in an unattended laundry cart - or in the trash - and helped himself to new ones from the supply closets. He could've done the same with his sheets, but that was too much like work. Instead, he just added a blanket now and then to keep the sweaty crusted linen from touching his body.

Now, he cracked the door and peered into the corridor. The night manager and that devil's spawn girl - were long gone. *Good riddance. Nobody tells me what to do, especially a nasty twat like Little Miss Fancy Pants. Nosireebob!*

Leaving the door ajar, he grabbed his Pall Malls and knocked one out of the red and white package. After corking it in his pie hole, he took the gold lighter he'd lifted from Mona Berger, the fat old cow who regularly rented the suite on the third floor because it was right over the restaurant so she could smell food all the time. Mona was a drunk and never even reported the lighter - or jewelry - missing, but she kept coming back to the hotel. Hell, she never even missed the cash he routinely lifted; all he had to do was give her that look - the one that said she was giving him a hard-on - and she wouldn't notice a crew of naked leprechauns hosing down a burning building.

He blew a smoke ring, then another one that bullseyed right through the first, and smiled. Old Mona Fur-Burger wasn't much to look at, but she was about as observant as a hemorrhoid in Indiana, and that's what mattered.

Coughing on the smoke, Arthur opened the door wider and waved it into the hall. His room wasn't a fit place to live - it was more like a glorified closet, maybe ten feet deep and not much over six across, except where the bump of a bathroom added another foot or two. He needed a better room, but Delilah Fucking Devine, Douchebag Queen of the Brimstone Grand, said he had to pay a lot more rent for a guest room. *Fuck that!* This room had one small window that opened right against the mountain - you could reach out and grab a handful of dirt if you wanted. Or a snake. One hot night last summer, he'd opened the damned window and woke up to find a family of ground squirrels gorging themselves on his bowl of peanuts. *Little fuckers.*

They'd all gotten away except for the one he'd flattened with his bare foot.

His mind returned to the Douchebag Queen's spawn-of-Satan granddaughter. *She can't tell me what to do!* The thing he'd seen - thought he saw - was impossible; nobody could change the color of their eyes like that. Maybe the kid had a hatful of magic tricks. Maybe not - either way she was the fucking devil's daughter.

"Who do you think you are, you little bitch, ordering me to stay in my room!" He stepped into the hall and crossed to a tall ashtray beside the elevator and stubbed his butt out in the sand. "Who the hell do you think you are, little Miss Fancy Pants?"

He took two steps toward her room then, inexplicably overcome with anxiety, turned on his heel and returned to his own, locking the door behind him. As he opened his window on the dark desert night, he told himself it was because he couldn't risk getting fired. But hidden deep inside his dark heart and darker mind, was the conviction that soon enough, little Miss Fancy Pants would be the one taking orders, not giving them.

DELILAH HAD SPENT THE EVENING ATTEMPTING TO GET MEMORIES OF the meeting at Gower's Drugs off her mind. She'd dined with Vera, then they'd watched *All About Eve*, a movie that inevitably reminded Delilah of Millicent McKensy, the tawdry little tart who tried - with a spectacular lack of success - to derail Delilah's career. In the end, all she took from Delilah was Clifton, and by then, she was welcome to him.

Vera, a very good friend indeed, had suggested watching the movie, as she usually did when she sensed something was bothering Delilah. Then she asked the questions meant to get Delilah to vent, and egged her on, bringing up everything from the hair-sprouting mole on Millicent's neck to the starlet's need for dress shields, even in winter.

Delilah smiled. It had all happened so long ago that there was no malice left, at least no more than you might afford a buzzing fly. She and Vera had killed a bottle of decent Merlot and had a lot of laughs. By the time Vera left, Delilah was in a good mood. Soon after, she got ready for bed. She put on her reading glasses and picked up *Airport* by Arthur Hailey, opened it and tried to read, but the words bypassed her brain. Today's encounter - and the memories it provoked - came flooding back.

Curse you, Adeline. I don't want to remember any of that nonsense.

But the thoughts wouldn't go away. The basement stairs. Carrie's desperate face, the hulking darkness below. How she'd raced from the hospital clutching the big black book to her chest, the shouts and screams following her into the desert.

They'd seemed so real. *But you couldn't have heard them, not outside.* Delilah put the novel down. She remembered now that she'd heard Carrie's voice in her head on more than one occasion. As a child, she'd assumed it was real, but now she knew it was nothing more than wishful thinking. Those screams had been echoes in her mind. Even now, she imagined she heard them. *Dee! Delilah!*

"Stop it!" Delilah rose and slipped her embroidered silk dressing gown over matching pajamas, belted it, and left her bedroom. The huge open living area was shrouded in shadows, relieved only by splashes of moonlight and a few dim amber sconces chasing darkness from the corners of the room. It was utterly silent in her penthouse; nary a creak nor a groan could be heard. That was the way of it in a building made of poured concrete, but she never got used to it.

Opening the French doors to one of the balconies, she stepped out into the night. It was summer-warm, humid, and the mild breeze held scents of mesquite and oak - and a coming storm. She looked up at the sky - to the east, the stars had been blotted out by roiling clouds and the nimbus around the sickle moon was growing by the minute. The eastern mountains lit with faint lightning. *The storm is over Sedona. It will be here before long.* Though she loathed thunder, she welcomed the rain.

Below, Brimstone slept in relative darkness, but lights twinkled along Main Street and the spotlights of the cement plant at Lewisdale five miles northwest shone bright. Here and there on the hillsides, amber light glowed in windows; in fact, there was a light still on upstairs over at the Granger house just down the road. As she watched, the light blinked out.

"Holly." Delilah whispered the word. The girl was over there tonight and, if Delilah heeded Adeline's warnings, she'd be there every night. "I have to remember where I hid that book," Delilah muttered. Then, "Utter, absolute, rubbish."

But she shivered all the same.

❦ 36 ❦

INSOMNIA

Holly lay staring at the ceiling, not a bit sleepy, even though she was exhausted. There was something about Becky Granger that sucked the life out of her. *Probably all those Barbie Dolls!* After they returned from the hotel, Becky had insisted on showing her the doll collection - again - and telling her stories about where Barbie and Ken liked to go on dates. Holly had glazed over more than once, and when Becky tired of Barbies and finally asked Holly a question - what TV shows were her favorites - the girl had rolled her eyes and called her a tomboy when Holly named *Dark Shadows, The Wild Wild West, The Man from U.N.C.L.E.,* and *Star Trek*. When Holly grinned and said thank you, Becky had rolled her eyes again.

Holly liked it really dark at night, but Becky couldn't sleep in the dark so there were two nightlights - one a dolphin, the other a unicorn - that made the room so bright that Holly could make out the pink paint on the walls. She wished she were in her own room at the hotel, or in the lobby talking to Steve, or maybe on a campout with Keith Hala. They'd roast marshmallows and tell ghost stories and look for arrowheads.

Finally, she began to drift, lulled by the scent of rain on the breeze that slipped through the open window beside her. Half-awake, half-asleep, she wandered through dreamscapes of leering faces and absurd creatures unafraid - she'd seen them all on a million other nights as she'd tiptoed into slumber.

Something tickled in her brain and then she heard wings, great wings beating the air, then one glowing red eye peered at her and the Beast's deep voice - called her name.

Go away! She thought the command so hard, she wondered if her eyes turned a little gold. Whether they had or not, the Beast retreated from her dreams.

UNABLE TO SLEEP, DELILAH SAT AT THE LITTLE ROUND TABLE IN HER bedroom and stared at the tarot cards spread before her. She hadn't asked a particular question, but rather sought a general look at what was happening around her.

It wasn't good. First, rather than using a face card for herself, she had left it to chance. The Page of Swords, reversed. It was the card, when upright, Aunt Beatrice had used to represent Delilah as a child, and she knew beyond doubt that this meant tonight's reading would concern the past.

The Page of Swords was crossed by Holly's card, the Page of Wands. *But how is she connected to my past?*

Then Delilah realized the card had to be referring to Carrie, not Holly. The thought comforted her.

Delilah shook her head and turned over the basis card. The Hanged Man. Carrie had given herself as a martyr before she died, and that backed up what Adeline had told her at the drugstore.

The Devil was in the near past - she was sure it referred to her grandfather.

Carrie's voice echoed in her head. *He's a bad man, Delilah, a very bad man!*

Delilah turned the near future card and saw the Chariot. For an instant, she thought - even hoped - it meant Holly would be traveling soon, traveling away from the danger Adeline warned of. *No. This is about the past. It means the reading is about the time when Boston was in the near future, around the time of Carrie's death.*

Quickly, she turned the crown card. Temperance reversed - lies and dishonesty. No doubt it spoke of her grandfather again.

He's a bad man Delilah!

The next card spoke of her role in the situation. It was The Hermit. She stared at the old man holding a lantern high as he peered into a cave. It told of inner wisdom, a search for the truth. At six, she'd had no inner wisdom, was searching for no truth beyond playing hopscotch and the possible existence of the Tooth Fairy. It made no sense.

The eighth card told her what others had expected of her. *Carrie counted on me to hide that book!* She flipped it to reveal The Fool. Youth and innocence. A fresh start. *Too bad I was the only one who got a fresh start. I'm sorry, Carrie. I wish you had, too.*

She turned the ninth card, which represented hopes or fears. The Tower. Disaster and destruction. *The end of everything.* As she'd run from the hospital that day, that was what she'd feared; the end of everything. Memories swirled up for a brief instant. She gasped as she felt a sharp phantom pain in her ankle and tasted dust on her tongue. Both were gone as quickly as they'd arrived.

The final card - the outcome card - was The Magician reversed. Trickery and cunning, manipulations and deceit. *Grandfather again.*

Before sweeping the cards away, Delilah looked them over once more. Carrie had given her life to stop Grandfather - the dark magician - hoping that Delilah would be able to find a place to hide the book from him and whoever else might have wanted it. A sudden image of Pearl Abbott clouded her mind. Delilah had been mildly amused when Ben Gower had called the woman Pinching Pearl, but there was nothing remotely humorous about that now.

Her eyes landed on the Hermit again, the one card she couldn't explain. His back was to her, peering into a black cave with a light perhaps incapable of penetrating such utter darkness. Perhaps it meant she'd never remember what had happened.

She swept up the cards and wrapped them in purple silk as the first drops of rain began to fall.

HOLLY, UNABLE TO SLEEP IN BECKY GRANGER'S BARELY SHADOWED pink room, steadfastly ignored the itch in her head that accompanied the phantom beat of wings and the deep voice of the Beast rumbling through her mind. Instead, she concentrated on Night Traveling. It was a trick she'd taught herself to evade nightmares and it almost always worked. In her mind, she would travel to pretty places, like a foggy redwood forest where pink rhododendrons grew, or up a snow-covered mountain, or to the Monterey Peninsula where she'd fly around the rocky cliffs and swoop over the ocean with the seagulls. She'd glide on invisible wings, smelling pine and fog, the ocean tang, or the clean cold scent of snow, looking for deer and mountain lions.

Tonight, she'd visit the Grand Canyon because, on the trip here Cherry had stopped there. They'd spent the sunset hour staring down into the colorful painted canyons before pulling into the campground and sleeping in the car. It was peaceful there, and really, really dark. *Not like here.*

The tickle and beat of wings faded, and in her mind's eye she took flight from the rim and soared and circled over the deep colorful canyon, dipping down to see the yellows, the reds, the ochres and blues of the craggy cliffs and gorges. She swooped down low over the twisting muddy river, then up again. For a long moment, she was lost in the beauty she conjured, but then, far above, a huge shadow blotted out the sun, and a voice whispered, *'Go home.'*

CHERRY DEVINE STARED AT THE HOTEL ROOM CEILING. SHE'D BEEN fucking all day and even though she'd just stepped out of a hot bath, she still felt dirty. Pete Hoden, the director, had taken a liking to her and had been making constant use of her, and even though the pay was pretty damn good, her body felt like it couldn't stretch another inch. Between takes, she'd had to use alum to tighten up her assets.

She sat up on one elbow, popped a sleeping pill, then washed it down with a sip of water. She wished it were gin, but it was too late at night to mix the two - she had to be back on the set at 7 a.m. and she didn't want Pete to give her a second warning about being hungover.

Pete was going to arrange a boob job for her, too, but now that she'd met Hugo Todger, she wasn't sure she wanted to go that route. Hugo was in real estate, and he was rich, with a ranch in Sedona, houses in San Francisco and New York, a summer home on Martha's Vineyard and even a place on the French Riviera. On the down side, he was a big fan of Nixon, Glenn Miller, and Benny Goodman, all of whom were huge snores as far as Cherry was concerned. He was also about sixty, bald as a potato and chubby, but cute like John Fielder, the actor who voiced Piglet and starred as a Jack-the-Ripper-type alien on *Star Trek* last December. She'd wangled a job as an extra in that episode, but it had been left on the cutting room floor. Still, she'd met Fielder and found him charming, so between the looks and the fact that Hugo even had that same high-pitched voice, she really couldn't count his looks as a negative. The fact that he was always chewing on a soggy cigar was a little gross, but she figured that was a small price to pay to have just about everything she'd always wanted.

Hugo was a sweet guy in his own way, generous and quick with his funny, high-pitched laugh. He was a long-time fan and had asked Pete Hoden for an introduction; the three of them went to dinner and had a good time.

The following night, on their first real date, Hugo had proposed, calling her his perfect woman, and promising to give her everything she ever wanted, and that she'd never have to work another day in her life. When he presented a ring with a rock that would make Liz Taylor jealous, she almost said yes. Almost.

She knew she had to play hard to get, so she didn't take the diamond - it was about the hardest thing she'd ever done, but she told him she had to think about it first. "Take all the time you want, Cherry, dear. This diamond isn't going anywhere."

The next evening, he took her to his ranch outside of Sedona. The Spanish-style house was a mansion with an atrium on the first floor that held a pool, a hot tub, and sweet-smelling tropical plants beneath its tall glass ceiling. After a dinner prepared by a uniformed chef, Hugo had taken her to the pool, presented her with a swimming suit and refused to watch her change. The two of them played in the pool for an hour, flirting and kissing, but he wouldn't let her go further. "Not until we're married," he said.

How someone, knowing what she did for a living, could be such an old-fashioned gentleman, Cherry had no idea. But it charmed her like nothing else, and after the swim, when he took her out to the stables to see the horses, she said yes.

Staring at the ceiling, Cherry waited for the sleeping pill to kick in. Despite her elation, she was troubled.

They'd celebrated their engagement with a bottle of champagne and talked - only talked - long into the night before Hugo had his driver take her back to her hotel so she'd be ready for work the next morning.

Just like now. Tonight, she'd returned to his ranch. He'd given her a tour of the whole place, told her she could redecorate the master suite if she wanted, asked her which horse she would like for her own. He showed her photo albums of his other homes and told her about the vacations they'd take, the places they'd visit.

There was just one problem - the problem that was keeping her from sleep now. When he'd told her he didn't like children, she'd said she didn't have any use for them either. He asked, shyly, if she had any, and she'd instantly lied. He'd laughed his laugh and looked her straight in the eye. "Good. I'd hate to have to call off the wedding." She knew he wasn't joking.

"Sorry, kid," she murmured as her eyelids grew heavy. "Them's the breaks."

BEN GOWER, IN HIS APARTMENT ABOVE THE PHARMACY, ROLLED over fitfully in his sleep as rain gently pattered on the roof.

Pinching Pearl chases him, her freak-strong hands grasping at him, leaving burning pain where her fingertips manage to brush his shirt. He's a boy again, strong and fast, but it's that day, the day he'd found everyone in the Clementine Hospital dead.

As H.H. Barrow, tall and broad in a suit as black as his heart, laughs and laughs, Pinching Pearl chases Ben back into the hospital. The dead are still there, but now they stare at him, their faces contorted with anguish, their bodies paralyzed in horrific spasms.

He skitters around a nurse sprawled on the floor and, before him, the elevator creaks open. An inhuman orderly, one with blue scales and coppery lizard eyes, leers at him and crooks a demonic finger. "Going up?" it croaks in a voice from the bowels of Hell.

Ben turns and races up the stairs, Pearl Abbott just inches behind him, her black skirts rustling like rattlesnake warnings, her breath hot on his neck. "Got you, boy! Got you, boy! Got you, boy!" Her laughter shrills, drowning out H.H. Barrow's.

Ben dodges convulsed bodies - one dead hand grabs his ankle, but he shakes it off. The second floor hall is blocked by a pile of corpses, all staring at him. The same at the third. Ben makes the fourth floor landing, climbs over cold, dead flesh, and enters the corridor. Pearl Abbott isn't far behind. He races past gowned patients half fallen from their beds, past nurses sprawled over beds or on the floor, past a young orderly fallen backward over his toppled cart, the pills and potions scattered across the floor like marbles. Ben keeps running, making for the stairs at the far end of the hall. Glancing back, he sees Pearl Abbott is farther back now, but he doesn't slow. Instead, he leaps over a pile of bodies on the landing and starts down, breathing hard, terrified. He makes the third floor, then the second.

But when he arrives at the first, H.H. Barrow - the Beast - massive in his black suit, booms laughter, and blocks Ben's way. His eyes glitter like a snake's and the left eye throbs gold. For an instant, the man's head becomes that of a dragon with eyes as red as blood.

SUDDENLY AWAKE, BEN GOWER SHOT STRAIGHT UP IN BED AND reached for the bedside lamp with a trembling hand. He slowed his breathing then rose, turning on every light as he made his way to the living room.

He pushed the curtains aside and stared up at Hospital Hill. For a single instant, he thought he saw a huge winged beast circling the top floors of the hotel.

He shook his head. "You're losing your mind, old man. You're losing your mind."

IKE CHANCE FOUND HIS WIFE STANDING ON THE FRONT PORCH wearing only her thin summer nightgown. Inhaling the scent of falling rain, he opened the creaky screen door and stepped out. She didn't acknowledge him as he draped her robe over her shoulders, but continued to stare up at the Brimstone Grand. Only the top floors were visible and no lights were lit, leaving the building a huge black mass against the midnight sky.

"It's happening, Ike." Addie's words were soft as silk. "It's happening." She turned to him, her eyes searching. "And I don't know if there's any way to stop it."

"You spoke to Delilah," he offered. "That's progress, isn't it?"

Her nod was all but imperceptible. "Yes, it is. But she remembers almost nothing."

"The way you told it, it might be coming back to her."

"She was barely more than a baby and it's been so many years. I don't hold out much hope."

He took Addie's hand and stared at the dark building at the top of the mountain. "Well, hopefully that little girl's mama will take her back to California soon and everything will settle down."

"I hope so. I hope so."

"See that, Addie?" Ike squinted into the drizzly night. "See that?"

"What do you see, Ike?" The words trembled on her tongue.

"Funny, it's gone now, but for a second there, I could've sworn I saw something flying around the hotel, something like a big old bat. My eyes are playing tricks again."

She turned to him. "You saw that?"

"Thought I did." Gooseflesh rose. The drizzle hardened into steady rain.

"You saw the shadow of the Beast. He's getting stronger." Addie squeezed Ike's hand. "Come on, old man. Let's go inside."

☒

SOME NIGHTS, STEVE CROSS HAD TROUBLE STAYING AWAKE DURING the long lonely hours in the Grand's lobby, but tonight wasn't one of them. He'd been hearing things for the last hour or so; one was distant thunder, creeping ever closer. The other was the elevator. He'd heard it go up and down, not once, but three times, the last time, not even a minute ago. He presumed it was the phantom lift, not the real one, since no one exited. Ever since Holly had seen Pearl Abbott on the elevator, he'd doubted the existence of the ghostly handyman, but now the air filled with the aroma of cherry pipe smoke - allegedly Jack Purdy's signature greeting. It wasn't the first time Steve had smelled it, but he'd assumed it was the remnants of a real cigar floating on the breeze. Tonight, though, the entry doors were shut and no one was smoking on the porch. He stood behind the tall desk, hoping for more signs that the long-dead handyman had come to call. It was a comforting thought after the frigid ghost of Pearl Abbott.

"Anybody here?" Steve kept his voice soft, friendly. The sweet smoky odor ebbed and flowed around him. "Jack Purdy? Are you here?"

The cigar scent vanished as lightning lit the desert night. The hotel seemed preternaturally quiet and Steve began counting. Finally, the thunder came, telling him the big storm was still miles away.

Steve lifted the latch and let himself out from behind the desk for the first time since he'd walked Holly and Becky to the Granger house. Uneasy in the heavy silence, he glanced toward the elevator lobby where the cab waited, gently lit, behind the door. *Good enough.* He turned and crossed to the glass entry doors and watched the rain pattering silently on the cement outside. Unnerved by the continued silence, he pushed open one door and stepped outside.

A cooling breeze plucked at his hair and sent a few raindrops to kiss his cheeks; the wind had picked up in the last hour. Another bolt of lightning revealed an angry, roiling sky; he scented faint ozone for the first time. Thunder rumbled, close enough that he imagined he felt the electric hum of it beneath his feet. Light, steady rain began falling.

Inside, the switchboard began buzzing. Steve toed the doorstop, leaving the door two inches open, then trotted to answer the elderly board. It was room 329. As usual, it was empty. He stared at the blinking light, willing it to stop.

It didn't. He picked up the headset and put it to his ear before connecting. "Lobby."

Only static answered. He hung up. Room 329 was rented out only when at capacity. The maids didn't like cleaning it - they claimed something whispered their names in their ears while they worked. Several times guests in 329 had shown up in the lobby demanding a different room for the same reason. Whispers in their ears.

The switchboard lit up again and he opened and closed the connection without listening. Ordinarily, he loved this electrical anomaly or phone-happy ghost - or whatever it was in 329 that set off the switchboard fairly regularly. It rarely happened on the day shift, but Meredith had experienced it once or twice. One night he trotted up to the room right after a call; it was dark and empty, of course.

The switchboard buzzed a third time - it had never gone off so many times in a row before. *There must be a short.* Anxiety growing, he ended it again then realized he no longer heard the rain.

He looked up; the rain was pouring now, but it made no sound that he could hear. *That's crazy.* He saw lightning flash bright and close, hitting the earth just below Hospital Hill. But he heard no thunder.

The air thickened around him. His arms pricked with gooseflesh. He felt like he couldn't breathe.

The switchboard buzzed again, loud and clear. Steve grabbed the headset and connected, demanding, "Who's there!"

Through the static, he thought he heard laughter.

He dropped the headset and returned to the front door, stepping out onto the porch. He could hear the rain again; it came hard now, sheeting sideways, hundreds of tiny sharp pins hitting his face. Lightning crackled and hit a scrawny tree at the edge of the parking lot. The air filled with ozone. The tree blazed then extinguished under the pounding rain. Thunder came immediately, like the mortar fire of the gods. Steve's hands flew to his ears.

He looked into the storm and thought he saw a dark glittering shape gliding in the night sky. A flash of blue, a blink of red. He squinted up through the pounding rush of water and thought, for an instant, he saw a dragon riding the storm.

IT WAS PAST TWO IN THE MORNING AND THE VOICE IN HOLLY'S HEAD made staying asleep impossible. It wasn't the deep scratching rumble of the Beast. This voice was an insistent whisper - *Go home! Go home!* - and as she came fully awake she realized it was her *own* inner voice trying to tell her something. It did that sometimes.

In the other bed, Becky slept peacefully, probably because she'd worn herself out from talking so much. Holly rose and dressed, her movements covered by the sounds of the storm. It would be foolish to ignore her own voice and stay here; she'd go back to the hotel and hang out with Steve Cross in the lobby. She could even catch a couple hours of sleep behind the desk and go back to the Grangers' house at dawn. Or not. It suddenly occurred to her that the voice might be warning her not to go camping. *That has to be it!*

She reluctantly sat down at Becky's desk and wrote an excuse on a piece of notebook paper by the glow of the unicorn nightlight. Then, filled with the need to leave, she quietly stuffed her pjs and toiletries in her knapsack and let herself out of the bedroom.

She tiptoed down the dark hall, the only sound that of Michael Granger's soft snores. Downstairs, the house was dark and silent. She paused, catching her breath as she realized she couldn't hear the rain anymore. *Maybe it's stopped.* As she entered the kitchen lightning flashed just outside and thunder followed immediately, but muffled, muted. It was as if the house were wrapped in a thick blanket. Fluffy sat on a kitchen chair, watching her with bright eyes. She patted his head. "Go back to sleep." He jumped down instead.

She unlocked the back door, stepped onto the porch and stared at the rain. It was plenty loud now that she was outside. It hit the driveway with tiny explosions. *I'm going to get soaked.*

Lightning flashed again - it hit somewhere near the hotel - and thunder cracked and boomed like a cannon blast. She thought about going back inside, but the voice came again. *Go home!* It almost never happened when she was wide awake, so she knew it was important to leave. She turned the lock on the knob and pulled it shut behind her.

"One. Two. Three!" Holly raced from the porch and along the long curving driveway, rain-soaked before she was halfway down. She loved going out in the rain in Van Nuys, but it had never rained hard and warm like this - nor had she ever been out at night. She'd expected to have fun running through the rain, but it wasn't fun at all, just scary.

As she reached the road, another bolt struck the mountain right behind the hotel. Thunder shocked her ears and shook the ground beneath her feet. The rain redoubled, blinding and deafening in its intensity, slanting sideways into her face, but she pressed on, determined, trotting along the gravel road as fast as she dared, almost falling when she imagined she heard great wings flapping above her. *It's just the wind.* But she ran faster and made it to the hotel in less than a minute.

Standing under the entryway roof, she set her soggy tote bag on the wrought iron bench and pushed hair from her eyes. She was shaking off like a dog, watching the rain and trying to get a little drier when the door opened behind her.

"Couldn't stay away?" Steve looked her up and down. "You're lucky you didn't get hit by lightning."

DELILAH DREAMED OF THE HERMIT.

The Hermit, surrounded by sagebrush and manzanita, stands beside a tall slender stone swirled with gray and red. He holds a lantern high in one hand and peers into an oddly triangular opening a couple feet off the ground.

Delilah approaches quietly and stands beside him. She's just tall enough to see into the little cave and what she sees takes her breath away. The walls are covered with primitive art, men holding spears and arrows and bows, all running deeper into the cave. Beside her, the Hermit lifts his glowing lantern higher and now she can see the giant winged snake on the ceiling - a dragon - raining fire down upon the figures, its talons full of bleeding bodies.

Delilah recoils.

"The Beast is on the hunt," the Hermit tells her. "They can't stop him." He looks down at Delilah and she sees his seamed face, realizes he is a native and

holds a flaming torch, not a lantern. His robe is buckskin and he has no beard, only long graying braids. His dark face is seamed with the sun and gold dust swirls in his eyes until they shimmer like the sun, holding her, mesmerizing her.

Delilah stares at him, unafraid. "Who are you?"

He looks at her somberly. "I am the one who holds the book for you. You asked me to keep it a very long time ago. Do you remember?"

She shook her head. "No."

"You must remember. It is time for you to take it back."

DELILAH'S EYES OPENED ON DARKNESS. SHE SWITCHED ON THE LAMP as she rose and crossed to the table where she'd left the Tarot cards. Pulling the Hermit from the deck, she peered at the card, thinking of the Indian in the dream. Closing her eyes, she murmured, "Who are you?"

And the answer slammed into her mind. She saw the petroglyphs in the little cave. Her cave. When she hid the book there she'd asked the long-dead artist for a favor: *Keep the book hidden. Promise!*

And she'd imagined she'd heard him reply on the wind.

Delilah returned to the balcony. She held a hand out, letting the hard rain batter it. There was no sign of the moon - the clouds were too thick - but still, she squinted through the sheeted rain, hoping for a glimpse of desert. Somewhere out there was the little cave with petroglyphs that, once upon a time, she thought of as her very own.

But where? She hadn't a clue.

"HEY, STEVE, I'M BACK!"

"That was fast." He looked up from the log book to see Holly dressed in dry clothing - shorts, sandals, and a faded blue T-shirt sporting a grinning Cheshire Cat. Her hair hung around her face like damp curtains. He was honestly glad she'd come back downstairs after changing clothes; he hadn't enjoyed being alone tonight. He grinned. "I thought you'd be in your robe and slippers."

"No way. I'm not going back to bed!"

"What about the camping trip?"

"I decided to stay home." She manufactured a smile. "Becky kinda drives me nuts, you know?"

"She can be ... pretty enthusiastic." He chuckled. "I'll leave a message for your grandmother, so she knows you're here."

"Okay, but not until morning."

"Sure."

Holly looked at him. "You don't mind me being here?"

"Take a guess." Steve brought two cold Dr. Peppers out from behind the desk. "I got these out of the cooler while you were upstairs. Want one?"

"Do I ever!" She waited while he removed the cap then she took a long pull and stifled a ladylike burp. "Thank you!"

"You're very welcome." Leaning against the tall desk, he opened his own bottle, and drank. "So, why did you decide to come back in the middle of the night? Becky doesn't drive you crazy while you're asleep, does she?"

"No." A real smile arrived and fled in an instant. "I couldn't sleep because I kept hearing a warning in my head. It kept telling me I should come home."

Steve nodded. "Do you think you were dreaming?"

"Not exactly." She gazed at the ceiling. "Every time I'd start to close my eyes, I'd hear it. Even with my eyes open, sometimes. And I heard it again when I saw how hard it was raining, when I was wide awake." She gave him a long, sober look. "It's good to listen to your instincts, you know?"

"It is."

She studied him. "Probably, I just wanted to leave, but maybe it was important that I did. I don't know."

Steve nodded. "I understand."

She glanced around, then straightened her shoulders and tried to sound confident. "Anyway, I didn't want to stay there and I realized I don't want to go camping. I mean, it sounded fun at first, but ..."

"Becky bugs you?"

She shrugged. "No. I don't know. I feel like I should want to, but I don't want to leave here."

"Brimstone?"

"The hotel," Her eyes were somber.

"Why?"

"It's like, this'll sound stupid ..."

"Try me."

"It's like I'm not supposed to go."

"Not supposed to?"

She pushed damp hair behind her ear. "It's like I'm not even supposed to be at Becky's house. Like I *need* to be here. It's dangerous not to be. Or something."

Steve nodded, worried that this little girl, with her ability to see ghosts, might be hearing one, maybe one that wasn't benign like Jack Purdy. "Holly, tell me truthfully. Are you sure it was your own voice you heard?"

She nodded. "Yes. I've heard it before."

All around them, the lobby seemed to be holding its breath. Steve shivered, feeling as if they weren't quite alone. "What do you say we sit on the bench outside and get a little fresh air? The rain's about done. I love the smell of the desert after a storm."

"Let's go."

37

IN THE SHADOW OF THE BEAST

As the storm fled the Brimstone Valley, the stars returned, clearer than ever. The sickle moon hung among them so bright in the clean night air that it hurt the eyes to look directly at it.

The town of Brimstone slumbered. Mayor Tom Hasenpfeffer and his wife, Brunhilde, snored peacefully; they had, as was their tradition, shared a bottle of peach schnapps and tubes of Ritz Crackers before repairing to the bedroom for their monthly maritals. Just buying the schnapps and snacks had made Brunhilde's panties feel tight, and Brimstone Billy at the market had leered at her purchases, waggling his eyebrows in a suggestive way.

AT THE WET WHISTLE, BARTENDER HEDISON HEDDY KELLER shared a few brews with Richie Shaw after the bar closed. The old friends had talked about baseball, politics, and the merits of various brands of beer before Richie finally brought up Ben Gower. "He's not been coming by much lately."

"Nope. It's the old business," Heddy said as he locked up the bar.

The two men started up the empty street. "Whenever he starts staring up at Hospital Hill, he's got something on his mind."

"He ever talk about it to you?"

"Not a word."

BEN GOWER SAT UP IN HIS BED, LAMP ON, BOOK IN HAND. HIS bedroom door was firmly shut, and would stay that way because he had no intention of looking at the old hospital again tonight; he might be a coward, but that was just the way it was.

He stared at the book. It was his favorite from childhood, *King Solomon's Mines*. He thought revisiting it might chase away the bad dreams, but tonight, the story couldn't keep his attention. His mind was on his afternoon conversation with Addie Chance and Delilah Delacorte Devine. He dwelled, too, on his lost love, Carrie, as well as on Dee's little granddaughter, Holly. She was the very image of Carrie, and the sight of her both delighted him and filled his heart with sorrow.

AT THE HALA HOUSE, YOUNG KEITH AWOKE FROM A NIGHTMARE about being drowned in thick cold Jell-O inside a haunted house and that outside, something, maybe a pterodactyl, flapped huge leathery wings as it circled overhead and laughed at him. He came bolt upright, sure he'd screamed in real life, but neither his mother nor grandfather came to him. Glad he hadn't disturbed them, Keith sipped from his glass of water, then turned on his side and shut his eyes, thinking of Holly and her golden eyes. He hoped she was okay.

In another bedroom, Abner Hala awoke from a dream he hadn't had since childhood when his grandfather had told him the story of the Hellfire Serpent. In the dream, it flew out of the bowels of the earth, straight up into the sky, then back down to snap up screaming people in its jaws and crush them. It swallowed, mouth dripping fire and blood, then trapped Abner in its coppery eyes and came for him.

DEAR OLD IKE FELL ASLEEP MINUTES AFTER THEY RETURNED TO BED, and he'd stayed that way, sawing logs neatly and efficiently. Addie had never minded his soft snoring - usually the rhythmic sounds helped her fall right to sleep - but tonight was different.

She'd seen the Beast. She and Ike both, but he thought his eyes were playing tricks on him, and she hadn't argued. *Best to let him believe that.*

A far-off shadow passed across the moon. Addie rose and peered out the window. The Milky Way spanned the night sky, twinkling like a diamond bracelet, but behind the Brimstone Grand, the sky was solid black save for an occasional flash of lightning. "Stay safe, Holly. Stay safe." That the girl was spending the night at the Grangers was small comfort; it wasn't far enough away to be truly safe.

DELILAH DEVINE, HAVING GIVEN UP ALL PRETENSE OF SLEEP, WAS curled up against the forest-colored cushions of her favorite easy chair, her feet drawn up like a little girl's. The chair sat near an open window and as the cool breeze danced with the sheers, she reflected on memories that were only beginning to draw to the surface.

Outside, the storm had traveled south into the mountains, heading for Prescott. The lightning was unseeable from the living room side of the penthouse, the thunder too distant to rattle windows. She could see the moon, almost feel its brilliant white smile as it played among the shadows cast by the gently blowing sheers.

Delilah had thought a lot about her conversation with Adeline Chance and continued to tell herself that what her cousin had said about Holly being endangered by long dead spirits was absolute rubbish.

But try as she might, she couldn't convince herself of it. She knew Adeline was correct in her assertion that Holly should leave the hotel - and Brimstone - behind. But the moment Addie had spoken the words, Delilah also knew, at last, that she did not want Holly to leave.

A single tear ran down her cheek. Delilah felt torn in half; she didn't know what to do.

ON THE FOURTH FLOOR, IN HIS SKINNY, FILTHY ROOM ACROSS FROM the elevator, Arthur Meeks dreamed that a golden-eyed girl with Satan's hooves and a whipping devil's tail stood in his doorway staring at him, through him. He was in equal parts frightened and furious, and in his sleep, he turned, rubbing Methuselah against the filthy blanket, excited by his fury, his fear, and the thought of humiliating the golden-eyed daughter of Satan.

STEVE AND HOLLY SAT ON THE BENCH OUTSIDE THE LOBBY SO LONG that their backs were imprinted with the swirls of wrought iron flowers and leaves. Neither wished to go inside, to feel the still silence of the lobby, to wonder what might visit them there. They counted stars and talked about how man would go to the moon someday soon, as JFK had promised. They talked of alien worlds, of Isaac Asimov, of Robert Silverberg, of anything but ghosts and phantoms. Finally Holly looked at her wristwatch.

"It's past three," she said softly. "Ray Bradbury said that at three a.m. you're the nearest to death you'll ever be except for dying."

Steve nodded. "'By the pricking of my thumbs...'"

"'*Something Wicked This Way Comes*,'" Holly finished. "I love that story. Do you think it's true? About 3 a.m.?"

"I don't know. It seems like it. Everything's so quiet."

For the blink of an eye, something dark filled the sky, blotting out the stars and moon. It was a huge black silhouette, shaped vaguely like a bird of prey. Here and there, it seemed to shimmer with blue incandescence. *It's the dragon from my dream.* But it moved too fast to be sure. It flew west, circled above something - *Becky's house?* - then swooped down and became one with the darkness.

"Did you see that?" Steve asked.

"Yeah." She felt suddenly numb and cold. "It looked like a dragon."

"It did at that." Steve attempted a smile. "I saw something like it earlier tonight, too, during the storm. It was a lot higher up. I thought it might be some sort of weird weather thing."

"Do you still?" Holly asked, eyes bright, face pale.

"I ... I don't know. Maybe. What do you think?"

"I think maybe it was the Beast." She stood up. "Let's go in."

THE BEAST CIRCLED THE GRANGERS' DARK HOUSE AT THE TOP OF their long driveway. After a moment, it landed weightlessly on the roof, dissolved into a cold black cloud, and sifted into the house through an open window.

38

IN THE MORNING

After Holly and Steve retreated into the hotel, they'd sat hidden behind the tall walnut lobby desk. Holly said it felt like a fort and Steve had to agree. They were able to relax, and talk of everything except bruises and beasts, ghosts or dragons. Everything sounded normal again.

The switchboard lit up once with a phantom call from Room 329, but they were both too tired to care. Holly soon began yawning, but refused to go up to her room, so Steve retrieved a sleeping bag from the back office and rolled it out behind the desk. Holly climbed in while he dozed in the chair.

He awoke with a start. It seemed like seconds had passed except for the crick in his neck. He glanced at his watch. "Hey, Holly!"

Her lids barely opened. "Hi." She rubbed her eyes and sat up, looking around, getting her bearings. "What time is it?"

"It's almost seven. Peg will be here in a few minutes to take over."

"Okay." She started to lie back down.

Steve grinned. "Do you want to explain to Peg why you're sleeping down here?"

"Oh!" Her eyes opened wide and she pulled her sandals on while

Steve rolled up the bag. She followed him into the back office where he stowed it back under a table. "Steve?"

"What?"

"Are you going to tell anybody I came here in the middle of the night?"

"That's our secret. I did leave a message for your grandmother that you came home this morning instead of going on the camping trip." He smiled lightly. "I just didn't say what time this morning."

Holly smiled. "Thanks. The Grangers are probably already gone by now, right?"

"I'm sure. They're early risers." He paused. "Holly, are you worried about napping in your room now?"

She shook her head. "No. Nothing happens in the daytime, right?"

"Right." But *he* was a little worried. "Listen, look around and come right back if you, you know, see any weird symbols drawn on your mirror or anything."

"I will." She hesitated. "That bellhop probably did it."

"You mean Arthur Meeks?"

She nodded.

Steve rubbed his chin. "You might be right. Maybe he wrote on the mirror with some kind of trick disappearing ink." The thought brought relief along with a few new worries.

"I bet he did do it." She gave him a smirky smile. "He doesn't like me."

"What makes you think so?"

"Because right before you came upstairs last night I caught him in my mother's room."

"You did? You need to tell Miss Delilah. He's not supposed to be in anybody's room unless he's handling luggage."

Holly looked pleased with herself. "I told him if he ever bothered anybody again, I'd tell on him and get him fired." She hesitated. "I was a little bit angry, so, well, you saw my eyes right after that happened. They change color when I get mad."

"So, he saw your eyes? What did he do?"

"He put her underwear back in her drawer and practically ran to his room." She grinned. "And he wet his pants."

Steve started to laugh, then cut it off. "He had your mom's underwear? Holly, this is serious!"

"Cherry wouldn't care."

"That's not the point. Has he bothered *you*?"

She hesitated just long enough for Steve to worry. "No." She drew the word out. "I think he was going to peep on me once - I caught him drilling a hole in the wall between my room and the next one-"

"Holly!"

"I blasted his eye with hairspray."

Despite his concern, Steve couldn't help laughing this time. "I noticed his eye was red a few days ago. I was afraid he had pink eye and told him to see the doctor - that stuff is contagious."

She gave him a gamine smile. "No. It was just hairspray eye."

"Holly, I admire your ability to take care of yourself, but you really do need to tell your grandmother about all this. That man shouldn't be working here."

Holly considered. "Probably. You won't tell her, right?"

"I won't as long as you promise me you'll tell her. And soon. I always had a bad feeling about that guy. So, do you promise? I'll go with you to see her if you want."

"I'd like that. And I promise."

The front door creaked. "Good morning!" Peg Moran's cheery voice echoed into the stairwell where they stood. "Steve?"

"Be there in a sec!" he called, then whispered. "Get going. But come back down if anything's wrong. I'll hang around for a few minutes."

"Okay." She hurried up the stairs.

HOLLY WASN'T QUITE AS SURE OF HERSELF AS SHE'D LET STEVE think, but she straightened her shoulders and marched up to the fourth floor without hesitation. Last night, when she'd come up to change her clothes, she'd been twenty kinds of nervous, but this morning it really wasn't bad.

She let herself into her room, flipped on the lights, and opened the drapes and blinds to flood the room with sunshine before looking around. When she did, she was happy to see nothing out of place, no more weird symbols drawn on the dresser mirror, and that her discarded rain-soaked clothing and tote were still in the tub exactly as she'd left them.

She poured a glass of milk, took it out on the balcony, and stared across the high desert. It was starkly beautiful in the soft morning light. To the east, the sun, still low on the horizon, glowed with the promise of another hot day, but right now the air was still nice, even a little crisp, and she almost wished she had pulled a jacket on over her T-shirt. But not quite. Straight down the hill, beyond the ridge of trees, Brimstone was coming to life. She spotted several vehicles moving along the streets like little Matchbox cars. A motorcycle passed a red pickup, its *vroom* echoing. A horse whinnied somewhere below and Holly thought of Becky, and how, last night, she'd thought, for one brief instant, that the Beast had circled the Granger house. *Maybe it was looking for me.* She shivered at the thought.

Maybe I should have gone camping with them - then it couldn't find me!

She remained baffled about why she hadn't gone - she'd really wanted to. She still had no idea why she'd been driven to come home. It all seemed silly now. Yawning, she went inside, rinsed her glass and plopped down on the bed, not even bothering to close the drapes.

But just as she began to drift into sleep someone knocked on the door. "Holly?"

She groaned and pulled the pillow over her head.

Another knock. "Holly? It's Frieda. Miss Delilah wants you to come have breakfast with her."

"When?"

"Ten minutes."

"Okay, I'll be there." She tried to sound happy about it, but it wasn't easy.

"HOLLY, ARE YOU ILL?" DELILAH SAT ACROSS FROM HER granddaughter at a small round table near a window overlooking the

Brimstone Valley and studied the purple bags under Holly's eyes, the pale face, the barely-combed hair. And her clothing - shorts and a decidedly ratty T-shirt.

"I'm fine." The girl's smile was forced. "Just a little tired."

"Did you sleep in your clothes?"

"Um, a little, I guess. I got up early and came home from the Grangers' house then fell asleep again."

"Yes, Steve let me know." Delilah heard stridency in her own voice and softened it. "Next time, change for breakfast. Why didn't you want to go camping, Holly? I was under the impression you would love to go. Fishing, hiking, horseback riding, roasting marshmallows over the campfire."

The girl shrugged, a pained look on her face. "I don't know. I just wanted to come home."

Frieda set toast and Denver omelets before them, then brought a teapot and pitcher of orange juice to the table and proceeded to serve. "Anything else, Miss Delilah?"

"That will be all for now, thank you." Delilah waited until Frieda left. "Holly, did I understand you correctly? You didn't want to go camping because you wanted to come home?"

Her granddaughter nodded.

Delilah hesitated. "Do you mean you consider this your home?"

Holly studied her hands a long time before nodding. Then she looked Delilah straight in the eye. "Yes. I mean, I would like it to be my home."

"I would like that, too but your mother will likely take you back to California eventually. I can't stop her."

"Has she called you? Is she still in Sedona?"

Delilah's heart broke for the girl. "I haven't heard from her. She's probably working very hard." She nearly choked on the words.

The look Holly gave her was too adult, too knowing, and her words were almost inaudible. "If you asked her, she would probably let me stay."

"She might. But Holly, this isn't a good place for you to live. It's dangerous."

"Why? Because I can see ghosts?"

Delilah studied her. "I guess you could say that. Holly, I spoke with my cousin Adeline, yesterday for the first time since Carrie died. I know you've spoken with her as well. She's very concerned for your safety. She has eyes like yours, you know."

Holly sipped orange juice and looked uncomfortable. "I know. Adeline said you didn't like her because you think she killed your sister."

"I was mixed up, sweetheart. I blamed her because she was with Carrie when she died."

"But–"

Delilah, cheeks flaming, reached across the table and put her hand over Holly's. "I blamed her because I was a little girl and I wanted her to die instead of my sister. I was angry. So angry." Tears threatened but she fought them back. "Carrie was everything to me. Our mother died when I was three and so, to me, Carrie wasn't just my sister, she was my mother. She protected me. She loved me. I didn't think I could survive without her."

Holly held her gaze. "What did she protect you from?"

Delilah studied the 11-year-old, seeing maturity beyond her years and ached for her. The girl didn't even know what childhood was. She'd been nothing but a latchkey child, left to fend for herself while her mother did whatever she wanted. She went to school, the library, and the park. She cleaned and cooked. She was Cinderella. Holly had admitted that Charlotte had never taken her to an amusement park, to the beach, or the mountains. She'd never ridden a carousel or seen the astronomy show at the Griffith Park Observatory despite the fact it was so near Van Nuys. She'd never even been to the zoo. The highlight of her life, thus far, had been a class field trip to a local dairy. It was unconscionable, and how she'd survived - indeed, thrived - baffled and impressed Delilah no end.

Charlotte had had every advantage, and Delilah wondered what would have happened if she'd been stuck with just a library and a park. *She'd probably have run away and become a criminal.* Charlotte had never willingly read a book in her life.

"Miss Delilah?" Holly was watching her.

"The other night, in the restaurant, you called me Gram." Delilah spoke haltingly.

"I'm sorry."

"No, don't be sorry. You may continue to call me that if you'd like."

"You don't mind?"

"Not at all." Pride be damned. This girl needed someone, even if she couldn't stay with her forever. "In fact, I'd like you to."

Holly's somber, tired little face lit up. "Me, too. Thank you, Gram."

Delilah nearly teared up again. "I'm proud of you, Holly."

"Thank you." She took her first bite of omelet and grinned. "What did Carrie protect you from, Gram?"

Delilah studied Holly, tempted to gloss everything over, as she always had, but there was no sense in it. "My grandfather, your great-great-grandfather, was a powerful man. A sick man."

"Sick?"

"Mentally sick. Carrie told me over and over he was a bad man and to stay away from him." She paused. "I don't know why - I was too young to know much of anything - but I did know it was true. Carrie died because of him, Holly. Adeline has promised to tell me why." She squeezed her hand. "To tell *us*."

"He's the Beast," Holly said somberly.

"What?" Delilah felt dizzy. "Who told you that?"

"He talked to me in a dream. He looked like a black dragon with burning eyes and blue fire under his scales. He had a horrible deep dark voice."

She didn't want to ask, but she forced herself. "What did he say to you?"

"He wanted me to climb on the dragon and fly with him. And that nurse, Pearl Abbott, she tried to push me over the balcony and get me on the dragon's back." She hesitated. "That's how I got the bruises."

Delilah shivered. "Pinching Pearl. Yes, Adeline and I talked about her."

"You know about her?"

"I do, but only because Addie and Ben jogged my memory yesterday. I was barely six when everything happened. I don't have many memories of my time here." She smiled. "Ben told me Carrie used to bring me to the drug store for ice cream when I was little. I almost recall it, but not quite. It was so many years ago." Her smile broadened. "And do you know what else?"

"What else?"

"Ben was in love with Carrie back then. He was in his mid-twenties and was just waiting for her to turn sixteen so he could declare his intentions. He wanted to marry her and bring us both to live with him. I remember that she was sweet on him, too. She told me *she* was going to marry *him*."

Holly beamed. "It's so romantic!"

"Yes, it was." Sadness nearly overwhelmed her as she thought of what might have been. She spoke brusquely. "But it wasn't to be. Instead, I went to live with Aunt Beatrice in her grand townhouse in Boston. That was quite an adventure. She took me to Europe every summer vacation, sent me to the finest schools, and taught me about some rather strange things."

"I want to know more about that, but first please tell me what bad things your grandfather did. You're still afraid of him."

"You know your mind, don't you, Holly?" Delilah shook her head. "He was truly frightening - I think small children pick up on such things."

Holly nodded.

"From my six-year-old point of view, Henry Hank Barrow was as tall as a pharaoh and as broad as Paul Bunyan. He always wore stiff black suits and polished black shoes and he carried a gold pocket watch with that symbol of his engraved on it."

"*Infurnam Aeris?*"

"You don't miss a thing, do you, young lady? Yes, that symbol. He liked to twirl the watch and tell me to stare at it and now I wonder if he wasn't attempting to hypnotize me with the thing. At any rate, he had bushy salt and pepper hair and big white mutton chops, and his eyebrows were black with long white hairs curling through them and they arched over his eyes like the devil's own brows. I thought of him as a big dark hulk, and the day Carrie died, that's how I saw him that last time, down in the basement at the foot of the stairs. He was nothing but a horrible mass of darkness and a pair of glinting eyes in the lamplight, glaring up as Carrie gave me his book." She paused. "I never saw my sister again ..." She swallowed. "Holly, it's too dangerous for you to be here."

"What book?" Holly replied.

Delilah shook her head. "I'd forgotten it until yesterday. It was big and black with the *Infurnam Aeris* symbol on it. Do you know anything about the symbol, Holly?"

"Steve told me he had a cult and that was its symbol. Pearl Abbott was part of it, too, and it wasn't nice. Henry Hank thought he was a wizard and he tried to make people do things. Bad things."

"Yes, that sums it up rather succinctly. Our forebear was a powerfully depraved man. And, Holly, he, somehow, in some way, is why you are not safe here. It sounds ridiculous, but I know it's true. Adeline says you shouldn't even be in town, let alone here at the hotel. That's why I wish you'd gone camping with the Grangers. It might have given us time to figure out something to keep you safer."

"What do you mean? Figure out what?"

"Well, I'm not sure about this, but Adeline says that if we could find that book, we might be able to use it to stop, well, to stop whatever is going on. To keep you safe."

"What happened to it?"

"I hid it for Carrie that day, but I don't know where. I threw the cards last night, trying to remember."

"The cards?"

"Aunt Beatrice was a Spiritualist and she taught me how to read the Tarot." Delilah blushed. "I don't believe in it like she did, mind you, but I think it can help us see into our own minds."

"I know about the cards. I read a book about them."

Delilah stared. "Tarot cards? However, did you even find out about them in the first place?"

"*Dark Shadows*. Remember, I told you about *Dark Shadows*? It's a soap opera and they have witches and vampires, and cards, and time travel, and ghosts, and-"

Delilah laughed. "I'd like to see that!"

Holly dimpled up, delighted. "We can watch it together. It's on every weekday."

"Then we shall." She squeezed Holly's hand.

"So what did your cards say, Gram? Did they tell you where the book is?"

"I'm not sure, but I think I got a hint."

"Gram?"

Delilah, unused to her new title, hesitated. "Yes?"

"Could you show me the cards? Could you show me how to read them? Maybe together we could figure out where the book is."

"I suppose there's no harm in that. It's sort of a silly game, though, Holly. You must keep that in mind."

Holly nodded. "And can we go see Adeline or invite her over? I bet she can tell us all sorts of things."

Shivers traveled down Delilah's spine. "Very well. Shall we invite her for afternoon tea?"

Holly grinned. "Yes, please."

ARTHUR MEEKS HAD JUST EXITED THE ELEVATOR WHEN HE SAW Little Miss Fancy Pants enter the fourth floor from the western stairwell. He knew she spotted him, too. Never taking her beady little eyes off him, she continued to her room and pulled her key from her pocket, then just stood there, staring. She gave him the ever-loving creeps, that's what she did, and even though he couldn't see the color of her eyes from halfway down the hall, he figured they were devil's-spawn gold.

It was all he could do to tip his cap as if she didn't scare him a bit, but he did it. She didn't smile or nod, just turned and unlocked her door. He waited to hear it slam, but it closed with barely a sound. The locks *snicking* into place were louder.

See? She's scared of me. And she should be. She's going to pay! She thinks she's such a hot little shit because her granny is the Queen Supreme Douchebag. But she's nothing but a little slut, just like her mommy.

He entered his own room and locked the door securely behind himself, not out of fear of Miss Fancy Pants, nosireebob. It was because fat Mona Furburger had just checked in again and it was

Christmastime in Arthur's pants pockets. Ol' Mona, pleading a bad breakfast or two, had asked him to unpack for her while she raised a big noisy stink in the john. He'd been glad to; not only had she given him a five dollar tip for all his hard work - which included smiling through the reeking green death that followed her out of the bathroom - he'd helped himself to one of the two dozen fifty dollar bills she always had tucked away in her jewelry bag. Just one - he knew better than to be greedy. He'd also walked away with a gold wedding band that had slipped halfway into a broken spot in the lining of the jewelry bag. It'd probably been there for years, a souvenir of one of her former husbands.

Arthur tucked Ulysses S. Grant into a hidden compartment in his wallet - he'd consult with the president later - then slipped the gold ring into his underwear drawer. He was no fool - he'd hang onto it a couple of days on the off-chance Mona Furburger reported it missing. In that case, he'd come to the rescue, finding it somewhere in her room, out of reach of her stubby fingers, and get a nice fat tip in the process. If nothing was said, he'd take it to that sleazeball Donald down at Horne's Pawn Shop and make a few bucks. "Win-win," he muttered as the phone rang.

"Arthur," he answered in his best butt-kissing voice.

"We have new arrivals." Peg Moran's nasal voice was as snooty as a twenty-dollar call girls on Christmas Eve.

"Be there in a jiffy."

Adjusting his cap, he raced out the door and ran straight into Little Miss Fancy Pants, who was watering a fern beside the elevator. She ignored him as he pressed the call button, so he licked his lips and looked her up and down.

"Better stop it." She spoke under her breath.

"Didn't do nothing."

She looked straight at him then and for an instant, he was afraid he'd see those gold eyes again, but they were blue save for that big speck like the old lady at the Humble Station had. "You ain't Miss Delilah's granddaughter, no. You got more basic roots than that. You're related to the old witch at the gas station. I can tell by the eyes."

Something sparked in the girl's gaze, but it was gone before it took.

"Adeline Chance is our cousin and she's not a witch. You better not say things like that." She strutted past him, head in the air, snotty as you please, and began watering the ferns on the other side of the elevator.

Little bitch. You'll get yours. "Where's your mother?" he asked as the elevator arrived.

The girl looked up, surprised. "Working."

The elevator opened. He undid the accordion door and looked at Little Miss Fancy Pants. Seeing a certain insecurity, he spoke. "You know what your mother does for a living? Does she tell you what she does for a living?"

Fancy Pants glared and he didn't think she had a clue.

He smirked and let one hand glide over Methuselah as he shut the elevator cage with the other. He gave himself a little squeeze. "Do you know, little girl? Does she tell you what she does at work? Does she show you her movies and teach you how to do things?" He licked his lips. "How to do things to men?" He winked. "I bet you wanna be just like her when you're all grown up." His eyes travelled up and down her body. "Won't be long now and you can be just like your momma."

She stared at him, her face unreadable. He pushed the lobby button. As the doors closed, he groaned with need but didn't dare touch himself for fear of staining his uniform pants.

"Little whore," he whispered. "Dirty little whore."

✵ 39 ✵

HOLLY TAKES A SHORTCUT

After her run-in with Arthur Meeks, Holly's mood soured. She quickly finished watering and reported back to the penthouse, happy that Frieda met her at the door with five crisp one dollar bills - her week's pay. The housekeeper explained that Miss Delilah was working on hotel business with Vera and the Commodore and expected to see Holly back at three-forty-five, dressed for afternoon tea with Adeline Chance.

In her room, Holly changed into shorts and a clean blue tank top, happy that the bruises on her arms had faded enough for it - it was going to be too hot for a shirt with sleeves. She folded four of the dollars and slipped them inside her Friar Tuck bank then tucked the fifth into her pocket.

She sat down at the little dinette table and took an apple from the blue bowl she'd glued back together after the earthquake. Chewing, she looked at the presents her grandmother had brought her. There were three spiral notebooks with bright purple, green, and red covers, a pack of Bic pens, another of pencils, a sharpener, a dictionary and a thesaurus, and even several paperback novels. Gram had explained that since she liked to read, maybe she'd like to write, too, and Holly knew it was true. Her mood lightened. She had already written down her dream and other things that had happened since her arrival, but now she thought about how much fun it might be to make up a story. She smiled; her grandmother was so thoughtful.

She finished her apple then made it downstairs without running into Arthur Meeks. Peg Moran smiled at her from the reception desk. "Holly, how are you today?"

She smiled. "I'm fine."

"I was just wondering, hon, why don't you take the elevator?"

Holly shrugged. "I dunno."

"It doesn't frighten you, does it? It's old, but it's safe."

"I'm not scared of the elevator." That was true - it was what might be in it that frightened her. "The stairs are faster."

"I see." Peg smiled. "A girl your age. That makes sense." She laughed. "At my age, elevators are faster."

"Peg, can I ask a question?"

"Sure, Holly. Ask away."

"Um, have you ever seen any ghosts?"

"Here?"

Holly nodded.

"No, sweetheart. I'm afraid not. Not even that nice one in the elevator. I don't think he's real at all."

"Me, neither."

"Why do you ask?" Peg leaned closer. "Have *you* ever seen a ghost, Holly?"

She hesitated, decided it was best not to say more. "Maybe I heard the ghost cat." She made a face. "But I probably just dreamed it."

Peg smiled over her reading glasses like a satisfied school teacher. "I'm sure that's all it was. Your imagination. Nothing to worry about." She paused. "I love cats. I don't think I'd mind a ghost kitty at all."

"Me, too." Holly moved toward the door. "Well, bye."

"Where are you off to?"

"The drugstore for a root beer float."

"That's nice, dear. Are you riding your bike?"

"It's too hot. I'm taking the path."

Peg didn't look pleased. "Don't talk to strangers. And you should wear long pants. There are snakes."

"Don't worry, I'll be careful."

THERE WERE PUDDLES ON THE GRAVEL ROAD FROM THE LAST NIGHT'S storm and when Holly came to a big one at the edge of the hotel parking lot, she looked down at her tennis shoes and smiled; she'd worn her old ones, grayish-white and frayed with a hole over one big toe. She jumped right into the middle of the puddle, soaking her feet in three inches of cool water. It splashed almost to her knees and felt so great that she jumped one more time before moving on. A moment later she passed the Grangers' long curving driveway and paused, half-tempted to go up to see if they'd left yet. *But that's silly.* They'd be long gone and probably even had their camp all set up by now. She wondered again why she hadn't wanted to go with them - splashing around in a creek in her swimsuit would be heaven.

Sighing, she walked another hundred yards, only slowing when there were puddles to wade in, then crossed the road as she approached the old playground. She'd been half-hoping that Keith Hala might be there so they could walk to town together, but the place was deserted and the swings and monkey bars and slide gleamed in the hot sun, looking ready to burn her if she so much as touched them.

Just before the playground entrance was a brown sign that said, "Brimstone Trailhead" in dusty white letters. She hesitated, knowing that she would pass fairly close to the abandoned house where that - that *thing* had gone after her and Keith. But, she reminded herself stoutly, that cold dark mass hadn't followed them outside. Not only that, she wouldn't even lay eyes on the house as long as she stayed on the trail that led down to town, so there was no reason not to take the shortcut. It was too hot to do anything else anyway.

Still not as happy as she wanted to be thanks to that creepy bellboy, Holly stepped onto the path and within a few steps was surrounded by scrub oak and manzanita, creosote and cat's claw, white and yellow daisies, some small intensely pink blooms with silvery leaves, and an occasional yucca plant. Everything looked bright and smelled fresh thanks to the storm as the wide steps began their sashay down the hillside and soon became the simple path. She moved slowly, trying hard to lighten her mood. She forced herself to pay attention to the plants - to the variety of greens, the shapes of leaves and thorns, the delicate curves of flower petals, the scents of earth and shrub and rain puddles, even the way the sun angled across the trail. She memorized them, promising herself she'd write it all down later. *Maybe I'll write a story about them and how they reach out and grab a creepy bellboy and drag him underground where they all wrap him in their roots and then feed off him until he's shriveled up like an old apple core and never bothers anyone ever again!*

Holly smiled a real smile at last. Meeks' words about her mother - *and about me!* - had shocked her and she'd continued to feel weird, but now her anger was growing, and that helped. A lot. Maybe Steve was right; she should have gone straight to her grandmother the day she caught the bellboy drilling a peephole into her room. But Holly was used to solving her own problems - she took pride in it - and it had felt *so* good squirting him in the eye with hairspray that she'd been glad she'd handled it herself. She still was.

But she'd thought that was the end of the problems with the creep until she caught him coming out of Cherry's room. She'd felt good about how she'd made him put her mom's underwear away, and how she'd forced him to go to his room and stay there, using the newfound power that came when she got mad and her eyes changed color. But this morning, it hadn't happened.

A rattlesnake lay sunning itself on a smooth stone near the trail and she passed by so cautiously that it never even moved. *Why did Arthur Meeks say those things? Why didn't my eyes change at the elevator this morning?* She knew the answer to the second question even as she thought it - she'd been too upset to get mad. He'd frightened her. "I can't ever be off guard around that creep," she told a yellow daisy. "Never ever."

I won't let him get me again! I'll get mad instead. And I'll write that story about plants dragging him underground and eating him! That'll feel good. Maybe Steve would like to read it.

She smiled again, her mood lifting another inch. Maybe she'd really better tell her grandmother what Meeks said, like she'd promised Steve. Gram would fire him for sure. *But then what would happen?* Holly didn't think he could be arrested, so would he hang around waiting to get revenge? *To do something to me?* To Cherry? To somebody else? *Sheesh.* Holly knew about bad things men did because Cherry had explained to her why the school teachers always said not to talk to strangers. In fourth grade, Holly had raised her hand and asked Miss Piper that question after the teacher had given the caution, but Miss Piper sort of hemmed and hawed and finally just said it was dangerous and not to do it. So Holly asked Cherry, who was always forthcoming, and found out that bad men liked to touch little girls and boys on their privates, and sometimes forced them to do things - nasty things - with them. And they might kill them, too.

Holly hadn't needed to know more than that but now she stopped cold. *Arthur Meeks wants to do things to me.* Her stomach lurched. She stared at the ropes of jimson weed and their beautiful poisonous white flowers. With a start, she realized she was at the cutoff to the haunted house.

She shivered despite the heat, then took a deep breath and straightened her shoulders. Glancing around, she thought that if Arthur Meeks had followed her today, she'd march right into that house and shove him into that cold black mass. He wouldn't just wet his pants, he'd poop them, too. *Maybe I'll write a story about* that!

Holly grinned, feeling better, braver. She turned off the main path and took one step toward the haunted house. Then two, deciding she'd like to take another look at it. Just the outside; no way was she going near it, of course, but since whatever was in there hadn't followed them out before, she figured that it had to be safe to look from a distance.

She arrived and stepped just a foot beyond the shrubs and flowers, onto the dead, poisoned land where nothing stood but the two skeletons of the trees standing guard in front of the old house. She looked up at the second floor windows. Vacant blind eyes stared back at her, and she shivered, thinking she saw movement, then realizing it was just the reflection of a dead tree limb trembling in the warm breeze.

She stuck her tongue out. "I'm not afraid of you."

The rusty-gray house just sat there, staring, silent as a tomb. Then there was a creak - the old wooden screen door - screen long gone - moved just a little. Holly stepped back, staring. It had to be the breeze, but there wasn't very much, probably not enough to make the wooden frame move. *Maybe the house is settling.*

It happened again. The door frame creaked and softly slapped the jamb as if someone was getting reading to go in.

Or come out.

"Crap." She stared at the house, at the big first floor window with its raggedy drape. There was nothing to see. She glanced down, spotted a stone the size of a plum, and picked it up.

The door creaked again. Holly took aim and flung the stone at the mostly glassless big window. It went in, missing the framing and drape shreds, and she heard the rock hit an interior wall. "Take that!" she called.

One second passed. Two.

She stepped sideways, thinking she'd find another rock to throw.

Three.

The plum-sized stone came flying back through the window and if she hadn't already moved, it would have hit her. She stared at the stone and started to reach down to touch it. Then the screenless door slapped against the jamb again. Hard.

Holly ran.

"HOLLY!"

Out of breath, she emerged from the trailhead onto Main Street's sidewalk and pulled up just short of plowing into Keith Hala. "Keith! Sorry."

Keith stared at her. "It's okay. This is my grandpa, Abner Hala."

She looked up into the man's sun-seamed face and put her hand out. "Nice to meet you, Mr. Hala."

His big hand engulfed hers and he shook it solemnly. "Call me Abner."

Holly smiled, still breathing a little hard. "I'm Holly."

"I know. My grandson has told me about you." He raised an eyebrow. "Where are you going in such a hurry?"

"Oh, um, I was going to the drugstore for a root beer float." Her heart continued to pound even as she tried to calm down. "I'm really thirsty." She felt foolish.

Abner smiled. "You look very thirsty. My grandson and I are, too. Perhaps we might join you?"

"I'd like that," she said, still panting. "A lot."

"Good." Abner gestured at a bench beneath a shady cottonwood tree. "But why don't we sit a moment first so you can catch your breath?"

Grateful, Holly sat, Keith perching on her left, Abner on her right. She saw now that the old man wore his salt and pepper hair in a long braid that hung down his back. He saw her looking, and gave her a small, quiet smile.

"I'm glad you guys were here." Embarrassed, she spoke quickly. Her bangs were stuck in a sweaty sheet to her forehead. As she pushed them away, the breeze felt good.

"Why were you running?" Keith blurted. "What happened?"

"Well, I ... I guess I spooked myself. It was silly."

Abner spoke softly. "Did you go back to that house?"

"House?"

"I told him what happened. It's okay." Keith paused. "Did you? Is that why you were running?"

Holly hesitated. "Kind of."

"What happened?" Abner's soft voice calmed her.

"Did you go inside?" Keith's eyes were wide.

"No, of course not!" She glanced at Abner. "I'll never go inside again!"

"Very wise," he said. "It's a bad place."

She nodded. "I just looked at the outside. And then, well, I threw a rock at the window ... It was already broken," she added quickly.

"Why did you throw it?" Keith asked.

"I don't know. Because the house was staring at me, I guess." That was true enough.

"So, what happened?" Keith sat forward.

"Something threw the rock back at me." She told them about the screen door moving. "Probably there was someone in there, some creep or something."

"Maybe." Abner studied her. "If it was a person in there, he could have been more dangerous than any old spirit. But it might have been a spirit. We can't know that so easily. But our hearts know some things. What does yours say about that place, Holly?"

She honestly didn't know what she thought about who - or what - threw the rock, but she realized that Abner was asking about the house itself and he was right - her heart knew the answer to his question. "It's, well, it's wrong. It's bad."

Abner nodded. "I thought you probably figured that out."

"Do you know why everything around the house is dead?"

"Well, according to my tribe's legends, that land is cursed."

"Cursed?"

"Indeed. You yourself sensed it's a bad place. So did my ancestors."

Holly nodded, and looked to Keith. "Did you know it was cursed before we went in?"

Keith shook his head. "I don't think so."

"I doubt Keith connected it," Abner said. "Do you remember the story of the great flood?"

Keith nodded. "How the first people came here from under the ground?"

"Yes." Abner looked at each of them in turn. "It is said that our tribe once lived under the earth. A flood came and to save the people, they turned to the daughter of the leader, a beautiful and powerful young woman with a name that's very hard to pronounce." Abner smiled. "We'll call her White Hare. They put White Hare and her great love, a young shaman named Inyapa, in a canoe and sealed it with pitch so that it would float. But there was a very powerful, very bad sorcerer named, Nezochi who was outcast by the tribe. He wanted to marry White Hare and rule the new land at her side, so he tried to kill Inyapa. He failed and the entire tribe united to stop him. Nezochi turned himself into a creature whose name translates loosely into 'Hellfire Serpent' - and in that form, he would kill many, many times." Abner cleared his throat. "But I'm getting ahead of myself. Or maybe you're bored with this old story?"

"No! I'm not bored!" Holly said.

"Very well. After the Serpent was imprisoned, the canoe was

launched and White Hare and Inyapa floated up and up, through a hole in a long sacred rock. I guess you could say it was a sort of a tunnel, a portal to this world. They arrived safely and wove long vines and sent them down so the people could climb them and escape the coming floods.

"Nezochi, the Hellfire Serpent, remained beneath the earth, imprisoned not only by the tribe, but by the serpent flesh he had chosen. You see, try as he might, he could not change back into his human form thanks to a powerful spell that Inyapa and White Hare cast together. Because of the nature of the spell, he soon lost his human mind and became a dark element of nature intent only upon death. As the last of the tribe fled to the surface, he finally escaped and in his serpentine form, chased after them. At the portal above, Inyapa, White Hare and the warriors helped the survivors escape the rising waters and fought the Hellfire Serpent back with the help of Inyapa's magic. They knew they could not destroy him themselves, so their goal was to keep him from escaping the underworld, knowing that he would eventually drown.

"The last of the tribe escaped, and the portal was covered to keep the Hellfire Serpent imprisoned beneath the earth, but he would not die. First, they used skins and woven bark mats and had to replace them almost daily, such was his strength. Eventually, a stone cover was fashioned and set into place. It is told that after a time, the Hellfire Serpent drowned, but even water could not kill its spirit. The Hellfire Spirit had become a thing of nature, of the earth, of water, of wind and fire. It had become a powerful elemental, which would not be so bad if it was an ordinary elemental." Abner paused. "In our lore, elemental spirits are neither good nor bad, they just *are*, and they respond to the good and evil in men's hearts. But because the Hellfire Serpent was originally the dark spirit of a very evil and powerful man, that made it different; it would never respond to goodness in kind as a natural elemental would.

"So, the Hellfire Spirit continued to plague the people. Whenever it came near the surface, the earth trembled and shook and Inyapa and White Hare did what they could to stop it. But it cost many lives and before it was done, only a handful of the People of the Sun survived.

White Hare and Inyapa did medicine to put the Hellfire Spirit to sleep, but sometimes he awakens, and to this day, attempts to escape. Whenever he does, the earth trembles."

"So the earthquakes are the bad spirit trying to get out," Holly said. "I get that, but I don't understand what that has to do with that creepy house."

Abner chuckled. "I took the long path to answer your question. You asked why nothing is alive around that house. It is because it sits in a dead place where nothing grows." He looked from Holly to Keith. "But it is not the house that makes the place dead; it is the portal."

Holly was riveted. "It's under the house?"

Abner shrugged. "Maybe. Or perhaps simply under lots of earth - it's been many, many centuries since this supposedly happened." He smiled the smallest bit. "And you must understand that what I've told you is a myth - but more often than not, there is truth to be found in such myths. Fairy tales are myths, too, and they teach us certain things."

"Don't eat candy houses in the forest." Keith smiled.

Abner nodded. "Is there really an opening and a powerful angry spirit haunting it? I doubt that, though anything is possible. I do know that our people have considered that spot a bad place and have avoided it for as long as the tales have been told. There are very few of us here now - we began moving away during the days of the copper mines. And I don't just mean when the white man came, but before that, when *my* people were the miners."

"Why?" Holly asked, her fears forgotten. She burst with questions.

"Why don't we go get those drinks now?" Abner rose and putting his hands to his waist, stretched his back to one side then the other with a satisfied grunt. "It's too hot. I'll tell you when we get there."

Holly and Keith stood up and Holly spoke as they began their walk to the heart of town. "How did you know I was going to come down the trail when I did?"

"I didn't," Keith told her. "I mean, you said you would come today, but I thought you'd be on your bike."

"So, it was just coincidence that you were there?"

Abner cleared his throat. "That was not a coincidence, young lady. That was synchronicity."

"Synchro-what?"

"Synchronicity. The universe saw to it that we met when we were supposed to."

Holly nodded. She liked that idea very much.

40

FRAGMENTED SPIRITS

Ben Gower smiled as Eddie Fortune set root beer floats in front of Abner Hala and the kids. Eddie did everything with a flourish and a smile and Ben wished he could keep him around forever, but the boy was destined for bigger things than jerking sodas.

Abner looked up just then, saw Ben, and nodded. That was as good an invitation as any. Ben strolled up. "Abner, it's been a while. How's life treating you?"

"I can't complain." Abner chuckled. "You've addicted these kids to your floats. I thought I'd see what all the fuss is about." He sipped from his straw and nodded. "Not bad, Ben. Nice sharp root beer. You can taste it through the ice cream."

Ben grinned. "We use Barq's. None of that wimpy stuff around here." He turned to Holly. "Good?"

"Great!" She smiled, looking so much like Carrie that it about broke his heart.

"I'm glad to see those bruises are fading." He spoke quickly, afraid of turning maudlin. He saw Abner look at her arms, eyes narrowing.

"They're almost gone." Holly smiled.

"No more bad dreams?"

She shook her head.

"Bad dreams?" Abner asked.

Holly hesitated. "I dreamed this woman was grabbing my arms."

"Pinching Pearl," Ben said. "She dreamed about her and woke up with some nasty fingerprints."

Abner glanced at Ben, then fixed his eyes on Holly, who stared steadfastly at her float. "Pinching Pearl. I haven't heard that name in a long time."

"Do you remember her?" Ben had a good twenty years on Abner, probably more.

"I saw her a couple of times when I was a little kid. She'd ride into town with Henry Hank Barrow in a big shiny Mercer Touring Car like they were royalty. Which I guess they were, back in those days."

"I recall them parking out front of the pharmacy now and then." Ben Gower shook his head. "They'd occasionally come in. To tell you the truth, even as a young man, if I saw Pearl coming I always tried to make myself scarce. My father, God rest his soul, understood."

"Why were you afraid?" Holly spoke with the bluntness of a curious child.

"When I was a boy I, too, was pinched by Pearl." He didn't elaborate.

"She's scary," Holly agreed. "Were you afraid of my great-great-grandfather, too?"

"Yeah." Memories crashed over him. Frightened horses, death in the hallways, H.H. Barrow and Pinching Pearl looming over him.

"Everyone was afraid of him, Holly." Abner watched Ben. "Now, do you two want me to finish that story about the Hellfire Spirit?"

"Please, Grandpa!" Keith said as Holly, mouth full of ice cream, nodded.

"Hellfire Spirit?" Ben spoke quickly, relieved Abner had changed the subject.

Abner gave him half a smile and Ben turned, poured himself a cup of coffee, and rejoined them. "I'm all ears."

"I was telling the kids how our tribe came here long ago and about the angry spirit of a medicine man who tried to stop them. He turned himself into the Hellfire Serpent and got trapped beneath the earth. The serpent died, but its spirit did not." Abner looked at Ben. "The portal the Hellfire Spirit used is at the old haunted house on the trail to the hotel."

"I can believe that," Ben said. "I haven't been up there in years. You mean to tell me that old house is still there?"

"It is. People sense it's best to leave it alone."

"Makes sense," Ben said. "I remember when that house wasn't so old, when it looked good, fresh paint and all. The trail used to run straight past it from the Clementine Hospital to town back then. It was meant to be a boarding house for the nurses and Pearl Abbott herself was the mistress of the place, but it didn't last long." Ben sipped coffee. "The young women didn't like staying there. There were rumors of strange goings-on, as well as a few deaths, as I recall. Until today, I'd assumed all the problems at that house had to do with Pearl Abbott." He paused. "They moved the trail in the mid-twenties so it came out at the new school - where the playground is now. The hike is longer, but no one's ever complained."

"It's good they moved it," Abner said. "The place where the portal is - where the house was built - attracted bad people. Good people thought it was haunted and stayed away, but it was really the elemental presence of the Hellfire Spirit they were sensing." He looked at Keith and Holly. "By now, I'd venture to guess it has its share of ghosts, too."

"Go on." Ben sipped his coffee.

Abner cleared his throat. "From the beginning, our people avoided living near the portal, and the stories say that everything was quiet until we began mining for copper. Then, occasionally, when men dug a little too deep, the Hellfire Spirit would awaken and shake and rattle the earth, sometimes killing our people. The medicine men would work to put the spirit back to sleep.

"By the time the white man arrived and his mining operations began to grow, most of our people left for what is now the Verde Valley, Sedona, and Prescott. A few stayed, like my grandfather. He was a good blacksmith and his ironworks thrived and grew. That was around the time the camp was christened Brimstone.

"But the white man's explosives and tools dug much deeper than our people ever had."

He looked at Holly and Keith from beneath lowered brows. "The earth shook whenever the angry spirit stirred and many, many miners died over the next few decades. It's said that there are still hundreds of bodies trapped beneath the earth, all captives of the Hellfire Spirit."

"Captives of the Brimstone Beast." Holly's words were as solemn as a priest's. Ben nodded, glad she realized they were one in the same.

"Indeed." Abner stirred the dregs of his float. "In the old days, there were deaths every day, but man's greediness knows no bounds, so the mining continued, growing until the camp was a town covered in a yellow pall of sulfur, as if to welcome the Spirit. The Beast. There were three big mining companies at work, and there were three hospitals too - each company ran its own. Between accidents and illnesses, the hospitals were always full-up."

"Illnesses?" Keith asked.

"The air was no good in those days, thanks to the mines, so lots of people got sick. The whole of Brimstone Valley reeked of sulfur - of brimstone." Abner shook his head. "It went on a long time, but the mining companies ultimately failed because it became impossible to dig deeper without disaster. As it was, Brimstone shook all the time, whether they were blasting or not. My grandfather and a few others had told the stories of the Hellfire Spirit to the white men because miners had been claiming to see things in the tunnels before disaster struck, and some townsfolk said they saw a serpent flying in thunderstorms. They named it the Brimstone Beast.

"Two of the mining companies closed - they were destroyed by earthquakes. Their hospitals crumbled, too, and no one tried to rebuild or clear the caved-in mines. The ores were buried too deep. It was too dangerous. But also, at that point, even the white man believed in the Hellfire Spirit." He glanced at Holly. "That is, the Brimstone Beast."

"The Clementine is the only hospital that didn't fall down." Holly stared at Abner, waiting.

"Indeed. Only the Clementine Mining Company - and its hospital - went unscathed."

"Why?" Holly took the word right out of Ben's mouth.

"Well," Abner said, "There's a theory, but you might not care for it, Holly."

"Does it have to do with *Infurnam Aeris*?"

Abner's eyebrows shot up. "You know about that?"

She nodded and spoke by rote. "It means 'copper hell' and it was my great-great-grandfather's secret cult. He called himself the Brimstone Beast and they did really bad things."

"Do you know what kind of bad things?" Abner asked carefully.

"Not exactly."

"Some believe he used sorcery to get rid of the other mining companies. Who knows?" Abner smiled. "So what else have you heard, Holly?"

"Not much. Can I ask you something?"

"Go ahead," Abner said.

"Well, when Pearl Abbott pinched me in my dream, I saw her. And I saw her when I was awake, too - she was in the elevator staring at me. And when Keith and I went in that haunted house, I saw something there, too, but not her. It was this big misty thing, kind of like a tall, black, skinny cloud."

"And it was *super* cold," Keith said.

"Did you see it, too?" Ben asked.

Keith shook his head. "No, but I felt the cold. It was like ice cold goo or something."

"Anyway," Holly continued. "Both times I saw Pearl, she looked real. Alive."

Abner nodded. "So what are you asking, Holly?"

"Well, I saw Pearl Abbott twice. But in the dream, I only *heard* my great-great-grandfather - I didn't see him. Instead I saw this big shiny black dragon with blue fire under its scales and these orangey-red eyes. I knew that was the Brimstone Beast. But I heard a deep voice in my head telling me to climb on the dragon. I know it was Henry Hank's voice, but it felt like the dragon was talking. It was weird." She paused. "Anyway, I wouldn't do it and that's when Pearl grabbed me."

"How did you get away?" Abner asked.

Embarrassment flashed across Holly's face. "Miss Annie Patches. She's a ghost cat. She jumped on me and woke me up."

"Holly has a spirit animal, Grandpa," Keith said. "Isn't that neat?"

"You're very lucky, Holly. But you still haven't asked your question."

"Why did I see Pearl Abbott but not my great-great-grandfather?" She hesitated. "Or why did he look like the Brimstone Beast in my dream? Adeline said he's dangerous because he's strong enough to *show* me the Beast. Is he the Beast or isn't he?"

"Very good question, Holly." Abner rubbed his chin. "Have you ever heard of a tulpa or a thought-form?"

"Yes. Adeline said the Brimstone Beast is a thought-form and that Henry Hank wanted to be 'one' with it. I don't get it though. Does that mean he *is* the Brimstone Beast? Is that why he looked like a dragon?"

"It's very hard to understand," Abner told her. "I'm not sure myself, but I think Adeline is right, or mostly right. A tulpa or thought-form is what we call a creature created by a man's imagination. But Henry Hank only *thought* he created the Brimstone Beast. He assumed he was giving existence to a purely mythical creature - to something *he* created himself. He probably didn't know that the Hellfire Spirit - the Brimstone Beast - already existed.

"But it did. It existed independently and Henry Hank tried to bend something very powerful to his will. He assumed it was his own thought-form, but it was much more. If there is any truth in my people's legends of the Hellfire Spirit, it's that it is an elemental that has always carried human negativity with it. First the shaman's, then Henry Hank's, too." He paused. "I hope this is making some sense?"

"Kinda." Holly stared at him with impatience. "But what does it mean?"

"It means that your great-great-grandfather bit off more than he could chew. In trying to meld with the Brimstone Beast, he fractured his own human spirit. It's fragmented, broken. I think that's why it can't be seen even by someone with your - or Adeline's - gift."

Holly nodded. "So that's why I saw him as a dragon?"

"Maybe. Or maybe it's a projection. The Brimstone Beast is unbroken and he is in some way part of it, so he can communicate through it. Do you understand?"

"Maybe. But the black cloud-"

"I think that is how you see his broken human spirit. I have heard that black clouds are sick spirits. It would make sense."

Holly's eyes grew wide and her words came out in a torrent. "Do you mean that black cloud in the haunted house is my great-great-grandfather's ghost? I mean, if Pearl lived there, it seems like it should be her, but wouldn't I see her like a real person since I did before? I mean, I've seen a few other ghosts and they always looked like real people-"

Abner put up a hand. "Slow down. I think the black cloud is a fractured spirit, so it is probably your great-great-grandfather."

"Really? Why is he there instead of at the hotel like Pearl?"

"Powerful spirits are not confined to one place," Abner explained.

Ben spoke up. "For many years, Pearl and Henry Hank kept company at her house. It's said they conducted many of their depraved *Infurnam Aeris* rituals there."

"Holly," Abner said, "the black cloud is almost certainly Henry Hank Barrow. You must not go in that house again. Either of you. Promise me."

"I promise." She paused. "Steve and I saw something else last night."

"The Beast?" Ben asked.

She looked at him, surprised. "Yes."

"I saw it, too," Ben said. "Or thought I did. I was looking up at the old hospital. My eyes were probably playing tricks - it only lasted an instant. Something big and dark in the sky over the Grand. Might've been my eyes." He smiled and lightened his tone. "But it was probably just a plane."

"It wasn't a plane. I dreamed about it," Keith said.

Abner nodded gravely. "So did I."

As soon as Arthur Meeks saw Little Miss Fancy Pants sashay out of the hotel, he grabbed his Polaroid camera and let himself into her room. He knew the maids didn't clean her room - she did it herself - so he didn't have to worry about being interrupted. Those maids thought the devil's spawn was just the sweetest little thing, so clean, so polite, with a smile for everyone. *Why she even knows our names, already!*

Arthur knew better. Little Miss Fancy Pants never had a smile for him, nosireebob, and as he went through her laundry basket, checking her dirty clothes with eye, nose, and occasionally, tongue, he knew she was a dirty little girl.

Dirty enough to keep Methuselah at attention, that was for sure. Maybe even dirtier than that because, while there were two pairs of capris, two pairs of shorts, a dozen socks, and six shirts in the basket, there was no underwear. The beast in his Jockeys throbbed as he sniffed a last pair of shorts. "Don't you wear your panties, little girly-girl?" he muttered as he dropped the shorts back in the basket and opened her dresser. "Are you studying to be a bad girl like your momma?" He took a Polaroid snap, so Little Miss Fancy Pants wouldn't find anything out of place.

There were several neatly-folded pairs of panties there, all clean - he gave each pair a disappointing sniff test to be sure. He put one pink pair in his pocket and continued looking. There were several under-shirts and two little lace training bras. He picked up one - pale blue with white lace - and rubbed it against his cheek, then replaced it before checking the other drawers. There were regular clothes in those, nothing the least bit entertaining.

In the bathroom, he found the missing underwear - three pairs hung over a towel rack. He took a photo then fondled and sniffed each pair in turn. One - lavender with purple elastic - was newly washed and quite damp. He pocketed that one then headed back into the living area and paused in front of the dresser again, his eye caught by a figu-rine. It was a smiling brown-robed monk with a bald head and rosy cheeks. He picked it up and realized it was a bank. He shook it and heard coins rattle and movement of paper. She had bills in there. *Who knows how much money Miss Fancy Pants has socked away?* He started to take it then decided to wait until his next visit; caution always paid off.

Next, he opened her refrigerator to see what she liked to eat. There wasn't much in it, and it was all boring, but he opened the milk carton and spat in it, carefully returned it to the shelf, then did the same to a pitcher of orange juice.

Standing back, he smiled. "There you go, Little Missy - you're going to swallow some Arthur Meeks and you're going to like it."

Momentarily, he returned to his room, and barely able to contain his excitement, he phoned down to the lobby and told that old bitch, Piggy Moran, that he had a sour stomach but would be back at work within half an hour.

He sat down on his filthy bed, unleashed Methuselah, and baptized Little Miss Fancy Pants' underwear with his own special brand of holy water and rubbed it into the material.

Less than fifteen minutes passed before he hung the lavender panties carefully back up in her bathroom and folded the slightly sticky pink panties into the drawer. He'd return later to get an unwashed pair to add to his collection. Meanwhile, he consulted his Polaroids and made sure everything was back in place.

Five minutes after that, Arthur Meeks, in the best mood he'd been in since he'd beat off while spying on Cherry Devine, was downstairs flirting with Piggy, who ate it all up like the stupid sow she was.

HALFWAY UP THE TRAIL, HOLLY STOPPED TO ADMIRE A COMPACT plant coated with so many little yellow flowers that it looked like someone had dropped a bouquet at the edge of the path. She looked up at Abner and Keith. "It's really nice of you to walk me back up the hill," she told them. "You didn't have to."

Abner nodded. "I want to be sure no one throws any more rocks at you."

"Are you afraid I'd go back to that haunted house?" Holly asked. "Because I wouldn't. Not alone, anyway."

"I'm glad. You're a brave girl, Holly, that's obvious." He glanced at Keith. "And sometimes those who are young and brave do foolish things."

"I already did," she said simply. "On the way down."

"Not too foolish, at least, but don't even go look at it alone again. Things are worse than I thought and even if you aren't frightened of ghosts - though I think in this case you should be - remember that bad places attract bad people." He paused, hooking into her and Keith's eyes with his somber gaze. "It's a magnet for bad that way."

"You mean maybe a bad person threw the rock, not a ghost?"

"Possibly," Abner said. "If you two hadn't told me about what you experienced yesterday, I wouldn't even consider that a spirit had done it. Just a person."

"Maybe it was Lonely Boy." Keith made a face.

"Who?"

"That's not funny, Keith." Abner looked at Holly. "Lonely Boy is what they call a killer that comes around now and then. Have you heard of him?"

Holly shook her head.

"He killed a young girl just last fall."

"Right before Halloween," Keith said. "Our parents all went trick-or-treating with us. They think he killed Connie Mendoza. She was a third grader and she lived on my street." His eyes widened. "But they never found her body."

"That was a long time ago," Holly said. She remembered seeing a yellowed "missing" poster in the Humble Station's window.

Abner shook his head. "Not so long. They think he's killed a number of children. Once a year at first, then he killed two in 1966 and two more in 1967. No one this year."

"It's August already," Holly said remembering the poster. "Maybe he's gone."

"He may be," Abner said, "or maybe he's dead. Or in jail. But he might live here, too. And if he does, he probably goes to the market and to the movies, just like the rest of us. He could've been in the drug store with us today. There's no way to know."

"But wouldn't he have killed someone again by now if he's here?" Holly asked.

"Maybe. Maybe not. It's not like he has a schedule. I don't recall many details, but he doesn't do it at a certain time. In 1966, the two girls were killed within weeks of each other, and then nothing happened for over a year. Everyone thought he was gone until it happened again. So, Holly, you be careful. You make sure you're with Keith or another friend when you're out anywhere isolated like the playground." Abner paused. "It would be best if you stayed off this trail by yourself, too. Take your bike to town. I can always give you a lift back up in the pickup if it's hot out." He smiled. "Or even if it isn't."

"Thank you, but I'm pretty safe. I'm from the city, so I know how to take care of myself."

"I told you how she made those bullies run, Grandpa." Keith's eyes gleamed. "I bet Holly could scare just about anybody if she wants to."

Abner nodded, then looked at her. "Is that true, Holly? Would you be able to think fast enough to scare someone if they surprised you?"

Thinking of her run-in with Arthur Meeks this morning, she looked at her feet. "Yes."

"Look at me, Holly. Do you really feel safe because of your gift?"

She looked up, suddenly on the verge of tears. "Not really, not yet. I mean I probably need to learn more about using it. Adeline promised to help me."

"Good. You talk to her. And you ride your bike and let me give you a ride back up the hill next time, okay?"

She opened her mouth to protest, but he cut her off. "Just until you *know* you can protect yourself."

"Okay. Thank you."

They began walking again and soon came to the cutoff masked by jimson weed. Keith halted. "Grandpa? Did you ever go inside the house?"

"A few times, a long time ago." He chuckled. "When I was seventeen, a few of us guys came up after high school graduation and dared each other to go inside. We thought we were so smart."

"Did you?" Holly asked. "Go in?"

"We went in through a window. Some of the guys were so drunk they didn't notice anything at first, but I sobered up real quick because my grandfather and father had told me the stories so often. I was afraid, but I wasn't about to say so." His smiled grimly. "There were five of us. Two went upstairs and the rest of us started looking around downstairs. We didn't have flashlights, just matches and Joe had a big lighter he'd filched from his uncle. It's lucky we didn't burn the place down. Or maybe not so lucky." He looked from Keith to Holly. "To be honest, I don't think we could've burned that house down if we'd tried. It wouldn't let us."

"The house wouldn't let you?"

"Whatever was in the house."

"Did you see it?" Holly asked. "The black cloud?"

"No. But we felt the cold. It was a warm night but inside that house, it was like ice. I went in one of the downstairs rooms and it was so cold my teeth chattered. Whatever made it cold came close to me. I backed out of that room so fast that I knocked one of the guys down. I saw his eyes as I helped him up - he looked like a spooked horse. Just then, there was a lot of noise on the stairs, and a yell. Joe - he was the varsity quarterback - tumbled down the stairs and broke his leg in five places." Abner shook his head. "He said something pushed him."

"What'd you do?"

"Well, we started to tell him to just stay still while we got a doctor, but he screamed and insisted we carry him out." Abner shook his head. "He was the bravest guy I knew, and he was crying like a baby. We brought him out and ended up carrying him out of sight of the house before he'd let a couple of us leave to go up to the Clementine to get help. He was so scared that despite the pain, he begged us to carry him all the way up the hill. Maybe we could have if we hadn't had so much beer that night." Abner eyed Keith. "That was the last time I ever had more than one beer in a night."

Keith nodded. "Did you ever go back?"

"Oh, I've looked at it a few times from the outside. I took your daddy there, Keith, and told him the old stories - and the story I just told you, hoping he'd stay away."

"Did he?"

Abner looked sad. "I don't know, but I doubt it. He wasn't very cautious." He smiled and squeezed Keith's shoulder. "I'm glad you take after your mother. She's sensible."

Keith smiled then nodded toward the cutoff. "You want to go see it now, Grandpa?"

Holly half hoped he'd say yes.

Abner gave her a look that said he knew what she was thinking. "No, I don't, not today. But if you both promise me you'll never go there by yourselves again - not even to look - I promise we'll go look together sometime. Deal?"

"Deal!" they echoed.

THEY HIKED ANOTHER TEN MINUTES AND FINALLY EMERGED AT THE trailhead by the playground. "You two want to play for a few minutes?" Abner plunked himself down on a bench shaded by a struggling scrub oak. He'd forgotten how steep the trail was and wanted a short rest.

"Sure!" Keith said, "Come on, Holly!"

Abner watched the kids swinging higher and higher, laughing and shrieking, and marveled at how quickly the young recover from frights. *Or seem to.* He was genuinely concerned for Holly and was glad when she admitted she wasn't as sure of herself as she acted. He hoped Adeline would be able to help the girl harness whatever power she had - and from what Keith had told him, it was considerable.

Abner was a lot younger than Addie Chance - he was barely older than Holly's grandmother - but he remembered Addie and Carrie from his boyhood. He'd seen both young women around town - often with a little girl holding their hands - *that must've been Delilah.* They were pretty and kind but he noticed them mainly because of the gold in their eyes. His father had told him it meant they could see ghosts and that had fascinated him. When he was grown - long after Carrie's death - he became friendly with Ike and Addie Chance and asked her if it was true. She said it was, so he told her about a problem at his house - the one his father and grandfather built, the one he still lived in. He was a newlywed, and he and Mary often heard whispering at night near their bed. They thought it might be a ghost, and it frightened Mary so much that they could not do the things most newlyweds enjoyed doing; the whispering became worse whenever they were intimate.

Adeline came to his house that very day and wandered through the stone and wood structure. She spent time in the bedroom by herself and he heard her talking to someone. When she came out, she smiled and sat down at the kitchen table with Abner and Mary. "Have you thought of adding on to the house?" she asked. Abner, surprised, nodded. Mary smiled and explained that her groom had promised to build on a nice new bedroom with a picture window that looked out over Brimstone Valley. It was to be complete by their first anniversary. Smiling, Addie suggested he build it more quickly or move into the smaller bedroom for the time being if they wanted privacy. When Abner asked why, Addie explained that his mother - who'd passed away only two years before - had not yet moved on and remained in the bedroom she'd shared with her husband and that seeing her son in the bed with his wife disturbed her.

Abner and Mary had looked at each other, slightly horrified and mildly amused. That same day, he and Mary moved into his tiny boyhood room and shared his twin bed. The new bedroom was ready for their six-month anniversary. Mary left fresh flowers in the bedroom for his mother and sometimes he went in to talk to her, though his visits came less and less frequently. The last one was after Mary's own funeral and he knew, without asking Addie, that his mother had finally moved on.

"It's too hot!" Keith ran up to him, Holly trailing. Both kids looked like horses ridden hard and put up wet.

Abner looked the kids over. "If your grandmother says it's okay, I'll drive you two to the public pool over in Lewisdale for a swim next weekend. Would you like that?"

Keith grinned happily and Holly lit up like the fourth of July. "There's a pool? I'd love it!"

"You ask permission and let us know. Just call Hala Metalworks. We're in the book." Abner stood, hands on hips, twisting his aching back. "I think I just might take a swim right along with you."

"Will they make you wear a swimming cap?" Holly asked, her eyes sparking with curiosity.

"Of course," he said somberly. My hair's longer than yours." He smiled. "Holly, Keith has promised to help me with a project this afternoon, so we're heading back down now. Make sure and call us about going swimming."

"I will. Thanks." She turned and began trotting toward the hotel.

Abner, shading his eyes against the sun, watched her. He was about to turn, but just past the Grangers' driveway, she stopped dead in her tracks. Her body was stiff, legs slightly spread, arms at her sides. He thought her hands were fisted.

"Something's wrong," he murmured.

"What?" Keith stared. "What's wrong?"

"She sees something."

"No!" Holly yelled. "Get out of my way!"

"Holly!" Abner began trotting, Keith following. "Holly," he called. "What's wrong?"

And then Holly started zigzagging back and forth as if she were avoiding something.

"Holly!" Abner cried. "Come here! Run!"

The girl turned to him, but before she could move, she flinched and screamed, then tore herself free of something he couldn't see. "No!" she screamed. "No!"

PEARL ABBOTT GLIDED FROM THE BRUSH ONTO THE ROAD, AS IF she'd been waiting for Holly. Her dark hair, severely pulled back from that hard-planed face, and the long black dress and white apron looked the same as always. Time stopped for Holly and she stared at the little red cross pinned to Pearl's bosom; it seemed to glint in the sun.

Holly heard the woman's harsh voice in her head even though the ghost's lips never moved. *"Come to me, girl."*

"No!" Trembling, Holly summoned all her courage and stared back defiantly. "Get out of my way!"

Dodging to one side then the other, Holly tried to run past her, but Pearl moved with her, gliding with preternatural speed, almost as if she knew where she was going before Holly knew herself. But Holly kept moving, dodging back and forth, trying to outwit the ghost.

Then she heard Abner's voice. "Holly! Come here! Run!"

She turned and saw him trotting toward her and took one step his way before Pearl Abbott's freezing fingers dug into her shoulders.

"No!" Holly screamed, tearing out of the painful grip. "No!" She heard Pearl roar with rage as she ran toward Abner, two steps, three. He was still so far away.

And then Pearl appeared in front of her, blocking the way. Holly smacked into her - a wall of frozen ice - and jumped sideways, heading for the center of the road. Just as Pearl grabbed for her, Holly leapt and ran - and her ankle caught in a rut. She fell flat, barely aware of the stinging gravel as she got up.

Pearl caught her by the arm and that frozen grip hurt more than the gravel or her ankle. She looked up into the ghost's rock-hard eyes. Black and soulless, they drilled through her.

Get mad! Holly told herself. *Get mad!* She tried to concentrate but her arm felt full of icy daggers. *Get mad! Get mad!*

Pearl's voice filled her mind. *"You're mine. You belong to me, now, girl. You belong to the Beast. You will ride with him!"*

"Holly!" yelled Abner, coming at a run.

The phantom let go of Holly.

"Watch out!" Holly cried.

But Pearl pushed him with both hands.

Abner flew backward, grunting as he landed on his back.

Holly's anger stuttered beneath her terror. She saw Keith helping Abner up, pulling him toward the side of the road. A car appeared in the distance.

Holly stepped back, keeping her eyes on Pearl. "You're nothing. You're nothing but a ghost. I'm not afraid of you!"

Pinching Pearl opened her mouth so wide she looked like a snake unhinging its jaw. Laughter exploded from that gaping black maw, so loud that Holly slammed her hands over her ears.

"You don't know anything, girl. That will change."

As the car approached, Holly took another step back, fear finally giving way to anger. "You're just my great-great-grandfather's assistant. You're nothing. You just do what he says. And *he's* nothing! He can't even be seen - he's nothing at all! He's broken!"

Holly recognized the clarity coming into her vision, felt the power beginning to surge into her blood. She pictured her eyes turning to gold. "You're just Pinching Pearl and you like to scare little kids. You're just a bully, Pinching Pearl. Nothing but a big fat bully!"

And in that instant, Pearl's contorted face turned cold and calm. Holly knew she'd rush her now and stood firm, hoping she was strong enough to stop her.

Before Pearl could move, the driver of the car - a big old Rambler - punched the gas and slammed into the ghost.

But Pearl, looking like she was standing in the engine compartment, simply glanced at the driver, then returned her attention to Holly.

The car door opened and Adeline Chance stepped out.

"Hey!" Addie called, her voice strong. "Pearl Abbott, you insufferable old bitch. Why don't you pick on somebody your own size?"

Abner and Keith flanked Holly, as she watched the ghost turn and study Addie.

"The one that got away." Pearl cackled again and Holly knew Adeline could both see and hear her. *"You'll get yours, old woman."* The ghost moved toward Addie.

The thought that Pearl would hurt her friend was just what Holly needed to get angry enough to stop her. She stepped toward the car. "Pinching Pearl!" she yelled, "don't you hurt my friend!"

Pearl turned and stared hard at Holly as she neared. Addie came around the other side of the car, moving silently closer, and for the bare instant she dared look beyond the ghost, Holly saw the gold spot in Addie's eye pulsing, and thought, *I'm not alone.*

"Pinching Pearl!" Holly said. "You go back where you came from. You leave me alone! You leave Adeline alone!" She had no idea what she could do to the ghost - none at all - but her vision became so clear and close that she could see a chipped spot on Pearl's red cross pin. She could see the pores in her ghostly face and darkness sifting behind the mask. "Go away, you bully, go away or I'll make you go away forever!"

The apparition wavered, staring at her. *"You will not win."*

"Yes, she will win," Adeline said. "And *you* will lose."

Pearl Abbott let loose that horrible snaky laugh again, but slowly, like a degrading photo, she faded, the laughter with her.

Holly just stood there, breathing hard, heart pounding, yet calm as Abner, Keith, and Adeline surrounded her.

"Holly?" Abner spoke softly.

She looked at him.

He stared into her eyes for a long time. "That was amazing," he said at last. "You are truly gifted."

Adeline gently hugged Holly and smiled at Abner. "She is."

"You must teach her everything you know, Addie."

Adeline nodded. "I will." She looked at Holly. "Are you okay? Look at all those bruises. She gently touched one of the new fingerprints on her shoulder. "Cold as the devil."

Holly nodded. "It hardly hurts," she lied. "It'll go away pretty fast. It did before." She glanced at the five-inch wide reddish mark on her arm where Pearl's whole hand had clamped onto her. That really hurt.

"Well, let's go inside and clean up those skinned knees and elbows before your grandmother sees you." Addie smiled. "I'll bet soaking that arm in warm water would feel pretty good." She smiled at Abner and Keith. "Are you here for tea?"

"Tea? No."

"I think you should join us," Adeline said. "We're going to talk about Pearl Abbott and Henry Hank and the things that happened. It would be good for Dee to hear from you."

"Yes, please come, Abner!" Holly said. "You and Keith. You know so much."

"Okay, for a few minutes." Abner rubbed his back. "Then I need a good hot soak. That ghost threw me a good six feet." He touched his chest. "I couldn't see her, but I sure did feel her. Like ice. For a second there, I thought she stopped my heart."

"I'll just get my car parked." Adeline returned to the Rambler.

Holly stepped away from the car, realizing for the first time that her ankle hurt from the fall. Abner saw. "You want a lift?"

She tested the ankle and grinned. "No, I'm okay. I'll walk it off." It hurt, but not too bad, and she needed to move. She was so full of adrenaline that she could hardly stand still.

As Addie parked, a little delivery truck pulled up next to her, a Metro, white with the Gower's Pharmacy logo painted on it. Holly smiled as Ben Gower exited. He nodded at them, then retrieved something from the vehicle - a big, slightly bedraggled orange cat.

"Fluffy!" Holly exclaimed. She held her arms out and Ben placed the cat firmly in them. Fluffy began purring.

"I see you're acquainted. He's Meredith's, right?" Ben glanced nervously at the hotel.

"Yes." She kissed the cat's forehead, hoping she hadn't let him out when she left in the middle of the night. *Probably not. They would've missed him. He must've gotten out when they left on their trip.* She hugged him close.

"Well," Ben said. "I know they're gone for a long weekend and I found him down the road a ways when I made a delivery. He looked hungry and miserable. Meredith told me he's a house cat, never goes out." Another anxious glance at the hotel. "She once told me that she keeps a spare house key behind the registration desk. I thought maybe if you'd fetch it, Holly, I can borrow it and put this fellow back in his home."

"Sure! It's not safe for cats to be outside." Holly hugged Fluffy close. "Because of coyotes and owls." She paused. "If the key isn't there, he can stay in my room until they get home!"

She handed the cat back to Ben and ran inside. Peg knew exactly where the key was and a moment later, Holly returned just in time to hear Adeline inviting Ben to tea.

The color drained from the old man's face as he looked toward the lobby door. "I ... I haven't been in there since I was a boy."

Fluffy, as if sensing his discomfort, put his paws around his neck, pushed his cheek against Ben's, and purred.

Abner nodded understanding. "That happened a long time ago."

"What happened?" Holly asked.

Ben acted like he hadn't heard her and Abner gave her a nearly imperceptible shake of the head.

"What do you say, Ben?" Adeline asked. "It would be very helpful. We'll all wait right here until you get back."

Ben hesitated, looked at Abner, then Holly. "Maybe, for a little while. My delivery man is home sick today, so I couldn't stay long. But first things first, I need to deliver this furball."

Holly smiled. "I'll go with you. We should make sure he has food and water and I know where it is." She put her arms out for the cat.

Together they got in the van. Adeline smiled. "We'll wait right here."

Ben tipped an invisible hat and pulled out, Holly cooing to the cat as they turned toward the Granger home.

BEN GOWER GLANCED AT HOLLY AS HE DROVE SLOWLY UP THE Granger's twisting driveway. She had her face buried in ginger fur and was explaining to the cat that she'd feed him and brush him and that he had to stay inside. "I'm sorry we found the key, Fluffy. I wish you could stay with me. I'd brush you until you don't have a speck of dirt on you."

Ben could hear the cat's purr. He was already sorry he'd agreed to Adeline's invitation to have tea with Dee and the others. He never wanted to set foot in that building again. But he'd agreed because it sounded like it would be helpful, both to Dee and Holly, and he was a grown man now - an old man, for Christ's sake - and it was time to let go of boyhood fears. There would be no dead bodies in the hotel. Just nice people, friends, he might be able to help.

They rounded the last hairpin turn and pulled past the cobblestone walk that led through a perfect garden to the front door. The place was beautiful, Ben thought as he continued on past the kitchen door to the broad area in front of the garage where he could turn the truck around. "Look!" Holly pointed. "Their car is still here."

It was true. The station wagon sat beside Mike's pickup in the covered carport beyond the house.

"That's a little odd." Ben turned the truck around and pulled to a stop by the kitchen door.

"They were supposed to leave before dawn." Holly absently petted the cat. "They went to bed early and everything." She looked worried.

Ben smiled. "Maybe they're out looking for the cat."

Holly brightened. "I bet you're right." She pulled the house key from her pocket and handed it to Ben. "I'll carry Fluffy."

They climbed from the truck and Ben rapped on the kitchen door. Receiving no answer, he tried the doorbell. They heard it chime deep in the house, but no one came to the door. Holly clutched the cat to her, looking worried again. Ben gave her another smile as he put the key into the knob. "Guess we'd better use this. They're probably out looking for that big fellow right this minute."

"Probably." She didn't sound convinced.

They stepped into the silent, shadowed kitchen. Holly put the cat on the floor and he immediately ran to a bowl of kibble and began eating. The poor guy was half-starved.

"Becky?" Holly called. "Meredith?"

No replies. Ben glanced around, saw nothing out of place. No breakfast dishes in the sink. Nothing to indicate anything was wrong. "Maybe the car broke down and they rented one in town."

"Maybe." Holly kept her eyes on the ginger cat. "I hope so."

Ben left her in the kitchen and walked through the living areas downstairs, and pulled up short when he saw a half dozen sleeping bags piled by the bottom of the stairs. *Something's not right.*

In the kitchen, Holly was putting fresh water in the cat's bowl. "I'll be right back," he told her. "Don't go anywhere."

"Okay."

Outside, he hurried past his truck to the garage where he peered into the back of the station wagon. It was full of camping gear. Coolers, tents, knapsacks, a bag of charcoal. *Something's definitely wrong.*

He trotted back to the house as fast as his old legs would carry him.

Holly wasn't in the kitchen. Neither was the cat.

"Holly!" he called.

"Upstairs. I have to catch Fluffy!"

"Holly! Wait for me!" Ben climbed the stairs and came to a sudden halt at the top. Holly's back was to him - she was staring at the cat. And the cat, a dozen feet into the hallway was standing stiff-legged, tail poofed, back arched Halloween-style, glaring at something Ben couldn't see. Hissing at an invisible something.

"Holly?" Ben murmured as he joined her. "Do you see what he's looking at?"

"No. I don't see a thing."

Looking at the closed bedroom doors, fear prickled down Ben's spine. "Holly, go downstairs."

"I have to get Fluffy."

"He's upset and he'll bite you. Let him come on his own."

She looked up at him, her eyes sparking with a promise of gold. "No."

"Then stay right here. Don't move."

He stepped to a set of double doors, figuring this had to be the master bedroom. He tried a knob. It was freezing cold but turned easily. "Stay put, Holly," he called as he opened the door and slipped inside. Something made him pull the door almost closed behind him.

The blinds were drawn; the room was dark and chilly. He could barely see the bed, couldn't tell if it had been made or not. "Meredith?" he murmured. "Mike?"

His bowels turning icy, he switched on the light.

Everything looked normal. He could see the Grangers were still in bed, asleep.

No, not asleep.

THE NURSE WAS SPRAWLED ON THE FLOOR BEHIND THE REGISTRATION desk. In the hospital corridor beyond, more nurses, doctors, patients, some collapsed on the floor, others draped over wheelchairs like laundry on a line, eyes open, staring, fear etched on their lifeless features.

Now, he forced himself to move closer to the bed. Beneath a cheery yellow and white patchwork quilt lay the Grangers. They were on their backs, eyes half open, dull with death. Mike's jaw hung open as if he were screaming and Meredith's hand was a stiff claw over her mouth.

It's happened again.

Outside, Holly screamed.

Ben raced from the room, past the hissing cat, and saw another door gaping open. He ran in. The first thing he saw was a wall full of model horses in a pink, pink bedroom. The second was Holly standing beside a peppermint-striped twin bed, staring at a little blond girl whose frozen features nearly stopped Ben's heart.

"Holly," he said.

"Becky's dead." Holly turned to him, her voice soft but strong.

"She's dead." She pulled the candy cane bedspread up, covering Becky Granger's corpse-white face.

Now all Ben could see was blond hair, like sunbeams, fanning over the pillow.

"They're all dead, aren't they?"

Ben nodded and put his hand gently on Holly's shoulder. "We need to leave."

She let him lead her to the door. "Now I know why I had to go home last night," she murmured.

"What?" he asked, about to shut the door.

"I had to come home. I was sleeping over and going camping with them. And then ... Wait a minute." She rushed back inside, grabbed a paper off Becky's desk, and returned. "Here. Read this."

Ben shut the door then read the note. *"Dear Becky, I left early because I forgot to water the plants yesterday and want to do it before my grandmother wakes up. I forgot that Miss Delilah and I were going to do some things together tomorrow, so I've decided not to go camping with you. I'll come next time. Please tell your mom? I hope you have lots of fun!"*

"I'm glad you left, Holly. Was this the real reason?" Ben glanced at the note.

"No." Holly reached down and picked up the frightened cat, who not only allowed it, but clung to her, burying his face in her hair. "My inner voice told me to leave, but not why." Tears ran down her cheeks. "I wish it had. I would've made them leave, too. I would've woke them up. I- I didn't know. I'm so sorry."

"Of course you would have. But this isn't your fault. Let's take Fluffy and get back to the hotel."

❧ 41 ❧

FLUFFY TALES

Adeline smiled at Holly as she came around Ben's delivery truck, the cat snug in her arms. "Did you decide to have Fluffy stay with you until Meredith gets back?"

But Holly didn't even look at her. She disappeared into the hotel without a word.

Then Addie saw Ben's ashen face as he approached.

"What's wrong?"

Ben's voice trembled. "They're dead."

"Who's dead?" Abner asked.

"Dead in their beds." Ben's voice was hollow. "Meredith and Mike. I found them. Their little girl." He paused. "Holly found her. I told her to stay downstairs, but ..."

"What about the boys?" Addie asked.

"I didn't check their rooms because I wanted to get Holly out of that house." Tears brimmed in his old eyes. "The house feels like a tomb."

"I'll go check on them," Abner volunteered.

"Here." Ben gave him a key. "Kitchen door. Wait." He extracted another key. "Take my truck."

"Thanks." After ordering Keith to stay put, Abner took off.

338

"Can I go in the lobby?" Keith asked, looking a little shell-shocked.

"Of course you may, but leave Holly be," Addie said. "She'll talk to you when she's ready."

"Okay. I'll just look at the souvenirs." The boy trotted away and Addie turned to Ben. "We'd better call the police. And an ambulance."

"I'll bet my soul there's nothing alive in that house." Ben's voice sounded as thin as the air.

Addie ran a hand over her hair, remembering. "Holly was supposed to spend the night with the Grangers. Thank God she didn't!"

"She was there," Ben told her. "She left in the middle of the night." He shook his head. "I don't begin to understand it, but she said she knew she had to go home." He pulled a folded paper from his pocket and handed it to Addie. "She left this in Becky's room."

"Holly's very intuitive." Addie read the note.

She started to hand the note back, but Ben said, "No, you keep it. Destroy it. Addie, she's blaming herself for their deaths, for not warning them to get out."

"I'll talk to her." Addie's mind raced with questions.

"I wonder what killed them," Ben said softly. "I didn't see any marks. It was just like when I was a boy. When I went to the hospital and they were all dead. Just like it." He glanced up at the hotel then fixed his gaze on her. "Addie, I saw the dragon fly last night."

"So did Ike. The Beast is growing stronger." Suddenly she understood. "Ben, I think I know why the Grangers died."

"Why?"

"The Beast knew they were going to take Holly away from here and Henry Hank couldn't allow that to happen."

Ben nodded. "I'd never tell that to the little girl."

"I won't, but she's smart. She's likely thought of it already."

Together, they entered the lobby. Ben joined Keith in front of the T-shirt display while Addie approached the desk. Holly, hugging the cat to her chest, stood just beyond, her face buried in Fluffy's fur. She didn't acknowledge Adeline.

Peg had been watching the girl and now she turned to Addie, her dark eyes shocked and sad. "What-"

"I need to call the police."

"I just did," Peg said.

"Thank you."

"Would you like some coffee?"

"Not right now." Adeline glanced at the girl. She hadn't moved. "I need to speak with Holly-"

A chime announced the elevator's arrival and Adeline watched the heavy doors open. A slim hand pushed the accordion gate aside, then Delilah Devine stepped out, searching eyes passing over Addie without seeing her. In an instant, they found Holly and Dee ran to the girl, enveloped her in her arms, murmuring to her, raining kisses on her brow. At last, she led her toward the stairs.

Relieved, Adeline turned to Peg. "I'd love that cup of coffee."

DELILAH SAT AT HOLLY'S LITTLE DINETTE TABLE POLITELY DRINKING the cup of orange juice her granddaughter insisted on serving her. The girl was maintaining herself by keeping busy, by acting as if nothing were wrong. Delilah understood - it was the same coping mechanism she used.

Holly had put a dish of water on the floor for the cat and as she finished cutting up some leftover chicken for him, the phone rang. Holly glanced up, her eyes alive with terror in her otherwise stony face.

"I'll get it. Fluffy needs you to finish making him his meal." Holly looked grateful and went back to work as Delilah picked up the receiver. "Holly Tremayne's room."

"Miss Delilah, Frieda thought you might be there," Peg Moran said. "I wanted to let you and Holly know that Steve is coming in a little early. He's bringing up some supplies for Holly's guest. Kibble, a litter pan..."

"That's very thoughtful of you, both of you. Thank you. I'll let Holly know." She hung up. Peg wasn't overly fond of people, but she dearly loved cats. Delilah gave Holly the news. The girl nodded and petted Fluffy as he wolfed down the chicken.

Delilah watched her granddaughter shred newspapers then take them into the bathroom. A moment later she returned and carried

Fluffy in. "See, Fluffy? You can pee on the paper in the bathtub until you have your own litter box."

Delilah cringed a little at the thought but made herself stay silent - it was really a very logical idea.

When Holly returned, Fluffy trailing her, Delilah stood. "I think Fluffy will be just fine if you and I go up to the penthouse for a while."

"I don't want to leave him." Holly looked at the cat.

"Just for a little while. Just for a sandwich."

"I'm not hungry."

The child was clearly trying to hide her suffering. "Holly, couldn't you consider coming up for a little bit? I really don't want to be alone. Do you?"

The girl looked up. "You don't?"

Delilah shook her head. "I really don't. Please come keep me company for a little while."

"Well, okay." Holly set Fluffy on the bed and kissed his forehead. "Don't worry, I'll be back soon."

AN HOUR LATER, HOLLY SAT CROSS-LEGGED ON HER BED, FLUFFY IN her lap. His deep rumbling purr soothed her and she wondered if she should have asked her grandmother to come back down with her. The purr would make her feel better, too; it would make anyone feel better.

Up in the penthouse, Frieda had served a tray of dainty sandwiches that had been intended for the tea with Adeline. Holly and Delilah had nibbled at them, but everything had tasted like cardboard. She'd brought a sack of them back to her room. They were in the fridge now. Even the heaping plate of cookies Frieda sent along sat untouched on the neat kitchen counter. Holly wasn't sure she'd ever want to eat again.

After their small meal, Delilah disappeared into her office to make a phone call, so Holly had stepped onto the western balcony. From there, she saw a police car blocking the entrance to the Grangers' driveway and, much higher, a few upstairs windows. Now and then she caught glimpses of movement. That was the worst. Or at least it was until Delilah joined her just in time to see the police car move out of the way and two ambulances slowly pull onto the road and drive off without lights or sirens. Soon after, Delilah reluctantly let her go back to her own room.

"I'm sorry, Fluffy," Holly murmured, fighting back a fresh round of tears as she remembered Becky's bluish-white face once again, the dulling eyes half open, full of terror despite the slack features. Holly knew that face would haunt her for the rest of her life.

Three sharp raps on the door sent Fluffy flying for cover. Holly jumped up and stared. Maybe it was the police wanting to know why she left in the middle of the night. Or maybe it was that bellhop come to tease her about her mother. Maybe-

"Holly?" called Steve. "It's me. Are you in there?"

Relieved, she pulled the door wide. "Come in."

"I've got everything your kitty needs right here." He smiled around two grocery sacks and headed for the table. She shut and locked the door before joining him.

As Steve began unloading the bags, Fluffy leapt onto the table, and with a trilling meow, tried to climb into one of them. Steve laughed as he pulled out a box of Friskies and shook it. "Is this what you're after?"

"I'll get a bowl," Holly said.

"No need. Look in the other bag. I bought him his own bowls."

The kindness almost brought tears again, but she refused to let them fall. "Thank you." She filled the dish and set it on the floor by the water bowl. Fluffy bounded down.

"I got a few cans of food, a catnip mouse and a ball." Steve placed the items on the table. "And here's a litter pan and a sack of Jonny Cat." He smiled. "I almost bought a little bed, but then I thought he'd probably sleep with you. Chester always sleeps with me."

"Chester?"

"Chester's my roommate. He's almost as big as Fluffy and looks a lot like the cat on the litter bag, only with longer fur. We have dinner together most nights," he added as Fluffy returned to the table and batted at the catnip mouse before picking it up in his teeth and running off with it. "Is there anything else you need?"

"I don't think so. Thank you."

"How about a Dr. Pepper?" Steve pulled two bottles out of the bag.

"Yes, please." Holly picked up the litter box and bag of Jonny Cat. "I'll be right back. There's a bottle opener in that first drawer and cookies on the counter."

THEY SAT AT THE TABLE SIPPING SODAS WHILE FLUFFY BATTED THE catnip mouse around. Twice, he'd picked it up and dropped it at Holly's feet. She chuckled as she tossed it for him. She hadn't known that some cats liked to play fetch. Steve watched, his heart breaking for her. He only knew what Peg had told him; it wasn't much, but it was enough.

"She didn't look asleep," Holly said.

"She?"

"Becky. I saw her. I always heard people look asleep when they die. Becky didn't."

"Holly?"

She wouldn't look at him.

"I'm sorry you saw that. I know it's hard."

She stared at her hands. "How do you know?"

"Well, when I was about your age, I saw our neighbor, Mr. Rogers, sitting on his front porch one evening. I waved but he didn't wave back. He was old; I just thought he was dozing. But he was still there the next morning and I wondered if he'd slept in his rocking chair. I yelled hello but he didn't answer. Something felt wrong so I walked up on the porch and tapped his shoulder and said his name. He toppled over. I just stood there and stared. He was so stiff he looked like he was still sitting in the chair. His face was - well, like you said, Holly. He didn't look asleep."

"What did you do?"

"Well, I backed away and ran home and told my parents. Later we found out he'd had a heart attack the day before." He paused. "But do you know what the worst part was?"

She shook her head.

"I thought that it was my fault that he died."

343

Now her eyes met his. "Why?"

"Because I didn't check on him that first night. I thought he might still be alive if I'd paid attention. That maybe I could have saved his life."

"I feel like that, too. About the Grangers." She hesitated. "But it's worse. Like I told you last night, I knew I had to leave. But I should have told them to leave, too."

"Even if you had known to tell them, do you think they would have listened?"

Holly considered. "Probably not."

"It's called 'survivor guilt,' Holly. I had it and so do you. It's natural and normal."

"You mean I feel guilty because I'm not dead, too?"

"Pretty much. And you can't do much about it except wait for it to go away. It will, I promise."

Holly looked dubious. "I don't think s-"

Fluffy jumped on the table and meowed.

Steve scratched him behind the ears. "Holly, you did save a life, you know." The cat head-butted his cheek. "Right Fluffy?"

"You mean-"

"This guy, right here," he said as the cat trilled and purred. "You saved his life."

"All I did was not notice that he sneaked out when I left. He could have died in the storm."

"But he didn't, Holly. He's here now because of you."

"I guess."

"You had a feeling you needed to leave. I think Fluffy maybe had the same feeling. Animals are smart that way. If you hadn't been there to open the door, he would have been trapped. Holly, you saved his life. Think about that. You saved him."

A ghost of a smile appeared on her lips as she reached out and stroked the cat. "I guess."

"No guessing. You did. And now he's here with you. You're tied together forever." He smiled. "Will your grandmother let you keep him?"

"I think so. At least if I get to stay. But if I have to leave, I can't.

344

Cherry's allergic." Tears spilled down her cheeks. "What will happen to him if I have to leave?"

"Don't worry about that. Chester and I would welcome him."

She wiped her eyes and smiled. "Really?"

"Really." The cat batted the little ball off the table and streaked off after it. "It's very sad that the Grangers are gone, but Holly, I believe you were saved for a reason. And so was Fluffy."

❦ 42 ❦

THE TEA PARTY

"Thank you, Frieda," Delilah said as tea was served. Though outwardly composed, she was frazzled as she looked around the table at her guests. All were dressed in black. At Adeline's suggestion, she'd invited them back to the penthouse for refreshments following the funeral. Addie, Ben Gower, Stephen Cross, Abner Hala, and Holly sat around the table. All were friends of the Grangers, but the real reason they were here was that Adeline thought they'd be able to help figure out what to do about Henry Hank Barrow and the missing book.

Adeline had insisted that if they didn't find the book and their grandfather captured Holly's power, it would destroy her, and make Henry Hank unstoppable, and that was a chance that they couldn't take. As much as Delilah didn't want to listen, as much as she didn't want to believe anything her cousin said, she couldn't discount it. What if Adeline was right?

But now, as she nodded at each somber guest, Delilah wondered why she had agreed; the days and nights since the Granger tragedy had been quiet. Neither Holly nor Steve had reported any strange incidents or sightings in the hotel. She believed them; Holly's color had returned and her eyes had lost the hollow look she'd had from lack of sleep.

The Grangers' deaths had been tentatively attributed to a freak gas leak from an old tunnel running under their property. Maybe, Delilah thought now, they should leave well enough alone.

But here we are.

Holly caught her eye and gave her a sad little smile as she sipped her tea. She hadn't cried at the services, but had stood hand-in-hand with Delilah as brave as a soldier - despite the fine tremble of her hand.

Most of the town had attended the funeral; the Grangers had been popular, active members of the Brimstone community. And not only adults had come - the children's friends came out en masse. There must have been fifty kids there, and that was the saddest thing of all, save for the small caskets of the children.

"I'm glad to see all of you," Delilah said, "but I'm sorry we're here under such sad circumstances."

They responded with polite murmurs and Delilah realized that Abner and Ben, and possibly even Steve, didn't know why they'd been invited. She should have explained.

Only a few days ago - just before the original meeting with Adeline was scheduled - Delilah had seriously considered packing Holly up and taking her away on an impromptu vacation - a month in Hawaii, perhaps. She'd gotten as far as picking up the phone to call her travel agent before realizing that without Charlotte's permission, she couldn't do it - and Charlotte seemed to have disappeared off the face of the earth.

Now Frieda returned with a cart bearing tiered trays - one of finger sandwiches - half cucumber, half ham - and the other laden with scones and petit fours. With a smile for Holly, Ben reached out and snatched up a chocolate petit four with a plump raspberry on top.

"While we're here to remember the Grangers," Delilah said, "we're also gathered for another reason. Last week, Holly and I invited Adeline over to help me remember where I hid a book my sister gave me. Our grandfather's book. It's important that we find it now." She glanced around the table. "Adeline believes Holly's safety may depend on this book. For a while, I believed it as well, but now that things have quieted down, I'm not so sure we need it."

"The quiet won't last." Adeline spoke softly.

"Well, I'd like to think it will and-"

"Dee," Adeline interrupted, "I hope you're right but we can't risk it."

"I know why Ben is here - you were an eyewitness to some of what happened. And you, Steve, you're practically the town historian." Delilah's eyes settled on the Indian. "But Abner, how are you involved?"

"Your granddaughter ran off bullies who were picking on my grandson. Keith saw her golden eyes and I've caught a glimpse as well." Abner gazed steadily at Delilah. "I know that Holly has the same gift as your sister and grandfather did, and as your cousin does. She sees spirits." He paused. "I also know that your grandfather was teaching Addie and Carrie to use their gifts to nudge people into doing his bidding. I believe that is his interest in Holly as well."

"What-" Delilah began.

"That was something that we found very difficult to do," Addie interrupted. "Almost impossible."

"But you did it when Pearl attacked me," Holly said.

"You did most of it, sweetheart." Addie smiled at the girl.

Delilah looked from one to the other, confused. "What are you talking about?"

Adeline cleared her throat. "Dee, Holly is far more gifted than your grandfather, sister, or me. Your grandfather figured out that if he concentrated very hard, he could sometimes incline others toward his will. But he wanted to bend them completely to it. The ability seems to be tied to the gold in our eyes. Henry Hank's talent, like his gold spot, was smaller than Carrie's or even mine, and I think that fact made him even meaner and angrier."

Adeline sipped her tea. "Grandfather began training Carrie and me to nudge people. I had a little more flair for it than he did, but Carrie was markedly better at it." Shaking her head, Adeline added, "If Carrie concentrated really hard, the fleck in her eye would do more than pulse - it swirled and sometimes her iris would appear both blue and gold. Henry Hank wanted ..." Adeline stared at the ceiling, pondering. "Well, he wanted to possess that power. I'm not sure how he expected

to get it, but I believe he had plans to somehow take physical possession of one or both of us." She paused. "After all, he'd already tried to
create a thought-form in the form of the Brimstone Beast. Honestly, I
think that he wanted to inhabit Carrie, to take her body for himself.
He was a crazy old man, mad for power." She glanced around the table.

Abner pondered. "What Barrow didn't understand was that he
wasn't creating a thought-form. He was tampering with a natural yet
very negative force. The Hellfire Spirit of my people's lore." He looked
at Delilah with raised brows. "The Brimstone Beast of yours."

"I know he *called* himself the Brimstone Beast," Delilah said.

Abner nodded. "He did more than that - he tried to become one
with the creature. It was more than he could handle and that's why he
is a fractured soul, a broken spirit. That's why Holly sees his ghost as a
black cloud. He has lost his form." He glanced at Holly. "Henry Hank
Barrow is at his most vulnerable; a fractured spirit is relatively weak. It
means now is our best shot. If we wait ... it may be too late."

Ben Gower nodded thoughtfully. "You know, I've always thought
that Henry Hank was mimicking Aleister Crowley with all that
Infurnam Aeris nonsense."

"Now that you mention it," Abner said, "I have to agree. Both were
depraved cult leaders with delusions of grandeur."

Delilah said dryly, "It sounds as if they both belonged in
Hollywood."

Abner grinned.

Ben Gower finished a cucumber sandwich in one bite and reached
for another, a twinkle in his eye. "Henry Hank no doubt studied
Crowley and resented his wider fame. He was a bitter man; his gold
fleck was smaller than his own granddaughter's. He was nothing but a
big fish in a very small pond. Everything about Crowley was bigger. No
wonder Henry Hank was such a sour piece of work." He paused. "No
offense, Delilah."

"None taken," she told him. "I was just six when he died, but I was
terrified of him. Carrie always told me he was a bad man." She gave her
granddaughter a little smile. "Holly, you haven't been nudging *me* to do
things, have you?"

Holly looked shocked. "No! I mean, I knew before that lots of times people were nice to me, like Cherry would let me have a double scoop at Thrifty's or stay up late when I really wanted to, but I never even thought ... you know, that *I* did it. I don't think I did. And I swear, until Keith saw my eyes change color, I didn't even know that could happen."

"You used your talent to help me, too," Delilah said." She looked around the table. "After the earthquake in the restaurant, she made the waiters and other guests look away while we left." She smiled at Holly. "You saved me from a great deal of embarrassment and I should have thanked you then. I'm thanking you now."

Holly blushed. "You're welcome. I think that was the first time I ever did it. I was really upset. I can only do it if I'm mad, like when those bullies picked on Keith and me or when those waiters wouldn't listen to me when I said to leave us alone. I can't do it if I'm scared."

"You're wrong on both counts, sweetheart," Adeline said. "At the gas station, you caused Ike and me to guess the exact candy bars you concentrated on. And when I drove up while Pearl Abbott was attacking you on the road, you were terrified but you did just fine."

"What happened on the road?" Delilah demanded. "What haven't you told me?"

Holly swallowed. "I was coming home to get ready for tea and Pearl Abbott attacked me. I had to concentrate really hard to get mad."

"It happened right where the old trailhead used to be," Abner said. "Straight up from Pearl Abbott's house."

"Pearl Abbott?" Delilah looked from Holly to Abner.

Holly stood and slipped off her black jacket, showing Delilah the newest bruises, and a painful-looking purplish welt on one forearm.

Delilah gasped. "Holly! I think we should take you to the doctor."

"They're just bruises." The girl pulled her jacket back on. "They're already a lot better. They'll go away."

"Pinching Pearl Abbott." Ben spoke softly. "Head nurse at the Clementine and high priestess of *Infurnam Aeris*." He caught Delilah's eye. "She did the same to me once. Evil woman. That was the last time I ever came up here. Until the other day." He glanced from Addie to Abner. "Do either of you have any idea how powerful Henry Hank and

Pinching Pearl were? I mean, just how powerful were their *Infurnam Aeris* rituals? There were always rumors but until now I've discounted it all as utter nonsense."

Adeline nodded. "I heard rumors too, particularly about nurses who boarded at Pearl's house disappearing under mysterious circumstances."

"Sacrifices, I heard," Ben said. "Sounded ridiculous at the time."

Abner scratched his chin. "I guess we all heard those things. Babies went missing from the maternity ward. My father talked about that. My siblings and I were born at home. My son was born at the hospital in Lewisdale. I wasn't taking any chances, either."

Addie said, "I didn't have my children at the Clementine, in part because of what happened there the day Carrie died, but mainly because of the missing babies. I had a friend who had a healthy baby there. The next day, they told her it died, and wouldn't let her see the body. I'm sure something awful happened to it."

Delilah was horrified. These were things she had managed to avoid but now, glancing at Holly, she knew she no longer could. "Ben, what happened that day?"

The elderly druggist turned pale. "It's not something I like to talk about. I was just a boy the day Pearl pinched me. I ran out of the hospital straight into her and Henry Hank."

"You were running because you'd just found the bodies," Abner said.

Ben's hand trembled, sloshing tea. "How did you know? That was before your time."

"I heard about it from my father some years later. He was one of the men who went up to investigate with your father and the constable."

"You're talking about the gas leak that killed everyone in the hospital?" Delilah asked.

"Yes," Ben said, his face stricken.

"But it wasn't a gas leak," Abner said. "And I don't think the Granger's died of a gas leak either. They blamed a leak then, just as they did today, because they couldn't find any other explanation."

Abner looked at Ben. "My dad said something about the Beast being responsible for the deaths."

Ben nodded. "My father said that if it had been a gas leak from the mines, they would've located and capped it. Or they would've closed the hospital down and rebuilt it somewhere safer. But they didn't. The incident was swept under the rug and all but forgotten." Ben shook his head. "Just like the Granger deaths will be. That's how it works around here." He sighed. "Abner, when your father said the Beast might be behind it, did he mean the mythical creature or did he mean Henry Hank himself?"

Abner rubbed his chin. "He didn't say, but I believe he meant Henry Hank."

Ben nodded. "Makes sense to me. Barrow called himself the Beast even before the century began. My dad was a druggist, so there was a scientific bent to his thinking, and he thought Henry Hank was behind the whole thing, that he'd somehow dispersed a deadly gas into the hospital. It happened on a morning when the Clementine was mostly empty of patients and was attended by a very small staff. But what always confounded me was why Barrow would wipe out all those people in his own hospital."

"To kill his enemies," Abner said. "A man like that would surely have plenty of them."

Adeline asked, "Would he harm innocent people just to kill an enemy?"

Steve Cross cleared his throat. "I might have an answer to that. One of the doctors who died was Virgil Endicott, the chief surgeon. Including Endicott, there were six senior medical staff on the board that Henry Hank ran. Endicott and three of the other doctors were continually at odds with him over finances and patient care. They fought a lot."

Steve folded his hands. "All four died that morning. The two surviving doctors were in Henry Hank's pocket. After the deaths, Barrow was able to cut corners as he saw fit. He replaced the dead doctors with new ones who worked cheap and the death rate at the Clementine skyrocketed."

"There you go," said Ben.

"It makes sense," Delilah agreed. "Perfect sense. Carrie was right about that bastard. So was my aunt. She loathed him."

"Dee," Ben said, "did your aunt tell you anything about him?"

"She only met him twice," Delilah said. "Aunt Beatrice once told me that Henry Hank was the devil's right hand. I believe those were her exact words. She felt he was vulgar and coarse despite his fancy clothing. She wasn't crazy about my father, either - which isn't surprising since he was Henry Hank's protégé and right-hand man. Bill Delacorte became the chief administrator at the hospital after Henry Hank's death, and the building was deeded to him when Frank Langley Clementine - head of the Clementine Mining Company - died." She looked around the table. "But the important thing is that Carrie feared and hated Henry Hank."

Ben cleared his throat. "All we really know now is that the hospital didn't have many patients and only a small staff on duty when it happened. That's what the local constabulary and preachers talked about - how much worse it could have been. And it never happened again in all these years. I think you've solved the mystery, Steve. Somehow Henry Hank killed everyone in the building to get rid of his political enemies."

"I think it's likely," Steve said. "Though gas leaks weren't uncommon in the mines. It could've been a happy coincidence for Henry Hank."

"True enough," Ben agreed.

"There were rumors that it happened in Pearl's house, too," Steve said.

"I remember that." Addie poured herself more tea.

"Given what I saw in the Clementine that morning, I'm inclined to believe it was intentional," Ben said. "People had dropped dead right where they stood. I remember seeing a nurse slumped over a wheelchair in the hall. She was as dead as her patient. None of them looked like they'd been choking or suffocating. It was as if they'd simply stopped being alive." He paused. "Just like what happened to the Granger family. It was the same." He looked to Holly. "I'm sorry."

She nodded darkly. "The Beast killed them. He killed them all."

ARTHUR MEEKS HADN'T GONE TO THE FUNERAL, THOUGH HE WAS sorry that a piece of ass as fine as Meredith Granger had died in her prime. She was a lot more fun to look at than Piggy Moran. He'd been polishing luggage carts in the lobby when the Queen Douchebag, Little Miss Fancy Pants, and that motley crew of locals took the elevator up to the fifth floor. Piggy said they were having a wake. *Well, whoop-de-doo!*

Now, twenty minutes later, he used his passkey to let himself into room 429 to take the monk bank and hopefully find some dirty panties in Fancy Pants' laundry hamper.

He walked through the shadowy room, past the empty laundry basket, and into the bathroom where, sure enough, three pairs of underwear were drying on the towel rack. He grabbed a pair of pink ones and stuffed them in his pocket, then returned to the dresser and snatched up the monk, sliding it into his T-shirt. "Come to Daddy."

"Meow!"

Go to sleep, Arthur, or the lion will eat you! His mother's voice.

Panicked, he turned and there on the bed was a gigantic long-haired orange cat. It glared at him. Arthur's blood ran cold. Then the cat stood up and hissed, ears back, showing long white fangs and gold devil's eyes.

"Go back to hell where you belong!" Without taking his eyes off the cat, Arthur backed out of the room and pulled the door firmly closed, made sure it locked. *Fucking Satan's spawn has a fucking cat!* He wondered if somebody had told the girl that he hated cats. Probably. Probably that fucking dead Meredith. Or maybe one of the maids. They all knew he didn't like to hear about the ghost cat, and sometimes even teased him about it. *Fucking cunts!*

He'd get them all. But first, he was going to get Little Miss Fancy Pants.

THE ADULTS KEPT TALKING AS THE LOWERING SUN SLANTED LONG

beams across the Oriental rugs. Holly stared into her tea, but she was carefully listening and storing up a million questions. She thought she'd ask Steve most of them since he was really into history. And what he didn't know, Adeline probably would.

"Holly?" Delilah asked, "Are you with us?"

"Yes." She sat up straighter. "I was just thinking ..."

"About what?"

"The book Adeline says we need to find."

"That's a good thing to think about." Adeline peered around the table. "After all, that's the primary reason we're here."

"This must be a very important book," Abner said.

Delilah nodded. "The day my sister and grandfather died, Carrie brought a book up from the basement - a big black book with the *Infurnam Aeris* symbol on it. She told me to hide it. I did, but I can't remember where." She glanced toward the windows. "I have recalled one thing that may or may not be true. I think I hid it in a small cave in the desert out there somewhere. It couldn't be too far away since I was on foot."

"What is the importance of the book?" That was Abner.

"It was Henry Hank Barrow's grimoire," said Adeline. "A book of spells. Carrie and I managed to look through it a few times. It contained all manner of crazy stuff including spells that we thought we might be able to use to protect ourselves from our grandfather's abuses, along with spells that might weaken him. There was also an incantation that would stop restless spirits from making trouble for the living; that's the one we hope to use on him now. If it works, it would put Henry Hank - and any other spirit, including Pinching Pearl - back in the grave for once and for all. Otherwise, I don't think Henry Hank will ever stop trying to possess Holly."

"Go on." Delilah said.

"Henry Hank kept the basement of the hospital locked. He considered it his private office and I don't think he ever brought anyone but Pearl Abbott - and Carrie and me - down there. But it was a lot more than an office. He had all kinds of lab equipment, books, horrible things floating in jars. There were beds and an operating table down there. Other things." Adeline paused. "Not that we understood much of anything. But he kept the book down there, too."

"And?" asked Holly.

"Well, that last day, Carrie and I had gone to the basement with the intention of taking the book. We knew Grandfather was planning something - something awful - and we knew it had to do with us. We meant to use the grimoire to destroy him that night. But he caught us." She glanced at the others. "Carrie managed to run upstairs and give it to Dee to hide before he could stop her." Addie looked at Delilah. "Providence must have seen to it that you opened the door at that precise moment, Dee."

"Synchronicity," Holly said, glancing at Abner.

"Yes," Adeline said. "And Delilah must have run like the wind because Henry Hank rushed up those basement stairs behind Carrie and grabbed her - I was trying to pull him back, but he was huge and strong and even with both of us fighting, we were no match for him physically." She looked to Delilah. "It was only a minute before he threw us off and opened the door to go after you. Fortunately, Dee, you were long gone."

Terror flickered across Adeline's face. "How he roared with rage! We clung to the railings so we wouldn't fall down those stairs as he slammed out and locked us in. A few seconds later we heard the creak of the copper door. And he was gone.

"We stood there clinging to each other absolutely terrified that he was going to catch you, Dee. We prayed you were safe. How we prayed." Adeline paused. "Then we came to our senses and prepared for his return. We knew he'd be back and if he'd caught you, Dee, we had to save you - and if he hadn't, we still had to save ourselves. Either way, we knew we had to destroy him. To somehow kill him, even if we didn't have the spell book anymore."

"I don't remember seeing him," Delilah said.

"And he didn't see you, Dee. When he returned, he came down the stairs, coldly furious. He had Pearl Abbot with him. They couldn't see us because we'd put out the lanterns and had hidden in the empty storage closet under the stairwell. Carrie held a length of pipe and I had a big claw hammer." Adeline held up her hands. "Look at that. I'm trembling. It's as if it happened yesterday.

"But no matter." She took a deep breath. "We waited, listening. Grandfather stood cursing while Pearl fumbled around lighting the lamps. We were so afraid. In the book, there was a spell that was supposed to stop him from wanting to do ... physical things ... to us, but we hadn't copied it out either, and now the book was gone. We were so terrified - for ourselves, and now for Delilah, too. We knew he would punish and ... abuse us. Physically."

"Do you mean he'd hit you?" Holly sat forward.

Adeline glanced at Delilah, then looked at Holly. "Has your mother or teacher ever told you not to accept candy or rides from strangers?"

"Yes," Holly said without a blink. "She told me why, too. Did your grandfather do things to you and Carrie?"

Adeline could only nod. Holly looked to Delilah. "Did he do bad things to you, too?"

"I ... I don't think so. I was very young." Her beautiful face looked pale, shocked by the question.

Holly nodded. "Cherry says how young you are doesn't matter to men like that."

"Holly," Adeline said quickly. "He didn't lay a hand on your grandmother. Your great aunt Carrie saw to that - she guarded her with her life and never let him near her."

"Adeline?" Holly set her teacup down.

"Yes?"

"What happened in the cellar? Did he find you?"

"He did. We were in that storage closet and he pulled the door open and shone a lantern in our faces. He called Pearl over. I remember her standing behind him with a smile on her face that would frighten Lucifer himself."

"What happened then?"

"Well, Carrie and I had no spells to cast so we came out swinging."

Adeline no longer trembled - now there was fire in her eye. Golden fire. The fleck shimmered and pulsed, and Holly watched, fascinated. "Carrie hit Henry Hank across the back with the iron pipe, but he didn't go down - he just roared and turned, trying to grab the pipe, but

Carrie stayed just out of reach, parrying and thrusting like it was a sword. I nearly lost my hammer because I was watching her, but Carrie yelled just as Pearl grabbed the business end and tried to yank it out of my hands. I managed to hang on. I got loose of Pearl and ran, but she was on me like a steamroller, throwing me to the floor, pulling my hair, pinching me with those talons of hers and trying to wrestle away the hammer. I just huddled over it, catching my breath, watching Carrie as she struck Henry Hank and struck him again.

"Pearl wouldn't stop. She pulled my head up and tried to pound it against the cement floor, so I curled into a ball, counted to three, then exploded at her, pulling her over until I was sitting on top of her, staring into those beetle-black eyes. I've never seen such hatred, not even on Henry Hank's face. That woman was pure evil.

"Right then, Henry Hank got hold of Carrie's iron pipe and swung it at her. He caught her across the stomach and she flew backwards, landed on her back. Before she could catch her breath, he was standing over her with the pipe, laughing.

"And then Pearl grabbed my throat and started squeezing. Without a thought, I raised the hammer and bashed it into her forehead with all my strength. Once, twice, and the third time, she let go. I heard Henry Hank bellow and knew he'd watched me kill Pearl. As I stood up, I saw her face in the lamplight covered in blood, the life in those black eyes dimming. Then Carrie screamed. Henry Hank had raised the pipe and was about to do the same thing to her.

"I leapt on him and his blow missed Carrie. He went after me now and I'd dropped my hammer. As he came at me with that pipe I thought I was dead, but I jumped out of the way as he swung. When he swung again, all silent fury, I saw something - the Beast. It appeared over him, like a ghost. Henry Hank's eyes seemed to glow red, and I saw black scales tinged with blue flame all around him. He swung again and this time he shattered my arm. I fell.

"That's when Carrie cursed him for a coward. She had the hammer raised, Pearl Abbott's gore and hair dripping from it, as she came at him. At that moment, I saw her eyes and the one with the gold mark swirled with power. It wasn't like yours, Holly, not by a long shot, but it was more than I'd ever seen. It was molten.

"Henry Hank saw it, too, and I think that's why Carrie managed to hit him - he was so shocked that his Beast-shadow vanished. He let her hit him again because he wanted her to come closer and I realized he wanted to possess her now more than ever, to take her body and power for his own." Adeline shook her head. "He didn't need the Beast if he could have her.

"As she rained hammer blows on him, she kept telling him he was nothing and he'd never touch either of us again. She said it over and over, her own incantation, and I managed to stand up and say the words along with her.

"Carrie bashed his cheek in. I saw teeth fly. She'd broken his jaw. How he screamed his pain and rage as he raised the pipe and slammed it into her side. I saw blood splash and heard bone crack as it hit her ribs. I thought she was done for, but Carrie didn't drop, not yet. Instead, she raised that hammer one more time, and with the gold in her eye blazing, she cried out 'Never!' It was a voice not of this world and nearly burst my eardrums - my ears rang for weeks after that. Carrie had found her power.

"She stopped Henry Hank in his tracks. He stared at her, and I saw his face. It was a mix of lust and fear, of envy and greed, it was every deadly sin all rolled into one. But he hesitated, no doubt as deafened as I was, and then Carrie swung the hammer and struck him square between the eyes, bursting his nose, caving his face. She struck again, and he fell dead."

Adeline met Holly's eyes and Holly understood. "You killed him, but that didn't stop him."

"It did for a while, but not forever." Adeline spoke quietly. "We needed the book to truly stop him. We still do."

Tears rolled freely down Addie's face as Delilah took her hand. "Carrie fell then," Adeline continued. "I put a pillow under her head and tried to stop the bleeding, but it was so bad ... I told her I was going for help, and as I turned to go up the stairs, the door opened. It was your father, Delilah. Carrie's preternatural scream had been heard by the nurses in the lobby and he'd come to see what was going on. He took one look at me and locked the door behind him.

"Bill Delacorte might've been a hard man, but he loved us, especially Carrie and you, Dee. I trailed him as he passed Pearl's body without a glance, then Henry Hank's, and knelt beside Carrie, took her hand in both of his. 'I'm sorry, Father.' That's what Carrie said to him as she lay dying. 'I'm sorry.'" Adeline wiped her tears. "'I couldn't let him hurt us anymore,' she said. 'He was going to hurt Delilah, too. I'm sorry, Father.'" Addie shook her head. "Those words will never leave me. Carrie called for me then and I knelt beside her. 'Tell Delilah I love her,' she said. She looked back at her father. 'Send Dee away from here, Father. Promise me.' He promised and then with a single sigh, Carrie passed in his arms." Addie wiped away tears.

"Uncle Bill didn't ask me what had happened, but he told me not to say anything to anyone, that he would take care of things. And he did. "Uncle Bill told the constable that Henry Hank and his nurse had lured us downstairs to try to do horrible things to us. Sexual things having to do with *Infurnam Aeris*. That there'd been a fight.

"There were funerals, and Bill Delacorte wouldn't let anybody see the bodies of Pearl Abbot or Henry Hank. Not at all. Uncle Bill took over as chief administrator of the hospital the same day. No one dared question him - Barrow had many enemies and some had already suspected he was abusing his granddaughters. Uncle Bill's story held up because it was true.

"And Delilah, that day, your father found you wandering in the desert west of here and brought you home. He was not a demonstrative man - he didn't know the meaning of the word - but he arranged for you to go to Boston to live with your aunt. You never spoke a word after that day, and he told me that your aunt wrote the following year to say you'd found your voice once more and that you were doing well with her. That was all I ever heard of you until he died and you came back to town."

Delilah wiped her eyes. "I'm sorry, Addie. I don't know how I got it in my head that you were the reason Carrie died. Can you forgive me?"

"There's nothing to forgive. You were just a child. I'm glad we can be friends again."

"ME, TOO." DELILAH SAT UP STRAIGHT AND FORCED THE SADNESS from her face, replacing it with determination. "And now we must find the book and get rid of Henry Hank Barrow for once and for all." She hesitated, then said, "Aunt Beatrice taught me to read the Tarot and while I don't believe in fortune telling, I do think the cards can open our minds up to certain things we may otherwise overlook. The other night, I threw the cards on the question of the book's location and one card stood out and followed me into my dreams. It's what helped me recall the cave. Perhaps if I tell you all, it would help. You, especially, Abner. You might know."

"Tell us, Dee," Addie said.

Quickly, Delilah told them about the throw, about the Hermit who stood looking into a dark cavern that his lantern couldn't illuminate. She kept an eye on Holly as she recounted the dream. The girl took in every word, eyes so intense that Delilah thought she caught motes of gold dust swirling through them. "And the Hermit morphed into an Indian and he showed me the inside of the cave. It wasn't very big and it was above the ground. I had to climb up into it. But when I saw inside, I recognized the petroglyphs on the wall. A hunt." She paused, her mind dredging up another fact. "I left the book there, under a flat rock, right under the art and I asked the long-dead artist to watch over the book for me."

She looked at the others. "I know that sounds absurd, but I was only six."

"It doesn't sound absurd at all." Abner leaned forward. "There are many caves containing glyphs nearby. Did you see anything else?"

"In my dream, the Indian pointed at the ceiling of the cave and there was art there as well. Men running. Only they were the hunted, not the hunters. There was a huge monster, like a dragon, flying after them, and killing them."

"The Hellfire Serpent," Abner said. "I know this place. I haven't been there since I was a boy, but I might be able to find it. There's a strange stone near it, two-toned. It stands like a guard."

Shocked, Delilah said, "Yes, I remember!"

"We must go there soon," Abner said. "Tomorrow."

"Yes," said Adeline, "and we must also be prepared for another attack."

"It's been quiet for days." Delilah clung desperately to that fact. "It may be over."

Adeline squeezed her hand. "I pray you're right, Dee, but we can't take a chance; we must be prepared."

✣ 43 ✣

SLIGHTLY QUIET NIGHT

ittle Miss Fancy Pants is going to get hers. Oh, yessireebob, she is going to get hers. Arthur Meeks waited for the obnoxious couple - the Dixons - to exit the elevator. The man, - Dickhead - wore a safari suit and horn-rimmed glasses as he yapped about hiking up Brimstone Peak to see the ancient Indian dwellings first thing in the morning. The beehive-haired wife sported a pair of unrestrained silicone titties that stood at attention, gravelly nipples straining against her thin white top. *Sugartits.* They were way too big for his tastes, but fake or not, they looked good and he imagined her getting it on with Cherry Devine.

"Bellboy, let's go," Dickhead said. "We haven't got all day."

"Tick tock." Sugartits' glazed red lips spread in a suggestive smile and Arthur wondered if they were married or if she was a hooker.

He smiled back. "Straight down the hall to your left. Room 401." The pair began walking as he pulled the accordion gate closed, pausing to look back toward Miss Fancy Pants' door. Still nothing going on that he could see. The townies were still upstairs - their cars remained parked out front. *What in hellation are they doing up there?* Then he hurried to catch up with the Dickheads. There were asses to kiss and tips to wrangle.

✠

HOLLY LET HERSELF INTO HER DARK ROOM AND JUMPED AS something soft rubbed against her ankles. "Fluffy!" She picked up the huge orange cat and held him. Immediately, he began purring and gave her a soft contented meow.

"Did you meet Miss Annie Patches yet?" Holly set the cat down and got him a last bite of chicken from the refrigerator. She'd been a little worried, but Fluffy had either not met the ghost kitty or got along famously with her. Either way, Holly was happy.

Fluffy made short work of the food and asked for more just as someone rapped on the door. Holly looked out the peephole. No one was there. Thinking maybe it was the door-knocking ghost, she opened it and was surprised to see Arthur Meeks moving quickly down the hall. *It was him!* Irritated, she stared hard after him.

Suddenly, he turned, feeling her gaze. He smiled, mouth closed but wide, like a rubber-faced clown without makeup. "Hello, Miss Devine."

"Tremayne," she muttered, refusing to look away.

"What was that? I didn't quite hear you." A lock of thin dishwater hair had escaped his little round cap and hung over his forehead, making him look like a gigantic ten-year-old with his pale round face and potato-shaped body. But his watery blue eyes, so light that at this distance they looked like black pupils in a sea of white, those were *not* childish. They were hard and bright and mean. He took a few halting steps toward her. "Can I help you with anything, Miss Devine? Any little thing at all?" His tongue poked out to lick his lips.

She didn't answer, just stared at him, anger growing. Fluffy poked his head out of the door at that moment, rubbed against her ankle, and meowed. As she bent to scoop him up, Meeks' pasty face turned even pastier. He turned and hurried to his room, slamming his door behind him.

"That was weird." She kissed Fluffy's forehead and went back into her room. "How about I go down to the restaurant? They have chicken and biscuits tonight. I'll bring some up and we can have dinner together, okay?"

Fluffy answered with a purry meow.

"But first, I need to do a couple things." She scooped his litter pan then took the underwear she'd left on the towel rack to dry back to the dresser. There were only two pair; she thought there'd been three; the pink pair with the embroidered flowers was missing. "Huh." Maybe she was remembering wrong. With a sigh, she started to open the drawer.

Goosebumps prickled her neck. Something wasn't right, but she didn't know what. The door was locked. Fluffy sat on the bed energetically cleaning his face. *I'm just being weird.* Holly replaced the underwear, shut the drawer firmly, then stopped.

Something *was* wrong.

Her Friar Tuck bank was gone. She moved the stacks of books and notepads, but the little Hummel monk was nowhere to be seen. "Fluffy?" She looked at the cat. "Have you seen Friar Tuck?"

The fluffy feline chirped at her.

"You're a lot of help." Holly smiled then began searching. She checked the other dresser drawers and the bureau that held the little black and white TV. Then the counters and drawers and cabinets in the kitchenette. Finally, she got down on her hands and knees and peered under the bed. Fluffy came and looked with her but there was nothing there, not even a dust bunny. She scritched him behind the ears. "I wish you'd tell me where Friar Tuck is."

Fluffy just looked at her and when she crawled across to the dresser, he padded along beside her, talking in his funny little purr-meow. She put her head down and peered under the furniture, thinking maybe it had somehow fallen behind the dresser.

But it hadn't. It was gone.

IF THERE WAS ANYTHING THAT GOT METHUSELAH ROARING, IT WAS rage - and Arthur Meeks had plenty of that.

Little Miss Fancy Pants - an eleven-year-old girl, for Christ's sake - was pushing all of his buttons ... and he knew she absolutely relished his discomfort. No, his fear. Yes, fear - *Call a spade a spade.* But in his defense, there was something truly creepy about the little girl and her weird eyes. And when that demon cat of hers looked at him, too, he'd gotten out of there fast. He didn't need two sets of gold eyes staring at him.

She and her damned cat were enough to scare anybody and Arthur took comfort in that. *Fucking Satan's spawn.*

But he still felt like a pussy and that made him mad. And *that* made Methuselah throb.

He lay on his bed, staring at the ceiling, the pair of stolen pink panties balled in his clenched fist. Closing his eyes, he brought the underwear to his nose and took a deep whiff. They were too clean but under the fragrance of soap, he detected the ever-so-subtle tang of sweat, of tender young skin, of virginal territory. The smell of little girls.

It was his favorite smell in the world. It lacked the yeasty, used smell of grown women. He enjoyed that, too - but not like this, never like this. *Clean as the driven snow.* He took another deep whiff, pushing down a giggle as he touched the fabric to the tip of his tongue. *So tender, so young, yes, yes, yes.* He had no memory of setting Methuselah free, but his rigid cock throbbed hot and hard in his hand now as Meeks slowly stroked and sniffed, stroked and sniffed.

44

CHERRY PICKING

Holly sat at her little round dinette table finishing a plate of hot chicken and dumplings; she hadn't eaten anything at the tea and for the first time since the Grangers died, she was really hungry. On the chair across from her, Fluffy sat neatly eating from his own plate. She'd piled books up to give him a makeshift booster seat so he had no trouble reaching his dinner. Holly smiled, watching him. "You're so polite. You never put your elbows on the table."

Fluffy looked at her and chirped.

"Yes, I agree." she told him. "It's very good. I brought extra so you can have it for breakfast, too." She watched the cat eat, hoping against hope that he would be hers forever. It was fun knowing Miss Annie Patches hung around, but a ghost kitty was nothing like having a warm, furry cat to hold and pet.

Holly finished her milk. "I'm still thirsty, Fluffy. Are you?" She poured herself another quarter of a glass then refilled Fluffy's saucer. "There you go."

Fluffy gave her a chirpy meow and two long, slow blinks then started lapping the milk.

"You're welcome."

A moment later, she heard the elevator chime halfway down the hall. She waited, listening. After a few seconds, footsteps approached and then Arthur Meek's voice calling, "Miss Devine! You dropped something!"

She jumped, stomach fluttering, and then realized he wasn't talking to her.

Cherry's back! Holly crossed to the door and stood on tiptoes to peer out the peephole. Her mother, wearing what looked like a silvery mink stole, stood at the door across the hall staring at Arthur Meeks who was pushing a pack of cigarettes at her. He fumbled and dropped them then bent down and took forever retrieving them because he was ogling her mini-skirted legs.

"You're pathetic," Cherry said, grabbing the smokes.

"Can I help you with anything Miss Devine?"

"I'll call you to take my bags down when I'm ready."

"Yes, Miss Devine. Anything else?"

She looked at his proffered paw. "Scram. I'm in a hurry." Entering the room, she slammed the door in his face.

Holly returned to the table in a daze. "Fluffy, I think I might have to leave, but Steve will take care of you, I promise."

The cat gave a questioning meow.

Holly's throat felt thick, her eyes burned and tears threatened to fall. She swallowed; she didn't want to go back to Van Nuys and hadn't wanted to since she'd arrived. She loved it here where she had her own room, good food, and didn't have to wash cigarette smell out of her hair and clothes every single day. She loved not hiding in a dingy corner of that stuffy, stinky studio apartment while Cherry entertained her boyfriends. And she loved her grandmother. She didn't want to leave her, or for that matter, her new friends.

The tears streamed now and she fell onto the bed, giving herself over to them. After a few minutes, Fluffy meowed at her and nuzzled her cheek. She rolled onto her side and he curled up against her, purring and chirping, trying to tell her it would be okay, but it just made her cry harder.

STEVE CROSS OFFICIALLY CAME ON DUTY ONLY MOMENTS BEFORE Cherry Devine had flounced into the lobby wrapped in silver mink. She'd been so perfectly balanced on ridiculously high white stilettos that she looked like a ballerina on point. She'd blown him a crimson-lipped kiss as she strutted to the elevator, but returned immediately, requesting his aid.

Cherry was a poor man's Jayne Mansfield and since that recently deceased actress had been a poor man's Marilyn Monroe, the picture wasn't as pretty as Cherry seemed to think. It reeked of the cheap perfume that she managed to rub on his clothing as he showed her which button to push for the fourth floor before pulling the cage closed on her. She'd given him a breathless "bye bye" then blew him another kiss before the main doors shut.

"Good riddance," Steve muttered as the elevator ascended. He was sorry she was back. She might be easy on the eyes, but she was hard on the soul.

He watched the elevator ding up to the fourth floor then went back to the registration desk, his mind on Holly, hoping the woman wouldn't do her daughter any damage. A few minutes later, new guests arrived, then another set, and he was so busy that an hour passed before he thought of Holly again.

Guiltily, he called up to her room and as he was about to hang up, she answered, her voice thick. "Holly? You okay?"

"Yeah." She sounded nothing like her usual self.

"Did you know your mom is here?"

There was a long silence, then she said, "Cherry."

"Yes. She arrived maybe an hour ago."

"Okay, thanks." Holly hung up.

Her flat tone disturbed him. Holly had never sounded that way before.

CHERRY HUMMED AS SHE FOLDED CLOTHES AND PLACED THEM IN THE suitcase. It kept her calm - or so she told herself. But her mind was a busy mess. She didn't know what to tell the kid and after overthinking it a while, decided not to say anything. *This is for the best.*

And then Cherry began thinking about her future with Hugo.

Cherry Todger. It had a nice ring. *And speaking of nice rings ...* She looked at the massive rock on her finger - *it would make Liz Taylor jealous.* She felt as giddy as a schoolgirl.

She thought no more about Holly. Or Delilah. She had a wedding to plan.

"An hour," Holly told Fluffy as he watched her wash her face and brush her hair. "She's been here an hour and she hasn't even said hello. Ouch!" She put down the brush and forced herself to carefully unsnarl the knot in her hair. She wanted to rip it out by the roots. "Can you believe that? An hour!"

Holly was trying to get angry. It was the only way to drown the sadness that had enveloped her when she heard Cherry say she'd be needing her bags taken down.

The thought of leaving Brimstone was too much. Straightening her shoulders, she stared at her reflection. "You can do it. You can tell Cherry you don't want to go." And then she thought of her newfound gift, wondering if she could *make* Cherry leave her here. She knew it wasn't right, but she really didn't care. *I can do something for myself just this once.*

"I'll be right back, Fluffy." She marched across the hall and knocked on Cherry's door.

"Hold your horses, hold your horses!" Cherry called.

Finally, still swathed in mink, Cherry opened the door. She stared, mouth half open. "Hey, kid, what're you doing here?"

"Steve told me you were here." Holly kept her voice neutral.

"Oh, yeah. I just got here."

Holly eyed the open suitcases on the bed, all of them nearly full. "You got here an hour ago."

"No I didn't. And don't talk back, kid. It's not nice."

Real anger rising, Holly pushed past Cherry into the room. "You've been here an hour."

Cherry shut the door. "How do you know?"

"Steve told me-"

"Steve's a liar."

"No, because I heard you."

"If you heard me, why did you wait so long to say hello?"

Holly crossed her arms. "We're leaving, aren't we? We're going back to Van Nuys."

"No-"

"I heard you tell that creepy bellboy you're going to call him to get the bags."

Cherry stared at her and shook her head. "No."

Something in her mother's face cracked, softened, for just an instant. "Holly, *we're* not leaving."

"Then why are you packing?"

Cherry grabbed Holly's hand and led her to the bed. "Come here, kid. I have news. Great news. Sit down and I'll tell you."

Holly sat and Cherry lifted an end of the silver fur and held it out to Holly. "Feel it. Isn't it nice?"

Holly touched it without enthusiasm. "I guess."

"And look at my clothes. This skirt is real leather. Isn't it beautiful?"

"It's just a black skirt."

"Feel it. It's leather."

Holly did as she was told. "Okay, so you have a new boyfriend?"

Cherry shook her head. "Guess again."

"You made a lot of money on a movie?"

"One more guess."

"I don't have another guess."

Cherry grinned and stroked the mink. "Come on. One more guess."

"You robbed a bank."

Laughing, Cherry rubbed the silky fur against her cheek.

"Better be careful, you'll get makeup on it."

"Who cares!" Cherry extended her left hand and shoved a giant ring in Holly's face. "I'm getting married!"

"That's fake," Holly said.

"No, it's not! It's real."

"Okay, so your boyfriend's rich."

"He's not my boyfriend. He's my fiancé. We're getting married next week in New York City! He has a penthouse there."

"We're moving to New York?" Holly asked, unimpressed.

"He has a ranch in Sedona, and houses all over the country."

"So where are we going to live?"

Cherry's smile changed into something else. It was the crack again, bigger now. Holly saw darkness flit through her eyes.

"Where are we living?" she asked again.

"You, my lucky, lucky daughter, are going to stay right here in Brimstone. Hugo and I are going to go on an around-the-world vacation before we do anything else."

"Okay. But where will we live when you're done with your honeymoon?"

"Why, you'll stay right here, kid. With your grandmother. I know how much you like her." Cherry grabbed a sealed envelope from the dresser and pressed it into Holly's hands. It was addressed to Delilah.

"How would you know? You're never here." Holly spat the words. "You don't know anything."

Cherry put a finger under Holly's chin and made her look into her eyes. "But I'm right, aren't I? You love your grandmother."

Holly refused to give her the satisfaction of a reply. "How would you know?"

"Because I know. You're like her, kid. You're nothing like me. She couldn't stand me and I hated her. But you - you two - you're going to be fine together."

"You don't know that," Holly said. Although it was true, there was no way Cherry could actually know that - she was just twisting things the way she wanted, just like she always did. Holly glared at her. "So, you're just dumping me here? Are you going to visit me? When will I meet my new stepfather?" Part of her was overjoyed - *I'm staying! I'm staying!* - but hurt and anger smacked her down like a Mac truck. She couldn't think.

"Holly, sometimes things just have to end," Cherry was saying. "I think maybe we came here because you were supposed to meet your grandmother and I was supposed to meet Hugo."

"Bullcrap!" Holly stood, the envelope still clutched in her hand. "Bullcrap! Why won't you answer my questions?"

Cherry hesitated, her eyes filling with tears. "Because if Hugo knew I had a child, he wouldn't want to marry me. Believe me, kid, this is best for everybody." She reached out to run her fingers down Holly's cheek.

Holly flinched back. "You were going to leave without even saying goodbye, weren't you?"

A lone tear escaped. Cherry wiped it away. "It's for the best, kid."

***.

ARTHUR MEEKS, HIS FACE PRESSED AGAINST THE WALL AS HE PEERED into the room next door, grinned and suppressed a rising chuckle. It had made his day, that stupefied look on the creepy little girl's face as her mother told her she was abandoning her. *Poor Little Miss Fancy Pants. Nobody loves you. Nosireebob!* But she was nothing if not stoic and he was disappointed by how quickly the little bitch regained her hard edge.

Come on, Mom, he thought, *make it hurt!*

But alas, Cherry Devine had let her daughter down easy - far too easy for Arthur Meeks' tastes. He wanted tears, Goddamnit - big fat, juicy, rolling tears, a quivering chin, a crumpling face. Some serious sobbing would have been ideal, of course, but Meeks knew he was dreaming if he expected that much from the soulless little slut.

All he got was that brief flash of confusion, a few "Bullcraps!" and a flicker of remorse, there and gone as quick as a snake's tongue - and then nothing. Nothing but that goddamned self-assuredness that Meeks had come to hate clear down to his bones.

That's when he decided to take matters into his own hands. *If you want something done right, you gotta do it your goddamned self.* He pried himself away from the spyhole and stepped from the vacant room into the hall, where he struck a casual pose, one shoulder pressed against the wall like he had all the time in the goddamned world. And he did.

Not that it took long for Little Miss Fancy Pants to leave Mommy's room.

She slammed Cherry's door behind her then saw him standing there. She froze.

"Well, well, well," Meeks drawled. "Looks like even your own mother can't stand the sight of you." He grinned, relishing her surprise. "I guess Old Queen Douchebag's gonna be your new mama now. How long do you guess it'll be before *she* can't stand you, either? Probably, she'll ship you off to some orphanage somewhere. I know I would." Meeks brought his 75-watt smile up to a full, beaming hundred. "I give it four, five months tops before she-"

"Shut up, creep."

Something in the girl's eyes dried up his words. His grin faltered as he saw a flash of gold fire so bright and strong it felt like a hot wall of hate pressing against him. Hate and something else. Something dangerous. Deadly. His breath caught. For an eternity, she just stood there staring and Meeks was paralyzed, suffocating like a fly trapped in a web.

"Just shut up and leave me alone." She spat the words and at last, that flaming gaze slipped from his face.

The spell broke as she brushed past him and Meeks bent at the waist, sucking air into his oxygen-deprived lungs. *Breath, precious, precious breath.*

Stunned, he watched her disappear into her room.

Evil, he thought. *Not of this world.*

Evil.

Evil, evil, evil.

She must be punished!

45

LEMONS AND LEMONADE

olly felt as if there were an earthquake inside her. Emotions flickered like flipbook pages; shock, sadness, anger, happiness, excitement. Joy. They all collided, roiling up and down, up and down. She sat cross-legged on her bed and stared at the envelope addressed to Delilah. "My mother's leaving me here, Fluffy," she told the cat. "She's leaving me."

Tears threatened then disappeared as if a cloud had lifted from the sun. "Fluffy, you know what? I don't have to go! I get to stay here with my grandmother like I wanted. And *we* get to stay together."

Then Arthur Meeks' voice intruded. *She'll ship you off to some orphanage somewhere. I know I would.*

A tear fell, followed by an instant righteous fury, red and hot; fury at the bellhop, fury at Cherry. "You're poison. You're both poison." Everything sharpened to crystal clarity and she heard a sharp sound and looked as a long thin crack ran down at the edge of her dresser mirror. She saw it so clearly that she could even see the tiny bright motes of shattered glass at the edges. Then she noticed her eyes, ablaze with gold. The cat was at the foot of the bed staring at the mirror, hissing, back arched, tail huge.

Instantly it was over. "Oh, Fluffy, no! I'm sorry, it's okay! I didn't mean to scare you!"

The cat gave one hiss then relaxed, though he remained at the foot of the bed.

She rose and approached the mirror. "I did that, didn't I, Fluffy? I really did." Now, she felt a kind of wonder. People had told her about her golden eyes, and she knew it was true, but it had never seemed so real.

Something moved within her, like a great gear shifting.

"I really did that."

Relaxing her grip on the envelope, she stood utterly still, and thought about how much she wanted to stay here with her grandmother. With her new friends. With Fluffy. Finally, she sat back down on the bed and after a few minutes, the big cat returned, curled up in her lap, and began to purr.

She concentrated on the soothing rumble, telling herself it was the sound of happiness and she should always remember it when she felt bad. Closing her eyes, she willed her emotions to settle. Last month, she'd read an article about how the Beatles learned transcendental meditation and how good it made them feel. She wanted to learn that, too.

A little while later she heard Cherry's door open, the bellhop's voice and Cherry's, then the cart creaking down the hall toward the elevator, and the click of her mother's high heels as she walked out of her life.

She saw Fluffy looking at her, concern in his golden eyes. She scratched him under the chin. "It's okay. It's fine. I'm not going anywhere."

The cat resumed his purring.

And Holly opened the envelope.

❧ 46 ❧

SOMETHING WICKED

S teve Cross sat reading, feet propped on the switchboard desk - a rare, rebellious pose - relishing the silence and solitude. This was his favorite time of night. Cherry was long gone and guests were settling in, no one was coming or going, the phone wasn't ringing, and there was nothing to be done except relax.

Engrossed as he was in his reading - *The Electric Kool-Aid Acid Test*, Tom Wolfe's new release - something was bothering him, niggling at the back of his mind like a quiet itch on the bottom of his foot.

The last few nights had been peaceful, quiet, but now it felt a little too quiet. A little too peaceful. *Nonsense,* he told himself. *Nonsense.* He returned to his book.

But when the elevator dinged, he jumped, dropping the novel.

Embarrassed, he cleared his throat, picked up the book, then stood, brushing off invisible lint, ready to greet a guest.

But when the elevator doors opened and no one exited, dread filled him. He knew he wasn't alone. He froze as the air shimmered like a heatwave before the open elevator doors. But it was no heatwave - the lobby had turned preternaturally cold. Colder than before. *Oh, no. Not now. Not again.*

Then Holly Tremayne came around the corner from the stairwell.

She stepped into the lobby, up to the reception desk, and stopped, staring at the shivery patch of air.

"Steve? Do you see it?"

"NOT EXACTLY, BUT I FEEL IT."

"Don't move." Holly stared at the black mist hovering in front of the elevator. It was what she and Keith had seen in Pearl's house. Teeth chattering, she watched the dark form glide slowly forward, praying it wouldn't notice her. Or Steve. As it moved from the elevator alcove into the lobby the cold intensified.

Holly put a finger to her lips. Steve's breath puffed white vapor as he nodded. She couldn't tell him Henry Hank was directly across from them now; she didn't dare speak. But she sensed the malice in the spirit of her great-great-grandfather. It wanted to hurt him. It wanted to hurt her. *It wants to hurt everybody.*

Quietly, she lifted the latch on the gate to the tall lobby desk and joined Steve behind the counter, jumping as the sound of the latch closing resounded like an explosion in the quiet lobby.

Suddenly, the black mist darkened and glided toward them. The air in her lungs froze. She felt Steve's hands on her shoulders, trying to tug her toward the front gate, toward the front doors. "Come on!" he whispered.

Holly swallowed, staring at the mass as it bore down on them. She willed herself to focus, to bury her terror beneath a blaze of golden fire that she imagined came from her eyes. But it wasn't working. She was too frightened.

Threads of blackness, like gelatinous strands of freezing slime began to crawl across the desk. "No!" she cried. "No!" A slimy tentacle touched her hand, a cold burn. Steve yanked her back and she let him.

Then bells jangled as someone entered the lobby.

"My goodness," cried a large woman Holly recognized as a guest. "It's cold enough to freeze the devil in here!"

The mist turned and glided across the room to the copper door where it disappeared with a rattling shake. A fine frost coated the metal in its wake.

"What was that?" The woman huffed at Steve.

"I'm sorry. It's the air conditioner, Miss Berger. It's been acting up. We're having it repaired in the morning."

"I should hope so!" She eyed Steve with beady eyes done up with way too much penicillin-blue eyeshadow. "Will this affect my comfort tonight? Because if it does, I-"

"No, Miss Berger, it affects only the lobby. You have nothing to be concerned about."

The woman patted her platinum bubble-bob. "I certainly hope not. Are there any messages for me?"

While Steve checked, she eyed Holly as if she were a block of stinky cheese.

Holly just smiled, glad the woman had scared off the spirit of Henry Hank.

"No messages." Steve said.

"Humph. Well, ring me if there are. I'm expecting one."

With that, Miss Berger - clad in a magenta and white paisley muumuu that made her buttocks look like a pair of wrestling bear cubs - headed for the elevator.

They watched. Once the door closed, Holly turned to Steve. "That was close."

He smiled, just a little. "If only she knew what she stopped." He paused. "Holly, what did you see?"

"Henry Hank Barrow."

"YOU SAW HIM, THEN?" STEVE GESTURED HER INTO A SEAT BEHIND the tall desk and took the other chair, amazed at her calm.

"I saw the big black cloud, yes." Holly spoke somberly. "He's very dangerous even though he's broken."

"So I gathered at the meeting. Did you come to talk about that?"

"Kind of, but first I need an envelope," she said, not looking at him. "For this." She pulled a folded sheet of paper from her pocket and Steve saw a shimmer of tears when she looked up.

"Holly? What's wrong?" He bent forward, put a hand on her shoulder.

"This." She held the paper out to him. "Read it."

Steve nodded, took the letter, and began reading.

"Mother,

I have an opportunity to turn my life around. A wonderful man has proposed to me. He's very wealthy and he is taking me around the world on our honeymoon. We leave next week. The only thing is, I have to leave Holly here with you. He can't know about her. Ever.

I am giving her to you. She'll be the daughter you always wanted. I know she already loves you. She said so.

I'll write when I can.

Cherry

PS If you can't take care of her, I think her father's brother is living in Peoria, IL. He should be in the book."

A second page, signed and dated, was clipped to the letter:

"I, Charlotte Cherry Beatrice Danvers Devine Tremayne hereby give my mother, Delilah Delacorte Devine, full legal guardianship of my daughter, Holly Evelyn Tremayne."

"Dear God." Steve looked at Holly. She stared at her shoes. "How could ..." He was going to ask how Cherry could do this to her own daughter, but when he saw the pain on Holly's face, he thought better of it. "Hey," he said, hunching to make himself eye-level with her. "It's not so bad here, is it? Think of all the fun we're going to have. I think you're just what this place needs to brighten it up."

"I know. I mean, I'm really happy. I was going to tell her I wanted to stay." Her lip trembled. "I was going to *make* her let me stay. But what if Gram ... what if ... what if she doesn't want me? What if she sends me to an orph - an orphanage or something?"

Another piece snapped off Steve's heart. "Of course she wants you, Holly. She loves you. She's talked about nothing else since you arrived. As much as this old hotel needs you, your grandmother needs you more." He tried a smile but it felt tight and out of place on his lips. "And I think you need *her* too."

Holly nodded. "I do. But-"

"But nothing. You're right where you belong, Holly. Life has a way of doing that - putting you where you belong. It's painful sometimes, but it's right. You'll see. And your grandmother is going to be thrilled to have you."

Her wide blue eyes became pools of hope, the gold motes glimmering like stars. "Do you really think so?"

Steve nodded. "I promise." He handed her an envelope.

Holly took it. "Thank you."

Steve watched her. "Fluffy needs you, too."

Holly almost smiled. "I need him more."

"Then it's settled. Welcome home, Holly Tremayne." Steve could see the light returning to her eyes and he prayed to God he hadn't made things worse, that Delilah would be as happy with the arrangement as he'd promised Holly she'd be. He thought she would. "As for ... whatever it was we just saw ..."

"Henry Hank?"

Steve nodded. "Yeah. As for *him*, will you be okay tonight?"

She nodded. "Will you?"

Steve forced a grin he didn't feel. "Who's afraid of the big bad wolf?"

"I don't think he'll be back tonight," Holly said. "It feels like he's gone."

"I hope you're right."

❧ 47 ❧

MEEK AS A LAMB

A fter an hour playing Scrabble with Steve, Holly, considerably
happier, took the stairs back up, pausing at the third floor
landing when she heard a door close nearby. Arthur Meeks
had just come out of a guest room and was holding something small
wrapped in tissue. She stayed hidden until he headed for the elevator.
He looked as furtive as a rat with a piece of purloined cheese.

He's stealing!

She raced to the fourth floor and slipped into her room just as the
elevator arrived. Cracking the door, she watched him cross the hall and
go into his room then turned to Fluffy. "He's a bad man," she told him.
"Don't you go near him. Promise?"

Fluffy eeled around her legs.

"Good kitty." She locked the door then her eyes fell on the long
crack in the dresser mirror, traveling down to the stack of books and
notepads, to the spot where her missing Friar Tuck bank was supposed
to be.

"He took it." She felt like Sherlock Holmes. "Of course he took it!"

And she was going to get it back. Tonight. After she saw Delilah.

382

"I WOULD HAVE ASKED YOU TO SUPPER TONIGHT, HOLLY, BUT THE Commodore and I had a dinner meeting."

Holly nodded. "That's okay. Can I ask a question?"

"Certainly."

"I know he helps you with business, but is he your boyfriend, too?"

Delilah studied her granddaughter, then laughed. "He's my lawyer and an old friend."

She saw relief on the girl's face. She'd probably seen far too many boyfriends come and go in her short lifetime. But she could see that there was something else on Holly's mind. "What's that in your hand, sweetheart?"

Holly handed her an envelope with an expression so anguished that Delilah found herself unable to speak as she accepted it. She turned it over. It was blank.

"It's from Cherry," the little girl said. "She said to give it to you."

"She's here? Now?"

"No. She left. But I heard her, so I knocked and she let me in but..." A single tear rolled down Holly's cheek.

"Oh, sweetheart, what's wrong?" Delilah pulled Holly close. "Come on, let's sit down." She led her to a velvety rose loveseat. "Tell me everything."

"She said she didn't want anybody to know she was here. Not even me." More silent tears escaped, but Holly wiped them away, her back straight, refusing to bow under the weight of Charlotte's cruelty.

"I am so sorry, Holly. How anyone could-" She silenced; Holly didn't need this. "Let's see what she's up to, shall we?" She smiled and kissed Holly's cheek. "Who knows? It might be good news."

She quickly read the letter, then set it aside. Holly was staring at her own lap. "Holly, you read this already, didn't you?"

She nodded, not looking up. "I'm sorry."

"In your position, I would have done the same."

"Really?"

"Look at me, Holly." Despite the fury building against Charlotte, she found it easy to smile at her granddaughter. As the girl looked up, Delilah pushed hair from Holly's face and pulled an embroidered linen handkerchief from her own pocket. "Use this." She waited. "I apologize for Charlotte's behavior. I must have been a horrible mother to raise someone who could just abandon a child." She slipped her arm around Holly and pulled her close.

"I bet you were a great mom."

"Well, I tried. But nothing I did ever worked. It was like your mother was a little Martian or something." Delilah wanted to say she was a chip off her thoughtless self-centered father, but that was something else Holly didn't need to hear.

"Cherry isn't like other moms," Holly said. "It's kind of like she's a little kid or something. Like she's always playing dress-up. I know she does some bad things, things that aren't nice, and I just try not to think about them." Finally, she strung her fingers with Delilah's and looked straight into her eyes. "I never felt like I had a mom. She always told people I was her little sister, or that she was babysitting me."

"I'm so sorry, sweetheart. I'm so sorry you had to go through that."

Holly looked away again. "I understand if you don't want me. I really do."

Delilah pulled the girl into her arms and squeezed her tight. "How can you even think that? Don't ever say that again! Never! Do you hear me? Never!"

Holly sobbed freely, her arms around Delilah's neck, hugging her until she could barely breathe. Delilah held on to her for dear life.

As the sobs subsided, she smoothed Holly's hair. "I love you, sweetheart."

"I love you!"

They sat together for an hour, saying little, just getting used to the feel of one another. Finally, Delilah took Holly into the kitchen for ice cream. They took the bowls out onto the balcony and sat enjoying the warm summer breeze and the taste of strawberry ice cream.

She looked at Holly, who smiled back. Delilah knew that whatever lies Charlotte had written in her letter, she'd been right about one thing: Holly was born to be her daughter.

HOLLY HAD RETURNED TO THE FOURTH FLOOR IN A RARE STATE OF

euphoria. Her grandmother wanted her! That knowledge had taken almost all the sting out of Cherry's abrupt departure and after the ice cream, Holly asked if she could keep Fluffy and Gram had said yes, and that Fluffy could even move upstairs with Holly where they'd have their own bedroom. For tonight, though, Holly opted to stay downstairs.

After she promised to return for breakfast - and sooner, if she got scared - Delilah bade her goodnight and Holly had returned to her room, happy that no one had seen her. After a few minutes with Fluffy, she put on her new, silent sneakers, pocketed her keys, and trotted down to the lobby, where she told Steve the good news and managed to find out Arthur Meeks had the night off and had gone to the movies. That made her doubly glad she hadn't told Gram about seeing the cold, dark cloud in the lobby; she needed to stay in her room tonight.

After telling Steve she'd come back to visit in a little while, she started back upstairs, her heart pounding. As she made the fourth floor, she pulled the skeleton key from her pocket, the one her grandmother had given her so she could get into the housekeeping closets to get the watering cans.

The key felt cold and heavy in her hand as she approached Meeks' door, but she didn't falter. She'd never done anything like this before and didn't even know if it would work, but after a final glance in each direction, she slipped the key into the lock and twisted.

When it clicked and unlatched she felt both relief and disappointment - a part of her had been desperately hoping the key wouldn't work and she could forget the whole plan.

But no such luck. Arthur Meeks' door yawned open like a stale, dirty mouth, exhaling rancid odors: sweat, spoiled food, and dirty socks. And the stink was no wonder; the place was a sty.

Steeling herself, Holly stepped inside and closed the door quietly behind her. For a moment, she stood against it, unable to move, unable to breathe for fear that the stink might infiltrate her lungs. *Just hurry.* But now that she was here, she was sure she'd made a terrible mistake. *What if he comes back? What if someone saw me and reports it to Steve? And Grandmother?* That fear got her moving.

Find Friar Tuck. She knew Meeks had it. Knew it the moment she'd seen him stealing from the other guest. She stepped across a pile of rumpled jeans, shirts, and underwear, stacks of food-spattered plates and bowls, and several purses Holly was certain did not belong to the bellhop. "Disgusting," she mumbled, stepping past several opened, half-emptied cans of baked beans, their remaining contents now dried and hardened and stinking to high heaven.

The bed was unmade, and on it were strewn magazines of naked ladies and a jumble of crusty-looking rags - white with yellowish stains. Holly refused to think about that.

As she scanned the room and toed things carefully out of her way, she saw more of what she was sure were stolen items: a gleaming pocket watch, two transistor radios, and a couple bottles of perfume.

But no Friar Tuck.

Her eyes lit on the night table beside the bed. Here, there was a lamp, an overflowing ashtray, and several empty beer cans. She stepped through the mess and opened the top drawer. Nothing but receipts, notebooks, pens, and pencils.

But in the second drawer -

"Friar Tuck!"

He smiled up at her as if happy to see her. She lifted him from the drawer and was pleased to feel the weight of the money still inside. She tucked the little bank under her arm, then began to close the drawer when something else caught her eye. Something familiar. Silky pink with embroidered flowers. He'd taken her panties right out of the bathroom! She snatched them up - they felt stiff and dirty - and stuffed them in her pocket.

Holly gaped at the drawer. Hers weren't the only underwear he'd stolen. There must have been dozens of them, most of them in girls' sizes.

"You creep ..." she whispered. She set Friar Tuck on the nightstand then carefully pushed the underwear aside. Beneath them, was something worse.

Photographs.

She picked one up and stared at it. It was a picture of a little girl. And there were more. Lots more.

They weren't wearing any clothes.

Some of them were crying. A few had their hands tied together. She thought a couple of them were asleep, then noticed their eyes were slightly open, unseeing. *Like Becky.* She pushed past those, then she picked up one photo of a child who looked familiar; she'd seen her face before. A little dark-haired girl with big sad eyes. She was probably no more than a first grader, still baby-faced.

The poster at the gas station! Holly gasped and let the photo tumble to the floor then grabbed her Friar Tuck bank and turned, nearly falling over a pile of dirty clothes. *I need to get out of here! Now!* Feeling like something dark and poisonous was creeping through her veins, she hurried from the room without another thought.

When Holly unlocked her own door, the phone was ringing.

ARTHUR MEEKS HAD ALWAYS HEARD THAT MESSY PEOPLE WEREN'T actually disorganized at all - not in their own minds, anyway - and that they knew where their things were, and could tell if someone had gone through their stuff. This, of course, was a hot load of bullshit, and Arthur Meeks was proof of it. He'd been a self-admitted pig his whole life and had never developed any system of organization. Once he put a thing down somewhere, it wasn't uncommon for him to lose track of it for good. And that was why, had it not been for the yawning night-stand drawer, God only knew when he would have discovered that someone had been snooping.

"Son of a whore." He looked around, seeing nothing else amiss and headed toward the nightstand. "Son of a motherfucking whore." He peered into the drawer and the moment he did, he knew *exactly* who the culprit was: Little Miss Fancy Pants. She'd come to take back her ugly-ass bank - and while that didn't piss him off in and of itself, it *did* piss him off that she'd found his purloined panty collection. And, he realized with a sick feeling, his photographs. On the floor, staring up at him with big dark eyes, was the little Mexican girl he'd picked up at the playground last year. She'd been a lot of fun. "Son of a whore!"

His bowels turned watery and he had to tight-cheek it straight to the toilet as he envisioned Little Miss Fancy Pants telling everyone in the hotel what she'd found. *Fuck! Fuck, fuck, fuck! I'm not going to prison!* "Son of a fucking whore!"

His mind raced as he hurried his body along. Cursing his damned delicate stomach, he knew just what to do about the little bitch. But he had to get to her before she had a chance to start wagging her slutty tongue.

As soon as he was finished, he dug paper and a pen from his top drawer and began writing. This would buy him enough time to get his plan in order.

HOLLY SET FRIAR TUCK ON HER DRESSER WITH SHAKING HANDS AND picked up the ringing phone. "Hello?"

"Holly, it's Steve."

"Hi."

"Is something wrong?"

"No."

"Are you sure? You sound kind of freaked out. I thought everything was great with your grandmother."

"It is-"

"Is the cat okay?"

"He's fine," she said, unable to bring herself to say more.

"Holly? You there?"

"Hang on a minute, okay?"

She set the receiver down and crossed to the door, slid the chain-lock into place and made sure the deadbolt was turned before taking a deep breath and picking up the phone again. "Okay, I'm back. What's up?"

"If you have time to come down, I just found something interesting in a book I borrowed from the historical society. There are pictures of a lot of your family and the hospital back in the day. It's pretty cool stuff. Interested?"

"I am. I'll come right away." She heard the elevator ding and glanced at the door again. "Hey, Steve, did Arthur Meeks come back yet?"

"Just a few minutes ago. Why?"

"Oh, I just heard the elevator is all and I don't think there are many guests on the floor tonight."

"Right. Just a couple down at the other end of the hall."

"Are they in their room?"

"No, they just went out, too. It's just you and Arthur up there right now."

Gooseflesh rose. "I'm going to feed Fluffy and make sure he's locked in tight, then I'll be right down." She paused. She had to tell someone about the underwear and photos in Meeks' room. Telling Steve would be the easiest and he'd go with her to talk to Gram. *But what if Meeks is listening at the door?* She realized she had to do it in person. She made herself sound cheerful. "If I'm not there in ten minutes, come and get me!"

Steve chuckled. "Yes, ma'am!"

She hung up and, after topping off Fluffy's crunchies and giving him fresh water, she checked the windows and balcony door to make sure the room was locked up tight. For good measure, she pushed a wooden dining chair under the balcony doorknob.

"Okay, Fluffy," she told the sleepy cat, "I'll be back in a little while. If any bad guys break in, you hide under the bed."

She opened the door quietly and peered out. The hall was deserted. Afraid Meeks might have a key to the deadbolt, not just the doorknob lock, she reached inside and put the Do Not Disturb sign on the door. As she was about to pull it closed, she saw Meeks' door start to open. She jumped back inside the room, turned the deadbolt, and hung onto the doorknob.

She waited, trembling, as his footsteps came closer and closer. The bellhop was whistling tunelessly between his teeth.

He stopped in front of her door. Trembling, she held the knob tight, but he didn't touch it. He didn't knock either. Instead, he pushed a folded piece of paper part way under the door. She stood there waiting and waiting, waiting forever, knowing he was watching to see if she'd take it.

At least five minutes passed before the paper was nudged completely into the room and his footsteps retreated. She waited until she heard his door close then picked the paper up.

It was lined stationery torn sloppily off a pad. She sat at the table and unfolded it.

"*I know you were in my room and if I tell your grandmother what a little snoop you are, I bet you'd get a spanking. But maybe I won't. Maybe instead it'll be our little secret, ha, ha. And if you tell anybody - anybody at all - your granny's going to die with her throat slit open. All your friends will die. That old lady from the gas station will get gas poured on her and I'll light a match and she'll burn up like a Roman candle. And that druggist, I'll just cut his head clean off, neat as a pin, and use it as a bowling ball. As for that injun, I'm gonna scalp him and stuff his hair down his ugly throat. I know you're sweet on that Stephen Cross fella, so I'm going to have him cut up into little bitty pieces and they'll be finding him for years and years. But you'll find his head in your bed real soon, snuggled right up to you. Yeah, he'll be just staring at you with his eyes all blue but he won't see a thing, ha, ha.*

But if you stay quiet, your granny and your friends will be just fine. If they die, it'll be all your fault, and don't you forget it.

You know who."

"HOLLY? HOLLY ARE YOU IN THERE?"

She jumped as Steve Cross' voice came through the door. "Yeah, just a second!" She wadded up the note.

"Everything okay?"

"Yeah, hang on."

Trembling, she opened a drawer and shoved the paper inside, then took a deep breath and opened the door. "Hi, Steve. What are you doing here?"

"You told me to come and get you if you were more than ten minutes, remember? It's been twenty. I would've come sooner, but we had guests checking in." He studied her. "You're really all right? Because you don't look all right."

"I'm fine. Let's go."

"Wait." He pointed. "Why do you have a chair under the balcony door? Did somebody try to break in?"

She thought fast. "I'm from the city. We always put chairs under our doors."

"Okay . . . If you say so."

She grabbed her keys and opened the door, waited for him to exit then did the deadbolt. "Let's go."

"You got it."

She glanced toward the elevator and saw Meeks standing there, staring. He tipped an invisible hat, eyes unblinking, then made a slicing motion across his throat before bringing his finger to his lips.

She wished Steve had seen but he was already walking toward the stairs. She hurried after him.

HOLLY WASN'T HERSELF, BUT SHE WOULDN'T TELL HIM WHAT WAS wrong. Steve Cross watched as she slowly turned the pages of the book he'd found today. It was about the Clementine Mining Company and had a lot on the hospital, even listing the names of those who'd worked or died there.

Holly stopped at a photo of a group of people standing together in front of the hospital doors.

"That's Pearl Abbott." Holly tapped a scowling busty woman in a long, dark dress. "She looks younger than when I've seen her. Ugh."

Steve squinted at lettering beneath the photo. "This was taken in 1900."

Holly nodded then pointed at the imposing figure of her great-great-grandfather. He was dressed in a black suit. His shock of dark hair was barely gray at the temples and his gaze bored into the camera. His eyebrows arched and tufted as if he were Satan himself. "That must be what the devil looks like."

"No kidding. See the man next to him? That's Bill Delacorte, your great-grandfather."

"He doesn't look very friendly either." Holly bent closer. "But Addie says he was kind of okay."

"She's probably right."

Holly nodded with a somberness beyond her years. "Remember how Adeline said that he wouldn't let anybody see Henry Hank or Pearl Abbott in their coffins? I wonder why."

Steve half-smiled. "Probably because they were gross looking. You know, all smashed up. It sounded like Carrie and Addie pretty much bashed in their skulls."

"They were really brave," Holly said. "I don't know if I could kill somebody." Her eyes widened. "I mean, Adeline's this nice old lady, but she ... I mean, wow!"

"They were like Wonder Woman," Steve said.

"They must've been really gross looking." Holly smiled, just a little. "Henry Hank and Pearl, I mean."

"Must have. So it's no wonder Bill Delacorte made sure they had closed caskets. I'm glad he turned out to be a better man than H. H. Barrow." Steve turned a page. "There's not a lot about him in the book. He remained as hospital administrator until it closed down in the thirties. He lived out the rest of his life here in town."

"Addie told Gram that he tried to write to her when she was little. But Gram never got the letters."

"Her aunt probably didn't give them to her," Steve said. "Maybe for the best."

"I don't know. Could be." Holly turned the page back to the group photo. "Steve, that day they all died? Does anybody know what really happened? Was it really a gas leak?"

"It's a mystery that's never been solved. It might've been a leak, but some thought Henry Hank was behind it - after all, the doctors that died had opposed his policies."

"If he did kill them, how could he have done it?"

"I don't know."

"Maybe with *Infurnam Aeris* spells or something? Or by getting the Brimstone Beast to help?"

Steve shook his head. "You wouldn't think so. But ... who knows? I sure don't." He shut the book. He'd given himself a massive case of the creeps. Every time he felt a hint of a breeze, he was afraid the lobby was going to turn icy cold again. He needed to get his mind off it for a while. "Want a soda?"

"Sure."

They drank pop and played Scrabble for an hour, and nothing more was said about H.H. Barrow or Pearl Abbott. It was past eleven when Holly started yawning. "I guess I should go to bed." She manufactured a smile. "I don't want to leave Fluffy alone with Miss Annie Patches too long. He might get scared."

"Shall I see you to your room?"

"That's okay." But she didn't move. He could tell she didn't want to go up alone.

"Have you talked to your grandmother about Arthur Meeks yet?"

She shook her head, not meeting his eyes. "Not yet, but I will."

"Good. I should go with you in case somebody went in and drew that *Infurnam Aeris* symbol on your mirror again."

She nodded. "Yeah. That's probably a good idea."

Together they walked upstairs and as they reached the fourth floor, he saw Arthur Meeks disappearing into his room by the elevator. *Good riddance.*

Holly saw the bellhop too and Steve thought her shoulders stiffened, but it was probably his imagination. She said nothing, just unlocked her door and waited while he went inside.

He switched on the light. "All clear."

"Fluffy!" she said as the cat came to greet her.

Steve checked the bathroom. "Everything looks fine."

"Thank you."

Then he noticed the mirror. "What happened?" He traced the three-foot-long crack with his finger.

"I dunno. Maybe the earthquake?"

"Could be," he said, thinking she looked embarrassed. "I don't think it's anything to worry about. The mirror won't shatter. It's a very shallow crack." He headed for the door.

"Steve?"

He turned, saw her face half hidden in the cat's marmalade fur. "What?"

"I did it."

"Did what?"

"Cracked the mirror."

"I'm sure it was an accident."

"Yeah, it was, but I did it with my eyes. I mean, you know... I didn't mean to or anything. I got really mad and it happened."

Steve nodded. "You must've been very angry."

"Yeah."

"I guess maybe you should let Addie help you learn how to control it better."

"I'm going to get lessons from Addie for sure." Her smile was small, uncertain. "Thanks, Steve. Goodnight."

Lost in thought, Steve strolled the long way along the fourth floor hall toward the elevator and when he came to Arthur Meeks' room, he slowed, seeing his door was ajar. He caught a glimpse of an unmade bed, clothes on the floor. "Arthur?" he called, tapping the door. "You in there?"

No answer.

"Arthur? Your door's open: Everything okay in there?" He leaned in, caught a whiff of old food and dirty laundry. Then Arthur Meeks, clad only in his birthday suit, burst out of the bathroom, red-faced, holding a wad of tissue over his groin. "Mind your own beeswax," he sputtered, and slammed the door in Steve's face.

✥ 48 ✥

THE CAVE IN THE DESERT

Once again, the inhabitants of Brimstone slept soundly. Delilah and Holly slept dreamlessly, and Steve Cross caught four uninterrupted hours behind the desk. Abner Hala dreamed he was on a picnic with his wife, Mary, and Ben dreamed of flirting with Carrie over chocolate sodas. Ike Chance slept well. Addie, though, was troubled by dreams of Holly calling for help.

When morning dawned the smell of rain drifted in on red sunrise breezes. Overhead, the sky gleamed salmon, lavender, and blue between ragged strips of gray clouds. Abner Hala, entered the lobby of the Brimstone Grand. "Hello?" he called. "Anybody here?"

"Just us chickens." Steve Cross appeared from the vicinity of the desk and smiled. "Mind if I tag along on the field trip?"

"I expected you to." Abner shook his hand. "I hope we can find the cave. It's been a long time."

"Coffee?"

"I'd love some."

Steve went into the back office and came back with two steaming mugs. "I tried doing a little research, but there doesn't seem to be much about any petroglyphs but the famous ones at Brimstone Peak."

Abner blew on his coffee. "And that's a good thing because there's

395

something special about that cave; I sensed it even as a kid. It's a place that feels like it can only be found if it wants to be found. Know what I mean?"

Steve nodded.

"It was virtually unknown even among my people. Today, we'll hopefully pass its location on to Holly. And you."

"I hope so. I promise to keep it secret."

Abner nodded. "Good. My grandfather showed me. I chose not to show my son because I didn't believe he would respect it." He looked hard at Steve. "I trust you and Holly."

"Good morning."

Abner looked up, surprised by Delilah's voice. Holly stood beside her. They were both dressed for hiking. "Good morning, ladies."

The lobby door opened and Peg Moran came in, Addie Chance behind her. Peg slipped behind the desk and Addie, dressed in jeans and a chambray shirt, smiled at Delilah. "I'm pretty fast for an old lady."

Delilah chuckled. "Faster than I am, I dare say." She looked at the others. "I wish I could tell you that I've remembered the cave's location, but nothing more has come to mind."

"I recall the general area," Abner said. "Between the two of us, I think we'll find it before it starts raining."

"I hope you're right."

"One minute." Steve Cross trotted into the storage room and returned with a plastic bag. "Glad you mentioned rain. We may need this for the book."

Delilah smiled. "You're an optimist, young man. I like that."

THEY LEFT THE HOTEL BY THE FRONT ENTRANCE JUST AS DELILAH had described doing decades ago. She and Abner led the way, and behind them, Adeline walked beside Holly and Steve, hoping she wouldn't slow anyone down. She and Ike took regular evening walks so she wasn't too worried.

She'd thought about begging off this hike, but felt she couldn't

desert Holly. Now she knew why. There was something - a new intensity - about the girl. Something was on her mind besides Henry Hank
and Pinching Pearl. She'd swear to it.

As they passed the curving driveway that led to the dark Granger
house, everyone fell silent, but once the playground was behind them
and they entered the old graveyard, Addie touched Holly's shoulder.
"How are you doing, sweetheart?"

Holly smiled perfunctorily. "I'm okay."

"Maybe when we get back I can help you hone your gift a little."
Addie's words were soft, gentle.

"That's a really good idea," Steve agreed when Holly didn't reply.
"Addie," he continued, "I had a little scare yesterday."

"What kind of scare?"

"Something very cold got off the elevator and traveled through the
lobby."

"I saw it, too," Holly said. "It was the black cloud. It was Henry
Hank."

They stopped walking. Abner turned. "You saw him yesterday?"

Holly nodded.

"What happened?" Delilah demanded.

Adeline spoke up. "Our grandfather is back, Dee. He's not
finished." She put a hand on Holly's shoulder. "And he won't be until he
gets what he wants."

Abner glanced at the lowering sky. "We don't have time to talk
about it now, but Adeline is right; your grandfather is a formidable foe
even without the Beast. We must get the book and banish him. For
Holly. For all of us."

Holly nodded without looking at Delilah.

"Let's keep moving," Abner said.

Far past the tall wooden cross, deep in the cemetery they came to
the small mausoleum, stern and plain except for the *Infurnam Aeris*
symbol carved above the name "Barrow" over the wrought iron door.
Delilah looked pale. "I've never seen this before. I haven't been back
since that day ..."

"Just as well." Addie had stood before the mausoleum a dozen
times over the years. Three bodies were interred in the mausoleum

building. The names read: Henry Harold Barrow, his wife, Lillian Lane Barrow, and Pearl Bathsheba Abbott. Granite grave markers for William Delacorte, his wife, Myrtle, and daughter Carrie were lined up to the left of it.

Delilah shook her head. "What in the world would possess them to put Pearl Abbott inside a family mausoleum?"

"I asked that question, too, Dee," Addie said. "Your father told me that Henry Hank decreed it in his will." She paused. "At least he had our grandmother's body reinterred here as well."

Delilah touched Carrie's stone. "I should have visited."

"She knows why you didn't," Addie said. "We'll bring her flowers after this business is settled."

"Yes." Delilah pointed north. "That old oak over there. I remember it. I think that's where I started down the hill."

Abner glanced at the dark sky. "Let's go."

THEY'D PASSED THE OLD OAK PERHAPS TEN OR FIFTEEN MINUTES before. Delilah shivered and drew her windbreaker tighter around her and wished she'd brought an umbrella; the rain was close now and she hoped they weren't on a fool's errand. The day had turned as dark as twilight and she recognized nothing. *Carrie,* she thought, *I wish you were here.*

"Dee."

She thought she heard her sister's voice, but realized it was only the wind. *Don't be a fool.* "Abner," she said. "Does anything look familiar to you?"

"Not yet, but it's so dark it's hard to see details."

"Dee," the wind sighed again.

And then a lone shaft of sunlight broke through the dark clouds, coming to rest halfway down the mountain slope. Delilah gasped; the beam shone on the red and tan standing stone outside the hidden cave.

"Do you see it?" Abner asked softly.

"I do. It's a sign."

Abner nodded.

As they began walking again, the clouds swallowed the sunbeam. Aunt Beatrice would have called it a sign and Delilah thought maybe she was right this time. *Thank you, Carrie.* As they slowly drew nearer to the sentinel stone she realized she'd never expected to find the cave at all. It hadn't seemed real until now. "There," she said, halting ten feet from the shadowed, nearly invisible stone. "There it is."

Abner squinted. "We're here."

"We're lucky," Steve said.

"It was more than luck," Delilah said as the five of them arrived at the stone.

"Synchronicity," Holly murmured. She touched the stone, wonder in her eyes. "Where's the cave? I'll go in and get the book."

"You're a brave young lady," Abner said.

"Thanks."

"You don't have to do this, Holly," Delilah said.

"I can go in and get it," Steve said.

Holly looked at Steve. "You're too big." She turned to Delilah. "I have to get the book. It's the only way."

"There's an alternative," Delilah said softly. "Come over here a moment."

Holly remained silent as they walked a few steps away from the others.

"How would you like to travel around the world with me?"

"What?" Holly asked.

"I have a small inheritance from my aunt - some money and her townhouse. When we're done traveling, we could live in Boston. You, me, and Fluffy. We could sell this place and never come back. No more ghosts."

"I like it here." Holly said. "And there are always ghosts. Everywhere."

"Okay. It's just something to think about." Delilah drew Holly into a quick hug. "Don't worry about anything." *I shouldn't have brought this up yet, damn it. She's upset enough as it is.*

"I want Brimstone to be my home now," Holly declared.

"Then it shall be, sweetheart." Delilah hoped it was true. "Let's join the others."

✠

AT FIRST, THE CAVE LOOKED LIKE NOTHING BUT A DARK ROCKY mound. The entrance was not only hidden in the stone's shadow, but masked by sage and mesquite. Still, there was plenty of room for Holly to climb up without getting scratched by the brush.

The wind howled louder as she clawed hair out of her face and peered into the darkness. She couldn't see more than a foot inside, but she could see it was dusty and dirty with rocky walls. It was maybe three feet in diameter - easy enough to climb into. She put her hands on the bottom to push herself up.

"No, Holly, wait!" Delilah stood beside her.

"Why?"

"Let's see what's in there first." Abner clicked on a flashlight and played the beam over the walls. Steve added his and Holly gasped as she got a close look. The cave ran at least a dozen feet before it became too small to travel. The light couldn't penetrate the darkness once the opening narrowed. Abner looked at Holly and said solemnly, "No bears. That's good."

"Wow," Steve illuminated the petroglyphs on the wall six feet in. Stick figures of men hunting a buffalo. Beneath the image lay a pile of rocks half-buried under a thick sift of dust.

"I put the rocks on the book to hide it," Delilah said. "It was wrapped in my pinafore."

"I'll get it," Holly said.

"Be careful," Delilah told her.

"Here." Steve gave her his flashlight.

"Thanks."

She pushed herself up into the cave. The light from Abner's flashlight shone steadily on the floor and Holly shined her light around the walls. It hit the ceiling and she gasped. "It's the Brimstone Beast!"

"Yes. It's always been here." That was Abner.

The Beast was chasing the hunters across the ceiling. Dead men lay everywhere and even though they were stick figures, the running ones looked terrified. Holly shivered, suddenly eager to get the book and leave the little cavern. She felt like she wasn't alone.

"The book should be there," Abner said. He pointed his light at the pile of rocks under the wall glyph.

Holly crawled to it and began moving the rocks. Finally, she uncovered something wrapped in shreds of dirty gray cloth. "I found it!" She pulled the book free of the dirt and pebbles.

Wind whipped outside, howling. Holly suddenly knew - *knew* - eyes were on her now, eyes hidden in the narrow darkness behind her. Near panic, she held the book to her chest with one arm and crawled forward. As she neared the mouth, a lightning bolt struck the ground somewhere toward the hotel. Thunder boomed like a cannon. The ground shook. She handed Steve the book and pushed herself forward as he placed the grimoire in the plastic bag.

Another flash of lightning, closer. A thundering of timpani. Holly scooted out of the cave, and Abner helped her to the ground.

The earth began to shake, but this time there was no thunder. "Earthquake!" Steve caught Addie as she lost her balance. Delilah looked like a deer caught in headlights and Holly and Abner ran to her.

"Come on!" Abner cried as something *cracked* and *roared* within the cave. "Follow me!"

The shaking slowed as lightning struck again, making the world brighter than reality. Thunder crashed, and then came another sharp jerk of the earth. Suddenly, the cave spewed dirt and rocks, barely missing Steve and Addie as it began to collapse in on itself. "Hurry!" Abner yanked Delilah forward. "Over here!"

They half-climbed, half-tumbled into an old streambed just north of the cave. "Holly, everybody, get down!" Abner cried as he pulled Delilah down with him. "Steve, Addie! Get over here! Get down!"

They obeyed just as lightning struck directly in front of the cave. Holly, momentarily blinded, saw jagged spots from the brilliant light. Then the rain came, buckets of it, cold and hard, soaking them. Delilah started to rise.

"No!" Abner put his hand on her back and shoved her back down. "Lie flat, all of you. Put your heads down. The rain won't kill you but the lightning will. Stay low until I say so."

❧ 49 ❧

THE BOOK

O nce the ground stopped moving and the thunder and
lightning let up, Ben Gower had braved the downpour to
make a delivery to old Mrs. Beezer, who lived in one of the
last houses before the turn off for the Grand. When he got back in his
Metro and flipped on the wipers, he'd squinted at a group of bedraggled people trudging up the road in the rain. "Damn fools," he
muttered, driving toward them. As soon as he saw who they were, he
had them pile into the Metro and ferried them up to the Brimstone
Grand.

Now he sat sipping hot tea in Delilah's penthouse with his passen-
gers. Delilah and Holly had changed clothes, and Steve, Adeline, and
Abner were wrapped in thick hotel robes while their clothing was
being dried in the hotel laundry.

They'd filled him in on their adventure and in the center of the
table was the book Delilah had hidden so long ago. "Another thirty
seconds, and we would have lost both Holly and the book to the cave-
in," Adeline told him.

Ben nodded at the book. "This all sounds very apocalyptic." He
could see the others were thinking the same thing.

"It may be just a coincidence," Steve said. "It's monsoon season and the quakes were probably just aftershocks."

"You don't sound very convinced," Ben said.

"I'm not," Steve admitted. "I'd like to believe it, though."

"The timing disturbs me," Abner said quietly.

"There was something in the cave with me," Holly said. "I felt it right at the end. It was watching me."

"Could be something elemental," Abner said. "It might have been warning you to get out."

Holly's face was a mask of impatience. "Let's open the book."

Adeline nodded. "All right, then. Why don't you do the honors, Holly?"

SHE WASTED NO TIME. WITH QUICK BUT CAREFUL FINGERS, HOLLY pulled away the decayed shreds of fabric to reveal the large book. On the front of the black cover was the tarnished gold *Infurnam Aeris* symbol. Goosebumps rising, Holly traced it slowly with her finger then lifted the cover to reveal the antique parchment paper and the hand-written words within.

But the words began to fade before she could make them out. It was as if the very air was erasing them.

The paper looked different now and bending closer, Holly gasped as realization dawned.

The pages were dust. No, not dust - ash, as if the entire thing had been burned to a perfect block of pale gray cinder. But the cover was still intact. Holly didn't touch it again. She just stared, not daring to breathe.

"My God," said Delilah.

And then a phantom breeze gusted through the room, a cool zephyr just strong enough to scatter the ash that had been the pages of the grimoire. It swirled up into the air, a dust devil that dissolved to nothingness before their eyes.

Steve Cross stared at the empty leather binding. "What happened?"

Abner shook his head. "It must have been magick from Henry Hank's arsenal."

Delilah stared hard at Holly. "I think it would be best if we get you out of Brimstone."

"I told you, I don't want to go." Holly's eyes sparked as she gazed at her grandmother. "There has to be another way."

"Whatever you decide," Adeline said, "Holly and I need to work on honing her skills immediately."

"Yes!" Holly cried.

Delilah opened her mouth. "That's not enough-"

"I might know another way," Steve interrupted.

"What's that?" Adeline's eyes were bright.

"We disinter Henry Hank and destroy - or at least scatter - his bones. It's supposed to work. We just have to make sure no one sees us in the cemetery-"

"You don't need to worry about that." Ben Gower folded his hands on the table. "H.H. Barrow isn't in that mausoleum. He's not even in the cemetery."

"He's not?" Abner sat forward. "I was just a boy, but I remember the funerals. The entire town turned out."

"Indeed," said Ben. "I was just back from college, working in my father's pharmacy. Dad was friends with Mort Dodd, the undertaker."

"I remember him," Addie said. "He had the dry goods store at the corner of Main and Rotzig. Used to sell caskets right alongside the dry goods."

"That's right. He and Dad played cards every Friday night. Anyway, not long after the funerals, Mort got drunk and told my dad that Bill Delacorte ordered five caskets. One for Carrie, and two each for Henry Hank and Pinching Pearl." Ben paused. "Bill swore him to secrecy and my dad swore the same to me, but they're all dead, so I don't see that it can matter now. The point is, Carrie was buried in sacred ground, but the caskets of Henry Hank and Pearl each contained a body's weight in rocks."

"Why?" Addie sat forward.

"Well, Henry Hank left a specific set of instructions with his son-in-law. He didn't want to be buried in consecrated ground, and he didn't want Pearl there, either. He wanted them both to be buried in their *Infurnam Aeris* robes, along with some funny knives and herbs and such, and interred in the basement under Pearl Abbott's house. Really shook up Mort. He told my dad that he and Bill Delacorte slid the caskets down through the old cellar door by themselves. He said that after they got the caskets inside, they nearly hightailed it out of there instead of moving them onto the pedestals in the room as prescribed in the will."

"Why?" Delilah asked.

"Dad said it was colder than a witch's tit down there. Real unnatural. He said Bill was as scared as he was even though he'd been Henry Hank's right hand man, and a member of his club, to boot." Ben cleared his throat. "Anyway, Dad was never quite the same after that. He said they got the caskets set up where they were supposed to but that there were *things* down there. They couldn't leave fast enough."

"Things?" Steve asked. "What kind of things?"

"I don't know. Dad wouldn't say anything more about it."

Abner rubbed his chin. "So, the remains are still down there?"

"As far as I know," Ben said. "Why?"

"Because Steve is correct; we may be able to defeat Barrow if we destroy his remains." He paused. "The portal is supposed to be under the house."

"The portal?" Delilah asked.

"The place where the Brimstone Beast came from," Steve said.

"That's the story my people tell," Abner explained. "I don't know how much is true, but the house was built on cursed ground. I think the serpent stories were made up to keep kids away. Whatever the truth is, there's something wrong with that place. Chalk it up to geology or elemental spirits, but chalk it up. If you've ever been in the house, you know there's a reason no one but the likes of Pinching Pearl and Henry Hank ever stuck around."

"A perfect place for such dark souls," Adeline said. "We need to destroy the bones right away."

"Indeed." Abner looked at each of them in turn. Delilah was pale, terrified. Addie appeared uneasy but determined, Steve was a little too intrigued, and Ben, Ben just looked old and tired and unafraid. But Holly. Holly wore a look that frightened him. Her blue eyes sparked with gold as she stared at the remains of the book. Her mouth was set in a firm line and there was nothing childish about her.

"Adeline," the girl said without a glance at her grandmother. "Let's go practice. I want to learn. I *need* to learn."

"In a minute." Addie looked to Abner. "When are we going to Pearl's house?"

"You don't have to come," Abner said. "This is a job for strong backs."

"We're coming," Holly said firmly. "Addie and I are the only ones who can see the ghosts. You need us."

Delilah stared at Holly. "You can't–"

Abner knew Holly spoke the truth. She'd been there and had the heart and courage to go in again. She was young and strong and their best hope. They needed her and she needed Addie. He told Delilah, "Nothing will happen to Holly. I promise you."

"Adeline can go, but not Holly. I won't have it!"

Abner heard the terror in Delilah's voice. "As you wish."

"But–" began Holly, eyes shimmering.

"She is your grandmother." Abner spoke gently. "You must honor her wishes. Addie, why don't you take Holly and help her work on her skills. They will be useful should she need to protect herself and Delilah."

"I *will* go with them, Gram," Holly said, eyes swirling. "I will."

Delilah looked confused. "I–"

"Holly!" Abner stood up, glared down at her. "If you use your talent to bend others to your will you are no better than your great-great-grandfather."

The girl turned her fiery gaze on him, then suddenly looked down. "I'm sorry," she said. When she looked up again, her eyes were blue once more. "I'm sorry, Gram."

✤ 50 ✤

DO NOT GO MEEKLY

R ain and dirt drizzled into Arthur Meeks' room from the open window abutting the mountainside. He'd called in sick, telling that bitch Piggy he had the stomach flu so that he could spend the morning in his room to plan his revenge on Fancy Pants. He'd gone through a whole pack of Pall Malls and was halfway through a second even though it was barely past noon.

He pushed a pile of dirty clothes off the footlocker, unlocked it, and removed his stash of chloroform. Now he studied the old amber bottle. He'd found it on one of his visits to the basement a couple of years back. He'd found lots of interesting things down there. Useful things.

Turning the bottle in his hands, he knew it worked despite the fact it was decades and decades past its prime because when he'd first liberated it, he'd removed the stopper and inhaled deeply until he began to get woozy. "Gonna go to sleep, little girl. Gonna sleep forever Little Miss Fancy Pants, but first, I'm going to punish you. Punish you real good."

Methuselah twitched and complained, so he set the bottle aside and opened the trunk again. He kept his most interesting photos in it along with ropes and handcuffs, gags, and other instruments he might need when punishing a small girl. He pulled a handful of photos out and released Methuselah. As he stroked, he thought about what he would do to Holly. About the last things he would make her see and feel before she died.

ADELINE DROVE HOLLY TO THE HUMBLE STATION AND SPENT THE next three hours helping the girl learn to control and use her talent. She was heartened by the fact that Holly had been practicing on her own, and while the girl wasn't at all sure of herself yet she did understand far more about the power than Adeline or Carrie had at that age. She was a natural.

They worked in the back office, where Holly practiced turning her power off and on at will. She had amazing prowess, though she didn't believe it, and when Ike knocked and asked if they'd like cold sodas, Addie said yes, and that Holly would tell him what to bring. Once he was out of earshot, Holly's eyes swirled the tiniest bit gold as she whispered, "Grape soda, Dr. Pepper, and Pepsi." In a moment, Ike returned with the requested sodas. He had no idea how he chose them - they just "felt" right, he said.

The three sat down and Ike looked at Adeline. "You've told me all sorts of things, but what haven't you told me yet?"

"That I'm going to Pearl Abbott's house. She and Henry Hank are buried in the basement and Steve Cross and Abner think destroying the bones is the best way to stop Henry Hank."

"Why are you going? I can't feature you doing much digging." He tried to smile but worry etched his face.

"I'm the only one who can see the ghosts."

Ike glanced at Holly, eyebrows raised.

"Dee won't let her go and I don't blame her. It's too dangerous."

Ike nodded. "I agree. It's too dangerous for you, too."

"It's too dangerous for all of us."

"Why not just burn the place down?"

"The bones must be destroyed or at least separated. Most fires don't burn hot enough to do that. They're taking sledgehammers and gasoline, I believe."

"I wish you wouldn't go," Ike told her softly.

"I wish I didn't have to, but I do."

"Then I'll come along," Ike said.

Addie patted his hand. "You don't have to do that."

"Haven't we always done these things together, darling?"

"We have."

"We're not stopping now. Besides, if something happened to you, I wouldn't want to live by my lonesome. I'm coming along. We'll all be happier that way."

Holly sipped her soda then looked at them, the gold in her eye a bare twinkle. "I'd better come," she said.

"No, you mustn't," Addie told her. "You promised your grandmother and you can't break that promise. If anything goes wrong, you let Dee get you out of Brimstone, and fast. You promise me that!"

"I promise. Let's practice some more."

"I FIGURE SEVERAL GALLONS OF GAS SHOULD DO IT," STEVE TOLD Ben. After Addie and Holly left, the men had driven back down the hill, Steve following Ben's Metro in his Mustang and Abner bringing up the rear in his F-250. The rain was slow but steady now, and Main was nearly deserted; parking was easy for a change. Abner drove on to his shop to pick up a few sledge hammers, promising to be back shortly.

"Will four cans be enough?" Ben called from the hardware section. "That's all I've got in stock. If we need more, we'd better go over to the auto parts store."

"Four should do it." Steve pulled out his wallet, but when Ben returned with the cans, he refused the money.

"We're in this together. You're contributing strength. I'll get the cans." Ben smiled. "Trust me, I'm getting the better deal."

"What are you going to do with all those gas cans?" Eddie Fortune, dapper in his apron and cap, approached them.

"Don't you have work to do?" Ben asked.

Eddie gave them a winning smile. "There's been almost no business while you were gone, Mr. G. I mopped the floors, cleaned the fountain equipment, swept the backroom, put all the new stock out, filled out reorder forms, got-"

"Very good, Eddie," Ben said. "But eavesdropping isn't on your work list."

"Mr. G, you've been gone most of the day, and heck, you've been gone a lot lately, and I haven't said a word. I've held down the fort, right?"

Ben nodded. "Are you asking for a raise, young man?"

"No, sir! I just want to know what's going on. Maybe I can help."

Ben glanced at Steve, a question in his eyes.

"You're too young," Steve said. "Your mother would kill me."

Eddie's face lit up. "You need another strong back? I'm your man,"

"No, Eddie."

"Just tell me what you're doing. You know I can keep a secret."

"Eddie's trustworthy," Ben said. "I vote we let him come along."

Steve raised his brows at Ben.

"We could use a lookout," he explained.

Steve had reservations, but he trusted Ben as well as Eddie, and the truth was, they *could* use the help. "Fine," he said, "but if your mom finds out, I had nothing to do with this."

Ben grinned.

"All right! When do we go? Where do we go? What's this all about?" Eddie started to take off his apron. "You said I could be a lookout. What am I looking out for?"

"Don't take that apron off yet. We're still open."

"Yes sir, Mr. G. What-?"

Steve hooked Eddie in his gaze. "Listen, Eddie, I know you like ghost stories."

The teen lit up again. "Ghost stories?"

"You may not like them so well after we explain what we're doing."

"I'll like them more."

"We'll tell you on the way."

"There're no customers, Mr. G. Can't you tell me now?"

At that moment, Abner walked in, the brim of his Stetson dripping rain. "Got the sledges," he said.

"Good." Ben locked the door behind him and turned the Open sign to Closed. "We need to tell our lookout here what we're up to."

Abner looked the boy up and down, unconvinced.

"He's my cousin," Steve said. "The kid's trustworthy and knows just about all there is to know about local ghosts."

"What do you know about Henry Hank Barrow and Pinching Pearl Abbott?" Abner looked Eddie in the eye.

"Barrow was a crazy hospital honcho. He had a cult. I don't know anything about Pearl except for what you told me."

"Well," Abner allowed, "I suppose most people don't know about Pearl. Her ghost never made an appearance before Holly Tremayne came to town."

"Delilah Devine's granddaughter?" Eddie's eyes widened.

"What do you know about her?" Abner asked quickly.

"I know she likes root beer floats."

"And that's all you need to know," Abner said. "As for the ghosts of Barrow and Pearl, they're going to hurt her if we don't do something."

"Something criminal," said Steve. "You know the old house below the hotel?"

"Sure. The haunted house. I've been in there. It's creepy as hell."

"You're going to stand guard while we go in, exorcise the ghosts, and burn the place to the ground. And that's *more* than you need to know, Eddie."

"I *thought* that place was haunted!" Eddie's eyes lit up. "What-"

Steve cleared his throat. "Rule number one: If you're going to be an accomplice to a crime, Eddie, the less you know, the better."

Eddie nodded, trying unsuccessfully to hide his glee.

HOLLY AND ADELINE RETURNED TO THE BRIMSTONE GRAND JUST AS rain began falling in earnest. Lightning ripped the sky and thunder shook the windows behind them.

"You made it just in time," Peg Moran said from the front desk.

"We surely did." Adeline glanced out; it was just past five but it looked like twilight out there.

Holly shuddered. Adeline pulled her closer and realized it wasn't the thunder that had made the girl shiver.

The bellhop had arrived, pushing an empty luggage cart before him, obviously trying to look busy while he eavesdropped. Something passed between him and Holly - something Adeline didn't like at all - and then, the unnerving glint still in his eye, the bellboy disappeared.

DELILAH STOOD AT ONE OF THE TALL PENTHOUSE WINDOWS overlooking Brimstone and watched the storm rage. She wrapped her arms around herself as thunder boomed and lightning spiked. *At least I'm indoors this time.* She wished Holly and Adeline had stayed here but Addie had insisted it was safer to work with Holly away from the Grand - and that was something Delilah couldn't dispute.

"Miss Delilah, you have company."

Delilah turned to see her granddaughter and Adeline. "Holly, I'm glad you're safely back. Frieda, bring some hot tea and cookies, please."

Frieda disappeared as Delilah forced a smile. "Adeline, you and Holly come sit down and get warm. Shall I have Frieda light a fire?"

Addie shook her head as she sat. "It's a summer storm. I think half this water is humidity."

"No thank you, Grandmother. I'm fine," Holly said, her voice a little too crisp. "And I don't want any tea."

Grandmother? She's still upset with me. "That's fine, dear. You don't have to drink it." She paused. "The men left shortly after you two did. They're in town picking up what they need to destroy the bodies and the house." She shook her head. "I don't understand any of this."

"I don't think any of us understands much," Adeline said. "We're just doing the best we can. And I want you to know that if things go wrong at the old house, Holly has promised she'll leave with you without argument, right Holly?"

Holly nodded without enthusiasm.

"Good." Delilah hugged herself, rubbing her arms. "I don't know why I'm so cold."

"You've had a shock," Adeline said.

"Well, I'd best get over it." Delilah sat down as Frieda brought a tea tray and placed it on the coffee table between them and poured. Delilah wrapped her hands around her teacup. "So, Holly, did you learn anything useful this afternoon?"

"Yes." She stared at her tea.

"Holly, give your grandmother a demonstration like we talked about," Addie said.

Still looking into her cup, Holly nodded.

Delilah rose and crossed to the tall windows - it was suddenly stifling hot. She cranked one window open and stood there, enjoying the rain-spattered wind blowing in her face.

"Gram," Holly joined her at the window, began cranking it closed.

Delilah looked at her granddaughter. "Whatever was I thinking? I must've lost my mind, opening a window in this weather!"

"No, Gram. I'm sorry. It was me."

"What are you talking about? I opened-" Delilah silenced, seeing the gold swirling through Holly's blue eyes.

Holly took her hand and led her back to the coffee table. They sat. "I'm sorry," she said. "I didn't want to, but-"

Adeline sipped tea. "I asked Holly to suggest to you to open a window."

Delilah looked flustered. "I didn't hear anything. I was just so hot all of a sudden."

"Because I told you that. It's telepathy or something." Holly looked guilty. "It's like what I did to those waiters in the restaurant - I told them they needed to not look at us. That's all. Gram, I wouldn't do that to you, but you asked what I could do." She paused. "I can do other stuff sometimes, if I'm mad enough. I cracked the mirror in my room a little. I didn't mean to-"

"Holly is incredibly powerful," Adeline explained. "We only practiced a little today and she's already learned so much about control."

"I'm very impressed, sweetheart, and I'm not angry." Delilah squeezed her hand.

"You are?" Holly asked. "Impressed, I mean?"

"Yes, I am." Delilah sat forward and took Holly's other hand. "Sweetheart, now I understand that you could make me let you go to that old house with the others - but you haven't done that." A single tear rolled down her cheek as she smiled.

"I almost did. I'm sorry!"

"No, Holly. I'm proud of you. Don't you see? You have more than a gift. You have honor. I'm so glad that you're my girl. My granddaughter. My daughter. I love you."

Holly stood and hugged Delilah as hard as she could. "Really? Really truly?"

"Really truly." Delilah hugged her back.

Adeline cleared her throat. "All Holly really needs now is a little more confidence, and I think you're giving her that, Dee."

Holly wiped her eyes and sat back down.

"You should have all the confidence in the world, sweetheart," Delilah said.

"She should," Adeline agreed. "Holly, you can't let your fears influence you. If Henry Hank or Pearl come again, your defense is your own power and confidence. That's all you really need and you have that. You just need to remember it."

Holly nodded then looked to Delilah. "So, can I go to the old house with Adeline?"

"No, I'm sorry."

"Listen to your grandmother, Holly," Addie said. "You have a lot left to learn and you're too young to risk your life. Do whatever she tells you. Don't question it. And remember, we don't know where Henry Hank and Pearl are, so you need to protect your grandmother every bit as much as she needs to protect you." Adeline looked grim. "Things may get crazy once we go to the house."

"I understand." As she spoke, gold shot through Holly's eyes again and Delilah knew Addie spoke the truth. They needed to take care of one another.

Although Arthur Meeks couldn't stand Piggy Moran, there was one thing about her he had to admit he liked: her great big rack. He never went out of his way to ogle the crotchety old bitch, but when he was bored and there was no eye candy around, he liked to fuck her between the tits with his eyes. It felt good, like a long-distance sexual assault that no one could ever prove. Wiping down the luggage rack several feet from the desk, he eyeballed her, chuckling as he fantasized about slapping her gigantic spiggoty tits with old Methuselah.

His laughter came out louder than he'd anticipated and Peg looked up, a challenge in her eyes that Arthur could not accept. He looked away and continued whistling and wiping and wishing he had the nerve to walk right over and sock her in those big, fat, middle-aged tits, maybe give 'em a couple Indian burns. *That'd give her something to scowl about.*

Just as another chuckle threatened to erupt, the front doors flew open and Steve Cross, along with that little shit relative of his, burst into the lobby, dripping wet. They headed straight for Pig Moran, spoke a few words, then the big-titted desk clerk made a phone call. One subtle motion at a time, Arthur moved himself closer, trying to find out what was going on. His interest was really piqued when, moments later, Steve and the kid were joined by the druggist, the Injun, and that old fuck from the Humble station, Ike Chance. Arthur suppressed serious laughter now, looking at the motley crew: with the ponytailed pretty boy, Steve Cross, and the mamacita, Piggy, the only things missing were a gypsy and a Jew.

Arthur Meeks edged ever-closer to the group.

"I want to go downstairs with Addie," Holly insisted as soon as Delilah ended the call from Peg Moran.

"Holly," Delilah began.

"Please?"

Delilah looked at Adeline Chance. Addie gave her a little nod. "Wouldn't it be all right for her to see us off, Dee?"

"I suppose," said Delilah. "We'll both come down with you."

✕

By now, Arthur Meeks was close enough to hear snippets of conversation - but not enough for it to make sense. The group in the lobby had been joined by Queen Douchebag, Little Miss Fancy Pants, and the old gas station fuck's wife.

Curiosity brimming, Arthur strained to make out what they were saying.

"... got the gas cans in the back of the truck ..." That was Steve Cross.

"... filled 'em myself," said Old Fuck.

"I grabbed a bunch of flashlights," added the kid.

"And I've got my eyes," said Old Fuck's wife.

What in creation are they talking about? If he didn't know better, Arthur would've guessed they were going to a Klan meeting.

"When will you be back?" the Queen Douchebag asked. She had her hand clamped on Fancy Pants' shoulder.

"As soon as we take care of Henry Hank," the Injun said.

"Gram?" asked Fancy Pants. "Are you sure I can't go-"

"No, Holly, we're staying here. Together."

The little slut shut her mouth.

"We'd better get a move on," said Steve.

Old Lady Fuck joined the men and her husband asked, "You're sure about this, Addie?"

'I am." She turned and smiled at Delilah and the little slut. "We'll be back before you know it."

"We'll be waiting," said Her Majesty. "Good luck."

"Be careful," Fancy Pants added. "Really careful."

Arthur stayed a few steps behind Delilah and Fancy Pants as they followed the others to the lobby doors and watched them pile into the pickup and the Mustang. Sunset was still a couple hours off, but the clouds were like pitch except when lightning lit them from within. Thunder rumbled somewhere behind the hotel, combining with the sound of the engines. Headlights lit the steady rain and the vehicles pulled out and turned back in the direction of town.

"Come, Holly," said the Queen. "We'll wait upstairs."

As the pair turned, Arthur slipped around a display of postcards and peered out the glass doors. He saw brake lights maybe fifty yards down the road as the vehicles pulled to a stop. The lights went off. They'd parked. *What the...* The rain lulled and he heard car doors slamming. It was too dark to see much, but he was pretty sure a couple of them were pulling things from the truck bed. *Crazy loons.*

"They're just taking care of a little business. Nothing to be concerned about."

Arthur, all ears, turned at the sound of the Queen Douchebag's voice. She was talking to Piggy Big Boobs, basically telling her that whatever was going on was none of her beeswax. *Cunty old douchebag!* His eyes fell on Fancy Pants and traveled up and down that little body. There were no titties under the pink t-shirt yet, just those tantalizing little buds that meant she was on the verge of losing her childish appeal. *But she sure hasn't lost it yet, nosireebob. Not by a mile.*

He moved swiftly back to the luggage racks and by the time Her Royal Highness and the slut-girl started up the stairs, he was polishing the brass with a vengeance. He counted to ten, then followed, careful to stay hidden behind each landing turn.

At the fourth floor, Fancy Pants spoke, "I'd like to go to my room for a while. Is that okay?"

The Queen Douchebag replied, "Let's go to the penthouse first. Frieda will have dinner ready in just a few minutes."

"But-"

Arthur's heart sank.

"You can come back down after dinner, Holly."

His frown turning upside down, Arthur listened as the two went on to the fifth floor, then trotted to his room and shut the door. *You're not going to have a very good night, Little Miss Fancy Pants. But I am. I'm going to have the greatest night of my life!*

❧ 51 ❧

IN THE BRIMSTONE GRAND

Peg Moran began shivering five minutes after Miss Delilah and Holly went upstairs. She didn't know why, but she was sorry she'd agreed to stand in for Steve while he did whatever it was he had to do. She hoped he'd be back soon.

She felt as if something unseen were looming over her, watching her - and waiting - though what it might be waiting for, she hadn't a clue. But the entire lobby felt heavy, cold, and ... pregnant. Yes, pregnant with something dark waiting to be born.

Peg stood behind the main desk, unable to motivate herself to do anything but wait. *Wait for what?* She didn't know. Mumbling a quick prayer of protection, she crossed herself, ignoring the cold of the lobby. And the air was getting colder, she was sure of that much. Colder and ... thicker. Heavier.

What's gotten into me? She tried telling herself it was her imagination - she'd always had such a vivid one, and it had often caused her grief when she was young - but tonight she couldn't convince herself it was all in her mind. She thought of Meredith Granger, of her death. And how that had resulted in her promotion to day manager. *Dear God, bless Meredith and her family, wherever they may be.*

She wondered if Steve ever noticed the cold at night.

And she wondered about Arthur Meeks, too. He'd been eavesdropping and had disappeared when the others left the lobby, and she wouldn't be surprised if he were up to no good. She didn't like to admit it, but the man made her nervous with his beady little eyes and rubber lips. The way he stared ... She never let him see how much he bothered her. Tonight, he frightened her, but she didn't know why. Peg shook off the thoughts, determined not to let her imagination get the better of her. *And that's all it is: my overactive imagina-*

DING!

Peggy jumped at the sound the elevator doors. They slid open and Peg watched, waiting for someone to emerge.

No one did.

Peg swallowed. "H-hello?" she called, her voice was weak and strained.

Only silence answered.

And then the ring of the switchboard. She gasped.

Room 329. Someone was calling from room 329. And 329 was empty.

She answered. "Hello?"

Static sounded.

"Hello? Who's there?" She remembered Meredith telling her about phantom calls from that room. Peg wondered if Steve had experienced it, too.

"Hello?"

Still nothing but a soft gray electric hum. Peg hung up and crossed herself.

Outside, lightning flashed and thunder grumbled. Peg's heart was a terrified little rabbit trying to escape its cage. The unnatural cold pressed hard against her. She felt an overwhelming need to get out. Now.

The guests are all in. I'll call Miss Delilah, tell her I have a family emergency and need to leave. She hated to lie, especially to Delilah, but when the elevator door dinged again, and once more, no one stepped out, Peggy picked up the phone and dialed the penthouse.

As soon as they'd arrived at Delilah's apartment, Frieda served Denver omelets and tea at the kitchen table. Holly hadn't even seen the kitchen until tonight, but it was instantly her favorite room, homey and friendly.

They ate quickly and in no time, were back in the living room, Delilah standing at the window with binoculars trained on the parked cars just down the road.

"Can you see anything?"

"Just the cars. They must be hiking down to the house." She handed the spy glasses to Holly.

"I'm glad the rain let up a little." As much as Holly wanted to be with the others, she was relieved to be here, safe with Gram. She peered at the cars.

"I'm glad, too, sweetheart. Addie, Ike, and Ben are too old to be hiking in this weather. I hope none of them breaks a hip."

"For sure!"

The phone rang. "Excuse me a moment."

Holly set the glasses down as Delilah hung up. Her grandmother smiled, though she didn't look very happy. "Peg had a family emergency. How would you like to go downstairs and help me man the lobby? We'll turn off the vacancy sign, but we ought to keep the doors open until nine in case any guests need to run out tonight."

"Yes! I'd love to! Everybody should be back from the house by then, too."

Delilah smiled. "Yes, they should."

✦ 52 ✦

THE OLD DARK HOUSE

There was something wrong with the house - something more than the eye could detect. The walls rose like normal walls, meeting the ceiling as squarely as any other room Adeline had been in before, yet there was something different about this place, something *wrong*. Even the shadows here were too dark, too thick.

She stood in the living room, searching that dense darkness, flanked by Ike, Ben, Abner, and Steve. Young Eddie, despite his protests, had been given guard duty and waited outside.

"Do you sense anything in here?" asked Ike.

Adeline nodded. Yes, she sensed something. A *lot* of something. Where could she even begin? "This is a terrible place. Terrible."

"Yes," Abner Hala agreed. "A very bad place."

Adeline played her flashlight over the center staircase, half expecting something to leap out at her, but nothing did; the shadows kept their secrets to themselves, and the house seemed to hold its breath, biding its time.

Something insubstantial passed by Adeline, something not quite human, at least not anymore. A rush of chilled, thick air. A frail presence, invisible. She glanced at the others. No one else had noticed, so Adeline said nothing. She turned, her flashlight cutting through the near darkness, and found a hallway to her right. Darkened rooms and debris lay beyond.

"We need to find the kitchen," she said. "That's where the cellar door will be."

"This way," said Abner, picking up a gas can. Adeline and the others followed, carrying more cans and sledgehammers.

"Ike," said Adeline, "hand me one of the sledges."

Ike did, and Adeline followed Abner up the hall, one hand clutched around the handle, the other around her flashlight. She shone her beam straight ahead, unnerved by the illusion of movement as they walked; it was as if the walls were breathing, the shadows crouching, preparing to pounce, but the looming ghosts were too faint to see. Shaking off the dark thoughts, she kept moving, aware that the hall was warming. Stifling, in fact. And it seemed to stretch on for an eternity before they came to the kitchen.

This room, too, was draped in shadows blacker than any Adeline had ever seen. Unlike the hall, it was chilly, and became colder as they moved further inside.

"Jesus," Steve Cross whispered behind her.

Adeline sliced her light around, saw nothing but broken tile and an old sink.

"There," said Ike, shining his on the cellar door at the far end of the room.

Abner approached. "It's padlocked to hell and back."

"Good thing we brought sledgehammers," Steve said.

"Well, Steve," said Abner. "Let's get to work."

53

THE ESCAPE

There was no family emergency at Peg's. The instant she and Delilah stepped into the lobby, Holly knew that for a fact.

"Peggy must have left the air conditioner on." Delilah rubbed her arms. "It's positively freezing in here. I'll turn it off." She marched purposefully to the copper door.

"No! Don't open that!" Holly yelled.

Surprised, Delilah whirled. "What?"

Holly took a deep breath. "Don't open that door, Gram. It's not the air conditioner."

"What is it, then?"

"Please, come back over here and I'll tell you."

At that instant, the elevator dinged and the door opened on blackness. Delilah stared. "The light burned out. I'd better call Meeks to bring a new bulb-"

"No!" Holly ran to Delilah and grabbed her hand as the black cloud oozed out of the cab, so cold it frosted Holly's breath. "Come away from there, Gram! Get away from the door!" She yanked her arm.

"What on earth-"

Holly's vision went microscopic. She could see every tiny particle of the cold black mist. "Come with me, Gram. Now!"

Delilah obeyed. The two of them ran out of the path of the frigid cloud, halting by the front desk. "What is that ... that cold?"

"Henry Hank," Holly said, watching the mass hover then disappear into the backroom, leaving hoarfrost on the copper door. "Come on, Gram. Let's get upstair-" Pinching Pearl Abbott, stern and upright, glided out of the elevator cab and headed toward the copper door. Holly held her breath.

"What do you see, Holly?" Delilah asked.

Suddenly, the spirit halted.

Holly gasped as the phantom turned its head backward and pinned her with its glittering black eyes.

Then, with a howl of outrage, Pearl shot toward them. Holly concentrated on driving her back, but there wasn't enough time and the spirit plowed straight into Delilah, who began screaming as red welts appeared on her arms and neck.

"Leave her alone!" Holly demanded, her power beginning to flow.

Pearl Abbot hesitated.

"Go away!" Holly cried. "Get out of here!"

The ghost wavered then shot into the backroom.

"She's gone," Holly said.

Delilah ran behind the desk, grabbed a small ring of keys, scribbled something on a memo pad, and cried, "This way!"

They ran through the elevator lobby, past the far staircase, and down the long hall toward the garage.

ARTHUR MEEKS WAS DESCENDING THE STAIRS WHEN HE HEARD THE screams. He ran down the last flight and entered the lobby. The place was deserted and very, very cold. He looked around. "What the goddamn hell?"

THE VIOLET PHANTOM AERO COUPE GLEAMED IN THE DIM GLOW OF the garage lights. "Holly, come help me get the garage door open!"

Holly ran to Delilah's side and together they pushed at the heavy door sideways. At first it didn't want to move - a blob of muddy gravel clogged the track. Holly snagged it out with her fingers and the door rolled open easily.

"Get in the car!" Delilah cried.

Holly climbed in while Delilah put the key in the ignition. "Damn, I wish Max were here. I haven't driven in years." She glanced at Holly. "Don't worry; it's like riding a bike. You never forget how."

The engine roared to life and Delilah turned on the headlights. "As soon as we get to town, we'll call the police to get the guests out."

"It's okay, Gram. They're not interested in the guests." She hoped Fluffy was safe.

Delilah nodded as she put the car in gear and inched forward.

"Where are we going?"

Delilah glanced at her. "We're going down to the Daisy Hotel for the night. It's too dangerous here." She pulled further forward and hard rain pounded the tip of the long hood, just past the naked lady ornament.

"But we can't leave! Fluffy-"

"I left a note so that Steve can call us as soon as they get back. He'll see to Fluffy." She looked at Holly. "If they're successful, these ghosts will be gone, isn't that right?"

"Right."

"Good." She gave Holly a sidelong glance. "I hope it works."

As Delilah began inching the Phantom further into the rain, Holly knew something was wrong. "It's getting cold in here, Gram. I think we better hurry." She saw her breath.

Delilah pushed the gas too hard and the car lurched forward, its long nose halfway out now. Stomping the brake, she stalled the car. "Damn it." She put the Rolls back in neutral and turned the key again; the engine came back to life. "We'll be downtown in a few minutes."

The car lurched another foot, the cab growing colder.

"Gram? It's really raining. Are you sure we should-"

Delilah eased off the clutch and tapped the gas just right, and the car moved forward at a snail's pace. "We can't stay here. It's not safe." Her breath formed white ghosts around her lips.

"We can go upstairs. It's safe there." Holly clung to the door. "It's not safe *here!*"

The itch in her brain was back; she realized Henry Hank was trying to get into her brain. She concentrated, willed her eyes to turn to gold. *NO! Get out!*

The garage door creaked and began rolling toward them as if shoved by an invisible force. "Watch out!" Holly yelled.

Delilah stomped the gas but the heavy wooden door slammed into the side of the Phantom, crunching into the long nose of the car only two feet from the passenger compartment. Wood splintered and Holly shielded her eyes as the windshield cracked and shattered.

Delilah gunned the engine until the car roared like a mad beast caught in a trap. The motor died and refused to start again.

An explosive sound rocked the car. "Someone's shooting at us!" Delilah pushed Holly down and covered her. There was another blast, then two more and the car rocked and sank. Then it was quiet; only the icy cold remained.

The scratchy itch in Holly's brain redoubled, but the intrusion angered her and helped her focus.

"Stay down." Cautiously, Delilah sat up, opened the driver's door, and peered out. She looked back at Holly. "It wasn't a gun. The tires are blown." She shivered. "I don't understand. How did the garage door shut on us? That can't be! And the tires! It doesn't make sense."

"He doesn't want me to leave, Gram." Holly's words were solemn and her eyes, preternaturally sharp in the dark. She could see the blackness looming beside the car now, could feel its rage and greed. Keeping her mind closed to his, she spoke. "He won't let me go. I have to stay here. He'll hurt you if we try to leave."

The chill began to lift. As Holly hoped, Henry Hank had heard what she'd told Delilah. "Gram, open your door and get out. I'll follow you. It's okay, we can go upstairs now."

Delilah slid out of the Phantom and helped Holly out after her. "How do you know?" she whispered.

"Because the cold went away. We can go in now. He wants me to stay here." She hesitated. "We'll be okay as long as I do. Let's go upstairs."

426

They reentered the hotel the same way they'd come. The temperature felt normal in the lobby. Delilah stopped walking. "I'd better see to the front door."

Holly hung back while Delilah locked up. The air wasn't cold, but it felt prickly, electric. She looked at the copper door, saw frost, and knew the spirits were nearby.

Delilah rejoined her. "Ready, Holly?"

"Yes. I'd like to go to my room and get Fluffy, clothes, and some other stuff."

"How about we both go? I can help you carry."

"Thank you, Gram."

FLUFFY CLOTHES? WHAT THE HELL ARE FLUFFY CLOTHES? STANDING behind the half-closed door in the back office behind the front desk, Arthur Meeks had been happy when Little Miss Fancy Pants had come back inside, but was now royally pissed off because the Queen was going to 429 with her and evidently moving her to the penthouse tonight. *Goddamnit, how am I going to give that little bitch what's coming to her?*

Staying out of sight, heart pounding, he followed them upstairs. He hid behind the landing, watching them turn off on the fourth floor, and after they headed into the girl's room and shut the door, he had an idea. As quick as a fox, he tiptoed to his own room, grabbed a rag and the bottle of chloroform. He gave a little groan as Methuselah throbbed to life; he wasn't sure if his plan would work, but the thrill of the hunt was worth the risk.

Stuffing the rag and bottle into his pockets, he opened his door slightly and peered

down at room 429, waiting. Hoping.

A moment later, the door opened and the Queen Douchebag came out carrying the little slut's suitcase and a cardboard box. She turned and spoke into the room. "Do you want me to come back down to help you with the rest?"

He couldn't hear Fancy Pants' reply, but his heart began to float on a wave of hope when Delilah said, "Okay, just get what you need for the night and hurry on up. I'll be waiting for you."

The door to 429 closed and she left. As her heels clicked up the stairs Arthur got to work. He moved down the hall and stopped behind two large potted palms near 429. There, he opened the chloroform and poured it on the rag, stoppered the bottle, and ditched it behind the planter. Then, he waited.

When Little Miss Fancy Pants finally came out, Methuselah strained against his navy corduroys. He couldn't see what she was carrying, but her hands were full, making her an easy target as she locked her door.

Arthur wasted no time.

He crept up behind her, his arm coming out and around her head, covering her mouth with the chloroformed rag.

It didn't happen as quickly as he'd hoped.

The little bitch began fighting and, horrified, Arthur saw the cat in her arms. Ears back, it yowled and climbed her shoulder as the girl struggled against him, against the drug. Growling, the orange monster bared its fangs and hissed - *the lion will come and eat you if you're a bad boy!* Black spots floated in his vision and Arthur nearly swooned as the yowling cat came closer, closer, across her shoulder, its front paws on his chest now, digging in. He was so scared he was barely aware of the crushing pain in his balls.

HOLLY, DIZZY AND SHOCKED, REMEMBERED WHAT CHERRY HAD TOLD her to do if she ever got grabbed by a man. "Twist his nuts off!" Her mother's words came to her just as she thought she was going to pass out, and now, hearing Fluffy's howls and growls, she yanked the cloth off her face, and pulled away from Arthur Meeks' limp hands just as Fluffy leapt from her shoulder. She stared.

The cat clung to the bellhop's face, claws dragging over his forehead and down his cheeks. Blood spurted as Fluffy sank his teeth into Meeks' nose. Powerful hind feet and claws pounded his mouth, turning his lips to raw liver.

Meeks made tiny terrified noises as his hands finally came back to life and flew to his face, grabbing at Fluffy, trying to tear him off. But the cat wouldn't budge.

Then, down the hall, the elevator dinged and the air went suddenly cold.

Fluffy pushed off and ran in the opposite direction. Arthur Meeks took a dozen staggering steps toward the elevator then stopped and just stood there.

❦ 54 ❦

IN THE CELLAR

The air was dank and heavy with dust and things long dead. Abner led the way down the cellar steps - thank heaven they were cement - into what felt like another world. He thought of the tales of the portal and the Hellfire Spirit and, in this massive vault of death, he realized there was truth to the stories. It felt as if something horrifying might rise out of the ground at any moment, as if eyes were on him, on all of them.

Halfway down, he paused to play his flashlight around the cellar. It was nothing but a huge crypt, the size of the house itself. There were open barrels, boxes, and trunks lining the edges of the room, and in the center, were two simple cement stands about two feet tall and four feet apart. Each held an ornate wooden casket blanketed in a thick coating of dust.

Abner did not want to keep going, but he did. He had to. Exchanging a glance with Steve, a pace behind him, he descended the stairs.

"Oh." Addie gasped the word, her hand tight on the bottom of the handrail.

Abner and Steve stepped onto the hard-packed earthen floor, then turned. Addie and Ike remained on the bottom step. Addie was staring across the room, looking at something the rest of them couldn't see.

"What is it?" Ike's arm circled his wife's waist.

"So many died here." Her voice trembled. "They're still here, bound to this place. Young women, babies, children." She put a hand to her mouth. "Some are sobbing. Some are screaming."

"Do you see them?" Abner asked.

"A little. They're calling out, but they're so afraid that they're hiding behind the boxes and barrels, and in the trunks. They're peeking out at us. They're angry, too. So angry." She raised her voice. "We're your friends and we're here to set you free."

Abner concentrated, saw nothing, but he thought he heard something. *It's just the storm.*

"It's okay." Addie spoke to the room. "You're among friends. We mean you no harm."

"I might hear something," Steve said, his voice tentative.

"They're here and they're listening." Addie lowered her voice. "They've been trapped here so long that their fear and anger has changed them. Be careful, be kind." She raised her voice again. "They want us to hear, to see, to know. Come on." She led them toward the boxes and trunks along one wall.

Steve shone his light into one of the wooden barrels and gasped. There was a skeletal hand poking up from what might've been a nurse's uniform.

"She says her name was Emma," Adeline told them. "And here," She trained her beam on the delicate skeleton of an infant, its ribs caved in. "This one is in great pain. She's so young she has no idea where she is and all she wants is her mother." A tear rolled down Addie's cheek. "She would kill to get to her mother." Addie moved away from the infant. "There are so many. So many. Henry Hank Barrow was a monster. I had no idea how evil he and Pearl really were."

"Addie, if we destroy Barrow, will his victims be freed?" Abner walked along, illuminating horror after horror; grinning skulls and skeletons and bodies mummified by the desert air, still with hair, red, blond, black. He now heard the phantom murmurs of women and the whimpers of babies, and realized the others did as well. *How strong their pain that we all hear them.*

"They will be freed, and Holly will be safe," Adeline said. "But both Henry Hank and Pearl must be destroyed. Pearl is an able jailer of these lost souls."

55

THE UNINVITED

Pearl Abbott glided out of the unlit elevator, her eyes as black as her dress and hair, her high cheekbones as severe as a Victorian schoolteacher's. Those burning eyes were on Arthur Meeks, who stood oblivious in the center of the fourth floor hallway. Holly ducked down between two big planters and peered between the leaves as the black cloud - Henry Hank - sifted into the corridor, a pulsing darkness beside Pearl. The electricity in the air prickled up goosebumps on Holly's arms and neck.

The ghosts advanced on Meeks, but Holly knew they were looking for her. Realizing they would soon sense her, she forced herself to remember Addie's most important lesson: *No fear. Ever. They feed on fear. Be resolute. Always. You have the ability; you will prevail.*

Meeks shivered and gawked around as if sensing something as the spirits bore down on him slowly, almost regally. With his torn, bloody face and shocked wide eyes, he was a pitiful-looking thing. *I should warn him,* Holly thought, then took it back. He didn't deserve a warning. He had stolen from her, attacked her, invaded her privacy and she knew he wanted to do to her what he'd done to those other girls.

She concentrated until her eyes sharpened to that crystal clarity that told her she had called up her abilities. Holly waited, her focus so great now that she could see the weave of Pearl Abbott's dress and the sifting darkness beneath her skin that betrayed her status as a spirit. She saw tiny red and blue sparks in the blackness that was the broken soul of H.H. Barrow, a glimmer of the Beast's red and blue lightning.

Pearl reached Arthur Meeks first. He gasped as she wrapped her arms around him and began pinching, pinching, pinching. Screeching now, Meeks flailed and Holly heard Pearl's dark laughter as she let go of him. He stumbled straight into the black cloud and struggled to move as if he were underwater. Everything was in slow motion and Holly listened to his muted, strangled cries with no pity. An endless moment passed then he popped out of the cloud as if it were Jell-O, fell, struggled to his feet, and stumbled toward the elevator.

At that instant, Pinching Pearl's cold gaze found Holly. She felt the invisible eyes of great-great-grandfather upon her as well. The phantoms slowly moved nearer.

You can do this. Holly, all but oblivious to the bellhop, walked to the center of the hall. *I have the ability; I will prevail.* She stared at Pearl Abbott, locking her pinpoint vision on the phantom as it glided closer. *They feed on fear. I will prevail.* She shivered once as the hall grew colder. Somewhere behind the spirits, Meeks was screaming in terror. Resolutely, Holly stepped forward to meet the ghosts.

56

DESECRATION

Steve stared at the caskets on their cement pillars. "Are we really going to do this?"

"We are," said Abner.

"Then I guess we'd better get to it." Steve felt unreal, outside himself, as he stepped toward the ornate boxes. The murmur of the dead grew louder, angrier, in his mind. He raised his sledgehammer and began banging away at the locks that sealed one. Abner brought his own hammer down on the other. Metal clanged, echoing through the vault as they hammered and beat. Steve was out of breath and working up a sweat. It took a few more good hard whacks, but at last, the lock broke off.

Abner's lock broke a moment later.

Addie's flashlight flickered, almost went out, then returned to life.

"We'd better hurry." Steve didn't look forward to what came next. And, judging by their faces, neither did the others. Ike joined Steve, and Ben joined Abner and they lifted the casket lids in tandem.

Steve recoiled from the smell of dust and fetid death, as the cloying, almost sweet reek of ancient rot reached deep into his lungs. Swallowing the urge to gag, he aimed his flashlight and forced himself to look down.

The corpse within was dressed in a cobalt robe, trimmed in red and gold, with the *Infurnam Aeris* symbol on the breast. A pointed hood covered the face, making it impossible to tell if this was Henry Hank or Pinching Pearl. Steve looked at the signet ring on a withered finger and the thin chain around the neck that held a lapis medallion set in copper, a blood-colored ruby in the center of the stone. Stomach turning, he pulled back the hood and stared into the mummified face of H.H. Barrow; there was no mistaking that huge mummified hawk nose.

"Stand back," said Steve.

The only sound was the weird murmur of long-dead victims. The sound was closer now, angrier.

Addie and the others stepped out of the way as Steve and Ike tipped the casket, spilling the body onto the ground. Dried skin ripped and powdered, bones scattered. Abner and Ben did the same and Pearl's corpse rolled to the floor in a clack and rattle of dust and bone. The smell of old death plumed out, saturating the air, and Steve's stomach tightened like a clenched fist.

The five of them gathered around the dried up remains of Henry Hank Barrow and Pearl Abbott and, without speaking, began to desecrate the bodies, kicking them, bringing their sledgehammers down to crush bone. H.H. Barrow's skull snapped free and Abner hurled it against the wall. It struck, cracked, and rolled toward Steve, stopping at his feet.

Steve raised his sledgehammer and, with a war cry, brought it down hard, turning the mummified head of H.H. Barrow into dust.

57

FLUFFY TO THE RESCUE

"What in the world?"

Delilah was about to open the door to head downstairs to see what was taking Holly so long when she heard the scratching. She saw nothing through the peephole, but the sound came again, followed by a loud, insistent *meow*. She opened the door.

Fluffy sat staring up at her, tail beating the floor.

"Did you jump out of Holly's arms?" Delilah asked, bending down to pet him. "Well, come on in."

"*Meow!*" The cat looked her in the eye, then stood, and turned around. He took a few steps away from the door and looked over his shoulder. "*Meow!*" he insisted.

"What do you want?" Delilah smiled.

He returned, tail whipping. "*Meow!*" He turned again, took two steps, and stopped, positively glaring at her. "*Meow!*"

Delilah chuckled. "Are you auditioning to replace Lassie? Is Timmy in the well?"

"*Meow!*"

"Oh, dear God." Suddenly, she understood, and followed the cat out. He trotted down the stairs, looking back to make sure she was

437

behind him. When they arrived at the fourth floor she saw Holly standing in the center of the hallway about halfway to the elevator.

"Holly?" she called.

The girl didn't turn, didn't move, but faced the other direction, still and stiff, and Delilah realized her granddaughter saw something she couldn't. Staring hard, she discerned something like waves in the air, the kind you see over a hot desert highway. Suddenly, the temperature dropped.

Fluffy hissed, tail fluffing to three times its normal size as he turned and bolted back upstairs.

Delilah heard Holly's voice, low and cool, intense. "You can't touch me," she said to the wavering air. "You can never touch me. Do you hear? I won't allow it."

It was a standoff. A moment passed then Holly yelped once, flinched, then cried "NO!" before going still again.

Delilah ran toward her.

"No," Holly said in a voice made of steel. "You can't touch me, Pearl. Neither can you, Henry Hank. NO!"

"Get away from her!" Delilah, trying to put herself between Holly and whatever threatened her, was suddenly in the grips of Pearl Abbott's freezing fingers once more. An instant later, something massive and thick engulfed her, made it hard to breathe.

"NO!" commanded Holly. "Get off her! Now! Get off! Get off!"

And it stopped. Just like that.

Even the chill vanished.

Coughing, Delilah saw Holly's molten gold eyes. "Was that Pearl Abbott?"

"It was both of them."

"Holly, you saved me! My God, I had no idea you could drive them away like that!"

"I didn't, Gram. They just disappeared. They're gone. That's why it's not cold anymore."

"Well, thank you." Delilah hugged Holly tight, then looked at her. "I don't understand."

Holly hesitated. "I was holding them off, but it was hard. Something else made them leave. They just stopped pushing at me and the itch stopped."

"Itch?"

"Henry Hank tries to get in my head sometimes. It itches."

"In your head?"

"He wants to get inside me and take over my body. Remember? We need to go–"

"I didn't understand... My God, he wants to possess you! We can't let him."

"He can't get in my head, Gram. I know how to keep him out."

"But–"

"Help!" a rasping voice called. "Help!"

Delilah looked up, saw nothing.

"Help!"

"It's Arthur Meeks," Holly said sourly. "He ran for the elevator when the ghosts came."

"We should go tell him it's safe now. He sounds terrified, poor man."

Holly stared at her, gold beginning to swirl back into her eyes. "He's a bad man, not a poor man."

"Help me!" came a muted shriek.

"Come on, Holly. We have to help." Delilah started for the elevator, Holly trailing

behind.

"Something doesn't look right," Delilah said as they approached. "Hurry!"

She ran and when she passed the huge planter that hid the bottom of the elevator, she gasped. The cab was about six feet above the landing. "Oh, dear God." Arthur Meeks had obviously been too frightened to notice and had fallen into the shaft. Now he dangled, his arms folded over the threshold, his only purchase.

He looked up at her. "Oh, thank heaven, Miss Devine! Please help me!"

She knelt. Hearing Holly behind her, she said over her shoulder. "We have to help Arthur up before he falls." When she looked back at

Meeks, he was staring past her, at Holly, his skin pallid as death, his lips bloodless.

"He tried to hurt me." Holly came no closer.

"He was probably just frightened and pushed past you without thinking. Give me a hand."

"No! Gram, listen to me! He tried to chloroform me! He has pictures in his room. He wanted to do things to me."

Arthur's eyes went wide. "That's not true! She's making up stories because I caught her snooping in my room."

"Because you stole my bank. And, Gram, he had my underwear in his room and a whole drawer full of girls' panties. And pictures. Naked pictures of girls. I ... I think some of them were dead."

Delilah couldn't think. "Holly, what are you saying?"

"Go look right now if you don't believe me." She glanced at Meeks. "He can wait."

"I don't need to look. I believe you." Delilah stared down at Arthur Meeks, thinking about the missing posters she'd seen in town, about the children who'd disappeared over the last few years. "If you want us to help you, Mr. Meeks, tell me the truth."

"I swear it's not what you think!" he sputtered. "I didn't kill anybody! I'm not Lonely Boy. She's just saying that! She doesn't like me!"

"Gram?" Holly spoke urgently. "I know where the ghosts went. They're at Pearl's house. We have to go now or Steve and Addie and the others, they're going to die! We have to go!"

"It's too dangerous."

"Help me!" Meeks pleaded. "Don't listen to her! She's lying! Help me!"

"They'll all die!" Holly said urgently. "We will, too! Addie and I have to be together to stop them! But we have to go now!"

"Okay, Holly." Delilah rose, never taking her eyes off Arthur Meeks. Now she could clearly see the glassy depravity behind the fear in his eyes. She prided herself on reading people but she'd never even taken the time to read the all-but-invisible bellhop before.

"You're not gonna leave me hanging here because of what that little slut of yours said, are you?" He spoke rapidly, his voice fired with desperation.

And there it was. Delilah stared down at the man, at his sweating face and terrified, pleading eyes. "Little slut?"

"You know she was asking for it! It's not my fault! She's been hanging around lifting her skirt to show me her privates. She doesn't wear underwear. She's asking for it. It's not my fault! You know she's-"

Delilah got back down on her knees and put her hands over Meeks' arms. "Are you sure, Mr. Meeks?" she whispered. "Are you positive that's true?"

"Gospel, Miss Devine! She's been rubbing up against me from the day she arrived. It's not my fault! She made me!"

"God doesn't like liars," Delilah said.

"Of course not, Miss Devine! Of course not. I'd never lie!"

"Tell that to the devil!" Delilah shoved, pushing Meeks' arms off the threshold. Screaming, the bellhop spiraled into the darkness below.

Delilah, still on her knees, said, "I pity the devil."

Holly grabbed her and pulled her up, tears streaming, hugging her so tight. "Thank you for believing me."

"Holly, I'm sorry for underestimating you. Let's go help our friends."

≈ 58 ≈

HOUSE OF THE DEAD

Steve had wanted Eddie to stay well away from the old house, but the rain made it too wet, and the lightning bursts too dangerous, to stand guard anywhere but on the front porch. Eddie had been pretty jazzed for a while, hanging out on the dark creaking porch of a haunted house while the storm rumbled around him, but now he grew impatient. It seemed like the others had been inside forever while he was stuck out here just because Steve was afraid of pissing off Mom.

Eddie shined his light through the big front window, but again saw nothing more interesting than cobwebs and dust. Even the old rocking chair that was supposed to move on its own was missing. *Maybe it got bored and moved to another room.*

He wanted to move, too, to go inside and see what the others were doing in the basement. *It should be one of the old guys out here, not me. I should be helping smash bones.* Thunder rumbled, nearer now. Damp and bored, Eddie wondered how it could take so long to mangle a couple of skeletons.

He leaned against the faded siding, yawned, scratched his chin, and sighed. Lightning flashed close enough to light the sky. Thunder followed on its heels, then a deluge. Suddenly, he had to pee like a racehorse. He considered whizzing off the porch, but he really wanted to see inside and there was probably an old toilet or a sink or something in there he could use. He smiled to himself; yes, peeing was a fine excuse to go in and poke around.

Carefully, quietly, he opened the torn screen door and stepped indoors; it was cold as hell, but after the warm humid night, it felt good. He shone his flashlight around the room, and saw only the weird blue walls and the center staircase draped in cobwebs. Nothing more.

He approached the hallway and played the light over the rooms beyond. The first doorway was partially blocked by the broken remains of an old chair. *The haunted rocking chair?* Curious, he started to step over it then stopped - the air was twice as cold in the room and his need to pee became excruciating. Turning, he saw an old bucket at the short end of the hall. Sighing relief, he used it then zipped up before grabbing the pail and returning to the main room.

The heavy main door had somehow shut itself. He opened it then, as he put his hand on the screen door, thunder cracked and lightning stabbed the ground directly in front of the house. Shocked, Eddie set the pail down - no way was he going outside to dump it until the lightning moved away. He watched the storm. The rain soon let up, but electricity danced in the whipping wind. The dead trees swayed. It was like *Night on Bald Mountain* in *Fantasia*. Eddie wished he were in the theater *watching* the movie instead of here in this creepy old place, *living* it. *That's not like me! I should love being in a haunted house. It's fun!*

But he didn't love *this* haunted house. It wasn't fun at all.

Lightning split open the sky, a huge, long bolt of it, and struck one of the dead trees. He watched it crack and flame. Half the tree broke off and crashed to the ground, smoking and sizzling, and then a gust of rain drenched the flames as the wind howled like a thousand banshees.

For an instant Eddie saw something darker than night, something that flickered with red and blue flames as it obscured the downed tree then rolled toward the house. "Holy shit!"

The screen door seemed to waver.

Ice cold air, crackling with static, engulfed him. It felt thick and slimy and Eddie tried to pull free but it was like running in mud. He could barely move. Finally, it passed by him, and again, he thought he saw tiny flashes of cobalt and scarlet in the wavering air. Then something else ice-cold was touching him, hurting, pulling, and pinching. He yelled, then it was gone, too, trailing a frigid train of air behind it.

Breathing hard, Eddie staggered to his feet and followed; he had to warn the others.

He shined his light but couldn't see beyond the frosted air as the all-but-invisible things - *the ghosts!* - headed into the kitchen. They moved to the far end, to a yawning door. *The cellar!*

"Watch out down there!" Eddie yelled as loud as he could. "Watch out!"

Staying close enough to frost his breath, he followed the entities down the stairs. He saw Steve and the others, then, their flashlights bobbing and blinding. He heard sounds like distant cries and sobs, faraway screams, unreal, unholy. "Steve! Watch out!"

Steve looked up. "I told you to stay outsi-" Then he became aware of the invisible cold.

"Henry Hank and Pearl are here," Addie cried. "Finish with the bones! Hurry!"

Steve and Abner smashed scattered white bones swathed in torn blue cloth. Eddie watched sparks fly as the hammers hit concrete.

Adeline stepped forward, her flashlight faltering as she raised her voice. "Stop! Stop right there, Pearl Abbott!" Then she screamed and dropped the flashlight, but not before Eddie saw red welts appearing on her face and neck.

Then it looked as if Steve were moving in slow motion, as if he were inside a force field, and Eddie realized the icy thing that had been on him upstairs engulfed his cousin now. Despite it, Steve kept hammering. Abner did too. Adeline Chance yelled something as Ike tried to pull her back toward the stairs. Ben Gower kept kicking at the bones.

With a *clang*, Steve dropped his sledgehammer, staggering. He looked like he couldn't breathe. Eddie sprang forward and leapt for the dropped sledge, pulled it out of the icy slime. Seeing a mummified leg, he smashed it. "Let go of him!" he cried, and crushed another "Let go!"

THEY MADE IT TO PEARL'S HOUSE IN A BLAZE OF LIGHTNING AND A herald of thunder. Rain half-swept them down the trail and Holly kept glancing back at Delilah, amazed at her sure-footedness, pleased at her speed. They'd lost too much time already and Holly had intended to run ahead, but she didn't need to.

Wet branches slapped Holly's face as she skittered toward the house. She pushed them aside, uncaring, determined only to stop Henry Hank from destroying her new family.

They arrived at the rear of the house and Holly led them around front. One of the dead trees had been struck by lightning and lay smoking on the barren ground. "This way." Holly and Delilah took the broad porch steps. Behind them, lightning torched the ground where they'd been standing a moment before. Thunder rattled the house and set the wooden porch moving under their feet. Holly pushed the screen door open and stepped into the cold blue room, her stomach twisting.

"Do you see them? Henry Hank and Pearl?" Delilah hugged herself against the chill air.

"No, but they're here somewhere." Holly squinted, her eyes getting used to the darkness. There were other spirits here, too, ones she hadn't noticed the day she and Keith had explored. They were watching, frightened. A few nearly invisible wisps peered from the hallway, but Holly sensed more watching from the kitchen. They were massing there, almost formless, mere suggestions of people. She could hear their voices, anguished, angry.

"Addie and Steve and the others are downstairs," Holly told Gram. "So are Henry Hank and Pearl. You should stay here. It's safer."

"Not on your life," Delilah said firmly. "Lead on."

Lightning lit the path to the kitchen, thunder rumbling as Holly felt the spirits of her great-great-grandfather's victims surrounding her, touching her, asking for help, demanding it.

"Do you hear voices?" Delilah whispered.

"Yes. Ignore them. They can't hurt us." Holly entered the long galley kitchen and even in darkness, could see the deeper dark of the open cellar. Crashes and calls came from below. The unmistakable ring of metal striking concrete. She heard Adeline's voice, commanding, then Abner's, cursing. A yell, a scream.

Holly clutched the handrail and started down into the frigid cellar, Delilah behind her.

Mad flashes of light lit the room as flashlights pointed here, then there. One briefly blinded her and Ben Gower cried, "Holly's here."

"Delilah," Addie ordered. "Stay on the stairs. Don't come down!"

"But-"

"Do what she says, Gram." Holly made the floor, her eyes first on Eddie, who was hammering stray bones as if he were Thor himself, then Abner, who stood amid a mound of white shards, half a skull glaring up at him as he took aim. Steve knelt, panting.

Along the walls, spirits watched from behind trunks and barrels. They were half-hidden staring at something beyond her. Holly turned to look.

At the other end of the room Pinching Pearl glowered from the cradle of the massive sparking blackness of Henry Hank Barrow. Holly gasped as the Brimstone Beast began to form, the black scales lit by cobalt fire, the eyes blazing rubies. Something scratched at her brain. *"Come fly with me, Holly,"* came that rumbling voice. *"Together we will rule the night and the copper moon shall be ours."* The Beast opened its mouth, breathing cold blue flames. A red forked tongue lolled out and Pearl Abbott stroked it.

"Did you hear that?" Eddie said.

"Hear it, hell, I see the damned dragon," said Ben.

Come with me, Holly.

Holly stared at the dragon, mesmerized.

"The Brimstone Beast." Steve got to his feet.

Join me.

It was strong, so strong. Holly stared into the dragon's eyes, watching the flames flicker within.

"The Serpent." Abner stared.

"My grandfather," Delilah breathed.

We will fly in the midnight sky.

"We will fly-" Holly whispered.

Then Adeline's voice cut through the Beast's cajoling rumble.

"Holly, don't listen to him! Don't let him in! Focus! No fear. You're in control, not him. Do *not* listen!"

Focus! Focus! Gathering her intent, Holly finally shook herself free. "Get out of my head!" she yelled, concentrating until the Beast dissolved back into an amorphous mass and she could once again see the darkness between the pores on Pearl Abbott's face. "You can't touch me!" Holly cried. "You can't move! You can't do *anything*!"

Addie was beside her now. "That's right. Don't let them get free. The bones are destroyed, but the spirits are still strong."

"Burn the bones!" Delilah called from the stairs. "Carrie says to burn the bones!"

"Yes," Addie said, "but first, Holly and I must trap them here, so even their spirits can't escape the flames."

She bent and looked into Holly's eyes, showing her that her own golden spot glinted and pulsed. "I don't have your power, sweetheart, but I'll help all I can." She glanced at the men, who stood together as if waiting to do battle. "Get the gas cans ready now. Who has the matches?"

"I do," Abner said.

"Soak the bones while Holly and I deal with the spirits. As soon as we're on the stairs, light the book of matches and throw it. And be quick about it." She nodded toward Henry Hank and Pinching Pearl, who continued to hover a dozen feet away. Addie laid her hand on Holly's shoulder. "You're doing great, Holly. Keep them pinned. Tell them they can't move, mean it with every fiber of your soul, and they won't be able to. Keep thinking it, or say it, anything you want. Just do it."

From the corner of her eye, Holly saw Addie turn toward the spirits of Henry Hank's victims, still watching along the far wall. "Go!" cried the old woman. "They can't hurt you anymore!"

The smell of gasoline filled the air as the men doused the bones. A beat passed, two, then with a rush of cool breezes, the spirits began to move. Some gathered closer, others disappeared, and from halfway up the steps, Holly heard Delilah gasp. "I feel them. They're leaving."

Suddenly, Pearl Abbott roared, her face enraged as she rushed forward and knocked straight into Addie, who cried out as the spirit began raising fresh welts.

"No! Stop it!" ordered Holly. "Leave her alone!"

And then Henry Hank was on Holly, suffocating her, wrapping her in icy slime, trying so hard to invade her brain that it hurt. Dimly, she heard Addie yell, "Take control! No fear!" Focusing all her power, all her anger, Holly forced Henry Hank out of her mind and off her body. The cold dark mass jerked away from her with shocking suddenness, thinning slightly, as if stunned, then regathering itself only a foot in front of her.

"You can't have me!" Holly's voice was as cold as death. Her vision sparked to perfect focus and new confidence filled her. "You can't have me or anyone else!" She glanced to the side; Pearl had stopped her attack on Adeline. "You're done, both of you. I won't let you hurt anyone, and you can't have me, either!"

The remaining spirits came closer.

She felt Addie's hand on her arm as the woman murmured, "Start backing up, but keep your eyes on them, Holly. Don't look away. You men, get ready to move."

Holly let Adeline guide her backward as she kept her unwavering gaze and thoughts fixed on the spirits of Henry Hank Barrow and Pinching Pearl Abbott.

At last they reached the bottom steps.

Now Ike and Ben joined them. "Go up," Addie told the men. "We'll be right along."

"Addie," said Holly. "Follow Ike and Ben. I can do this."

"No-"

"Yes!" She turned a tiny part of her mind toward Addie. "You can't run as fast as I can." Holly raised her voice now, pushing her will on them all. "Ben, Ike, Addie, Gram, get upstairs. All of you. Get out of the way. Go outside and wait for us. Go now!"

Silently, they obeyed. Steve, Eddie, and Abner stared at her. Eddie grinned nervously.

"Okay," Holly said as she took one backward step, then two, and three up the stairs.

"Steve and Eddie, come up here!" They obeyed.

As Holly mounted the fifth step, Henry Hank and Pearl glided forward. "Stop!" she commanded, pushing with all her might. "Stay where you are!"

They hesitated and the angry spirits of their victims loomed closer.

"Now!" Holly said quietly.

Abner struck a match, lit the book until it was all flame, and threw it at the trail of fuel that led to the bones two dozen feet away. "Run!" he yelled as he made the stairs.

And they did.

As they charged into the kitchen, they heard the first explosion. They ran faster, all four of them, across the blue living room. The floor began to shake, and the walls to crumble. Glass shattered. Timbers cracked.

"Earthquake!" Steve yelled. Scooping up Holly like a football, he bolted outside, throwing himself over the porch steps to the trembling ground, keeping her wrapped in his arms until they hit the earth. Instantly, Abner and Eddie landed beside them. All scrambled to their feet as the world shook. They ran to the edge of the clearing where Delilah, Addie, Ike, and Ben waited.

They stood together in the downpour, swaying with the ground, and watched the skeletal remains of the final tree topple as the earth shook it loose. A moment passed and they saw the flames kiss the first floor of the house, then the second, expanding until it was lit like a Christmas tree, bright and gay.

Holly covered her ears against the screams and roars coming from the house as the victims of Henry Hank and Pearl Abbott took their own revenge.

Finally, the sounds began to fade. Addie cried, "We got them!"

The fire cackled and spat as the screams died to low moans and mixed with the groans of the burning timbers.

Then there was silence but for the licking flames.

"They're nothing but dust now," Addie said. "They're gone."

"Delilah put her arm around Holly, "You did it."

Holly smiled.

"Carrie was there," Delilah said. "She helped."

"She did," said Holly. "I'm glad."

"I even saw her for an instant," Delilah said. "I thought it was my imagination, at first, but when I heard her, I knew it wasn't."

"She reminded us to burn the bones." Adeline smiled. "Carrie always kept a level head."

"Yes, but she said more than that."

"What else did she say, Gram?"

"That she loved me." Delilah wiped away a tear. "I can't believe it was real."

"It was," Addie assured her. "Carrie can rest easy now. So can the others. They're free."

"And Henry Hank and Pearl Abbott are on their way to Hell." Delilah looked at Holly. "Along with others who deserve it."

Holly stood on tiptoe and kissed her cheek.

They stood in the pouring rain watching the old house burn. It took a long time, but it slowly fell in on itself and darkened, at last extinguished by the rain.

For a while, they stood in silence.

"What will happen now?" Holly asked.

"When the town's powers-that-be discover the house has burned," Steve said, "they'll just assume kids did it."

Abner smiled. "Or blame the lightning."

Steve nodded. "Even better."

"No one will ever uncover the cellar again," Abner added. "The portal is closed now. May it stay so forever." He looked at Holly. "Thank you, young lady."

The others echoed his words.

Holly knew she was blushing.

"Well," Delilah said at last. "The rain's letting up. Let's go back to the hotel, have some hot cocoa, and relax. In the morning, I'd like to come back and salt the earth."

"We'll all come," said Holly.

EPILOGUE

PRESENT DAY

"**A**fter that night, I still saw the occasional ghost in the Brimstone Grand, though Henry Hank Barrow and Pearl Abbott never troubled any of us again.

"But my great-great-grandfather and his partner-in-crime weren't the only ones to disappear. I never saw my mother again either, but every Christmas for a dozen years, she sent me a crisp one-hundred-dollar bill. There was never a note or a return address, but she always left a kiss in her trademark cherry-red lipstick right beside the image of Benjamin Franklin. Many years later, I hired a detective to find out what happened to her. Surprisingly, she'd remained happily married until her death in 1981. I was - and am - happy for her, though I must admit that, initially, my happiness was purely selfish. I got to stay with Gram and Fluffy; I got my wish."

The fluffy marmalade cat sleeping in the sunlight beside the keyboard stretched, touching her hand with his paw. She smiled and continued typing.

"Did I feel like an abandoned child? Hardly. Cherry was right; Gram was the mother I needed, and I like to believe she needed me as well. We had many years together, and she saw to it that I was educated and well-traveled; and most of all, she encouraged me to write. We soon fell into a habit that lasted long after I was published.

Each afternoon, I read to her from whatever I was writing. It never mattered if it was about jungle explorers, a Martian invasion, or ghosts rattling chains, Gram's encouragement never wavered and she helped me become what I am today."

"Grandma?"

Holly turned from the computer screen and smiled at the little golden-haired girl standing in her office doorway. "Come in, sweetheart."

The six-year-old grinned and ran to her for a hug. Finally, she let go and looked at the screenful of words. "Did you finish your book, Grandma?"

"I did, just this minute. And do you know what that means?"

"What?"

"We have to celebrate! How would you like to go down to the village and have a root beer float with me?"

"Grandma! Can we?"

Holly looked into the little girl's face, smiling at the golden motes that danced in her blue eyes. "Yes, we can. Did you know, my grand-mother took me to town for my very first root beer float a long, long time ago?"

"Were you celebrating something?"

"We were." Holly smiled.

"What were you celebrating?"

"That's a long story." Holly tapped the computer screen. "In fact, I just wrote all about it."

"Will you read it to me, Grandma?"

Rising, Holly took her granddaughter's hand and led her from the office. She shut off the light. "Someday, you can read it for yourself." She picked up her purse. "For now, I'll tell you just a little while we have our floats."

ABOUT THE AUTHOR

Tamara Thorne's first novel was published in 1991, and since then she has written many more, including international bestsellers *Haunted, Bad Things, Moonfall, Eternity* and *The Sorority*. A lifelong lover of ghost stories, she is currently working on several collaborations with Alistair Cross as well as a new solo novel. Learn more about her at: http://tamarathorne.com

In collaboration, Thorne and Cross are currently writing several novels, including the next volume in *The Ravencrest Saga: Exorcism*. Their first novel, *The Cliffhouse Haunting*, was an immediate bestseller. Together, they also host the horror-themed radio show Thorne & Cross: Haunted Nights LIVE! which has featured such guests as Anne Rice, Laurell K. Hamilton, Chelsea Quinn Yarbro, Charlaine Harris, V.C. Andrews, and Preston & Child.

For book deals, updates, specials, exclusives, and upcoming guests on Thorne & Cross: Haunted Nights LIVE!, join our newsletter: http://eepurl.com/ckaBrr

BOOKS BY TAMARA THORNE

Candle Bay

Shrouded in fog on a hillside high above an isolated California coastal town, The Candle Bay Hotel and Spa has been restored to its former glory after decades of neglect. Thanks to its new owners, the Darlings, the opulent inn is once again filled with prosperous guests. But its seemingly all-American hosts hide a chilling, age-old family secret.

Lured to the picturesque spot, assistant concierge Amanda Pearce is mesmerized by her surroundings--and her seductive new boss, Stephen Darling. But her employers' eccentric ways and suspicious blood splatters in the hotel fill her with trepidation. Little does Amanda know that not only are the Darlings vampires, but that a murderous vampire vendetta is about to begin--and she will be caught in the middle. For as the feud unfolds and her feelings for Stephen deepen, Amanda must face the greatest decision of her life: to die, or join the forever undead.

Eternity

Welcome to Eternity

A little bit of Hell on Earth ...

When Zach Tully leaves Los Angeles to take over as sheriff of Eternity, a tiny mountain town in northern California, he's expecting to find peace and quiet in his own private Mayberry. But he's in for a surprise. Curmudgeonly Mayor Abbott is a ringer for long-missing writer Ambrose Bierce. There are two Elvises in town, a shirtless Jim Morrison, and a woman who has more than a passing resemblance to Amelia Earhart. And that's only the beginning.

Eternity is the sort of charming spot tourists flock to every summer and leave every fall when the heavy snows render it an isolated ghost town. Tourists and New Agers all talk about the strange energy coming from Eternity's greatest attraction: a mountain called Icehouse, replete with legends of Bigfoot, UFOs, Ascended Masters, and more. But the locals talk about something else.

The seemingly quiet town is plagued by strange deaths, grisly murders, and unspeakable mutilations, all the work of a serial killer the locals insist is Jack the Ripper. And they want Zach Tully to stop him.

Now, as the tourists leave and the first snow starts to fall, terror grips Eternity as an undying evil begins its hunt once again ...

Haunted

Murders and Madness

Its violent, sordid past is what draws bestselling author David Masters to the infamous Victorian mansion called Baudey House. Its shrouded history of madness and murder is just the inspiration he needs to write his ultimate masterpiece of horror. But what waits for David and his sixteen-year-old daughter, Amber, at Baudey House, is more terrifying than any legend...

Seduction

First comes the sultry hint of jasmine...followed by the foul stench of decay. It is the dead, seducing the living, in an age-old ritual of perverted desire and unholy blood lust. For David and Amber, an unspeakable possession has begun...

Moonfall

Moonfall, the picturesque town nestled in the mountains of southern California, is a quaint hamlet of antique stores, cider mills, and pie shops, and Apple Heaven, run by the dedicated nuns of St. Gertrude's Home for Girls, is the most popular destination of all. As autumn fills the air, the townspeople prepare for the Halloween Haunt, Moonfall's most popular tourist attraction. Even a series of unsolved deaths over the years hasn't dimmed Moonfall's enthusiasm for the holiday.

Now, orphan Sara Hawthorne returns to teach in the hallowed halls of St. Gertrude's where, twelve years before, her best friend died a horrible death. In Sara's old room, distant voices echo in the dark and the tormented cries of children shatter the moon-kissed night.

But that's just the beginning. For Sara Hawthorne is about to uncover St. Gertrude's hellish secret...a secret she may well carry with her to the grave.

Bad Things

The Piper clan emigrated from Scotland and founded the town of Santo Verde, California. The Gothic Victorian estate built there has housed the family for generations, and has also become home to an ancient evil forever linked to the Piper name. . .

As a boy, Rick Piper discovered he had "the sight." It was supposed to be a family myth, but Rick could see the greenjacks--the tiny mischievous demons who taunted him throughout his childhood--and who stole the soul of his twin brother Robin one Halloween night.

Now a widower with two children of his own, Rick has returned home to build a new life. He wants to believe the greenjacks don't exist, that they were a figment of his own childish fears and the vicious torment he suffered at the hands of his brother. But he can still see and hear them, and they haven't forgotten that Rick escaped them so long ago. And this time, they don't just want Rick. This time they want his children ...

The Forgotten

The Past ...

Will Banning survived a childhood so rough, his mind has blocked it out almost entirely--especially the horrific day his brother Michael died, a memory that flickers on the edge of his consciousness as if from a dream.

Isn't Gone ...

Now, as a successful psychologist, Will helps others dispel the fears the past can conjure. But he has no explanation for the increasingly bizarre paranoia affecting the inhabitants of Caledonia, California, many of whom claim to see terrifying visions and hear ominous voices. . .voices that tell them to do unspeakable things ...

It's Deadly

As madness and murderous impulses grip the coastal town, Will is compelled to confront his greatest fear and unlock the terrifying secret of his own past in a place where evil isn't just a memory. . .it's alive and waiting to strike ...

Thunder Road

The California desert town of Madelyn boasts all sorts of attractions for visitors. Join the audience at the El Dorado Ranch for a Wild West show. Take a ride through the haunted mine at Madland Amusement Park. Scan the horizon for UFOs. Find religion with the Prophet's Apostles--and be prepared for the coming apocalypse.

Because the apocalypse has arrived in Madelyn. People are disappearing. Strange shapes and lights dart across the night sky. And a young man embraces a violent destiny--inspired by a serial killer whose reign of terror was buried years ago.

But each of these events is merely setting the stage for the final confrontation. A horror of catastrophic proportions is slouching toward Madelyn in the form of four horsemen--and they're picking up speed.

The Sorority

They are the envy of every young woman--and the fantasy of every young man. An elite sisterhood of Greenbriar University's best and brightest, their members are the most powerful girls on campus--and the most feared ...

Eve

She's the perfect pledge. A sweet, innocent, golden-haired cheerleader, Eve has so much to gain by joining Gamma Eta Pi--almost anything she desires. But only a select few can enter the sorority's inner circle--or submit to its code of blood, sacrifice, and sexual magic. Is Eve willing to pay the price?

Merilynn

Ever since childhood, Merilynn has had a sixth sense about things to come. She's blessed with uncanny powers of perception--and cursed with unspeakable visions of unholy terror. Things that corrupt the souls of women, and crush the hearts of men. Things that can drive a girl to murder, suicide, or worse ...

Samantha

Journalism major Sam Penrose is tough, tenacious--and too curious for her own good. She's determined to unearth the truth about the sorority. But the only way to expose this twisted sisterhood is from within ...

And check out these haunting titles by Thorne & Cross!

Darling Girls

Fang Meets Fang ...

The vampires of Candle Bay and Crimson Cove come together for the Biting Man Festival in Eternity, California, to celebrate a centuries-old tradition that quickly turns murderous as they're faced with old enemies, uncontrolled bloodlust, and the unpredictable antics of a self-proclaimed vampire slayer who is hellbent on destroying them all.

Mother

A Girl's Worst Nightmare is Her Mother ...

Priscilla Martin. She's the diva of Morning Glory Circle and a driving force in the quaint California town of Snapdragon. Overseer of garage sales and neighborhood Christmas decorations, she is widely admired. But few people know the real woman behind the perfectly coiffed hair and Opium perfume.

Family is Forever. And Ever and Ever ...

No one escapes Prissy's watchful eye. No one that is, except her son, who committed suicide many years ago, and her daughter, Claire, who left home more than a decade past and hasn't spoken to her since. But now, Priscilla's daughter and son-in-law have fallen on hard times. Expecting their first child, the couple is forced to move back ... And Prissy is there to welcome them home with open arms ... and to reclaim her broken family.

The Past Isn't Always as Bad as You Remember. Sometimes it's Worse ...

Claire has terrible memories of her mother, but now it seems Priscilla has mended her ways. When a cache of vile family secrets is uncovered, Claire struggles to determine fact from fiction, and her husband, Jason, begins to wonder who the monster really is. Lives are in danger - and Claire and Jason must face a horrifying truth ... a truth that may destroy them ... and will forever change their definition of "Mother."

The Cliffhouse Haunting

When the Blue Lady Walks...

Since 1887, Cliffhouse Lodge has been famous for its luxurious accommodations, fine dining ... and its ghosts. Overlooking Blue Lady Lake, nestled among tall pines, Cliffhouse has just been renovated by its owners, Teddy and Adam Bellamy, and their daughter, Sara.

Cliffhouse has not always been a place of rest and respite, though. Over the years it has served many vices, from rum-running to prostitution - and although the cat houses have been replaced by a miniature golf course and carousel, Cliffhouse retains its dark history; darkest during the Roaring Twenties, when a serial killer called the Bodice Ripper terrorized the town, and a phantom, the Blue Lady, was said to walk when murder was imminent.

Death Walks With Her...

Now, there's a new killer on the loose, and the Blue Lady sightings have returned. The Bellamys are losing maids, and guests are being tormented by disembodied whispers, wet phantom footprints, and the blood-chilling shrieks of mad laughter that echo through the halls of Cliffhouse in the dead of night.

The little mountain town of Cliffside is the perfect hunting ground for a serial killer... and the Blue Lady. Police Chief Jackson Ballou has bodies piling up, and between the murders and the mysteries, he can hardly pursue his romance with Polly Owen. And Sara Bellamy may lose her true love before they even have their first kiss.

The Ghosts of Ravencrest

Book 1 in The Ravencrest Saga

Darkness Never Dies ...

Ravencrest Manor has always been part of the family. The ancestral home of the Mannings, Ravencrest's walls have been witness to generations of unimaginable scandal, horror, and depravity. Imported stone by stone from England to northern California in the early 1800s, the manor now houses widower Eric Manning, his children, and his staff. Ravencrest stands alone, holding its memories and ghosts close to its dark heart, casting long, black shadows across its grand lawns, through the surrounding forests, and over the picturesque town of Devilswood, below.

Dare to Cross the Threshold ...

Ravencrest Manor is the most beautiful thing new governess, Belinda Moorland, has ever seen, but as she learns more about its tangled past of romance and terror, she realizes that beauty has a dark side. Ravencrest is built on secrets, and its inhabitants seem to be keeping plenty of their own - from the handsome English butler, Grant Phister, to the power-mad administrator, Mrs. Heller, to Eric Manning himself, who watches her with dark, fathomless eyes. But Belinda soon realizes that the living who dwell in Ravencrest have nothing on the other inhabitants - the ones who walk the darkened halls by night ... the ones who enter her dreams ... the ones who are watching ... and waiting ...

Welcome to Ravencrest ...

Who is the man digging in the garden beyond Belinda's bedroom window? Who - or what - is watching her from the vents? From ghostly screams and the clutching bony fingers of death in the indoor pool, to the trio of gliding nuns in the east wing who come at Belinda with black blazing eyes, to the beckoning little girl in the red dress who died more than two centuries ago, Belinda is thrust into a world of waking nightmares where there is no distinction between the living and the dead, and there are no limits to the horrors that await. Witchcraft is afoot at Ravencrest and as unspeakable terrors begin to unfold, Belinda realizes that her beautiful new home is a keeper of tragedy, a collector of souls. And it wants to add her to its collection ...

The Witches of Ravencrest

Book 2 in The Ravencrest Saga

Dark and Unnatural Powers

In a remote part of California just above the coastal town of Devilswood, Ravencrest Manor, imported stone-by-stone from England more than two centuries ago, looms tall and terrifying, gathering its dark and unnatural powers, and drawing those it wants as its own.

Murder Lurks in the Shadows

Governess Belinda Moorland has settled into life at Ravencrest and, as summer gives way to autumn, romance is in the air. She and multi-millionaire Eric Manning are falling in love ... but powerful forces will stop at nothing to keep them apart. And as the annual Harvest Ball is set to begin, evil abounds at Ravencrest. Murder lurks in the shadows, evil spirits freely roam the halls, a phantom baby cries, signaling a death in the mansion, and in the notoriously haunted east wing, three blood-soaked nuns, Sisters Faith, Hope, and Charity, tend to the demented needs of a maid gone mad.

Vengeful Spirits

Ravencrest has come to life. In the gardens below, granite statues dance by moonlight, and a scarecrow goes on a killing rampage, collecting a gruesome assortment of body parts from unwilling donors ... But Belinda's greatest danger is the vengeful spirit of Rebecca Dane. Once the mistress of Ravencrest, Rebecca Dane has a centuries-old axe to grind with the powerful witch, Cordelia Heller - and Belinda becomes her weapon of choice.

Made in the USA
Columbia, SC
22 July 2022

63828093R00286